A GOOD BUNCH OF MEN

A DICKIE FLOYD DETECTIVE NOVEL

DANNY R. SMITH

ISBN-13: 978-1-7322809-1-5
{Revised July 2018}
Third Edition

❀ Created with Vellum

For Floyd, my partner, brother, and friend.

Undercover cops blend well into their surroundings, disguised as construction workers, cab drivers, junkies, and bums. Yet their eyes can reveal their presence to the seasoned criminal. A cop tends to study everyone and everything, as does the predator. The two of them, in a crowd of a hundred, will often recognize one another, while the other ninety-eight remain oblivious to the presence—or threat—of either one.

PROLOGUE

SUSIE DIDN'T MIND playing the cops and hookers game, an unavoidable situation for a working girl. She would come out no worse for wear if she only played by the rules. She had learned to be friendly but respectful, even a little playful at times, and she knew to give the cops something they didn't have when they called her over.

Nothing happens on the street without these girls seeing it, hearing about it, or being directly involved in it. They know who peddles the dope, who runs the guns, who whacked the last guy, and who is getting whacked next, and why. If a girl wanted to stay on the street making her money, she would need to provide information to the cops from time to time.

Susie glanced toward the white panel van as it slowed, pulled along the sidewalk, and followed her as she sauntered north on the sidewalk of Long Beach Boulevard. The driver leaned toward the open passenger's window and looked her over. As the vehicle came to a stop, she drifted toward it, smiled, and said hello to the lone occupant while stealing a glance into the back of the van. It appeared to her only as a dark hole, her delicate frame standing maybe five-six in her four-inch heels.

She looked up and down the boulevard. This time, she looked for cops, as something bothered her about the man in the van. His cold eyes telling her nothing about his soul. There were none in sight; the local sheriffs who routinely cruised the streets and alleys like sharks searching for prey, were nowhere to be found. Nor could Susie spot any undercovers, the cops who dressed in jeans and sweatshirts and ball caps while driving vans and pickups and sedans of every make and model, invisible to all but those whose survival depended on street smarts and instinct. Not a single cop in sight at one of the few times Susie had hoped to see one.

The streets of South Los Angeles were alive late on this warm Friday night. Music played loudly from cars and apartments, the sounds of mariachi or rap setting the background to engines revving, tires squealing, an occasional burst of gunfire, and the shrill sound of police sirens.

Girls like Susie survived the streets by instinct and the grace of God. Vans were the red flag, though all too often, even they would be overlooked by the most desperate of the lot. Odds were on the side of returning unharmed—relatively speaking that is—but therein lies the grace of God.

Susie glided away from the van in her short red and blue sequined skirt, and black fishnet stockings. An evening breeze gently lifted the jet-black hair off her shoulders as she glanced back toward the van. The man inside snarled something as he pulled away, though it was indiscernible over the rumbling acceleration.

Like a drive-thru burger joint, one vehicle replaced the previous, customers abundant and hungry in this low-rent, red-light district. Susie tilted her head to the side, her eyes searching the interior of the vehicle with the next potential customer as the screening process began again. This time, it was another lone male, but in a compact sedan. She had felt uneasy throughout the evening, and not only with the creep in the van. It seemed there had been a steady flow of undesirables, which really said something in this market. The man in the sedan didn't seem right either, so she motioned for him to move along.

Susie forced a smile and picked up her stride as she stepped to the passenger's door of the next vehicle to arrive. She recognized the driver as an associate, one with whom she had recently had a disagreement. No matter, she thought, they could handle whatever business brought him here, and she would enjoy a short break from the freaks on the street. Maybe they would go somewhere to get coffee or a bite to eat if he were in a better mood now. Susie looked up and down the street, and across to the other side. This time she hoped to catch a glimpse of one of her friends, or maybe her roommate, someone with whom she could check in. It was a manner of keeping track of one another, an unwritten code for the girls on the street. But there were no friendly faces in sight.

She wondered where her roommate had gone. She hadn't seen her take a job, and it had been only a few minutes since Susie had seen her further down the block. Maybe the she had gone back to their room.

Susie was startled to see a second man sitting low in the back seat as she settled into the car. She looked over at the driver, who offered no explanation. Rather, he quickly pulled away from the curb before her door had even closed. Clearly, he was not in a better mood.

Unable to relax, her eyes scoured the streets as they rode away. She hoped to see a friend, or even a cop. Someone who might recognize the apprehension in her eyes and be able to report with whom she was last seen. But there were no friendlies, and no cops. Only darkness beyond the city lights, a vast emptiness of space that reminded her of the inside of the van she had earlier dismissed. She thought of her roommate and pictured her in the dark hole, gagged and tied, and considered it—however briefly—as a possible explanation for her absence. Then Susie pictured other girls from the street, and finally herself, replacing one with the other, each having her final ride in the van. But she dismissed these thoughts and refocused on the situation in which she found herself, and her feeling about it was not a good one. The familiar company of this tattooed man offered no relief from her anxiety, and the presence of his mysterious companion only validated her fear.

Susie believed in her Lord Jesus Christ, having been raised a faithful attendant of the Renewed Life Baptist Church in Compton. And on this night, as she sat unnerved in the presence of a familiar but dubious companion, she silently prayed that her Savior would watch over her, protect her, and forgive her for her sins. She thought of her mama, and asked that He watch over her too.

But sometimes, on the cruel and wicked streets of sin and Satan's rule, *Thy will* does not deliver one from all evil. For there shall come a time when *He* will bring all evildoers to a wretched end.

And the brothers and sisters in Christ said, *Amen.*

1

THE PROBLEM WITH the shrink was you couldn't tell her everything, really level with her about what went on upstairs. Not when you carried the baggage of a veteran homicide detective. I'd humor her with my feelings to a small extent, but mostly I'd tell her what I thought she expected or wanted to hear. Sure, I could tell her some things I wouldn't tell Val, but the stakes were higher in doing so. At worst, Val could pack her bags and leave, say I'm nuts, and maybe file for divorce. Who'd argue? The shrink, on the other hand, being employed by the Los Angeles County Sheriff's Department, is tasked with keeping the crazies off the job, and keeping those on the job from joining the ranks of the crazy. Which meant that with the stroke of a pen, this powerful doctor could have my badge, gun, and pension. With a single phone call, she could have me locked down for a psych evaluation. Seventy-two hours in four-point restraints, a danger to himself or others. And then what?

So, what I told her, recalling the session the best I could as I crept along the Pomona Freeway in bumper-to-bumper midday traffic, was: Yes, I do feel anger at times, but what cop doesn't? Do I drink? Of course I drink. Excessively? Not compared to my partner, Floyd. No, I don't feel the steady diet of death has taken a toll, though maybe I'm just numb after twenty years. Sure, dead kids get to me, but they always have. That's not a big surprise, is it, Doc?

Jesus.

Not even noon and thanks to traffic, smog, too many beers last night, and now this broad with the big sofas and hair, my head throbbed. Better a headache on my way to the office, than an escort to the Augustus Hawkins Mental Health facility. Which could have easily been the case, if the shrink really knew the half of it.

Maybe that's what I should have done, just laid it all out there. Tell her about the recurring, vivid sensory recall of crime scenes. Tell her about the persistent dreams where I see my victims in their final moments, hear their pleas and their screams and their final gasps of life, yet have nothing to offer, no way to help. Tell the good doctor that sometimes, while interacting with others, I envision them dead and see them naked on a metal slab.

These revelations alone could end my career, or at the very least make a strong argument for reassignment. Maybe during the next visit, I'd put it all out there and take my chances. Get a psych retirement out of the deal, start sleeping late and playing golf a couple times a week.

Or end up at Augustus Hawkins.

Goddamn shrinks.

I envisioned the snarky doctor telling colleagues over lunch about the crazy cop she sees, this one who sees people naked, as I turned into the parking lot of the Homicide Bureau to see Tommy Foster strutting toward the back door. He was dressed in his trademark short-sleeved dress shirt and tie, cowboy boots beneath double-knit slacks. His sleeves were tailored to fit snug, the fifty-something former bodybuilder who still regularly hit the gym. He was still confident, maybe cocky, as he neared retirement. Now that guy's nuts, I thought. And as I placed the car in park and prepared to face the day, I looked at my hat and shades in the rearview mirror and said, "As long as they grade us on a curve around here, you're probably okay, Dickie Jones."

"LET'S GO, DICKIE."

"What?"

"We've got a case."

Jesus, been in the office five minutes, on the shitter for two, and hadn't even had a chance to grab a cup of coffee yet.

"Where're we going?"

"They have a case for us. Where the hell have you been, anyway? You just show up at noon now?"

"It's like eleven, not even close to noon. And, I happened to have an appointment with that shrink you're so fond of. I swear I hate that woman."

"She loves me, Dickie. But we get along, have fun during our sessions because she knows I'm normal, just there to make the wife feel better. She's probably figured out that you're completely nuts."

"Yeah, you're the normal one."

Floyd said, "Jesus, what the hell are you doing in there?"

"What do you usually do in the head, dumbass?"

"Well hurry up," he said.

"What, like I'm in here reading the paper?"

"I'll meet you at the desk."

"Hey!" I said, folding the sports page.

"What?" Floyd said, then mumbled, "Goddamn zit on my nose."

I could see it, Floyd posing in front of the mirror—he'd never met one he hadn't liked. He was likely okay with the hair, but that zit . . .

"You didn't tell me where we're going."

"Malibu. Come on, let's go."

The bathroom door opened, closed, and moments later, reopened.

"I'm hurrying, asshole!"

"Excuse me?"

I didn't recognize the voice. The shoes were familiar; they looked like almost every other pair worn at the Homicide Bureau: unpolished, black leather wingtips.

"Uh, never mind, thought you were someone else."

The shoes left before I finished up in the stall.

I left the restroom, still drying my hands with a paper towel as I headed for the front desk at a fast clip. As I passed the captain's office I glanced in to see his feet propped on his desk; they were wrapped in brown loafers. Only guys who spent all day in the office wore loafers.

I passed through the reception area where phones ring non-stop as any combination of two or three homicide detectives and civilian employees work around the clock answering calls from all over the county and beyond. The calls could range from a deputy sheriff reporting a death, to civilians asking about the progress of their loved one's case, or maybe the media inquiring about the recent killing of God knows who.

I homed in on the package sitting atop the front counter that separates the desk personnel from a reception area, a small, tiled alcove with a few plastic chairs and a muted television suspended from the wall. I plucked a chocolate chip cookie from the foil-covered plate that had enticed me, and gave an indirect "Good morning" to the desk crew.

Sylvia Ramos, a civilian who works the desk on day shift, Monday through Friday, sat to the left of David Castaneda, a veteran homicide investigator who had apparently drawn the short straw and today had his turn in the barrel.

"What do you have for us, Davey?"

Davey laughed. The guy always seemed to be in a good mood despite the job, showing no signs of stress. A real exception among the otherwise terminally fatigued.

"Shit, hoss, your partner already grabbed it, said he'd handle it without you because you were powdering in the ladies' room."

"He's an asshole," I said. "So, what is it?"

Davey halted me with a raised finger as he reached for the phone, still grinning, enjoying life while dealing with death.

Two lines rang as Sylvia said, "Hold, please" into one and then punched another blinking light to tell someone else, "No, Detective Grimes is not in the office, would you like his voicemail?"

"Good cookie," I said to Sylvia.

She had the phone propped against her shoulder and reached for a message pad with her left hand, a blue pen hovering in her right. Her long, dark hair flowed over the phone, across her tanned arm, and came to rest on the cluttered desk in front of her. "Thanks," she said, now tucking the mouthpiece beneath her chin as she glanced my way.

I continued: "You made them?"

"I did," she responded.

Sylvia then turned her attention back to the phone, "No, but I could transfer you to his voice mail . . . uh-huh, you're welcome." She hung up and rolled her eyes. "Freaking morons." Then she looked at me and said, "What'd you say?"

"I asked if you made the cookies."

"Me and my daughter made them last night, thought we'd fatten you guys up a bit." Her smile at the end of the sentence was sincere, though maybe a bit forced, likely due to the stress of the job.

"Like we need the help," I said, and patted my stomach.

Davey dropped his phone into its cradle, leaned back in his chair, and looked up at me.

"Here's the deal, hoss. The case in Malibu's a little strange, may have some complications."

These were not words I wanted to hear. *Piece of cake, it's a walk-through*, those types of comments were preferred. *It's a little strange*, or *Jesus, hoss, this one's a piece of shit*, were the types of comments I could do without, especially on a morning that started as this one had.

"How strange, Davey?"

"Some asshole in Malibu decided to whack his old lady, then turn the gun on himself."

How tough could this be?

"Simple enough," I said, "murder-suicide."

"Problem is, she hasn't died."

"So, attempted murder-suicide," I said and shrugged, still not seeing the problem.

"Yeah, but—"

"But what, Davey?"

"Well, your lieutenant doesn't want to send a team since it's not actually a murder. He's thinking a one-man response for the suicide, and he said the attempted murder can be handled by the station dicks."

"What's he thinking?" I asked. "More than likely she'll eventually die too, and then what? We've got a homicide case handled like a suicide. It doesn't make sense to me."

"Your partner jumped on it, hoss, said he'd be happy to take it as a one-man response."

I chuckled, but not from being amused.

"He hates being on call," I said. "The asshole will probably unplug the poor broad, make sure we're credited for a murder just to get us out of the rotation for the weekend. I don't put anything past Floyd."

Sylvia rolled her eyes. "You guys are sick."

I could use the break myself, I thought, but didn't bother saying so. Thinking how ironic it was that when I first came to Homicide, it had been difficult to sleep for the anticipation of being called out in the middle of the night. After a few years, it began wearing on me, never knowing when the call would come or what kind of mess we would inherit. Just another asshole, or a dead kid? Some murders matter more than others. Some murders weigh more than others.

"Shit, hoss," Davey said, "last I saw, Floyd was headed out the back door, ice chest in hand. My guess is he's got a six-pack iced down for end of watch."

As Sylvia reached to answer another call, she said, "You guys are all alcoholics."

"Easy, hoss," Davey said, looking at Sylvia and smiling. "There's no reason to be casting stones here. A guy can get thirsty doing this job."

"So, what are we doing?" Lieutenant Jordan asked as he joined us at the desk, straightening his tie and adjusting the clip as he stepped alongside me. He liked the hanging, dangling, fancy gold tie clips. Most of us barely buttoned our collars or snugged up the knots of our ties, much less bothered with clips. The ones who did generally wore a simple sheriff's star, or maybe a bulldog—which was the Bureau mascot—or the numbers *187*, the California penal code for murder. Jordan reached for a cookie but changed his mind. I glanced at his feet: black wingtips, but they were polished, definitely not the pair from the restroom.

"We're still trying to figure that out," I said.

"Have one, Lieutenant," Sylvia said, "they're homemade."

"No thanks, watching my weight."

"They're low-carb," I said, reaching for another.

"You want this thing?" Lieutenant Jordan asked, looking over the top of narrow reading glasses, his blond brows pushing wrinkles across a tanned and freckled forehead.

"Apparently, my partner does. I say we go have a look, that won't hurt anything. If she doesn't die, you can put us back in the rotation. Chances are—"

"You feel like gambling," he said, "it's up to you. She doesn't die, you guys will be back up for murders tonight."

"Yeah, but if she does die," I said, "we get a walkthrough. I could use one right now. No follow-up, no court . . ."

"You got it, big boy," Lieutenant Jordan said.

So, there we stood, gambling on death like vultures. It was my move, but the lieutenant held all the cards. Davey sat content, not much invested in the hand. Sylvia seemed to be disgusted by her fellow mankind.

"Piece of cake, hoss," Davey said. "Couple of hours at the scene and you're having a cold one, out of the rotation for the weekend and another case in the Solved column."

Sylvia rolled her eyes as Davey took another call.

When he hung up, he turned his attention back to me and pulled the Dead Sheet from a tray, a form used by the desk crew to document every death case that comes through the bureau. He hovered a pencil over it, waiting. "What d'ya think, hoss, you want it?"

"Fine," I said. "We'll take it."

The drive from downtown Los Angeles to Malibu didn't take long, the red *excuse me* light flashing from the dash of my Crown Victoria as I headed west toward the coast. Floyd had had a head start, but I wouldn't be far behind him. He would likely be taking it easy, not a worry in the world. Probably listening to a rock station, thinking about everything other than the impending death investigation.

I raced across the southland, monitoring traffic reports and plotting my route while crowding the left side of the fast lane in an effort to clear the way. I thought about the woman who was fighting for her life, trying to hold on, in no hurry to join her husband in the afterlife. Their agendas were apparently very different. Then I considered the possibilities, how the case would be handled depending on her fate, and for a moment, I felt bad that I was betting on her death.

Nothing against her, I thought, now feeling a little guilty about being indifferent to her destiny. But, I reasoned, she'd likely be a vegetable if she did survive, and then die in a few months or years anyway. God had the master plan, right? It wasn't up to me, but since it directly impacted my life, was it a terrible thing to hope the good Lord called her home? Then I thought of the damned shrink again and wondered what she would say about these ideas. I decided it was best not to worry about any of it now. The poor old lady would die, or she wouldn't; it wasn't up to me. And there'd be no sense in mentioning this dilemma during my next session with the doc.

I hit the siren a couple of times to alert the driver ahead of me who apparently didn't know that a red flashing light meant *MOVE*!

TWO BLACK AND WHITE SHERIFF'S PATROL CARS IDLED IN THE STREET, marking the location in traditional crime scene fashion with emergency lights flashing. Yellow tape had been stretched across the driveway and sidewalk of 1455 West Sunset Place. As I pulled to the curb, I noticed a female deputy with her hair in a bun walking toward Floyd's car. Her dimpled smile offset the businesslike hairdo required by department regulations. Experience told me I'd be working this one mostly by myself, my partner easily distracted by the ladies.

"I'll talk to the deputy," Floyd said, as he stepped out of his car and pushed his fingers through his hair, facing me just long enough to say it. He added, "You can take care of the scene, right?" He turned with a big grin and headed for Dimples.

Pretty Boy Floyd. The looks of a Baldwin brother and the testosterone level of a Brahma bull. Add alcohol and prepare for everything from adult entertainment to Floyd-made disaster. It would be hours, or the end of *her* shift, before my partner refocused.

"I'll tell you what, slick," I called out to his back, "why don't I go ahead and take care of the scene." *Asshole.*

2

SOME DETECTIVES ABANDONED their pagers after the Homicide Bureau issued cell phones. I preferred the little beeping device and took it everywhere I went, like a sidearm and the American Express. The phone could stay in the car; if they wanted me, they had to page me first, which was an effective way to screen my calls. The only downside was the middle-of-the-night wake-up calls, as the pager only had two settings: vibrate, or an obnoxious beeping. Only one of which had any chance of waking me.

"Who is it?" asked my better half as the device came to life.

I looked over at the nightstand where the pager sat next to my badge and gun, not far from the alarm clock. The display light flashed as it continued to beep and flash in the otherwise quiet, moonlit room.

I swung my legs over the side of the bed and grabbed the pager, frantically pushing buttons until it stopped beeping. When I gathered myself enough to focus, I pushed the button again to illuminate the display: *187*.

When a gang member receives a *187* page, it's usually a threat. When a homicide detective gets one, it's time to go to work. Maybe a gangster had received one first.

"It's the office," I said around a yawn.

"You're getting called out?"

"Looks like it."

I arched my back through a series of audible pops.

Valerie sat up in bed, her arms wrapped around a pillow.

"I thought the Malibu case took you out of the rotation."

"It should've," I said. "I guess we get another, because that's my luck. Would you mind starting the coffee?"

"Sure."

Valerie scurried from bed wearing panties and an oversized Dodgers t-shirt. She grabbed a robe and wrapped herself in it as she disappeared into the hallway.

I sighed, stretched, and sat on the edge of the bed, now staring at the enemy. It read: 2:17.

Once the Malibu case became a murder, the unfortunate wife having succumbed to multiple gunshot wounds, I assumed we were out of the rotation. As such, I had not planned on being called out in the night. Normally, during an on-call period, I would have a suit, shirt, and tie set out, along with fresh underwear and socks in an effort to avoid the middle-of-the-night mix-and-match routine. But sometimes the callouts came without notice, the nature of our work being completely unpredictable.

The Los Angeles County Sheriff's Homicide Bureau is centralized to serve the entire county—28 patrol stations spread across 3,000 square miles of land—from a single office located near downtown Los Angeles. Each of the individual patrol stations functions almost as an independent police department, with the captains of those stations essentially assuming the role of Chief of Police. In addition to the patrol responsibilities in its assigned jurisdictions, each station has detectives who handle robberies, burglaries, rapes, frauds, and other miscellaneous crimes. However, when a death occurs, the call is made to Homicide Bureau's 24-hour line to report the case, and a team is dispatched to their location. The local deputies secure the scene and witnesses and await the arrival of Homicide.

To handle the caseload of such a large and populous county, the Homicide Bureau is staffed with approximately 80 investigators. Most of these investigators are assigned to one of six teams, each team having approximately 12-14 investigators and a lieutenant. Those investigators are paired into two-man teams, or partners. Each of the six teams is rotated through on-call periods, which generally occur every ten calendar days. The pairs of partners are placed in a call-out order by the team lieutenant, generally based on who caught a case during the last rotation. There were always exceptions to the rule, such as when an investigator was unavailable, tied up in court or on vacation. In that case, the investigator, and usually his or her partner, would be pulled out of the rotation. But generally, each team would have five or six pairs of partners in every rotation to handle murders throughout the county for their on-call period of a few short days. All too often, there were more murders than the five or six pairs of partners could handle, so detectives would sometimes be recycled. Which meant that even though they had already caught a case during a particular rotation, they'd be up for another. Being called out twice in an on-call period didn't occur often, so I never planned for it and always hoped against it.

Valerie returned to the bedroom, stepped out of her slippers and robe, and slipped beneath the covers as I still sat clearing my head and collecting my thoughts.

"Coffee's started," she said.

"Thanks. I better call the desk, then grab a quick shower."

She looked cozy with her dark hair draped over a pillow, her brown eyes showing sympathy as she watched. "Do you want me to pick out a shirt and tie?"

"It's okay. You might as well get back to sleep."

I hated her going through my shirts and ties, picking out several and replacing them in random order, not light to dark and from left to right as arranged.

MY CELL PHONE SAT PLUGGED INTO THE ADAPTER AND CRADLED AGAINST the dash of the Crown Vic, right where it sat when I parked just a few hours earlier. It illuminated when I started the car, showing six missed calls in the display. All were from my partner. He'd lose his mind if he couldn't reach me at any given moment. Some people would try calling once, maybe twice, but then they'd wait for a callback. But not Floyd.

The green digits on the clock read 2:49. I estimated my arrival at the South Los Angeles crime scene to be approximately 3:30. With that, I pulled out of the driveway, steering with my left hand which also gripped a mug of coffee, and I hit the speed dial of my beloved partner's cell.

"What in the hell is your problem?"

"Where the hell are you, dickhead?"

"Just leaving the house."

"What'd you do, take a bubble bath?"

"Where are you?" I asked, ignoring his sarcasm.

"Almost there. Not entirely sober, but I'm handsomely dressed and damn near back in our old stomping grounds. You should see the suit Cindy picked out for me."

"I'll never get that."

"What?"

"That your wife picks out your clothes."

"There's lots you don't get, Dickie, that's for sure."

"What's the story on this?" I asked. "I only got the basics from the desk."

"Our victim's a hooker, works Long Beach Boulevard. She may have been strangled, is about all I got. What the hell's taking you so long tonight? Shit, Dickie, I'm damn near there."

I ignored his question. "We know her?"

"Who, the hooker? Probably. Don't we usually? The scene's right there in the middle of that stretch we used to work whores, I think right near the El Pollo Grande, off the strip, the way I got it. Name didn't ring a bell though, Susan Wright. *Pollo* actually sounds good right now; I'm starving."

The memory of working hookers brought a smile to my face. Me and Floyd, undercover, two dirty-looking white boys—by design, at the time—cruising in a white Super Sport Monte Carlo confiscated from a drug dealer. It had amazed me at times that they paid us to do that job.

"I wonder how late they stay open." Floyd continued.

I recalled one night when we pulled alongside a black lady who strutted down the sidewalk wearing a short denim skirt and heels. I had slowed as Floyd leaned out and asked, "Hey baby, how much?" I could still see the look she gave us, her hands on her hips as she said, "How much what?" all pissed off. Floyd tapped his bare wrist and asked, "How much *time* is it?"

We didn't wear watches or wedding rings when working undercover. Handcuff keys were buried in our pockets, never dangling from a keyring beneath the ignition. Hookers stayed alive and out of jail by developing street smarts, and part of street smarts included sniffing out undercover cops. Sometimes we drove around with beers between our legs to enhance the cover, and because we could.

I had pulled away from the curb at Floyd's urging—*Get me the hell outta here!*—as the would-be hooker continued to voice her displeasure in colorful language. Floyd's parting shot had something to do with free advice about the way she had dressed.

Those were the days, I thought, as Floyd continued with the conversation, now saying through my earpiece, ". . . and if they're closed, maybe we can hit El Tecazo; I think they're open all night. What do you think, Dickie?"

Still recalling those days, I thought, man, it had been a good time, that was for sure. Very little stress, or so it seemed, and no middle-of-the-night call-outs or bloody crime scenes. The dress code of the day was whatever the hell we felt like wearing; shorts and t-shirts were not a problem. I looked back at that time in my career the way a young man remembers high school, seeing now how good he had it though at the time he couldn't wait to finish, get his life started, get out of the house.

But you can never go back.

Floyd continued, saying, "Dickie, why are you ignoring me?"

I tugged at the knot of my necktie and glanced at the clock on the dash. "I'll see you in twenty."

Floyd, not known for patience, said, "Hurry up."

A RED AND BLUE SEQUINED MINISKIRT, RED PUMPS, AND BLACK FISHNET stockings, removed any doubt as to the chosen profession of our latest victim, Susan Wright. *Susie-Q* was her street name, we were told. I guessed her to be in her mid- to late-twenties, though she appeared forty; I had learned to factor in the miles. The track marks on her inner arms—scars and scabs caused by intravenous drug use—provided insight into her lifestyle and proffered a second reason she may have been killed, the first of course being her profession. If not a serial killer or demented client who did her in, maybe it had been a pimp or dealer. These ladies of the night had many ways to end up dead. One minute they'd step into a van, just trying to make a buck, and the next thing they knew they'd wake up dead.

Floyd stood next to a uniformed patrol deputy on the outskirts of the crime scene, a small area cordoned off with yellow tape streaming across the sidewalk, part of the street, and an entrance to the dark, narrow alley behind a row of businesses.

"Nice of you to join us," Floyd said, as I approached the two of them.

"Thanks, partner."

I introduced myself to the deputy and shook his hand. Then I nodded toward the victim on the sidewalk and asked Floyd, "Did you have a look yet?"

"Waiting on you, Dickie."

"Let's do it."

Floyd held a cup of coffee in one hand as he reached inside his dark blue suit with the other to retrieve a pair of wire-rimmed glasses. The glasses weren't likely a necessity for one of the youngest guys at Homicide, probably more to enhance his appearance: mature, intelligent, distinguished . . .

. . . *Drunk?*

"Dude, you smell like a brewery."

"I had some beers, get off my balls."

"Some?"

"Some six or eight," he said. "I thought we were out of the rotation."

"Let me talk to the brass, anyone shows up."

"Your lieutenant called before you got here," Floyd said, "asked if we'd need anything. Said he was headed out to Lancaster on an officer-involved shooting. Some nutcase with a machete hacked up a motel clerk, then came after the deputies when they showed up. Six deputies, all locked and loaded, handguns and shotguns pointed at the dipshit who decides to take them on with a blade. You can figure out the rest of that story."

"Some crazy shit up there, you know it?"

"All them inbred people, desert rats. Those are your people, Dickie."

"Not my people," I said.

"The brass will be up there all night," Floyd continued, "sorting shit out and kissing ass with the media, trying to explain why the cops pumped sixty rounds into the idiot and why they didn't tackle him like they would in the movies. I don't think we'll be bothered."

"Well shit, then, have another beer."

"Don't think I haven't considered it. You know I have a cooler in the trunk."

"Of course you do."

A voice called out from behind, "*Dickie Floyd.*"

I turned to see Mike Ortega approaching, the ever-present grin and bounce in his step. The guy was full of energy and usually in a great mood. He had worked undercover with Floyd and me before we went to Homicide, but had since promoted and was now back in uniform. Mike had been the first to refer to us collectively as *Dickie Floyd*, saying we were one another's alter egos, each a figment of our imaginations. He swore it was true, though we knew better; there were two of us, and we were fairly certain of it.

"What's up, Miguel?"

"That's Sergeant Miguel to you, dickhead," Floyd said, brushing past me to shake Mike's hand.

I touched the stripes on one of his sleeves, exaggerating my enchantment as I bowed before him.

"I wondered if you two idiots would get this one," Mike said. The promotion obviously hadn't changed his personality. "I figured one of you'd probably know her, or at least Floyd would for sure. Floyd knows all the hookers."

"I don't have to take this abuse," Floyd said, turning back to Susie.

"Dude," Mike said, waving a hand across his nose, "you want some gum?"

"You can both kiss my ass," Floyd said, without looking back.

Mike chuckled and turned back to me, his teeth chomping gum. "Nice hat."

I lightly touched the brim, a tan felt with a dark brown band. The hats had become my trademark as I carried on the tradition of the Hat Squad, a group of old time homicide detectives the Los Angeles Times had made famous. There had been a front-page story with a photo of the well-dressed men at a notorious crime scene, suits and dress hats with big shiny sedans in the background. Decades later I remained one of a few who wore hats, mostly to protect my bald head, but also for nostalgia's sake.

I tipped my hat to Mike and said, "Why thank you, Sergeant Miguel."

"So, who is she?" he asked, standing with thin arms folded across his uniform shirt, a shiny new sergeant's badge pinned on his chest.

"Susie Q, someone told us. Looks familiar, but I don't know we know her." I called out to Floyd, "Do we know her?"

"She looks familiar," Floyd said over his shoulder. He was squatted next to her, taking a close look and trying to see beneath the scarf around her neck. He was careful not to touch anything before photographs and measurements documented the scene. "Maybe we've seen her out here, but I'm not sure we've ever arrested her. Maybe we've talked to her; I don't know."

Mike and I stood with the sounds of the city around us.

Floyd continued: "Susie Q, huh? I'm not sure, Dickie. I mean, she sorta looks familiar."

"Seems we arrested most of them over the years," Mike said.

"Except the pretty ones," I reminded him. "Floyd usually talked us out of busting the pretty ones, usually saying they'd make good informants."

Mike said, "Pretty Boy Floyd, the lady's man."

Floyd still studied the corpse, convincing himself. "I'm sure we know her. She's old enough, could have been tricking when we were out here."

The three of us quietly gazed at the dead hooker, trying to put life into her clouded, dead eyes for recognition. Trying to figure out the *who,* before getting to the *who did it* and *why*.

A loud scream erupted from behind us. The kind of wailing you knew right away had to be from someone who'd heard their baby was dead. Word seemed to travel quickly through the streets to mama. Then they'd come running to see for themselves, see with their own eyes it really was their baby. See that it had finally happened.

A uniformed deputy braced the black woman just outside the yellow tape. She appeared to be in her fifties, this distraught civilian who wore a blue robe and yellow fuzzy slippers. I envisioned wearing the slippers at the office. A thought of the captain coming into the men's room and seeing them beneath a stall, amused me. Then I pictured walking through the bureau to show them off, maybe wearing a yellow fuzzy dress hat to match.

It was this type of thinking that worried me at times. Would a normal person have these thoughts? Were other cops so twisted that while standing somewhere between a dead hooker and the devastated mother who mourned nearby, that they would humor themselves in this manner? I knew Floyd did at times, but that was no measurement of my sanity.

"My baby, my baby!" the woman wailed.

Two deputies now struggled to hold her back. A few civilians, a black man and two Hispanics, one male, one female, were trying to console the woman, touching her back and her head, telling her it was going to be okay. Telling her to calm down, and try to hold it together. They were just regular folks, residents of a violent city, doing the best they could under the circumstances.

"I guess we found the next of kin," Floyd said, stepping next to me and following my gaze.

"Looks like it."

"Should we talk to her?"

"Not yet," I said. "Let's give it some time."

"Oh God, no," the woman cried. "Lordy Jesus, please don't let that be my baby boy!"

Baby boy?

Floyd and I glanced at one another and turned to have another look at Susie.

I raised my brows, looking at Floyd, waiting to see what he would have to say about his girl, Susie, being a boy. He just shrugged, then turned back to Susie, all business now.

3

THE CROWDS DISPERSED over the hours and the sounds of a busy city faded to only the occasional passing vehicle, a screeching tire, or a distant siren. Floyd and I continued documenting the scene, jotting notes in our notebooks that would later be used to prepare our reports. We likely appeared indifferent at times to the violence and death which encompassed us, as the banter continued throughout the process. But between pokes and jabs, we would speculate on motive, contemplate evidence, and pose questions, usually arguing about the answers. Occasionally we'd reminisce about other cases or past times as we stood comfortably in our old haunts, a neighborhood where violence was the norm and an established police presence a necessity.

In the background a police radio broadcast the soothing voice of a female dispatcher who spoke in codes to the peacekeepers of the night: *10-4, Century 212-Adam Code-6 with a 925A, Alameda and 115th, dark blue Regal, California License two Adam William Boy, nine three eight . . . any unit to assist? . . . any unit, Century 212-Adam is out with a 925A-Adam, Alameda and 115th . . . Century 214 in two . . . Century 210 Sam from the station.*

The early spring morning dew settled in with a light fog as Floyd helped a coroner's investigator slide a metal gurney into the rear of a white van with *LOS ANGELES COUNTY CORONER* painted across the side. Two thuds confirmed the doors were closed, and Susie was secured for the ride downtown. Floyd thanked the investigator and shook his hand through the driver's window.

Century 210 Sam is Code-6 with 212-Adam, advising additional units, shut down your Code-3.

The Coroner's van crept into the darkness with a white haze slowly rising from the exhaust, obscuring the taillights that glowed in the night.

Century 212-Adam is advising Code-4 at their location, Code-4, 212-Adam. Frequency 22 is clear, KMA-628.

Floyd turned on his heel and walked back to me, his notebook propped open in his left palm. He jotted notes with a black and gold Mont Blanc pen, his eyeglasses now dangling from the corner of his mouth. He kept his head down and continued writing as he stopped in front of me. "What's up, Dickie?"

"Just watching Phil wrap things up." I nodded toward Phil Gentry, the crime lab technician at the scene. "Thinking we're about done here and how nice it would be to crawl back into my bed before dawn."

Floyd removed the glasses from his mouth, tucked them into his jacket pocket, and retrieved a can of Copenhagen. He thumped the can twice with his middle finger, removed the lid, and dug into the worm dirt with two fingers and a thumb. He continued studying me while he packed a chaw between his cheek and gum, as if waiting for me to continue.

"Strange case but that's nothing new for us, right?"

Floyd brushed his hands together, letting crumbs of tobacco fall to the sidewalk below us as his tongue fiddled with the tobacco in his mouth. He said through a full mouth, "They don't pay us enough, Dickie. You think about the shit we deal with on a regular basis, the weirdness that seems to follow us around. Tell me what normal assholes would volunteer for this job?"

"Us?"

"We're not normal, Dickie, that's my point. They should pay us more, like they should pay the coroners more. I mean, your patients are all dead, what doctor wants that job?"

"Have you *seen* those doctors without their masks? No way any of those guys would make it in private practice. Strange ducks, they are, the lot of 'em."

"Take Phil over there," Floyd continued, nodding that direction, "Phil's a good man, a great lab tech, and we're lucky to have him at any of our scenes. But then you take that idiot Barrios, the tech we seem to get stuck with on every other case, and that asshole makes our job twice as hard. He should get his paycheck from the public defender's office. Give him an hour in your crime scene, he makes the O.J. case look good. And you have a point about the medical examiners. I cringe when we need them to testify."

"That's my point."

"And that's why, Dickie, they should pay us more."

"Because the medical examiners are ghouls?"

"That and because nobody ever seems to get killed in the daytime. Just once, I'd like a case in the morning so I could drive to work like a normal human being and drive home in the evening, done for the day."

"Very inconsiderate of them."

Phil finished casting a partial shoe impression from a planter a few feet from where Susie's life came to an end, and he paused for a moment to look around the scene. Finally, he worked his way over to us. "Are we finished here?"

"What d'ya think?" I asked Floyd.

"I think that's it," he answered, looking around the scene from where we stood. "Did we get victim perspective shots?"

"Phil," I said, "we get victim perspectives?"

"Got them a while back," Phil said, his right hand buried in a pocket of tan-colored cargo pants. His camera hung around his neck on the outside of a dark blue windbreaker, *CRIME LAB* in gold letters across the chest and again on the back in larger letters. "Are you guys going to want aerials?"

Floyd shrugged. "I don't think so, Phil. I really don't see the value of it on this one. What do you think, Dickie?"

"We can always get them later."

Floyd spit tobacco into the gutter. "True. It's not like this area is going to change much if we need them in a couple years for trial."

"Trial, ha!" I said. "Figure the odds."

"Never know, Dickie. We've solved tougher ones. You remember how you felt about Clarkson? Said we'd have better luck with a mafia murder."

"We got lucky."

Phil ran his fingers sideways through a tuft of hair hanging over his eyes. "That sounds familiar, Clarkson. Is that the El Monte murder you guys handled a couple years ago, female found shot to death in her car?"

"That's the one," Floyd said, nodding. "We had you on that one too, huh?"

"We made the suspect," Phil said, "with a hit from a partial print from the passenger's side door, is what I remember. You guys nailed him on that?"

"Nope," I said, the contempt coming through as I spoke. "D.A.'s office said we didn't have enough on him, even though the guy copped to being with her that night in the park. Said he met her there and they had a couple of beers and hung out for a while, is all. His story is that when he left, she was alive and well, rolling a joint before she headed home to hubby."

"We matched him with DNA too," Floyd said, "his semen just happened to be in her vagina."

"And that wasn't enough?" Phil asked.

"His lawyer clarified it for us later," Floyd said. "Apparently, it was a big misunderstanding, an oversight that his client forgot to mention he'd banged this broad he'd had a beer with. The fact she just happened to have her brains scrambled by a hollow-point shortly thereafter, was just bad luck. Oh, and it didn't occur to him to let the cops know he had been there that night, not mentioning a thing until Dickie and I screwed the front sights of our pistols into his ears and introduced ourselves to him early one morning."

"Unreal," Phil said. "So, how'd you guys finally nail him?"

"Wiretap," Floyd said, "and a little bit of stimulation. Once we had the wire in place, we interviewed his ex and told her we had enough to arrest him. This was a couple of years later. She called him as soon as we left, and they got into a screaming match because now she's thinking maybe he really did do it. When they hang up, he calls a buddy—panicked now—and runs it by him. The guy asks if he did it, and you'll never believe what homeboy says."

Phil shrugged, "He did it?"

"Says it was an accident," Floyd said, "and that's all we needed."

"All they'd charge him with was involuntary manslaughter," I added. "Because now that he's said it was an accident, how are we going to prove otherwise? See, this is why we ought to be able to beat confessions out of these guys."

Phil chuckled while shaking his head. He looked around the scene once more, and said, "Okay guys, need me for anything else? . . . Last chance."

I lifted my hat, wiped perspiration from my shaved head as I took another look around before making that decision of crime scene finality. Deciding whether to break it down, knowing there's only one shot at it. On this case, we seemed thin on physical evidence, and so far, there were no witnesses identified. Sure, someone saw something, but identifying witnesses in this part of town was the most difficult part of solving murders.

"How the hell are you sweating?" Floyd asked. "It can't be fifty degrees."

"Feels like sixty."

I loosened my tie even more below the unbuttoned collar and pushed my sleeves up two turns. My suit jacket still hung in the back of the car. There was a different look to the veteran homicide cop than what they portrayed on television.

"You need to move to Nebraska," Floyd said.

"Montana."

"Whatever. Somewhere it never gets over thirty."

"Somewhere I don't have to put up with your shit," I said, then turned back to Phil. "I think that'll do it for us."

"Okay, guys, I'm going to get out of here then, give you two some privacy."

"Might be another murder here in a minute," Floyd said.

Phil smiled, turned, and waved goodbye, his equipment and evidence in hand. Moments later Floyd and I watched as his Taurus disappeared into the night.

"There he goes, with all of our evidence. Two envelopes."

"What've we got?" Floyd asked, "couple condoms—"

"Unused."

"—and a book of matches?"

"Maybe we'll get something from the autopsy," I said, trying to sound hopeful.

"Like what, semen? The broad's a whore."

"Guy."

"The guy's a whore," Floyd said. "Point is, if semen doesn't convict some asshole who kills a housewife in the park, it sure isn't going to convict anyone on a hooker case."

"It may get us close though, maybe help us get someone identified. This time," I said, my attention suddenly drawn across the boulevard, "we beat a confession out of 'em."

"What are you looking at?" Floyd asked, turning to follow my gaze.

I nodded toward the motel with the neon sign flashing *REGAL INN* and *ROOMS AVAILABLE*.

"What about the motel?"

"What about it?"

"Ever since we determined our girl, Susie-Q, was born Shane Clayton Wright," I said, "you seem to have backpedaled quite a bit, saying you'd never met that whore in your life. None of the uniforms copped to knowing her either, after that little tidbit of information surfaced."

"Yeah?"

"So, either everybody's lying their asses off, or Susie wasn't a regular on the streets. If she didn't work the streets, then—"

Floyd looked up again at the neon sign, "Well, dickhead, let's have a look."

A patrol deputy nearby tried to conceal a chuckle. The chuckle seemed to be in response to my partner's term of endearment. Floyd, having apparently caught the deputy's reaction as well, smiled and said, "It's short for Dickie."

The deputy only smiled in return, likely thinking these two old-timers were nuts.

Every year the deputies appeared younger and younger. There were some I wondered if their mothers knew they were out this late. Other times I realized this was just part of the process of getting older, being seasoned, and working around other seasoned cops. We all appeared old and worn out, compared to the younger deputies on the streets.

I wondered if this was the deputy's first murder scene, but quickly dismissed the thought. He was here at the scene without a training officer, so at the very least he had been at the station for six months. Six months in this district exposes young deputies to a lot of crime and violence. Most trainees working these beats would handle dozens of shootings and stabbings, and at least a handful of murder cases, before they were finished with their formal patrol training. Not a lot of time passed between murders in South Los Angeles.

I recalled my first murder scene as a patrol deputy, only a couple of miles north from where we stood. It had been a gang member who was shot and killed in his girlfriend's front yard. The locals had said he'd *been caught slipping*, as if that alone summed it up and there was no need for further explanation. The victim, a gang member from a rival neighborhood, came and went freely for several weeks without a problem. But then one night, as the locals said, he got caught slipping, and that was the end of that.

I stepped off the curb and started across the four lanes of Long Beach Boulevard.

Bernard Carey.

Yep, I thought, looking up and down the desolate road in the early morning hours, how could I forget that one? His girlfriend's grandmother had stood on the porch wringing a mop, glancing at the dead boy in her front yard and going about her business as we processed the scene. That had made a lasting impression. Yeah, Bernard Carey . . . deceased, cause of death: *Got caught slipping.*

The memories of Bernard Carey faded as I became aware of Floyd speaking to no one in particular, mumbling about the fleabag motel I had dragged him to and how pretty soon the sun would be up and traffic would be a bitch, and how I hadn't bothered to feed him yet, here it was nearly daybreak.

It took several minutes for the night clerk to answer Floyd's persistent buzzing of the service button. A female of Middle Eastern persuasion appeared on the other side of thick glass, her round, brown eyes glazed with sleep and disinterest. "Yes?"

I pulled the badge holder from my belt, displaying the six-point gold star, *DEPUTY SHERIFF – LOS ANGELES COUNTY* in gold letters against a blue background, a gold ribbon over the top: *DETECTIVE*.

"Can we have a word with you?"

She nodded in the affirmative but stood still.

"In there?" I suggested, motioning toward the door that led to a lobby behind her.

She slid a piece of wood to cover the small opening in the window, then turned and walked away. She reappeared moments later opening the lobby door.

"Thank you," I said.

As I followed Floyd inside, I winced at the smell of body odor.

Floyd retrieved a Polaroid picture of Susie's face, the scarf still wrapped around her neck, one eye open, the other half-closed, death obvious even to the untrained eye. He held it out for the clerk to see. The clerk's hand flew to her mouth, then drifted down across her chin and settled over her heart.

"You know her?" Floyd asked.

Her eyes remained focused on the picture, now alert and showing interest.

Floyd's hand shook slightly as he held the photo for her to see. "Well?"

I wondered what his body lacked: sleep, caffeine, nicotine . . . all of the above? Maybe alcohol.

"Yes, I know this one," she said, her finger touching the picture.

Floyd glanced at me, then back at the clerk. "How do you know her?"

"Upstairs," she said and pointed toward the ceiling, her speech thick with an accent but absent emotion. "Two-seventeen."

Floyd pocketed the picture and turned for the door.

"Could we have a key?" I asked, my hand held outward.

"I go," she said and walked past me. She put her hand on Floyd's arm and nudged him toward the door. "Go, you go now."

Floyd looked at me and grinned, then stepped outside.

The night clerk led the way up a gum-stained concrete stairway to the second floor. A black, wrought-iron rail enclosed the narrow walk with brown doors against tan stucco walls. Nothing stirred at the low-rent motel, not this early in the morning.

Floyd stopped the clerk as she reached for the door, held out a hand and gestured for the key. He took it from her and put a finger over his lips, the universal sign for her to be quiet now. I motioned for her to step back, and she did.

Floyd and I made eye contact, the only communication we would require before going through the door. Being partners off and on for the last two decades, we seemed to know what the other thought without a spoken word. He'd go in first and I'd follow, taking opposite sides of the doorway immediately inside. It didn't matter which way he went, it would be my role to move the other direction. We didn't view this as high risk, but we'd take a few precautions nonetheless; you never knew what you might walk into.

We drew our weapons and held them at the sides of our legs, made eye contact one more time, and nodded. Floyd keyed the door and pushed it open. He stepped in and crouched as he moved left, his Beretta leading the way. I stepped in behind him, flanked to the opposite side of the doorway, and positioned my back against the wall. I scanned the small room over the front sight of my H&K nine-millimeter, and almost immediately stopped to focus on a human foot. It was encased in a black, high-heeled shoe and protruded from beneath a mattress that sat halfway off its frame. I glanced at Floyd, and he at me; it was a silent communication confirming we both saw it.

We moved silently through the room toward the bathroom, watching our step, knowing evidence was likely everywhere. Our guns remained at the ready as we visually swept the interior. The main room was clear, and so was the bathroom. There was nobody here other than Dickie Floyd and another dead hooker.

"I'll call it in," I said to Floyd, sliding my pistol into its holster on my right hip. "See if they'll give us a fresh team out here to handle it."

"Christ, Dickie," Floyd said, now stepping out of the room. "How the hell do you manage to constantly get us into this shit?"

4

THE MORNING SUN glistened off of the burgundy-colored Caprice's windshield as Sandy Landers, another detective on our team, arrived at the Regal Inn. She stopped in the driveway near the office and parked the car there, partially across the sidewalk.

"They're killing me," I said to Floyd, shielding my eyes from the glare.

"Are you part vampire, Dickie?"

"I hate the sun," I said.

"And the heat. And the traffic. And—"

"My partner."

"—your partner. Why're you still wearing felts if you're so damn miserable?"

"Protocol. Can't switch to straws until Easter."

"Are there hat cops, someone who enforces these things?"

"Easter in the spring, Labor Day in the fall. That's when you switch, like women's shoes."

"Women's shoes?"

"Black and white, dumbass. Women aren't supposed to wear white after Labor Day. How does Mr. Fashion not know these things? Same thing with hats. Felts in the fall and winter, straws for spring and summer. In California, it can sometimes be a bitch—"

"Hey Sandy," Floyd said, as she walked up on our conversation.

"Hi Sandy,"—then to Floyd—"with how hot it can be in the fall."

"Hi Matt," she replied, then she nodded at me, "Richard."

Sandy seemed to study us both for a moment, the mirrored shades moving from one to the other, her round little face framed by straight, black hair. This very serious lady in her cop glasses, black slacks and a burgundy blouse to match her cop car.

When Sandy Landers first came to the bureau, I had told her to drop the formalities, telling her to call me *Dickie* and that Matt goes by *Floyd*, a nickname I had pinned on him many years before. She had locked the mirrors on me that day, new to the bureau but coming at me with the confidence of a veteran, saying, "Floyd's an old man's name, and Dickie is just obscene."

That was about two years ago and now she was breaking in a new guy. She was well liked, seemed to be a hard worker and a team player. And she was tough. Having been raised with four older brothers, she had learned to wrestle at first, and then box, all at an early age. She joined the department shortly after graduating from the University of California Los Angeles with a Bachelor's degree in business and a newfound love of mixed martial arts. It wasn't uncommon for her to show up to the office with a black eye, or worse.

"Who's your new partner?" I asked, nodding past her as the new face approached, a slender, dark-haired man slipping into a suit jacket.

"Rick," she said to him over her shoulder, "this is Richard Jones, one of the guys on our team."

"Nice to meet you, Richard," he said, stepping over to shake my hand. "Rick Davenport."

"Likewise. Call me Dickie."

"And his partner," Sandy nodded toward Floyd, "Matt Tyler."

"Welcome aboard. You can call me Floyd."

"Dickie," he said looking at me, and then at Floyd, "and Floyd?"

"As in *Pretty Boy*." I said.

He nodded, slowly.

"They're both nuts," Sandy said, holding the serious look behind her shades. "You'll call them little as possible, if you have any good sense at all."

"You can lose the jacket, Rick, there won't be any brass coming by. Plus, it's too damned hot." I glanced at my watch. "Barely seven and it's already what, seventy degrees?"

Floyd stared at me for a moment through his black-framed Ray-Bans, a slight grin on his face. His thoughts were anyone's guess. Probably something demented, sexual, or maybe violent, or some combination thereof.

Floyd then looked at the new guy. "Where'd you come from, Rick?"

"Gangs," he said, "up in Lancaster."

"Compton North," I said. "All the assholes they got up there now, are transplants from down here. You can thank the liberals for that. Housing and development, equal opportunity bullshit."

Rick Davenport stood silent, taking it in.

Floyd picked it up: "Long as you're not from I.A."—pausing to spit tobacco over his left shoulder—"Last three sergeants they transferred in were all from internal affairs. Two of them had personally tried to have our asses fired a few years back, me and Dickie here. This asshole," he said with his thumb pointed at me, "gets us in a gunfight at a shopping mall, of all places—"

"I *did not* get us into a gunfight," I said.

"—Johnnie Cochran slaps a lawsuit on our ass, says Dickie crippled his client, shot him in the ass while he was running away. You know the kid was going to be a football star or some shit, by the time Johnnie's told it."

"He turned when I fired," I said, "is why he was shot in the ass. But you're off the subject."

"Anyway," Floyd said, "then these guys from Internal Affairs, the same assholes who tried to nail us when they were working the dark side, they come to Homicide and now they want to be our buddies."

"House-fairies," I said, "is what they are. We've got no use for any of them."

"I told you they're nuts," Sandy said to her partner. Then she looked to me. "So, you stumbled across a murder?"

"Sorry to dump it on you," I said, seeing my hat in her mirrored shades, "but this would've been our third murder this weekend if we kept it."

"Third?"

I turned toward the motel and motioned for her to follow. "We picked up a murder-suicide yesterday out in Malibu," I said over my shoulder, now taking the flight of stairs to the second floor, "then we were called out on a murder across the road there last night." I looked across the street in reflection.

"This morning," Floyd corrected me.

"Whatever, it was dark. Anyway, that's how we stumbled onto this one. We were following up on our case from last night—"

"This morning."

"—talked to the manager here to see if she knew anything, and that led us to this room up here."

Sandy glanced at Floyd, then back to me. "What'd you get in Malibu?"

I paused at the top of the stairs and looked across Long Beach Boulevard. The traffic flowed steady now, morning commuters scurrying throughout the city, north and south on Long Beach Boulevard. People were headed north to downtown Los Angeles or south toward the beach, or to the various schools, factories, and businesses in between. A city bus came to a stop not far from where Susie took her last breath, its brakes squealing and motor growling as it settled to a heavy stop.

"Murder-suicide," I said, "retired engineer decides he's checking out, going to take the wife with him."

Floyd leaned on the wrought-iron handrail. "Made sport of it, the dumb bastard chasing her around the room, firing at will, if you can imagine that."

"The guy goes into the kitchen, points a gun at the lovely missus," I said. "She's just sitting there having her morning coffee, reading the paper. She looks up, can't believe it, says, 'What are you doing, Mel? Why, you're not going to shoot me, are you?' But ol' Mel don't say shit, just lets one fly—*blam!*—nails her in the shoulder. She says, 'My God, Mel, why are you shooting me?' He doesn't answer, just levels his piece at her again. She gets up, runs through the house, and dipshit chases behind, blasting at her with his .357—*pew, pew*. She's yelling, 'Mel, why are you shooting me?' . . . Yeah," I said to Rick who stood shaking his head, "she asks him,

'Why are you shooting me?' She finally drops in the downstairs bathroom. There's a trail of blood from the kitchen into the dining room, through the living room, down the hall, and into the bathroom where she's later found. This asshole goes back to his room and reloads. He gets a box of bullets from the closet—this we figured out from the evidence, she didn't know about it—and sticks the gun in his mouth. Drops the hammer, and he's done."

"Right there," Floyd said, "in the walk-in closet. Brains all over his suits."

"Man," Rick said.

"How did you learn all this?" Sandy asked, sounding a bit skeptical about the details.

"She was still alive when the deputies got there," Floyd said. "She gave them a statement on the way to the hospital."

"But she died?"

"Oh yeah."

"Son-of-a-bitch wants to off himself, fine," Sandy said, "but don't be shooting my ass too."

I nodded in agreement. "I hear ya."

Rick asked, "What set this guy off?"

"Don't know yet," I said. "Everyone we've talked to said they were like Ozzie and Harriet, a picture of bliss. Doesn't make sense."

"Unreal."

"Tell me about it," I said.

"So, why're you guys back in the rotation after catching that?" Sandy asked.

"Ask Jordan," Floyd said, "that's his call."

"He knew Harriet Nelson bit the big one, yet he gave us this dead cross-dresser," I said, nodding across the street. I paused, looking at the sidewalk, seeing Susie still there in my mind as people walked over her, unmoved by the sacred ground over which they passed. Busy with their own lives, human rats trying to thrive in a concrete cage, or maybe just get by.

Sandy and Rick stood facing me again, waiting. I looked from one to the other. "Strangled with his scarf, is how it looks so far. No other obvious signs of trauma."

"Who's your victim?" Sandy asked.

But my mind had stayed on the crime scene. "Wait—"

Floyd said, "What's up, Dickie?"

"—what time did our murder go down?"

"Just after midnight. Or at least that's what time someone found her and called it in."

"Did you notice the bus stop?"

"No, you?"

"No," I said, and held it for a moment. "Wonder what time the buses stop running down here."

"Well," Floyd said, "I'll just put that on our *shit to do* list."

"The victim?" Sandy asked.

"What?"

"I was asking who's your victim, what do you know about him?"

"Shane Wright," I said, "known as Susie Q on the street."

"Stays in the motel?" Sandy asked.

"Recently, yeah," Floyd said, "at least according to the night clerk."

"We came over, thinking maybe our victim's doing tricks out of the motel," I said.

"He is," Sandy guessed.

"Well, he's staying here anyway. Night clerk knows him, so she took us up here to the room," I said, moving farther down the balcony in the stillness of the morning. People here were unaware of the time of day with no place to be anytime soon.

"Two-seventeen," Floyd said, pointing to the brass numbers on the door.

"This is how we found it, other than the door was closed and locked." I stood at the threshold and looked through the familiar scene once more. Taking in the soiled and stained carpeting, burn marks, and beer stains leading my eyes to the foot under the mattress. "We cleared the place, confirmed she's dead—or maybe he?—then sealed it off and called for another team. Floyd needs a beer."

"Not anymore. Now I need breakfast, coffee, then beer."

"You get a statement from the clerk?" Sandy asked.

"Just some preliminary information," I answered. "We can send Floyd back if you'd like. He loves her."

"She must be hot, huh?" Sandy surmised.

"No," I said.

"Not hardly," Floyd added.

"But since when does that matter?" I added. "She's the only one here with a dress and no—"

"Easy," Sandy said.

"—coroner's case number?"

"Nice recovery."

"Okay," I said, "we're out of here. Call us if you need anything. Otherwise, we'll hook up at the office tomorrow, compare notes, or maybe see you at the autopsy. We should probably work these cases together."

THE SUN ROSE LAZILY OVER THE CITY OF ANGELS, AS DID HER CITIZENRY, neither in a hurry on Sunday morning. Soon the roads would bustle with Angelenos scurrying toward the beaches, toward Hollywood, toward the Garment District in downtown, or maybe heading north or east to the mountains and beyond. Floyd and I drove to 1104 N. Mission Street and walked through the service entrance of the Los Angeles County Coroner's Office to attend the postmortem examination of Shane Clayton Wright.

By the time we arrived and donned our protective clothing: paper gowns, booties and skull caps—all in matching blue—latex gloves, and our county-issued respirators, and entered the autopsy room, the examination had already begun. Susie had been examined with the aid of an ultraviolet light to detect and recover any physical evidence that might exist. Samples of her hair and nails had been collected, and then she was undressed, weighed, washed, x-rayed, and wheeled into the examination room where four other autopsies were in progress.

We stood table side and watched as the doctor and a technician recorded details of the subject: her ethnicity, the color of her skin, hair, and eyes, the presence of any marks, bruises, or scars, and her sex, which caused considerable pause. And soon the table was surrounded by other examiners, technicians, and detectives who came to opine or observe an uncommon specimen.

Muffled conversation persisted through respirators and paper masks and then the internal examination began. Her organs were extracted. The condition and weight of each were noted and recorded. Dr. Thurman then removed two plastic liquid-filled casings from beneath the skin of her breasts, held each up for a closer examination, and asked the tech to record the numbers that he prepared to read aloud.

Floyd said, "What the hell?"

"Serial numbers," the doctor replied, "required by law."

"I'll be damned."

EVERYWHERE WE WENT FLOYD SEEMED TO *LIBERATE* SOMETHING THAT didn't belong to him, certain he couldn't live without it. Hotels? Floyd would fill his suitcase every day with hotel shampoo, conditioner, body soap, face soap, shower caps, tissues, coffee—caffeinated and decaf—hand towels . . . *Hey Dickie, you have any room in your bag?* The guy has a cabinet full of stolen hotel supplies at home that he'll never use. But he's all stocked up, just in case. Floyd: the original prepper.

Following the postmortem examination of Susie, Floyd and I stood in the coroner's office supply room where we discarded the paper gowns, booties, headgear, and gloves. Floyd began stuffing a supply of new booties and rubber gloves in every pocket of his gray pinstriped Joseph Abboud.

"What the hell are you doing, retard?"

"Stocking up," he said, holding his suit open, looking for another pocket. "I used my last pair of gloves yesterday on your drag queen. Here, stuff a couple of these in your pockets, would you?"

"Booties?"

"Keeps the blood off the bottom of my shoes, Dickie."

"You've never worn booties at a crime scene," I said. "You mentioned one time, after the O.J. trial I think, that maybe we should start, but you've never—"

"There's always a first, Dickie."

"I hope a news crew catches it, first time you decide to put that shit on. See what that does to your image."

"I might just step out of a crime scene stark-raving naked, Dickie, stand there in front of the cameras in my blue booties. You'd be in the background doing that detective shit you do, I'd be all, *How do you like me now?"*

I tucked the booties in my trouser pockets. "Get me a couple pairs of gloves, would ya?"

When we cleared the loading dock on the way out, or more appropriately, the unloading dock, Floyd pulled four pairs of latex gloves from his jacket and handed them to me. "If that cheap captain of yours would supply us with the good stuff, I wouldn't be forced to commandeer this shit. The guy's making a common thief out of me."

"These *are* good gloves," I said, admiring the weight and feel of them, thinking I'd rather wear these the next time I touched bloody whatever.

"The thick ones," Floyd said, walking around to the passenger's door of my Crown Vic, "don't tear as easy. So, what do you think now, Dickie, about your girl?"

"Susie Q? I don't know, man. It's crazy."

I lowered myself into the driver's seat, started the car, and flipped the air-conditioner up full blast.

I looked over. "Operation must've cost several thousand, or better."

"I'd guess ten grand," Floyd said. "At least ten, now that I think about it. The implants were probably five, then you add the retro-fit for the plumbing down there. Jesus, the whole package. That's a man serious about being a woman."

I pulled out of the lot onto Mission Boulevard, scooting between dilapidated cars and buses emitting black smoke into the smoggy sky, taking in the street and surrounding structures that were old and in need of repair, one of the many rundown neighborhoods of Los Angeles County. I moved into the turn lane for the southbound Golden State Freeway, ignoring an irate driver's horn.

"Where's a street whore get cash like that?"

"That's my point," Floyd said, "maybe she's not a street whore. Maybe she's got something else going on, something bigger than what we're seeing."

I accelerated up the on-ramp, watching the side view mirror as I merged into traffic. When I settled in, making it to the fast lane and bringing it up to cruising speed—about thirty miles per hour this time of morning—I glanced over to see Floyd staring out his window.

"Did you know about those serial numbers on implants?"

"Nope, that was news to me, Dickie."

"Me too. Pretty cool though, if you think about it."

"Cool?"

"I mean, yeah, they can find out who made them, who installed them, and when. Think about it: if we get an unidentified victim who happens to have implants, we'd be able to ID her by tracking those numbers, theoretically. You don't think that's cool?"

"Or him," he replied, as he gazed out the window, looking off to the east. Maybe admiring the skyscrapers, maybe just contemplating the morning sun subdued by a gray haze, a new day dawning, the darkness and depravity now behind us for the time being.

At times she could be deceptive, this City of Angels that sparkled and shined in magazines and movies. But on the sweltering summer nights—especially—some of us saw her for what she had become, saw the hordes of undesirables who made her vile, decrepit, murderous, the Madonna now past her prime, the lady fallen from grace. The angels had been replaced by evil spirits. The city of devils. *Los Diablos.*

"You know what, partner?"

"What's that?" Floyd asked, finally coming back to me. His face showed no emotion, a blank stare, a mystery to the one who knew him better than most.

"This place has become nothing more than a freak show. Men becoming women, women going butch. Kids on dope and the so-called adults sit on their porches drunk or loaded as they watch it all happen, nobody in charge. Nobody getting their asses kicked for bad behavior."

"You should fix it all up, Dickie."

"You'd have to nuke the place, start fresh. Maybe make an announcement for the few remaining functional citizens to pull out, have them bring the flag."

5

IT MAKES NO difference how a person lived, there was always someone who cared about them. Telling that person that their loved one has been killed is among the most difficult tasks with which a cop is burdened, especially when that person is a parent of the deceased.

Floyd and I stepped into the modest home of Lucille Wright, the robust woman holding open a wrought-iron security door. I thanked her and brushed past, stepping into a tidy living room furnished in floral patterns and dark wood. She waved me to an armchair as she sank into the adjacent sofa. Floyd balanced on the edge of the same sofa, but at the opposite end of Ms. Wright, as if he hadn't planned to stay long. He opened his notebook and gave me the nod.

"Ma'am," I said and paused, "you were out there the other night, so you know about your boy being killed. We're very sorry for your loss."

She sat solemnly, nodded and said, "Thank you."

"Detective Tyler and I are responsible for investigating your son's case. It's our job to find out what happened and why, and try to figure out who's responsible."

She dabbed the corners of her eyes with a handkerchief. "What happened to him?"

"We're not sure yet," I told her. "It'll be a while before the coroner makes his report. In the meantime, we're talking to those who knew him, family and friends, hoping to learn more about his life. The more we know about how he lived, the better our chances to find out who killed him and why."

"You don't know *anything?*"

"He may have been strangled—"

"Oh, Lord!"

"—but we're not sure yet. They'll have to do more tests."

She didn't need to know there would be a microscopic examination of the tissue from his larynx which had been cut from his body just a few hours ago. She didn't need to hear about the bruises and marks consistent with manual strangulation, and the petechial hemorrhaging, the tiny, pinpoint red marks in his eyes, a further indicator of the manner of death. We graciously downplayed the violence.

"He didn't suffer much, ma'am, you should know that."

Her body jerked as she restrained her emotions. Her eyes drifted to a mantle displaying photos of a young boy. In one, he was maybe eight, wearing a green and white baseball uniform and holding a bat over his shoulder. He had a wide grin and a short afro sticking out from his cap. Another was of a handsome teenaged boy with smooth brown skin and a flawless smile, wearing a purple graduation cap and gown. Pictures of her boy before he became a girl.

"Is that Shane?" I asked, and brought my eyes back to Mrs. Wright.

A hint of a smile crept onto her face and disappeared a moment later. "That was my boy. Graduated right here, Lynwood High," she said, nodding as though we could see the school from where we sat. "Lots of boys around here never do finish up high schoo'. No, theys more'n likely to drop out and join a gang, or get to smokin' that dope. I was very proud of my boy."

"That's right, ma'am," I said, "he did good, graduating from high school."

"It seems like such a long time ago, now. Shane changed so much over the years, and then after . . ." She faded off and looked down at the carpet.

"After what, ma'am?"

"His daddy." She paused to dab her eyes again. "He never did show him much affection, you know? Always saying Shane acted like a little girl, called him a little sissy boy. Not the boy he had hoped for I guess, the type to play ball, get out and mix it up with them other boys.

"Shane was always a little bit different. His only real friend was a little girl down the street, Donna Edwards. He'd play dolls and dress-up with that little girl, let her put makeup on him, paint his eyes all silver and blue with sparkles . . ."

She shook her head, looking down again toward her calloused, bare feet. "Shane's daddy caught him one time getting dolled up. He had just put on his makeup, and I guess he was putting on some red lipstick—"

Tears rolled down her cheeks. She lifted her head toward the heavens and stared off for a moment. "He gave that boy a beating that day. Beat him with his fists."

I shook my head and felt my lips draw tight and my jaw clench, the Irish temper about to be lost. Most times I could control it, but there had been a few occasions when a vulnerable victim had suffered at the hands of a bully, and the temper had gotten the best of me. Hearing of a full-grown man beating a boy—a soft boy at that—as if he were another man, made my blood boil. I made a mental note we'd be talking to this man, this bully, this little boy's daddy. I glanced at Floyd and saw we were on the same page.

"He's lucky I didn't have no gun up here in this house, is all I can say," she said. "Probably for the better, I guess, or else I'd be spending my life in prison.

"I had the po-lice lock him up that time, 'cept they didn't keep him long. Let him go on bail. I think his mama posted it."

She wiped her cheeks, drew a long breath, and let it out slowly. "That was the end of him being here, Shane's daddy. I told him if he ever lifted a hand to that boy again, I'd kill him in his sleep. I meant every damn word of it too, forgive my language.

"Shane was never the same after that. Pretty soon he started not being around here, staying out all night, doing what he wanted. I couldn't do anything about it. I tried talking to the boy, but he wouldn't talk to me much for quite a little while."

"How old was he then?" I asked.

"Let me see," she said and glanced to the mantle again, "I'd say about thirteen, maybe fourteen? Yeah, probably thirteen or fourteen. He matured slowly, never did have to shave his face. Maybe he was older, now that I think about it. Fifteen?

"After a while—and with his daddy out the house now—Shane and I had mended our relationship and got real close again. Maybe 'cause I took up for him with his daddy, maybe just 'cause I understood him. But truthfully I think it's 'cause I accepted who he was and allowed him to be just that. Pretty soon he got to where he'd talk to me about how he felt, and then one day he said he just didn't feel like he was meant to be a boy. Lordy it broke my heart at first, but I still loved the boy, couldn't imagine not loving him no matter what he turned out to be. Then he told me he wished he'd just been born a girl," she said, and looked up with a smile to finish, "and by God, I wished it too. I know he'd been happier if he had, and his little life wouldn't have been so hard."

I reached over and covered her hand with mine. She drew a deep breath and paused to gather herself.

I retreated and asked, "He stay in touch at all, Shane's daddy?"

"I never heard from that son-of-a-bitch—'scuse my language—after I threw his ass outta here for whoopin' up on Shane." She paused and then came right back, some excitement now in her voice. "Wait, one other time he got hisself locked up for something else and had the nerve to call me. Called me collect of all things, asking would I come see him, and would I put some money on his books down at the county jail. I told him he could rot in hell and hung up on that fool."

"What's his full name, the father?"

"Charlie Wright. Charlie Lincoln Wright. His mama stay right over here in Inglewood," she said, and pointed across the living room, "Leilana Wright, nasty ol' thing she is. He's probably living off her, when he ain't in jail."

"That should be helpful," I said. "We need anything else we'll—"

"Did you know about the sex change?" Floyd blurted out.

It really didn't surprise me, though I had hoped this one time Floyd might avoid working sex into the conversation.

"Shane started dressing like a girl every day 'bout two years ago, right after high schoo'. He'd leave here all dolled up, had them fake boobies I'd seen on his bed one time, you know?" she said, looking at Floyd now, "thems ones molded from plastic, like a girdle with boobies. You know what I mean?"

Floyd nodded, "Yes ma'am."

I frowned at my partner, pondering.

"Came a point," she said, "I gave up thinking he'd change, grow out of it, so I decided to support him. I'd tell him he looked nice and it seemed to make him happy. That's all I ever wanted for him, was to be happy. Then one day he tells me about having real boobies now. I said, 'Oh Lordy Jesus.' He showed 'em to me, says, 'I'm gonna have the rest done too, mama. Be a complete woman.' I didn't ask what he meant, didn't wanna hear no more of all that."

"Do you know how he paid for all of this, Mrs. Wright?" Floyd asked.

"I don't," she said. She thought for a moment and then showed a puzzled expression, as if she had never thought about it before. "Do you?"

I quickly spoke up, "No, ma'am."

Lucille Wright, now gathered and composed after stepping off of that roller coaster—for the time being—looked at Floyd and then me, and said, "That boy loved his mama, and he loved the Lord."

"I'm sure he loved you very much, ma'am," I told her as I stood, digging in my pocket for a business card. I handed it to her and said, "Best way to reach me is on the pager. Just punch your number in at the beep, or leave me a voicemail, either way."

Floyd told her, "We're sorry for your loss, Mrs. Wright."

Floyd looked at me over the top of his Ford Taurus, each of us hanging a suit jacket in the back seat where they'd likely stay the rest of the day. He said, "Do we hate Charlie Lincoln Wright?"

"It's what I'm thinking."

We ducked into the front seats and closed our doors simultaneously. Floyd glanced over as he started the car. "Shall we pay him a visit?"

I opened my cell phone and said, "We shall."

An instrumental jazz version of some pop song from the seventies played through my earpiece as I waited on hold for Sylvia, the perpetually busy receptionist at our office. I had asked her to check the computer for an address on a Leilana Wright, probably living in Inglewood.

The music stopped and Sylvia's voice was back. "Are you still there?"

"I'm here."

"10119 South Inglewood Avenue, Apartment 201. Do you need me to check for a phone number?"

"No thank you, dear, me and Floyd are going to pay her a visit. I appreciate the info."

"Be careful, guys."

When I disconnected, Floyd said, "Well?"

"Inglewood Avenue, take the freeway."

"You're not the boss of me, Dickie."

"Jesus."

Fifteen minutes had passed without conversation, the radio tuned to a rock station for Floyd's listening pleasure.

"This is it," I said as we passed the lime green apartment complex where gangsters loitered out front. "Nice place."

Floyd whipped the car to the curb and looked through his window at the gangsters who were now looking at us. No doubt they knew *who* we were; they were probably only wondering *for whom* we were there.

"They're going to love us," Floyd said.

I studied the gangsters, black men or boys in baggy jeans and wife-beaters, the small sleeveless undershirts fit tightly to their bodies. Most of them either wore a cap or had a bandana on their head, though one sported a sixties-style afro with a comb sticking out on one side. There were two who could have been concealing weapons, based on their dress. Those were the two I'd watch the closest. I didn't have to say anything to Floyd, knowing he'd be with me or ahead of me on that.

"Oh yeah," I said, "wait until they get a load of us."

We walked into the courtyard in our shirts and ties; the jackets remained in the car. Floyd rolled up his sleeves as we passed by them, letting the gangsters know we meant business.

"How you girls doing today?" Floyd asked.

"Ah man, that ain't right, po-lice," one of the boys said.

Floyd smiled. I glared as we continued past. Each of us had our own way of letting them know we were unafraid and had no intention of playing games. No gangster had ever intimidated either of us.

We had heard tales of Chicago and Detroit, maybe a few other places scattered across the country where the cops would refuse to go into certain neighborhoods or housing projects. Maybe it had been exaggerated or completely made up, but Floyd and I had scoffed at the idea of it. There wasn't a city, neighborhood, street, or alley in the entire country the two of us wouldn't travel into or through to do our job, as long as we were together, and armed.

I listened to the low-toned banter behind us as we headed up the stairs, paying it no mind but listening for any warning signs. We paused outside 201. I looked back and saw the fellas had followed us to the bottom of the stairs.

"Curious little guys," I said.

Floyd glanced down at them and back to the door.

A middle-aged female appeared a few moments after Floyd rapped his knuckles against the black iron door.

"Can I help you?"

"Are you Leilana Wright?" Floyd asked.

She frowned a little. "Who wants to know?"

Floyd pulled his badge off his belt and held it up for her to see. "We're with the sheriff's department. May we come in?"

"I'm not sure—"

"It'll just take a minute, Mrs. Wright," he said.

She opened the door, slowly stepping out of our way as we moved inside. "Does y'all have a warrant or somethin'?"

"Is Charlie here?" Floyd asked.

"*Charlie?*" as if she had never heard the name.

I walked to the hall and looked in a bedroom just as a man stepped into that room from an adjacent bathroom. His eyes showed surprise when he looked in my direction.

"Hey, how's it going?" I said, casually.

"What's up?" was his response.

He seemed to be sizing me up, though he didn't seem nearly as surprised or alarmed at seeing a white man in his hallway, as I would have been if the roles were reversed. His eyes paused around my midsection where my badge and gun were openly displayed.

I looked him over too, taking in the bare chest and feet under loose-fitting khakis. His thin frame showed some definition, no doubt the result of incarceration. He didn't appear to have any weapons on his person.

"What's your name?"

"Huh?"

They're always getting ready to lie when they give you the *huh*.

"What is your name?" I asked slowly this time.

"Keith."

"Keith what?"

"Um, Jones . . . Keith Jones. What's this about, man?"

"That's funny."

"What?"

"That's my name, Jones."

"Oh yeah?"

"Yeah, only I don't think I've ever seen you across the dinner table."

"Huh?"

"You suppose we're related?"

He chuckled, seeming to loosen up a bit. Maybe it was my grin, or perhaps he thought I was funny.

"Us, related? Nah, I don't think so, man. You's too light skinded."

"You're probably right, Keith. Listen, my partner and I would like to speak with you for a minute, if you're not too busy. Outside would be best."

"What about?"

"I'd rather not say, not in front of the lady. I assume she's your mother?"

"Yeah, dat's right."

"Why don't you grab some shoes, we can talk outside."

"Yeah?"

"Yeah, Keith, why not?"

He turned and took a couple steps into the room.

I called out at his back, "Hey, Charlie?"

He turned to answer and instantly realized the mistake he had made.

Charlie paused for a second then ran back into the bathroom, flinging the door closed behind him. I caught it with the bottom of my foot and it sailed open. Floyd's presence seemed instantaneous, suddenly on my heels. Charlie reached into a clothes hamper next to the tub as Floyd had come alongside and then past me. He collided with Charlie, sending an elbow across the back of his head which instantly dropped him to his knees.

Charlie pushed himself up, using the tub for momentum, and turned toward us ready to fight. Floyd punched him in the face four times, hard and fast, but the blows didn't seem to faze Charlie Lincoln Wright.

I had seen Floyd hit bigger men and knock them down—sometimes out cold—with as little as one punch. The thought suddenly occurred to me that maybe we were in trouble with this guy.

Charlie tucked his head low and began to run past us, determined to escape from the two uninvited guests in his bathroom. I grabbed his shoulders as he passed, in an effort to tackle him, and Floyd went lower, wrapping his arms around Charlie's waist. He drove through us, high-stepping and spinning like Walter Payton going through a defensive line. He shrugged out of my grasp of his bare shoulders, and pushed through Floyd's grip.

Suddenly we were behind him, reaching for him again, but now going through the bedroom and into the hallway as he continued to break our grasps and gain more ground.

We chased Charlie into the living room, knocking his mother out of the way and falling over furniture. I grabbed him around the neck as he hit the door and struggled to unlock the deadbolt. Floyd hit him low again, but Charlie didn't go down. He opened the door and dragged us with him onto the balcony.

Leilana Wright screamed from the doorway, telling us to leave her baby be, let him go . . . screaming for help, but not from the cops.

There was movement at the bottom of the steps, which I assumed to be the gang members who had been curious about our presence. It seemed they were moving in our direction. Charlie gripped the balcony as we pushed and pulled him and pounded on his hands, trying desperately now to release his grip so we could get back inside before he had help. Once inside, I reached up and bolted the door, for our safety.

Charlie broke my grasp and dragged Floyd across the room as my partner hung on Charlie's legs. I stepped over a couch and landed on Charlie's shoulders, hanging on as he spun in a circle. Floyd came up to his feet, ready for more standup fighting. I still rode on Charlie's back, trying to get a grip around his neck so I could choke him out. Floyd continued throwing punches, striking him multiple times in the face and body, quick combinations that Floyd practiced daily for just this type of opportunity. It had been said that Floyd had always trained for the ultimate confrontation, and the thought that this may have been just that occurred to me as Charlie whirled me around the room.

Charlie stumbled backward, and we tumbled with him over a coffee table, landing on the floor. Floyd grabbed one arm and I reached for the other which Charlie held under his body. The three of us now lying on the tile floor, face down. The action had slowed while Charlie seemed to focus on keeping his hands beneath him. Floyd and I were content for a moment just to hold him down.

After a minute, I grabbed a lamp that now lay on the floor, apparently knocked from the coffee table during the ruckus. I lifted it above Charlie's head where he would see it. Panting, I told Charlie if he didn't put his hands behind his back, I'd break the lamp over his head.

Charlie paused for a moment, but finally complied, allowing his arm to be placed behind his back. He repeatedly said he didn't know what all this was about.

Nor did I, at this point.

Floyd said between gasps for air, "You got handcuffs?"

"Me?"

"No, Charlie, you idiot. Yes, you! You got hooks or not?"

I reached for the small of my back where I kept a pair looped over my belt. They were gone.

"Where're yours?" I asked.

"In the car," he said.

I looked up and saw Leilana in the dining area. My handcuffs and hat were on the ground at her feet. Leilana stood still, looking at us but not saying a word.

I said to her, "Give me those cuffs."

She looked down and then away, her lips tightly sealed, her arms now folded across her chest.

"Lady," I said, while trying to catch my breath, "Junior's going to jail. Now give me those cuffs or you'll be going with him."

She stared away as if we weren't there.

Floyd pulled his gun and stuck the barrel in the base of Charlie's skull. "Dead or alive, lady," he said, "he's going with us. Now slide my partner those goddamned cuffs or say goodnight to Charlie."

6

NICE BLUFF," I said to Floyd. We had finally handcuffed our opponent, Charlie Lincoln Wright.

"Wasn't a bluff. Do you *hear* that crowd out there? I figured if we didn't get a handle on this in a hurry, we'd have a riot on our hands."

"Yeah, the girls downstairs. Why'd you have to antagonize them?"

"Your presence antagonized them, Dickie. Are they still out there?"

"Sounds like it. I heard a couple pops a few seconds ago, sounded like something breaking downstairs."

"Probably busted out my windows, the little bastards."

"Maybe you should have tried being friendly, rather than getting them all riled up."

"They didn't seem to be the friendly type, Dickie. I try to avoid people who aren't friendly. What are they doing out there?"

"Sit tight, I'll have a look."

I rolled off Charlie and pushed up onto a knee with a groan. I lifted my head just high enough to see over the ledge. "Shit!"

"What?"

"Your car's on fire."

"What the—"

"They torched your car. It's fully engulfed."

Charlie laughed.

Floyd shot a knee into his rib cage, then rose to look outside while resting his foot on Charlie's back. "Think we should call the cops?"

"Don't you call the fire department when shit's on fire?"

"I don't care about the fire," Floyd said. "I'm thinking about getting you and me and our friend, Charlie a ride out. Preferably without getting shot. Besides, you know I hate firemen."

"What's happened to your sense of adventure?"

Floyd lowered himself to a seat on Charlie's back. "I just happen to be more civilized than you, Dickie. That's your problem, you're uncivilized, always have been."

"I think that shrink's making a sissy out of you."

Charlie chuckled and Floyd slapped the back of his head.

"Ouch!"

"I'm just opposed to violence, is all," Floyd said. "Besides, Doc loves me. You know, most sessions, all we talk about is you. I'm not going to lie, we're both a little worried."

"Great."

"Make the call, Dickie."

"Okay, you stay here with Charlie."

"We'll be right here waiting for you, Dickie. Isn't that right, Chuck?" Floyd said, and slapped Charlie's head again.

"Asshole," Charlie said. The sound of another slap followed.

I went into the kitchen and asked for the phone. Mrs. Wright sneered at me, her short wiry hair framing a pockmarked face. She puffed a cigarette and flipped a finger toward the counter, indifferent now.

I picked up the phone and dialed 9-1-1.

"9-1-1, what is your emergency?" said a male voice suitable for radio broadcast.

"My name is Richard Jones and I'm a detective with the sheriff's department."

"What can I do for you, sir?"

"You have an address on your screen?"

"I have 10119 South Inglewood Avenue, Apartment 201 in Inglewood."

"There's a Ford Taurus on fire out front, an unmarked sheriff's vehicle. The natives here are a little restless over an arrest we've made, and it appears they've been playing with matches."

"I'll send the fire department right away."

"Sir, you need to send us a couple patrol units. We're going to have trouble getting out of here alive with our prisoner."

"Yeah, cause you started a riot," Floyd said in the background.

"What was that, sir?" the dispatcher asked.

"Just my smart-assed partner, sorry."

"We'll have someone there right away."

"We'll be the white guys in suits, barricaded in 201."

"How do you figure I started a riot?"

Floyd and I were sitting in a briefing room at the Inglewood Police Department Headquarters, waiting for a ride from our lieutenant. We had lost the car, Floyd's Taurus burned to a crisp in an overt act of civil disobedience. But we had made it out alive, with our prisoner, and were not too much worse for wear.

"You started it, the whole thing," Floyd said. "First, you antagonized the young men out front, got them all pissed off by giving 'em that Dickie stink-eye thing you do. You might have noticed I smiled at them, gave them a warm greeting, real neighborly like. Then, you start a fight with Charlie, then—"

"Wait a second here, asshole. First of all, you called them girls. That probably pissed them off to start with. Second, how'd I start a fight with Charlie? You're the one who started punching him in the face for no apparent reason."

"Your lieutenant's here at the counter, guys," an Inglewood police dispatcher said, poking his head full of red hair around a corner. "You want to follow me up there?"

"Sure," I said, "we can't wait to see him."

"Yeah," Floyd said, "he loves us."

I looked over my shoulder at Floyd as we walked out of the room. "You're such an asshole."

He laughed and said, "You still started it, the whole damn thing."

Lt. Jordan took the news better than expected, once I explained how Charlie Wright may turn out to be a prime suspect in our drag queen murder. Floyd corrected me, saying technically, Susie wasn't a drag queen, having had gender reassignment surgery. Nonetheless, I told the lieutenant, as he gave us a ride to Lennox Station, if Charlie was good for one, he was good for two murders, ours and the one in the motel room, the one Detective Sandy Landers and the new guy were handling.

At Lennox Station, we completed a pile of forms to report the damaged county vehicle and the arrest. Once finished, the three of us walked out to the parking lot.

"What are you boys going to do about your prisoner, this Charlie guy?" Lt. Jordan asked as we approached our vehicles, passing a row of black and white patrol cars and several detective cars along the way.

"We'll let him catch the bus to county jail," I said, "give him a few days to cool off and then go talk to him. Hopefully, we'll know more by then, maybe have something to go at him with."

"What are you holding him on?" he asked.

"For now, just assault on a peace officer, him beating up Floyd. That'll give us a couple of days."

"I could have taken him out if your fat ass wasn't in my way, Dickie." Then Floyd to Lt. Jordan: "Like a monkey humping a football, this asshole rolling around on top of the poor guy, huffing and puffing trying to catch his breath."

Jordan looked at Floyd and frowned, then turned back to me. "This guy have a record?"

I responded: "Who, Floyd?"

The lieutenant grinned. "The suspect."

"From what we've heard, yes," I said, "but we haven't looked it up yet. Floyd, definitely."

The lieutenant looked at Floyd who was staring off through the parking lot now.

"I think he's ignoring us," Lt. Jordan said, smiling at the usual banter between two old partners.

Floyd looked at him. "Who, me?"

"You seem distracted. Everything okay, big boy?"

"Just doing a mental inventory of my car," he said, "thinking of all the shit I lost from them assholes torching it."

"Damn!" I said. "Our suits—"

"And wallets," Floyd interjected. "I'm way ahead of you, Dickie. All my equipment in the trunk—"

"Most of it stolen," I said.

The straight-laced lieutenant snapped his head around to Floyd.

Floyd stared back through dark shades. "What?"

I PULLED OUT OF THE PARKING LOT WITH MY HAND IN FRONT OF AN AIR vent, waiting for it to cool. "I need to get the air fixed in this piece of shit."

"You really think Charlie whacked his own kid?" Floyd asked.

"He could've. Why's he running from the cops?"

"Look at us, Dickie. We came into my place, I'd run too."

I shrugged a concession. "The important thing is, Jordan doesn't need to know that. You see the way he eased up about us mugging Charlie, once he thought we might've solved the case?"

"You're the one that mugged Charlie," Floyd said. "You knew the minute Susie-Q's mama told you about that beating, that you'd be picking a fight with him one way or the other. You're not shittin' me, dickhead."

"Yeah, well, maybe. It's not like the asshole didn't have an ass whoopin' comin'. And it ain't like you didn't have the same thing in mind."

"That was hardly an ass whoopin', Dickie."

I turned right on Century Boulevard and headed east, done with the talk about Charlie. Thinking now about Susie Q and his mama and his childhood friend who played dolls and dress-up with the troubled young man.

I glanced at Floyd: "Let's go find Donna Edwards."

"WHAT DO YA WANT WITH DONNA?" THE BURLY MAN IN BLUE COVERALLS asked, holding the screen door open as he spoke. He looked from me to Floyd and back, and before we could reply, he said, "Y'all the po-lice?"

"Sheriff's Homicide, sir," Floyd told him, offering his hand. "I'm Detective Tyler, this here's Dickie Jones."

The big man shook Floyd's hand, then reached for mine. "Is everything okay?"

"We'd like to ask her some questions," Floyd said, "about Shane."

"Shane Wright?"

"Yes, sir."

"Something wrong?"

Floyd, looking through the shades, kept it low key. "Just need to talk to her, is all."

"Hold on," he said, and disappeared into the living room. The smell of smoke and barbecue escaped through the door as it closed.

I glanced at my watch. "Dinner time."

"So much for the gym today," Floyd said.

"Yep."

"Damn, my gym bag was in the trunk too."

"Sucks to be you," I said.

After a few moments of waiting, Floyd said, "You suppose he went to get a bat, gonna come back out here and whip our asses?"

I thought about it for a second. "No, I don't think he'd need a bat."

Floyd grunted. "Hmpf."

The large man reappeared in the doorway. "Here's Donna's address and phone number. She's living over there in Downey, far as I know."

"Thank you, sir," Floyd said.

"Are you her father?" I asked.

"I married her mama, raised her up like m'own."

"You know Shane very well?"

He nodded, grinning just enough to show some silver in his teeth and a dimple on one side of his mouth. "Confused little boy, he was. Good kid though. He in some kind of trouble?"

"He's been killed."

The big man's smile instantly turned to a frown as he studied me for a moment and then looked over at Floyd. His gaze came back to me, all business, his brows crowding together just over the bridge of his nose. He said, "He didn't deserve it, no matter what happened. That boy didn't have a mean bone in his body."

"No, sir," I said, "he didn't deserve to be killed."

"THAT ITALIAN JOINT'S RIGHT OVER THERE NEAR THE ADDRESS POPS GAVE us for Donna," I said. I turned into traffic, messing with the air-conditioner. "How's eye-talian sound to you?"

"Did you forget our wallets were torched, along with my six-hundred dollar suit jacket?"

"I thought it was two bills."

"Yeah, at the Rack. You buy it at Nordstrom, it costs you six, easy. At least four."

"I've got a fifty stashed in my badge wallet," I said, leaning to the side just enough to check, making sure it hadn't been lost during the rodeo in Inglewood. "What about you?"

"My informant stash? I can't ever just leave it alone. The last fifty I had got spent at the Outback."

"When was that?" I asked. "I don't remember an invite."

"One day last week. You had left early or something, I think. Tommy and I went over after work, had a steak and a few beers."

"You and Tommy Foster, huh?"

"Yeah, he's a good dude. You remember back in the day, back when we were working patrol and he was working gangs? He was doing that body-building bullshit, tanning and shaving his body and all that other homo shit."

"Yeah."

"I thought the guy was a bit strange, but, I didn't know him."

"Yeah, me too."

"But you know, that dude is solid, man. I mean, you get to know him, he's just a damn good guy. Loves to lift weights, chase tail, and drink beer, not necessarily in that order."

"Yep."

"Guy's been through about a half dozen divorces and he don't give a shit. As long as he has enough money to buy a steak and beer once in a while, nothing seems to bother him."

I had to agree. Tommy had grown to be one of my favorites over the years as well. We had picked up a couple cases together and not only did we work hard to solve them, we had a lot of fun doing so.

I said to Floyd: "Yeah, he's a good dude."

"That's for sure. Turn here."

I slowed for the corner, peering up through the windshield at the street sign. "Now where?"

Floyd studied a map with a penlight. "Hang on . . . two blocks up, turn left."

"Two blocks up, got it."

"It'll be on the right."

"Got it," I said. "Right here."

Donna's house appeared vacant. There were no lights on inside or out, and no cars in the driveway or on the street in front.

We knocked a couple times and rang the bell, but there was no response. Then we had a quick look through the front windows, peeking inside with flashlights to make sure nothing seemed suspicious. Before leaving, Floyd stuck a business card in the screen door, a gold star and *Matt Tyler, Detective, Los Angeles County Sheriff* on the front. On the back he had written a note, asking her to call.

WE SETTLED FOR A LITTLE MEXICAN JOINT NOT TOO FAR FROM DONNA'S house, thinking we'd be nearby if she called. Plus a good meal and a couple margaritas sounded good, and we could probably get both with my emergency fifty. We might even have enough for a tip.

After dinner was cleared, Floyd checked his watch, then ordered another round. "We'll give her a few more minutes, see if she calls."

"Probably a waste of time," I said.

"We've got booze, Dickie, it's not a waste of time."

"No, I mean Donna. What's she going to tell us? Shane was confused . . . Shane was abused . . . Shane stole her favorite blouse?"

"Maybe they stayed in touch," Floyd said, "girls do that."

"She's not a girl."

"She's not?"

"No."

FLOYD HAD A TENDENCY TO OVERCORRECT HIS POSTURE WHEN HE'D HAD A few. Maybe just a defense mechanism that kept him from falling forward. I followed him across the parking lot wondering if I leaned one way or the other, looking at the back of his wrinkled white dress shirt. It made me think about our suit jackets lost to the fire.

"Hey, where'd you keep that fancy pen and pencil set, anyway?"

He stopped, did a quarter turn with his body, and looked across his right shoulder at me. "You have got to be shitting me."

"That set you bought in New York."

"Mont Blancs. Son-of-a-bitch. See, that's another three bills there, Dickie. You suppose the county's going to reimburse me for all this shit?"

"I lost a Bic and a mechanical pencil," I said, brushing past him, continuing to the car.

"Do you see why I hate you?"

"Not sure of the brand," I said without looking back, the grin on my face unseen by Floyd.

"You really are a dickhead."

I held my hand up, working my thumb up and down. "It had one of those clicky things on the end there, the thingy gets the lead to come out?"

"This is why you have no friends."

"About a buck-fifty at Walmart. So yeah, make sure you let me know if they're going to reimburse us for this stuff."

WE DROVE BACK TO DONNA'S FIGURING SHE MIGHT BE HOME AND MISSED the card on the door or ignored it. It was a little past eight now.

The headlights of the Crown Vic washed across the front of the house as I turned into the driveway. Nothing had changed; there were still no lights, no cars, and Floyd's card remained where he had placed it.

"You got any other bright ideas?" Floyd asked.

"Yeah, one. Drop your ass off and head home."

A man appeared in my blind spot, startling me as I glanced over my shoulder to back out of Donna Edwards's driveway. The unshaven man stood silent, dressed in gray sweatpants and a stretched out, soiled, white t-shirt with a V-shaped neck. He scratched his head, a thick mass of black and gray hair going every which way. He stood watching us, his mouth partly open as if he had something to say.

I rolled my window down. "Good evening."

"Howdy."

He stepped closer to the car, leaned over, and looked toward Floyd with one eyebrow lifted. Then he rested his hands on the door. "Y'all looking for something?"

"The young lady that lives here," I said and nodded, leaning toward the center of the car in an attempt to put distance between us to escape his stench.

"The li'l nigger girl?"

"A young black lady," I said, and glanced over at Floyd. Then back to the stranger: "Name's Donna."

Floyd leaned forward to look past me, have a better look at the man. Floyd's right hand was to his side, out of my view and no doubt resting on his pistol.

"Yeah that's her. She's usually got a couple of them greasy Mexicans there with her," he said, sending stale beer and cigarette breath through the opened window. "Whole neighborhood's gone to hell."

"Okay, sir," I said, "you've been a big help. We'll see ya later, huh?"

"I oughta get out and kick his ass," Floyd said, "see if he's any tougher than Charlie."

"Except you don't like violence," I reminded him, as I dropped the shifter back into reverse.

The stranger still at the window: "You boys FBI?"

"No sir," I said, "Sheriff's department. Hey, we've really gotta run, see ya later, man."

"They ain't been here for a couple days. None of 'em."

I stopped. "Who's that? Who hasn't been here?"

"Probably selling drugs, what I always figured. The bunch of 'em always here, none of 'em work nowadays, not even the goddamn Mexicans. You'd think at least them beaners would work. If nothin' else, down there at the car wash, or maybe mowing lawns."

"You haven't seen anyone here for a couple days, you say?"

He leaned into the window. "Been a couple days now, yes sir. They was all here, like usual, and then *poof!*, they all just disappeared."

Floyd and I exchanged one of those glances, the kind that says neither of us liked what we heard.

The stranger straightened, placed his hands on his hips and stood gazing toward the house, or maybe beyond it. He shook his head and said, "Just like that,"—and snapped his fingers—"gone!"

7

MONDAY MORNING I awoke to silence, a welcome change from the turbulent weekend of death, destruction, and sleep deprivation. I rolled out of bed just after eight, feeling refreshed and energized. The priority at this point would be fresh coffee, so I ambled to the kitchen where a note waited beneath a clean mug. My wife would be gone all morning, it read, and she hoped I had been able to get some rest.

What I had actually hoped for was some time together before starting another fourteen-hour day. I tossed the note in the trash and reached for the pot.

As I poured a cup of coffee, I heard my pager beeping from the bedroom, the faint sound carrying down the hall. It amazed me I'd heard it at all, my hearing not what it used to be. I grunted and said to a steaming cup, "My idiot, no doubt."

The pager display read *10-21 007*.

Floyd, as predicted. A modern-day James Bond, sending a message to call him. I wondered if it would be work-related or was he wondering what suit or hat I planned to wear today. Our relationship was not unlike that of a couple school girls, at times.

I retrieved my phone from the county car. "What do you want?"

"Where are you?"

"I'm home. I just got up a few minutes ago."

"I wish I had your hours," he said. "You plan on working today?"

"What the hell do you want?"

"Coroner's office called on the Malibu case."

"Yeah?"

"The old man had terminal cancer."

"He knew about it?"

"According to the coroner's office, yeah. They've got his medical records."

My chuckle was not one of amusement, more of astonishment. "So he decided to do the wife a favor and take her with him."

"Looks that way, Dickie. Anyway, we'll have the report in a couple weeks and be able to close that one out."

"What about your transsexual murder?"

"*My* transsexual murder?" he asked.

"Yeah, did you solve it yet?"

"Yeah, dickhead, I solved it; Elmer Fudd did it."

"*The* Elmer Fudd? Elmer J. Fudd, the chubby little guy in the overalls who's always trying to whack the bunny?"

"No, dipshit, the fat dude across the street from Donna Edwards."

I laughed. "Your buddy."

"Yeah, my buddy. He's your cousin, more like it."

"I guess you never know, huh? Could've been that web-toed asshole. Maybe he figured he'd clean up the neighborhood, get rid of some of the colored trash."

"We find the burning crosses, we'll know where he buried the bodies."

I grimaced at the thought. "You think Donna's dead?"

"I don't know what to think, Dickie. She's gone, I know that. And I know you better get your ass moving, get to work at some point today, or you might discover I'll be gone too."

"I should be so lucky."

"Hey," he said.

"What?"

"Which hat are you wearing today?"

MAYBE FLOYD STUMBLED ONTO SOMETHING, I THOUGHT, WITH HIS flippant allegation that the creepy guy across the street had whacked Donna Edwards and her Mexican friends. I slowed in front of Donna's house and flipped my notebook open to copy the license plates of three vehicles near the property across the street. It was the place I attributed to Elmer Fudd, as my partner had named him, the house with the dead lawn and a serial killer's van sitting in the driveway over a puddle of motor oil. We had watched him walk that direction after our memorable encounter.

My mind flashed a scene of the disheveled man dragging a dead woman from the side door of the deathtrap on wheels, rolling her down a steep embankment. Seeing an attractive black woman in her twenties, the image I had of Donna Edwards, tumbling through the weeds.

I turned the Crown Vic around, parked on the street one house west of Donna's, and sat with the air-conditioner running as I jotted a few notes. I wrote down Fudd's address and a description of his house in the event we would need it for a search warrant later. Ditto for Donna Edwards's house. I noted the time, 0922 hours, and the fact it still appeared vacant: there were no cars in the driveway and Floyd's business card remained on the front door.

It seemed a good time to stretch my legs, so I figured I'd have a look around. I walked the perimeter, working my way through a wooden gate at the side of the garage. I tugged on a piece of rope coming through a small hole to release the latch. All the doors and windows were intact, nothing broken or unsecured. The small back yard held a patch of grass that butted up against a concrete patio with a Jacuzzi tub, the smell of chlorine hovering over it. An eight-foot, dog-eared redwood fence enclosed the rear property, affording privacy from the neighbors.

Except one, I thought, looking at the two-story house two properties west and one street over, the back of that house facing this way. I watched the upstairs windows for a couple minutes but saw no movement.

The sliding glass door of Donna's patio accessed a bedroom, I noticed while peeking through the partially open vertical blinds. A queen-sized bed with a floral-print comforter and pillows holding stuffed animals took up most of the floor space. Assuming it would be Donna's room, I twisted my head, looking one way and then the other, taking in what I could from the outside. Everything appeared to be in order with no signs of suspicious activity, other than the absence of life.

As I approached my vehicle, Elmer Fudd stood in his driveway, his arms folded across his chest as he stared in my direction.

I nodded as I reached the street and angled away from him, headed toward my car. "Good morning."

He stood silent, wearing what appeared to be the same soiled sweat-pants and t-shirt he wore the day before. His gaze went beyond me, absent of emotion; he didn't smile, nod, or even blink. Nothing.

I felt uneasy continuing toward my car, my back now to the strange man. I saw the scene again in my head, random girls rolling from his van down an embankment. Elmer spitting the words, *See ya later, bitches*.

I glanced over my shoulder while working my key into the driver's door and was surprised to see he had disappeared. *Poof!*

THE TWO-STORY HOUSE THAT SAT IN THE MIDDLE OF THE ADJACENT BLOCK and offered a view of the Jacuzzi, was easy to spot as it towered over the others. Unfortunately, nobody answered the door. Probably a working couple in this middle-class neighborhood; I'd have to come back in the evening.

I WALKED INTO THE OFFICE TWENTY MINUTES LATER TO FIND FLOYD reading his Horoscope in the *L.A. Times*.

"What's the forecast?"

"Forecast?"

"Yeah, what's it telling you about your future? Or maybe I should say, *our* future?"

Floyd folded the paper and set it on his desk. "It says that people think

I have all the answers, or at least, a viable plan. See, Dickie, you always have to have a plan."

"What about me?"

"What about you, Dickie?"

"What's it say?"

"You don't believe in this shit, so why would you ask?"

"Just curious."

"Well let's have a look," he said. He picked the paper up and scanned through it. "Let's see here . . . Cancer . . . *'Get your chores done early, Cancer, so you can have time to play tonight. Plan a romantic getaway with a loved one.'* Go figure, Dickie getting his chores done early to spend time with the little woman. We'll see about that."

"It could happen."

"They write these things for normal people, Dickie, not lunatics. They should have a warning on the bottom of the page, or maybe on the top, *Not Intended for Dickies*."

"Well speaking of me finishing my chores, and since the stars say you have all the answers, or at least a *viable plan*, what are you going to do about your buddy, Elmer Fudd?"

"What about him?"

"Dude gives me the creeps. I think we better dig into his background, see what he's about. But I'm not the guy who has all the answers, or a plan."

Floyd turned in his chair to face me, revealing a brown and gold, flower-patterned tie with hints of deep red against a light blue, freshly pressed shirt. He said, "The guy's just a derelict, plain and simple. He's a drunk and a slob. Probably never held a job. Probably goes to jail for drunk and disorderly, occasionally lewd conduct, maybe pissing in public. That's about all I think about Fudd, that and he might be your uncle. But I also think he has nothing to do with this case, so tell me, Dickie, why are you so interested in him?"

"I think he's a serial killer."

"You say that about everyone."

"Just white guys in vans that give me the creeps. Reminds me of those two cousins; what were their names?"

"Bono?"

He was close, the name rang a bell . . . "Bianchi. Ken Bianchi. Who was his cousin, Buono? Yeah, that's it, Bianchi and Buono, the hillside stranglers."

"That's what I said."

"You said, 'Bono,' like, Sonny Bono."

"Exactly. Sonny and Cher, famous serial killers. So you've been back over there?" Floyd asked.

"I dropped by on the way in. Let me get a cup and hit the head, I'll tell you all about it."

He spun his chair back to face a cluttered desk. "Hurry up."

"Nice tie, by the way" I commented, as I turned away from Floyd only to find my captain standing behind me.

"You could stand to run yours up to the collar, maybe button up that shirt," Captain Stover said, snugging the knot on his as an example.

"It's hot in here."

He shook his head, glanced from me to Floyd and back. I could see the wheels turning, the man dying to say something smart.

"So you guys caught that whore murder?"

Trying to not engage, I simply said, "Yeah, it's ours."

"You know why the two of you get these sick, twisted cases?" he asked, nodding to Floyd.

Floyd spun his chair back around to face us, his arms folded across his chest and the corners of his mouth turned up in a grin. Floyd's favorite thing in the world seemed to be watching his partner have a conversation with someone whose agenda differed from his own. Especially people like our captain, a natural smart-ass who lived to antagonize others. Floyd knew I would fall into the trap half the time and end up pissed off and arguing or going off, doing or saying something I'd later regret.

"Why?" I asked the captain and then glanced around to see who'd be listening.

The office sat nearly empty, not uncommon for a Monday morning. A third of the bureau on a day off, their teams up for murders next weekend. Another third coming off weekend duty, including me and my partner, the new cases scattering us throughout the county for the next couple of days. The last third would be equally divided among those golfing, those sitting at home, and those who had already crawled into a watering hole for the day, the stress of the job and all taking its toll.

Captain Stover grinned a mouthful of crooked teeth. No doubt he had hoped I'd ask. "Because you two nut-jobs are the only ones sick enough to relate to those weirdos and their friends, that's why. Wouldn't surprise me if one of you two perverts had been with one of them, whatever you call 'ems."

"Transsexuals," Floyd said, still grinning. "That's what they're called when they've gone through a gender reassignment surgery."

Working the captain into a frenzy.

"See?" Stover said, shaking his finger now toward Floyd, "That's exactly what I mean about the two of you. Most of the guys around here wouldn't even know about that. Most detectives, if they picked up one of these types of cases, would have the good sense to do the scene and be done, not waste any more time on a dead—what'd you call it?"

"Transsexual," Floyd answered. "Now, if they dress like a woman but still have all the boy parts, they're just transvestites. Or drag queens, cross-dressers . . . whatever."

"You guys are sick," the captain said, his smirk now completely gone. "I mean it."

"Us?" I pointed to Floyd, "him."

"You got real cases need solving, right?" Captain Stover asked, now showing some anger. "Cases with real victims?"

Maybe he could have this conversation with our victim's mother, I thought. Tell her how her son's death doesn't matter, since he isn't a *real* victim.

Floyd sat there smiling; he knew I'd be fighting to hold back. That son-of-a-bitch, I thought, he really enjoys this.

I recalled a dead baby case we had picked up a few years earlier. The captain had sauntered out to the floor mingling with detectives as he did today. He had asked why Floyd and I used so much overtime the month before. I reminded him of the complex baby murder we were working, and told him a little bit about the progress we'd made and the plans we had to shore up the case. I mentioned we were close to making an arrest, and hoped to have the case filed with the District Attorney in the near future.

And the prick had the audacity to hold his hands two feet apart and ask why we were making such a stir over a victim only *so big*.

It had been a mistake engaging him that time, and I knew better than to do it again. I'd only end up losing my temper, which never ended well. It had been said I have no filter when angry, and I wouldn't disagree.

"Anything of a sexual nature seems to keep Floyd's attention," the captain continued, still stuck on our new case. "Maybe this'll keep him out of trouble for a couple of weeks. The two of you perverts checking packages in the ghetto, looking for a missing carrot." The smirk back on his face now, probably thinking his comment was clever.

"Speaking of me staying out of trouble," Floyd said, "do I get reimbursed for all my shit that was burned up?"

Captain Stover frowned. "You got receipts?"

"My suit was seven hundred, and it's not like I can just replace the jacket. Dickie's probably cost him fifty bucks. Plus I had at least lost what, two, three hundred in cash?"

I walked away knowing Floyd would keep the captain entertained with his growing list of damaged personal property and its rapidly increasing value, hearing the captain say something about how we cost him more money than we were worth to him.

I walked into the bathroom thinking about how much I hated the bastard.

When I returned with a Styrofoam cup of black coffee, strong, the bottom of the pot stuff but it would do, Floyd sat entertaining Sandy Landers and her partner, Rick Davenport. The two detectives stood at Floyd's desk. I pulled the chair from my desk and joined them.

Floyd looked at me, and his eyes told me he didn't like it and neither would I. He and I could read each other's minds with merely a glance. It had been that way for years. Partnerships were like marriages: some worked, some didn't. Some were just better than others, and every once in a while one seemed perfect. Floyd and I loved being partners and it worked. We were best friends, and had been for nearly two decades. As with a good marriage, we both recognized it as a once-in-a-lifetime partnership.

"Sandy was just telling me their case is solved."

"What case?" I knew which case, but had to ask. "The motel room?"

"Yeah," Sandy said. "An informant gave us some information on a gangster who bragged about doing it. Apparently, our suspect went there to buy himself a piece of tail, finds out our girl isn't a girl, and whacks him."

Floyd and I looked at each other.

"That's it?" I asked.

She nodded her head. "That's it, plain and simple."

"So, you think it's a coincidence your victim is killed the same night as ours, right across the street?"

She shrugged. "Why not?"

"They know each other," I said, "obviously. They were staying together or at least using the same motel room, probably doing tricks there, maybe even tricking together. Not to mention both were strangled. I'm pretty sure we're looking at one suspect here, Sandy."

"We matched a partial print on our gangster, lifted from a beer bottle inside the room," she said, staying with it. "How much more do you need?"

"What the hell does that mean?" I asked. "He was there? So what? When was he there? That doesn't put him there when your victim was killed. Shit, probably half the gangsters in Lynwood have been in that room at some point."

I paused, running it through my head, wondering could she be this shallow or was she taking the shortcut and moving on, the way the captain liked things done. A solve's a solve, right? Jesus.

Floyd decided to deflect the hostility I had inadvertently directed toward Sandy. "Maybe that's how it went down, Sandy, but you have to admit, that'd be an awfully strange coincidence."

"Maybe," she replied.

"Yeah, maybe the story's true," I said, picking up on Floyd's message that I needed to cool off a bit. "Maybe your guy did go there to get a piece of ass, found out the trick was a dude and lost it, then left in a hurry, leaving his beer there . . . maybe. Or, maybe he went there knowing damned well your victim's a queen, and that's his thing, I don't know. But I honestly just can't believe he killed her, Sandy. I just don't see it being that simple."

"Him," Floyd said, keeping track of who's who in the transgender scheme of things, or maybe just trying to lighten it up a bit.

After a few moments of silence, I asked, "Did you guys interview him?"

"No," Sandy said, "he lawyered up on us."

"Did you take it to the District Attorney yet?"

"It was rejected," she said. "The D.A. said we didn't have enough evidence to convict him, though he said it sounded like a good start. Either way, it goes down as a solved for us. How does it get any better'n that?"

8

WHAT THE HELL was that all about?" I asked Floyd as we walked to my car later in the afternoon. "Is she lazy, or stupid?"

"Sandy?"

"Yeah, Sandy. How's she going to clear a case like that? She knows damn well there's a good chance that gangster had nothing to do with it. Doesn't she?"

"Surprised me to hear her say it, to be honest."

"Bullshit's what it is," I said, squeezing between my car and one just like it, only black, the two detective cars backed into their spaces behind the gray building in the City of Commerce. "Problem is, it'll jack our case up too, if she sticks with it."

"We won't let it," Floyd said. He slid into the passenger's seat. "Don't get yourself all worked up, Dickie. That's your problem, you let this shit get to you."

I dropped the car in gear and pulled out of the space, the tires groaning against the asphalt as I cranked the wheel. I glanced at my partner. "Who's on our list now?"

"Suspects?"

"Yeah, who are we looking at so far? Charlie Wright . . ."

"Charlie . . . Elmer Fudd, this gangster of Sandy's, I guess. Maybe he's someone we should at least consider. That's about it, as far as I can see. Unless you want to add the captain to the list. He seemed to have a problem with Susie's lifestyle."

"Wouldn't surprise me," I said, "the weirdo."

I watched as Floyd reached for the radio. He changed it from AM to FM, then began checking different stations. He settled on a classic rock station, then leaned back and opened his notebook. As he jotted notes, he read them aloud: "Interview Charlie Wright . . . and . . . do a background . . . ditto for Elmer Fudd . . . arrest the captain."

"Perfect."

He looked up from the notes. "We can't talk to Sandy's suspect. You do realize that, right? She said he lawyered up."

I glanced from the road to Floyd and back, twice. Not answering right away, thinking it through for a moment.

"We can do a background on him," Floyd continued, "maybe see if that gives us anything to work on. Talk to his homeboys, family members, work it that way. Hell, he might have an alibi. It's not like she bothered to check."

I turned the radio down. "What about the informant, the one who put Sandy onto the gangster? He doesn't have a lawyer. I say we beat his balls, see what he has to say. I mean, why did he give this guy up to begin with?"

Floyd read it aloud as he added it to the list. "Interview Sandy's informant. Beat balls. Oh," he said and looked up, "I sent a teletype out statewide this morning."

"Yeah?"

"Yeah, while you were sleeping in, enjoying your morning. Just a generic of what we have, the prostitute thing. Didn't even reference the queen angle. Maybe someone out there has a similar murder, LAPD, Long Beach—"

"You thinking serial killer?"

"Well, Dickie, you're always expecting it, we might as well explore it. Nothing gets you more excited than having a good old-fashioned serial killer running around the county. Still pissed off you missed out on all the Night Stalker fun."

"Yeah, too bad we were just pups back then."

I thought back to when Floyd and I were assigned to the jail and the Night Stalker case went down, each of us just young deputies not long out of the academy. I remembered them bringing him in, the big celebrity, Richard Ramirez. He had been escorted by half a dozen deputies and a few sergeants and lieutenants, everyone enamored with this sick bastard coming in wearing handcuffs and chains, the biggest killer of our time. I had been surprised to see he wasn't anything special, just a slimy looking stoner type. He looked like half the kids you'd see behind the bowling alley or hanging out in the park smoking dope. Nothing special about his outward appearance, which made me want to see inside his head all the more. His eyes were dark and empty, a contrast to the smirk he wore on his face. I remembered looking at the homicide dicks who led the way and thinking, those are the big leaguers right there, man. These were the guys who get to take on this vicious killer and try to get him to crack, tell his story and confess his sins. They'd hear the details of each case and go through it with him over and over until it's solid and until they knew they had him. They would get a close-up view inside the monster's head, a unique experience most would not be able to handle or comprehend. Then they'd see him through court and tell him, have a nice life, asshole. Or death, whatever.

"It would be a dream come true, for you, huh Dickie?" Floyd said and chuckled.

"You have to be careful what you wish for," I said.

The rock and roll music and our air-conditioner blowing full blast nearly drowned the sounds of traffic and road noise, the streets of L.A. badly in need of repair. My mind remained on the Night Stalker, the Satan-worshipping serial murderer and rapist who terrorized Californians for more than a year, some for maybe a lifetime. Floyd was likely thinking about fashion or beer or one of the secretaries, or maybe kicking someone's ass at the gym, the guy all over the place.

I glanced over and saw him leaned against the door, the A/C blowing his brown hair up on that one side. He was giving me a look through his shades, more of a smirk, really.

"What?"

"What's wrong with you?" he asked.

"What do you mean?"

"You know what I mean. Anyone know you better than me?"

He had a point. Of the two people from whom I couldn't hide my emotions, Floyd was certainly one; I had married the other.

"You don't know me for shit," I insisted.

"Something's eating you," he said, "or maybe it's your hat's too tight today. I like that color by the way. Kind of a taupe?"

"Something like that," I said, and glanced in the rearview mirror to see it. "I forget what they call it . . . Yeah, kind of a taupe, I'd say."

"Did I help you pick that one out? It looks too nice for you to have picked it out all on your own."

"No, asshole," I said, "you picked out that green piece of shit straw hat that I never wear because it is absolutely so gay Peter Pan wouldn't wear it to a fairy festival. You know the one I'm talking about too, the one you talked me into buying at that hat store in Inglewood, the one that specializes in pimp-daddy felts with big purple feathers. Remember?"

Floyd grinned.

"I swore I'd never take you to another hat store after that."

"There ain't nothing wrong with that green straw, Dickie. I happen to like it. You're just too insecure to wear it. If I were into wearing hats, I'd wear it to the office with a pair of shorts and a Hawaiian shirt, maybe flip-flops and a snorkel."

"If I ever have a manicure, I'll probably wear it that day, to the salon," I told him. "Or if I ever visit a gay bathhouse, I'll definitely wear it for that occasion. Otherwise, I think I'll leave it with you. Maybe I'll will it to you, along with all these cases you're not bothering to solve."

Floyd sat grinning, not saying a thing.

"I do like this one," I said, and glanced at it again in the mirror.

"Okay, but back to you, dickhead," Floyd said. "What's up? Something's on your mind and don't tell me there's not . . . Don't make me stop this car."

"That only works when you're driving."

I paused, glanced over, and then back to the road. Floyd held his stare. I knew he wouldn't let it go, and I couldn't bullshit him. "I don't know, man, just sitting here thinking about stuff."

"Like? . . ."

"The Night Stalker, right now."

He grinned.

"That's why I sometimes swear I'm nuts. It's like an obsession with me."

"That case is solved, Dickie, in case you hadn't heard."

"That's not what I'm talking about. I'm just saying, all of it, it all sucks me in. It's like an obsession, or worse. I can't stop thinking about the cases—any of them—ours, other guys', famous cases like the Night Stalker, Hillside Strangler, Ted Bundy. I mean, I even read about this shit in my spare time. I don't think that's normal. I don't dare tell the shrink this stuff either. But I'm telling you, it really worries me sometimes."

"Well yeah, Dickie, you're definitely nuts. Shit, I've been telling you that for years."

"Then there's guys who seem to just cruise through, not really worrying too much if they solve *their own* cases, let alone someone else's. Here we're trying to kill ourselves over each one, and some guys are out golfing. And it don't matter what they give us, either. Gangsters, pimps, junkies, whores—shit, transvestites—as long as there's a coroner's case number, we work it the same as if it were a cop or a senator."

"Yeah, your point is?"

"I don't know. Maybe I'm just feeling sorry for myself."

"Look, we give a shit, that's just how we're wired. It isn't about anyone else, Dickie, it's about us. And it's about the victims and their families and whether or not the bad guys get away with murder on our watch. That's why you take this shit so serious, Dickie, you want to solve our cases. We both do. We see it as a challenge and we want to win, see the son-of-a-bitch put away."

I gave it a slow nod, thinking it through.

"It's what we do," he continued, "stand over a fresh kill like we were dispatched from Heaven, there to do the Lord's work. Solve cases and take assholes like Elmer Fudd and Charlie Wright to jail."

"Yeah, I guess you're right."

"Hell yeah, I'm right, Dickie."

Maybe I just needed the pep talk. It was like going to the shrink, only something that actually made sense. This genius I work with filling in for the overpaid doc with her plush office, and doing a better job of understanding my madness.

I smiled. "Thanks, partner."

"We're a good bunch of men, Dickie," Floyd said with a wide grin on his face.

I chuckled at the memory. It had been fifteen years earlier, back in our uniformed patrol days, a hot and busy weekend night in South Central Los Angeles. Units were scattered throughout our jurisdiction, Firestone Park, chasing one hot call after another. The burglary-in-progress call Floyd and I were sent to seemed hardly a priority on a night when people were shooting one another at a record pace. We took our time, not expecting much as these types of calls were notoriously false reports. But we arrived to find the back door of the business wide open. We didn't bother to call for backup, knowing it would take one of us being shot, or at least bleeding, to get another car out there on a night like that one; every unit in the field was busy chasing the radio.

Floyd had covered the front while I stayed with our patrol car at the rear of the business and made announcements over the loud speaker, telling the would-be burglars inside that they were surrounded by the Texas Rangers. To my surprise, it worked. Two crackheads came out the back door, hands held high above their heads to surrender.

Floyd came back around as he heard me direct them on the loudspeaker to walk toward me with their hands up. We handcuffed the suspects and placed them in the back of our patrol car. Both of us were amazed that anyone was even still there. Shortly after the arrest, we were laughing and joking about the announcement while we headed to the jail with our prisoners. One of the crooks, a tall, slender black man with a joker's grin, said, "Y'all ain't no Texas Rangers, man . . . shit, I knew y'all was jus' playin' us." Floyd told him, "We're every bit as tough as those rangers though, you made the right decision giving up." The crook had laughed and said, "Sho' yo' right, Deputy, all y'alls a good bunch of men."

TURNING INTO THE NEIGHBORHOOD, FLOYD ASKED, "WE GOING TO Donna's or that other place first?"

I suggested we check the two-story I had told him about, the one on the street behind Donna's with a view of her backyard and Jacuzzi. I told him maybe we'd catch someone home, see if they know anything, maybe have a look at Donna's from that upstairs window. Who knows, I had said, maybe we'd see something interesting ourselves. Catch Fudd creeping around the back, maybe moving the bodies or chopping them up. I asked Floyd what he thought about that plan.

He shrugged and said, "You're driving."

I pulled the car to the curb in front of the two-story, pleased to see two cars in the drive and several lights on inside. An Asian woman in her forties answered the door with a smile, and warm, soft eyes. "Hello," she said, "how may I help you?"

Floyd showed her a badge. "We'd like to ask about a neighbor, someone from the next block over."

"Oh," she said, "I don't think we know anyone over there, but please," stepping back and allowing space in the doorway, "come in." She turned her head toward the back of the house. "Honey?"

Lanh Hoang, a man I immediately recognized, walked from the kitchen, wiping his hands on a dish towel. He smiled when he saw us. "Detectives, nice to see you."

I offered a hand as he neared. "Small world, huh?"

"What brings you here?" he asked, then looked at his wife. "These are the detectives from that case I helped with translation, a few months back. You remember, I told you about it."

"He was a big help," I added. "What'd we do, a dozen interviews in Vietnamese?"

"At least," he said, now shaking Floyd's hand. "Come in, come in."

His wife excused herself after the introductions, disappearing into the kitchen. The sounds of water running and dishes clanging brought an image of the petite woman busily cleaning after their meal. The aroma of spices and food wafted throughout the clean and comfortable living area, furnished in black leather and metal framed glass tables.

"We're looking for someone who lives on the next block," Floyd said, "might have some information on a case we're working."

I nodded toward the staircase. "You can see the place from your upstairs window."

"Oh?"

"We're pretty sure," I said.

"Well, let's go have a look," he said, "you can point it out."

The room with a view of Donna's back yard held a treadmill, a stationary bike, and a universal gym, the type with pulleys and bars going every which way, and a bench on one side. Rubber mats covered the floor, mirrors and bodybuilder posters hung on the walls. The room appeared recently cleaned, everything neatly arranged and organized.

I walked directly to the north-facing window and pointed toward Donna's house. "Right over there, the place with a Jacuzzi on the patio."

"Ah," Lanh said.

The pungent odor of garlic announced his presence at my side.

"Yes, I have noticed these people before. I don't know them, but I have noticed several people there on different occasions. Young people, you know?"

Floyd slipped over to take a look, see the view. Then he cut to the chase: "They have Jacuzzi parties?"

"Yes, often," he said. Then he looked over his shoulder and lowered his voice. "They don't always wear bathing suits either." He chuckled, but somewhat uncomfortably.

I glanced at Floyd, then back to Lanh. "Describe the people you've seen."

"Almost always, a black girl, young, probably early twenties, attractive, nice body." He paused, a slight smile on his face. Probably a bit of image recall taking place as he recounted the moments. "Sometimes there are men, different ones. A Spanish guy with some tattoos, muscular build, he seems to be there often. Sometimes a Spanish woman, too."

Floyd stepped closer, focused now, intense. "Who gets naked in the Jacuzzi, Lanh?"

"Always the black girl. Sometimes with the Spanish couple. Sometimes with men I don't see before, black men. One time a white man. Young like her, short hair, clean cut."

"When's the last time you saw them?" I asked.

"Few nights ago, maybe three or four. I exercise at night, ten, eleven o'clock. Last time I saw them, I heard the music first, so I had a peek. The black lady was there with the Spanish guy, the one with tattoos? There were also two girls I had never seen before, but they didn't go into the Jacuzzi. They sat on some chairs outside, smoking."

"Your wife ever see any of this?" I asked.

Lanh's eyes widened and he looked over his shoulder again. "Oh no. Um, she probably shouldn't know what I told you. She would maybe be a little mad at me, but it's not my fault I see them."

"No, Lanh," Floyd said, "I'd say you're completely innocent on this one, clearly a victim."

Lanh smiled, seeming to relax a bit.

"What did these two girls look like," Floyd asked, "the ones that didn't go in the Jacuzzi?"

Lanh giggled. "Hookers."

"Hookers?"

"To me, it's what they looked like. Short skirts, high-heeled shoes, those stockings, you know?"

"Fishnets?"

"I think that's what they're called, they're black, kind of lacy . . . really stood out from the red shoes."

"Red shoes?"

"Yes, one of them had red, the other black I think, both high heels."

Floyd scrunched his brows. "Did you see the color of that skirt, this one with the red shoes?"

"The skirt was dark, really that's all I could tell. But shiny too, you know, like glittery?"

"Sequins?"

"Huh?"

Floyd looked at me, then back at Lanh. "It sparkled, right, like a movie star's dress?"

"Yeah."

"She was black?" I asked.

"Both of the ones that looked like hookers, were black. Then the girl who lives there, she's black. Then the Spanish guy was there too, but he's not black."

Floyd rolled his eyes at me.

"But he was in the tub," Lanh said, "that Spanish guy, with the black girl who lives there. I remember thinking they probably got something going. But I never think that when the Spanish woman is there, you know? I think he's got something going with her, too."

"But the night with the hookers there," Floyd said, "the black lady who lives there and the Mexican weren't romantic, right?"

"No, not romantic, not that night with all those people there. But they didn't have any clothes on."

"And what night was this, Lanh, exactly?"

"I think Friday or maybe Thursday. I just can't remember for sure."

I PREPARED TO ASK FLOYD IF HE COULD BELIEVE HOW STRANGE THIS CASE was now that it looked like Susie Q and maybe her friend from the motel were with Donna the night she was killed, or possibly the night before that, and how everyone was either dead or missing. I was about to ask him that and what does he think about Elmer Fudd now, when we turned the corner in my Crown Vic to see the strange man crossing the street. He had stepped off the curb from the area of Donna's house and appeared to be headed home.

"What's your boy Fudd up to?" I asked, accelerating to get up there quicker.

"I don't know," Floyd said, "but I plan to find out."

I watched as the stranger stepped onto the curb, onto the dead lawn, and continued walking toward the door.

"The guy creeps me out. Look," I said, "he's still wearing the same outfit, those disgusting sweatpants, that t-shirt—"

"Pull over," Floyd said to me, and then through his window, "Excuse me, sir?"

"Mr. Fudd," I said behind him.

"Shut-up, Dickie, what's his name?"

"We didn't get it."

Elmer looked over his shoulder from the front porch, his hand now reaching for the doorknob. A large figure standing silently in the shadows, moving stealthily about, appearing and disappearing with ease, the mystery man we called Elmer Fudd. A serial killer.

Floyd jumped from the car, his door flying open and bouncing back as he stepped toward the sidewalk saying—in an assertive tone now—"Sir?"

I slammed the gearshift into park and moved out behind him, accustomed to Floyd taking off without much notice.

Elmer Fudd disappeared into the dark hole and slammed the door behind him. Floyd, hot on his heels, stopped at the closed door.

There were no lights on inside the house, no movement or signs of life. No Elmer Fudd. *Poof!*

"Well, now what?" I asked, standing slightly behind and to the side of my partner.

Floyd stared at the door. He was probably contemplating putting his foot through it; that would be my guess. He held that look on his face: contemplative, maybe a little pissed, ready for action and deprived of it.

After a moment, he turned just enough to send his words over his shoulder at me. "What about a door-kick?"

"Then what? Take him to jail for being ugly in public? Neighborhood nuisance? *Fleeing from Floyd?* That could be a book, you know. Fleeing from Floyd. Yeah, I think I like that. Maybe it would be about all the women in your life, that and serial killers like Fudd. I could write it, but maybe call it an autobiography."

Floyd turned to face me, his hands now gripping his hips, holding that posture he gets when something's eating at him or there's someone to impress. The forty-year-old detective with the build of a college athlete, light on his feet and quick with his wit. He said, "Dickie, if you're planning to write any books about me, you'd better come up with something better than that. Maybe you could call it, *How Dickie Ruined my Life*. Or, *How Dickie Drove me Half Nuts*."

"Half?"

He faced the door and said, "Let's go, Dickie, before I do some-thing stupid here."

I turned and walked across the dead lawn and onto the sidewalk where I paused to look across the street at Donna's house. I glanced back at Fudd's to see the closed door of a haunted house. Then I looked at my partner, who stood beside me, appearing to take it all in as well.

I asked, "This weird enough for you yet?"

"It's never weird enough, Dickie."

9

DONNA EDWARDS'S HOME appeared undisturbed since my earlier visit, still showing no sign of life. Having been left with no options or answers after the presumed outlaw Elmer Fudd had disappeared into the darkened home, we wondered what the serial killer had been up to. He had clearly come from the direction of Donna's home, and Floyd and I both were intrigued.

Maybe we would find an open door or window, evidence of a break-in or even prowling, anything that might give us a reason to haul Fudd down to the pokey and beat a confession out of him. Or at least come up with some probable cause, something we could put in an affidavit and present to a judge, try to get a search warrant for his house. Have a look in the dungeon. See the stiffs piled up in the basement, body parts in the freezer.

Standing next to the Jacuzzi, I looked up to the darkened window of Lanh Hoang's gymnasium and wondered if we were being watched. "Weird little bastard, that Lanh."

Floyd followed my gaze, then turned back to study the patio, the Jacuzzi, the bedroom through partially opened blinds. He said, "I don't know, I'd probably exercise more myself with a view of this place. Seems to be a constant source of entertainment. Shit, my neighborhood's boring compared to this place."

"We forgot to ask how it ended that night," I said, the thought just coming to me. "Were they still out here when he finished pumping iron, or did he see them leave?"

"You know what else we didn't ask him?"

"What?"

Floyd grinned. "Where's he keep his binoculars?"

"You think?"

"No way he's seen this show more than once and hasn't enhanced his vision, the little pervert."

"It's what you'd do."

"Hell yeah, Dickie, that's what I'm saying. This guy's getting off on this shit, probably up there every night waiting for the show. It's only natural to want a better look. Little perv probably has a telescope mounted on a tripod for this gig, had it hiding in the closet from us and the wife."

"Makes sense, right?"

"The thing is," Floyd said, going on with it, "he cops to using glasses, that'll go over big in court if he ever has to identify anyone. Could end up being an important witness, the weird little bastard. If it turns out those were our girls he saw, Susie and the one from the motel, Sandy's victim, this case just got real interesting, partner."

Interesting, I thought, yes, but then again we had wanted to talk to Donna because she's friends with Susie. Is it so odd to think that Susie had visited with her sometime before the murder? Probably not. Although, it did seem odd that not only is Susie dead, but so is her friend, Stephanie, and Donna's nowhere to be found.

And what about this guy with the tatts?

"What we need," I said, "is to see if Lanh can identify our girls. Bring him some pics. Also, get him to give us more on the Mexican asshole with the tattoos, the one that gets naked with Donna. If she doesn't turn up soon, we might want to get a composite drawing of that asshole, see if we can get him identified."

"That's another point," Floyd said. "How do you see a guy's got tattoos this far away, if you're not looking through glass?"

"I guess it depends on how tatted up he is," I said. "If he's fully sleeved and they're all over his back and chest, probably wouldn't be too hard. If you're talking just a few tattoos, you may have a point. Let's ask him, see how much detail he can remember, having had a good look through those binos."

Floyd glanced back toward Lanh's, then at the hot tub. Back to me and asked, "You done here?"

I had another look around the patio, the yard, the adjacent properties from where we stood. "I guess. Doesn't really look like anything happened here. No blood anyway, or any other evidence of foul play."

"At least nothing we can see."

THE PAGER VIBRATED ON MY BELT AS I PULLED INTO MY DRIVEWAY AT 10:30 p.m. I sighed, seeing the display held the number for my office.

I sat in my driveway, the Crown Vic idling as Frank Lewandowski, a homicide dick with less than a year to go before retirement, told me how the phones were driving him nuts: "The Chinaman guy from the training bureau, the one who translates for you guys, needs you to call him. The irritating little bastard called three times in an hour—for Christ's sake—asking if you or Floyd were in the office. I told him nobody's in the fucking office but me, and all I'm doing is answering the goddamned phone, thank you very much."

All this, Lewandowski said, while dealing with an attorney on one line and his girlfriend on the other, the broad on his ass telling him he needs to take the ex-wife back to court, get her off the retirement, and asking where they are in their relationship, for the love of God. Frank saying he didn't have time for all this shit and then have to deal with these goddamned foreigners on the job too, people he could barely understand on the phone, for Christ's sake.

When Lanh answered the phone I said, "Frank Lewandowski said next time he sees you, he's going to strangle you with those cheesy epaulets you wear on your uniform."

"The guy at the desk? He's upset with me calling?"

"Settle down, Lanh, he's just riled up over having to take his feet off the desk. Don't worry about that old grouch. What'd you need, anyway?"

"After you guys left, I got to thinking. The night the black girl was in the Jacuzzi with the Spanish man, and the two hookers were there—"

"Yeah?"

"—it was Friday, I know it for sure."

I searched my brain for the day of the murder. Today was what, Tuesday? No, Monday. The murder was Saturday, early in the morning, still considered Friday night for most.

"Are you sure?"

"Yes, I keep track of my workouts in a journal."

"You don't say—"

"I log what exercises I do, how many sets, how much weight—"

"Me and Floyd do that with beers."

"You do?"

"No, Lanh, we don't." Jesus, this guy. "You were saying?"

"Well, I remembered doing curls, standing near the window with thirty-pound dumbbells, one in each hand, doing sets of eight."

I wanted to ask if he grabbed the binos between sets. "And you know that was Friday?"

"It's right here in my journal: Friday night, curls, six sets of eight with thirty pounds. I don't know why I didn't think of it earlier, maybe I was too nervous when you guys were here questioning me. But I thought of it after you left."

"You're a stud, Lanh, and a big help."

"Thank you, sir. Also, I just wanted to make sure—"

"Yes?"

"Well, my wife, she won't know about this, right?"

"Your dirty little secret is safe with us, Lanh."

VALERIE JONES, THE TALL, SLENDER, GOOD-LOOKING BRUNETTE WITH whom I took a blind swing and hit it out of the park, playing way out of my league, looked up from the couch as I dragged myself through the front door, my briefcase in one hand, my jacket and hat in the other.

"Rough day?"

I kicked the door closed behind me. "Not terribly. Just tired from the weekend, mostly. Maybe I'm getting too old for these all-nighters. Why do you ask?"

"You have that look. The one you get when you're ready to kill something."

"Not at all, babe. Maybe just a little frustrated over this case. Plus I was anxious to get home but had to deal with two more phone calls right when I pulled up."

"I figured. I saw you sitting out there in your car. Need a beer?"

"A cold beer sounds great. You going to join me?"

Valerie set her book on the end table and stood from the couch, her long tanned legs straightening beneath loose-fitting pink shorts. "Tell you what, why don't you put your stuff down and get out of that suit. I'll make us a couple drinks and meet you on the deck."

"Jacuzzi?"

"You up for it?"

"You kidding?" I thought about my horoscope: *Get your chores done early, have a little time to play tonight* . . . Maybe Floyd was on to something with this voodoo shit.

THE PROBLEM WITH BEING A HOMICIDE DICK—OR MORE ACCURATELY, ONE of the problems with being a homicide dick—is the brain never takes a break. I wouldn't know if shoe salesmen think about new styles and stinky feet while enjoying an adult beverage with their significant other, or if a carpenter thinks about door frames and right angles while sitting in a hot tub with his best gal. Maybe the guy at the market dreams about fresh produce coming in, or has nightmares about merchandise falling from the top shelf, I honestly wouldn't know. But I do know that when the neighbor kids play out front unattended, I see them as vulnerable and I worry. When my wife drives alone at night, I fret about predators and remind her of all the precautions she should take to avoid being a victim. I can't go to bed or leave the house without checking all the doors and windows, and for some reason, I seem to allow all of the cases, their victims and the suspects, rent-free space in my head, 24-7.

And now, while having a cold beer with my hot wife, my mind drifted back to Donna Edwards and her Jacuzzi parties. Seeing it through Lanh's perspective in my mind, through his binoculars, the victims at Donna's house, Donna and the Mexican in the hot tub. I was thinking about the what and the why and then back to Susie, my latest victim, the transsexual lying on the sidewalk in a sequined skirt and red pumps, her lifeless eyes gazing up at the stars. Thinking about all of this and hearing my wife saying her book, by J.D. Robb, who, she said, is really Nora Roberts, has this chick detective, a lieutenant who is being stalked by the killer she's investigating . . .

And it occurred to me, this is exactly why they send us to the shrink, free of charge.

FLOYD AND I HAD JUST ARRIVED AT DONNA EDWARDS'S HOUSE TUESDAY morning, idling out front as we finished up the morning discussion as to whether or not we truly were nuts or could we maybe be normal after all, or perhaps relatively normal, all things considered. We had concluded there were guys much worse, like Bob Richards, who had been recently terminated due to a fistfight-turned-gunfight with a neighbor in his middle-class neighborhood. Or Jimmy Gross, who still plays ice hockey at 45 years old as a hobby, not that great of a player but makes the amateur team every year as an enforcer, a guy who is sent out on the ice when someone needs taken out. Then there was Nate Hollyfield, a former Marine Recon guy who recently took up skydiving from buildings in downtown Los Angeles—at night, since it is completely illegal—because being a cop in L.A. didn't offer enough excitement for him. We were discussing these guys and a few of the bad drunks in the bureau when suddenly our windshield shattered with the sound of a thud and a sonic crack.

The second impact immediately followed with a gunshot at about the same time, maybe just after, confirming to me that we were under fire.

By the third shot I had crawled across the seat and out the passenger's door, piling up with Floyd somewhere along the way and landing together at the side of the car. Though we hadn't confirmed the direction of gunfire, we had both instinctively identified the house across the street as our primary threat.

"You okay?" I asked, my speech rapid, my heart pounding in my chest.

"Yeah, you?"

I glanced down for a quick inspection and found my gun in my hand, though I didn't recall drawing it from its holster.

"I'm good, I think. Where the hell's it coming from?"

"Across the street, Fudd's house."

I scooted closer as Floyd crouched ahead of the door. We huddled together behind the right front tire, keeping the engine block between us and the asshole with the gun.

"Have you seen him?"

"No," he said.

"You sure that's where it's coming from?"

Floyd looked over at me. "Who else you think it might be?"

"You're probably right. Why don't you call nine-one-one, get us some help."

Floyd nodded toward the adjacent yard. "I lost it getting out, must've flown off my lap or something."

I looked to see his phone in the grass about ten feet from the car, out in the kill zone.

I said, "Looks like you tossed it out there. Guess you figured we wouldn't want to call for help."

"Where's yours, asshole?" he asked.

"In the car, where I keep it."

"Well good thinking there, partner."

Another bullet struck the car near our heads, and then the sound of a projectile tearing through metal forced us lower yet. Another impact shattered glass somewhere behind us near the back of the car.

"He's not sure where we are," I said, "that one hit in the back."

The next gunshot accompanied a heavy thud near our position. Moments later, a warm fluid was soaking my pants. For a moment, I wondered if I had wet myself.

Floyd glanced at the ground and asked, "Radiator?"

"Maybe. That or the transmission, or I pissed myself."

"We've got to do something, Dickie. Sitting here doesn't seem to be a good option."

"You got a plan?"

"Maybe put some rounds down range and move, get to the back of that house," he said, nodding the direction. "And I'd strongly recommend we move fast, none of that lallygagging shit from you this time."

"That's your plan?"

"Make it to that wall," Floyd said and nodded toward a wall dividing Donna's house and her neighbor's, "duck behind it and low-crawl to the backyard."

"Then what, we come out on the next block?"

"No, we double back and kill this son-of-a-bitch."

I winced when another projectile peeled through the metal of the hood, not far from where we huddled. I thought about my partner's so-called plan, then thought about the fact that the car was being torn to shreds, gunshots echoing through the otherwise still morning. I had yet to hear sirens, not even in the far-off distance. It also occurred to me that when help did arrive, they wouldn't be able to come directly to our location, not with an active shooter using a high-powered rifle. Not until a SWAT team arrived, and that could be hours.

I thought about Valerie and pictured her sitting at her desk, the perfect posture and a pleasant smile, the occasional sip of coffee from a mauve-colored mug with flowers, no idea about her husband's dreadful situation. Probably thinking he and his best friend were having a dandy time together at what they called work, maybe pictured us enjoying a cup at the office while talking about our gals or maybe someone else's.

Just hours before, she and I had enjoyed an evening under the stars, relaxing in the Jacuzzi with a couple of drinks. Now I sat in this gutter, the morning sun warming my back, the acrid smell of transmission fluid mingling with Floyd's aftershave, and bullets piercing the metal and glass around me.

We were pinned down, huddled together for concealment and cover. Both knowing the risk of trying to make it through the kill zone, and also knowing we couldn't stay where we were, our cover only affording us so much protection. We were not the type to hope for a good outcome; rather, we were the type to make something happen. And if we were to fall, it wouldn't be without a fight.

I looked Floyd directly in his Ray-Bans and said, "Say when."

10

NOW!" I POKED my pistol over the warm hood of the Crown Vic, held it sideways and started blasting in the general direction of Elmer Fudd's house. The thought occurred to me that after years of ranting about movies and video games where the gangsters and sometimes even cops shot their guns sideways—to look cool—here I was doing the same thing. But not to look cool, only to keep as much of my body behind metal as possible.

Floyd spun and ran to the wall, hunched at the waist, making it over the wall and out of view in an instant. I wondered if Fudd even saw him move.

When the slide of my weapon locked to the rear, I reached for a second magazine.

Floyd yelled, "Ready, dickhead?"

"No!"

"Go!"

Shit!

Floyd started shooting from behind the wall. I pushed off the fender of the now leaking and ventilated cop car with the only thought being, *this could be it.* I ran crouched toward the wall, reloading my weapon on the move, the way I had been trained to do during Advanced Officer Training courses. I recalled complaining about the exercise, telling the instructor as long as I'd been a cop, I'd never even heard of anyone reloading on the run; that shit was for T.V.

The twenty yards to the wall looked more like three football fields as I left the cover of my car, waiting to take a bullet to the back of my head. Floyd continued shooting until I tumbled onto his side of the concrete wall, my right elbow and then my body plowing into the turf like a lawn dart. I had envisioned a graceful tuck and roll, but this wasn't it.

The sulfuric odor of burnt gunpowder lingered as my partner and I huddled behind a mass of cinderblock, the moist turf beneath us and the warm, morning sun above. Two grown men in suits lying in the grass on an otherwise lazy SoCal morning.

Floyd said, "Cover me," and started fast-crawling toward the back of the house before I could protest or inquire as to his plan. The instant he left, I felt isolated, but also afraid for his safety as he entered the kill zone.

I peeked over the wall—just long enough to see that my gunsights were pointed in the general direction of our enemy—and began firing, shooting double taps, two shots at a time, in a steady, controlled pace. The way I had been trained.

That training staff may have been onto something after all.

Floyd reached the end of the wall and scrambled around the corner of the house. He came back around, looking over the barrel of his pistol through dark shades, and began firing over my head. "Move, Dickie!"

I rolled onto my belly and headed his direction, surprising myself with how quickly I could move on my hands and knees in a suit. A bullet strike on the block wall suggested I move a little faster, and I did. I flattened out and increased the speed of my crawl, now worried about Fudd *and* my partner, both of them shooting over my head. I hit the corner and scurried around the back of the house, rolling onto my back as I came to a stop. I flipped around and crawled alongside Floyd.

"Where is he?" I asked, breathing heavily.

"No idea," Floyd answered, his breathing now controlled. "Pick a window."

After taking several deep breaths to calm myself, I took careful aim and placed a couple of shots to the side of each window, picturing the assailant standing to the sides of a port. I shot until my second magazine was empty, then sat up behind the house and reloaded.

"No shots from him for a while now," Floyd said, also reloading.

"Maybe we got him."

"Maybe. This is my last magazine, what about you?"

"Same here," I said, tapping the bottom of the magazine and releasing the slide, driving a live round into the chamber. "We better make these last."

"Just make 'em count, Dickie."

The faint sound of distant sirens broke the moment of relative silence. "Hear that?"

"Yeah," Floyd said, his eyes scanning the two-story across the street, a determined look on his face now red and drenched with sweat.

"We need to get to a phone, let someone know what they're rolling into."

"Elmer Fudd with a high-powered rifle?"

"Something like that."

Floyd crouched and moved quickly but deliberately toward the back door of the house, peeking through windows along the back wall. I figured he was looking for the residents, likely prone on the floor by now. He checked the rear door, then looked at me and shook his head. It was locked.

I shrugged.

He responded with a shrug of his own, and then he kicked the door open and stepped inside.

Moments later, Floyd reappeared on the back patio holding a cordless landline, saying into the mouthpiece, "He's probably wearing gray sweatpants and a dirty t-shirt, same thing he's been wearing all week . . . No, we don't know the address, but it's a two-story with an ugly brown van in the driveway . . . The guy answers to Elmer Fudd."

I noticed a helicopter approaching. "Give them the Crown Vic for reference," I said. "We're behind the house south of it, Fudd's in the one directly north. We got a bird coming in."

Floyd nodded to me, then relayed the information into the phone, doing his best to describe our position and that of the sniper. Reiterating not to roll in too close, the shooter is using a high-powered rifle.

THERE HAD BEEN WORSE DAYS IN MY CAREER, THOUGH AT THE MOMENT I had difficulty recalling them. I leaned back in a leather office chair, chugging my Diet Coke in the air-conditioned conference room of the Homicide Bureau as I waited in my green- and brown-stained suit pants, both knees torn, exposing grass-stained knees beneath. My shirt was missing several buttons and it too was soiled by grass and dirt and was darkened by sweat. I'd have to give a statement before going home to clean up.

I thought about the day Adam Youngblood was killed in a shooting during a traffic stop back in '87. Kenny Goldhammer had been killed during a pursuit, his patrol car broadsided by a city bus in the intersection of Central and Martin Luther King. That must have been a year or so later. Then there was Mike Farley, shot to death during a Narcotics raid in Lynwood, a few years after that . . .

I then thought of my partner who sat in another room, probably in a similar condition physically and mentally. We would be separated until each was interviewed, per deputy-involved shooting protocol.

Yeah, there had been worse days, I thought, now in the comfort and safety of our office where suddenly, for the first time since the shooting had started a couple hours prior, I began to tremble. I had just choked back some emotion when Captain Stover walked into the conference room with a scowl on his face. He pushed the door closed behind him, walked over to the table and had a seat across from me.

His silence gave me pause and caused my mind to consider the possibilities of how the conversation would go. Was he here to tell me Fudd's dead? Did we kill him, or had SWAT? It didn't even matter, as long as he was dead. Or maybe he was in custody, confessing to all of the murders and now telling my colleagues about the missing Donna Edwards, describing where to find the corpse. I thought of all that and then it occurred to me the captain could be there to relieve me of duty, saying we were out of control, all the shit we seemed to be in all the time, all the death and destruction we seemed to attract. Or maybe he would chastise me about another destroyed county vehicle, as if it were my doing.

Finally, he slid a manila file folder across the table at me. "There's all the info on your boy, the guy who tried killing you and your partner this morning. Have a look."

I watched the captain's eyes while pulling the file toward me, still trying to get a feel for him. He seemed to be studying me also, making me think there might be something more to this.

When my eyes shifted to the paperwork, he began, "Have you seen your car?"

"Don't really care about the car, Captain."

"That's two cars in less than a week. You guys—"

"With all due respect, Captain," I said, looking up at him now with a scowl of my own, "you're not going to want to push this right now. I don't really care about the goddamned car."

"What did you say?" he snapped.

He heard me, of course. The point had been made, no sense in pushing it. I lowered my eyes to the file in front of me, hoping it would end there.

"Nothing to this guy, no criminal history, nothing," Stover said, quiet now, almost decent. "Looks like he's a veteran, but we don't have any information on his service yet. You guys can really pick them."

I hadn't yet opened the file; I sat fixated on the photo clipped to the outside. It didn't resemble this guy we called Fudd. Something was off.

"What about the house?" I asked. "Anything good, like dead bodies?"

"They haven't come up with anything yet, as far as I know. We have two teams and the crime lab out there now. Just got the warrant signed about an hour ago."

"He has something to do with these murders," I said, now looking up at the captain's smug face, "I can feel it."

"Can you prove it? Hunches tend to come up flat with the D.A."

I looked back at the closed file in front of me, choosing to hold my tongue. The captain had never worked as a detective, only supervised various detective teams. Now he was telling me what it would take to get a case filed by the District Attorney. *Whatever, man.*

"The house across the street from this asshole belongs to a girl named Donna Edwards," I said. "She grew up with our victim, Shane Wright—"

"The drag queen."

"Transsexual."

"Whatever."

"We're pretty sure they—Donna and our victim—were together the night before she was killed," I said. "The victim from Sandy Landers's case may have been there too. And now, Donna Edwards is missing."

"That seems a bit thin," he said. "Interesting, but thin."

"Maybe it is now," I agreed, "but it's a good starting point. We need to get a good interrogation with this guy. If you think we should stay clear, given the circs, you need to put a tough team on him, a couple of seasoned dicks, like Little and Lopes, or maybe Stanton and Gray. Make sure whoever you choose talks to us before they go in, get some background on our case."

Captain Stover sat with a puzzled look for a moment, and then he seemed to understand. He said, "You realize we don't have the suspect, don't you?"

"*What?!* What do you mean we don't have him?"

"He wasn't in the house. He was gone before SWAT made entry. What do you want me to tell you?"

"He escaped?"

"That's the way it looks," he said, his eyes darting away. "The dogs are out there now. Maybe they'll get a scent and track him down."

I looked back at the file without seeing it, trying to keep my composure though I wanted to scream. How did he slip out of there, and when? I hadn't expected that at all; I hadn't even considered it. It felt like being socked in the gut, knowing the guy who had been shooting at us—trying his best to kill us—had escaped and was out there somewhere.

"So there's nothing in the house?" I asked, trying to refocus.

"Not really."

"No torture chamber, body parts?"

"Nope."

"They check the freezer?"

"Some photos, papers, that's about it. There in the file," he said and nodded to the folder in my hand. "That's about it, really . . . so far."

I opened the file and thumbed through a couple utility bills. "That's his name, James Scott?"

"There's another photo in there, a few pages back."

I thumbed to it, and studied it. I told myself I could see the man we know as Fudd in that photo, though it really didn't look like him. Maybe fifty pounds ago, twenty years ago, whatever. The more I looked at it though, the more I put it on the man in the driveway.

"Yep, that's him," I said. "That's our boy, Elmer Fudd."

"Keep looking. There's some interesting photos in the back."

I flipped through pages of various printouts—DMV records, FBI and DOJ queries with no records, California Criminal History Report, again with no records—and finally came to the first of several photos which were printed on regular printer paper.

"What's this? Wait, what the hell?"

Captain watched as I continued.

I looked at the next three, each a photo of me walking around Donna's house. Two different days, evident by the clothes. Photos of Floyd, some zoomed in close and personal. "This is unreal. Why's he photographing me and my partner?"

"Maybe he likes you two," he said. Then he leaned over and pointed at the next picture. "Is that your victim there, the ugly bitch in the miniskirt?"

"That's Shane Wright," I said, flipping it over and looking at the next one. "This one here's probably Donna, or that would be my guess. The Mexican guy here—"

"Reed and Knight are handling the shooting. Fugitive's giving us a team, six deputies and a sergeant to search for this lunatic. You and Floyd keep the drag queen murder—at least for now—and monitor Sandy and the new guy on their case, in the event they do turn out to be related. I'm not so sure she's sniffing down the right trail on this."

"There," I said, still studying photos, barely hearing the captain's words. "This one here."

"What?"

"See the dress, the shoes, fishnets?"

"Yeah?"

"That's my victim—"

"Freak."

"—and she's wearing the same thing she wore the night she was killed. Looks like she's leaving Donna's house here. This girl behind her right here, this looks like Sandy's victim."

"Maybe the only outfit she has."

"Lanh Hoang, guy does our Vietnamese translations?"

"Yeah, little weirdo."

"He lives on the next block," I said. "He saw our victim at Donna's house, just a few hours before the murder. She was wearing these clothes. They were in the back, near the Jacuzzi, her friend here with her. We need to get a positive I.D. from Sandy on this photo, see if this is her victim."

"You need to give Reed and Knight a statement."

"Did they find his gun?"

"No."

"No?"

"No."

"Jesus. Well, what is it, anyway?"

"What do you mean?" he asked.

"The weapon. We've got expended cartridges, right? What's he shooting?"

"No cartridges."

"What? That doesn't make any sense. How do we not have cartridges? Who the hell's searching that place?"

"Calm down, Richard. Best we can figure, he policed his brass. Who knows why."

"This is crazy," I said, dropping my forehead into the web of my hand, supporting it with an elbow on the walnut conference table. I stared at the file, the photo of James Scott off to one side, the one of my victim wearing that outfit to the other. What was it with this guy, James Scott? Here he was in this D.M.V. photo, his hair slicked back, neat and trim. Clean-shaven, his pale blue eyes crisp and alert, a bit of a grin for the camera, just on that one side of his mouth. But what else was it? Something else about him, something different. The guy we knew, the one we called Elmer Fudd, fit the bill of a classic society dropout. This guy in the picture looked like the same guy, but somehow appeared very different.

"The statement, Richard, are you ready?"

"Sure."

"After you give them your statement, go by the crime lab and let Firearms test-fire your gun. You and your partner both. They'll need to figure out who hit what, if someone turns up with a county bullet in them. Hopefully, it won't be a neighbor, the luck you two seem to have. After that, I want you to go home. Stay there. Take a day or two off. We'll call if we need you."

"Right, boss."

"I'm serious. I don't want you back in the field tonight, or tomorrow."

"Long as someone keeps us posted," I said, "let us know if they find our boy."

"We'll keep you posted; don't worry about that."

11

WEDNESDAY MORNING ARRIVED with a headache, the result of an extended debriefing in Chinatown. Floyd insists on Bombay gin whenever we shoot someone. The fact we hadn't actually shot anyone, as far as we knew, mattered not according to Floyd. We would make an exception this one time, and hey, who knows, we may have shot him.

I pulled into the crowded office parking lot and backed into the nearest spot with a mental list of ideas and the sound of a passing train's whistle ricocheting through my aching head. The ground rumbled beneath my feet as it occurred to me how disorganized the hooker case had become.

On our *persons of interest* list, we had Charlie Wright, the victim's father. Who sat in county jail on charges of assault, contempt of cop, or something along those lines. We needed to clear him of the murder—assuming he didn't do it—and speak with a deputy district attorney about charges related to our scuffle with him. The fight with Charlie seemed insignificant after being nailed to the concrete by sniper fire. The truth was, Floyd and I wanted a piece of that bully, and we had our opportunity. It might not have gone the way we had hoped, but now it's done. And like settling a score with a school classmate, once the fighting is over, there were seldom hard feelings that remained. We could just about shake hands and forget it now, neither of us believing Charlie had committed the murder.

We also had the gangster issue to iron out, the misguided youth on whom Sandy Landers hung her case, as thin as the evidence was. Although the D.A. had rejected the case, Sandy's report named him as a suspect, something that could eventually cloud our case if not addressed early on.

Finally, I thought, we needed to find out what happened to Donna Edwards, and why Elmer Fudd, now officially known as James Scott, had tried to kill us.

I paused at the rear door, lifted the gray felt enough to wipe the sweat from my head, and then walked in to the sounds of a busy morning at the Homicide Bureau. The pecking of keyboards accentuated phones ringing and being answered. There was chatter, coupled with laughter, and then, "Hey Dickie, show us that dive and roll routine."

Laughter followed the comment and someone else said, "I've got a box of bullets for sale, if you're interested."

I launched an indirect *bite me, assholes* as I approached my desk, glaring at Floyd, the prick sitting there with that grin.

"What?" he asked.

"My dive and roll routine?"

"Hey, they asked what happened. I told them how you saved my life."

"Again."

"Yeah, again."

"You done telling war stories?"

"You know what your problem is, Dickie?"

"I'm sure you'll tell me."

"You don't know how to have fun. You don't even like fun. See, fun is my department, falling under the category of entertainment. This is just a small sample of the shit you don't know. There's a much larger list, but we don't have time for all of that right now."

"You know what I *do* know?"

"What's that, Dickie?"

"I know I liked you better when you were being shot at."

I tossed my hat onto my desk atop a stack of paperwork. The chatter behind me had faded to a few chuckles, I noticed while loosening my tie.

Next on the list was coffee. I turned my sleeve cuffs up as I rounded the corner into the hallway. I hoped to make it to the kitchen and back without encountering the captain. That was always a goal, but more so today than usual, since we were instructed to take a few days off.

Sandy Landers and her partner, Rick Davenport, were seated in the lunchroom having coffee. Both seemed happy, probably just pleased with themselves for solving another case. I put on the best greeting smile I could muster. "Good morning."

"Morning," Rick said.

"Hey, Richard," Sandy said. "We heard about that fiasco out there. The sniper?"

"Yeah, pretty exciting," I said, hoping to have it dropped there.

"Do you think that guy has anything to do with your murder?" she asked.

I looked over to see her blowing at the steam from her coffee as she awaited my reply.

"I think he might have something to do with *a couple* of murders."

"A couple?" she asked.

"If he's involved in mine, he's good for yours too. He may have even whacked Donna Edwards."

"Who's that, Donna Edwards?"

I turned to rinse a mug over the sink. "Best friend of my victim. I think both of our victims were with Edwards the night of they were murdered. In fact, now that I think of it, I need you to look at a photo, see if it's your victim with mine at Donna's house."

"Okay, but I told you our case is cleared, right?"

"That's what you said."

I swiped a paper towel through the inside of my favorite mug, the one with the chalked body outline and *My Day Begins When Yours Ends* on the side. I filled it with detective-grade caffeine, which is akin to high-test fuel and high-velocity bullets, only cheaper and more practical in a place like this one.

"I'll be at my desk when you have a second to look at that picture," I said on the way out.

"Bad news, Dickie," Floyd said when I passed behind him, pulling my chair out of the desk next to his. "Your buddy Charlie's been released."

"How'd that happen?"

"You forgot to do a P.C.D."

"Why's that my job?"

"Because you're the one good at making up probable cause. It's only fitting you should fabricate the declaration."

"So we'll go back to his house," I said, picking up my phone to check messages, "talk to him there."

"So you can start another fight?"

"Hang on."

"What?"

I tucked the mouthpiece under my chin, spun my chair toward Floyd and said, "Some asshole lawyer. Says he represents Charlie Wright and would appreciate any future contact be arranged through him."

"So, next time we go to kick his ass, we should do it at this guy's office?" Floyd asked with the ever-present smirk.

"I guess."

I dropped the phone into its cradle and stared at my desk, absently viewing photos beneath the glass: portrait of the wife, a couple hunting trip photos, Floyd . . . one, two, three . . . "You put another picture of you on my desk?"

"The one with Cody?"

"I guess that'd be the new one, I don't know. I can't keep track anymore. There's more pictures of you on here than of my wife."

"You love me more," Floyd said, confidently.

"I don't mind the ones of your kids, but I'm starting to get tired of seeing your mug everywhere. I see enough of you already, thank you."

"Dude, that was Cody's last game. They beat Whittier for the league championship. Didn't I tell you about it? I thought you'd like it, being his godfather and all."

"You didn't have one of him without you?"

"I almost brought you one from our Hawaii trip, me and Cody snorkeling. I'll have to remember to bring it in."

"That's what I need, a swimsuit edition." I leaned back in my chair. "I think you have issues, pal."

"How's your head?" he asked. "You always feel like shit after gin. Have you noticed that? I have, because you're hard enough to deal with day to day, Dickie. Add a night out, and you're downright miserable. I need a soda. Come on," he said, rising from his chair, "buy me a Diet Coke."

"Wait. I'd like for us to get organized on this case and get something done before our next on-call period. Plus we can't spend too much time in the office this morning. The captain's going to lose his mind if he sees us."

"See what I mean? Impossible to deal with. First, I already saw the captain. We had a nice little chat. I told him we just had a few things to take care of here in the office and then we'd take the rest of the day off. Now, buy me a soda and tell me all about your list of shit to do. I'm sure it's a dandy."

We walked back to the kitchen, past Sandy and her partner still enjoying the morning over a cup of coffee, nothing better to do. I slid a dollar in the vending machine and hit the button for a Diet Coke. Once Floyd had his soda, we turned and walked back through the office to our desks, remaining silent other than the occasional greetings with other detectives. We pulled our chairs out and sat to face each other.

Floyd, sounding annoyed with the prospect of hearing my thoughts, said: "Okay, Dickie, let's hear it."

Then he began looking around the office as I spoke, disinterested.

"What do we have for evidence?"

He didn't respond.

"Hey, dipshit, can you pay attention here a minute?"

"See," he said, "you're all grumpy, probably because I kept you out late. I don't know how Val puts up with you."

"Do we have any evidence? Yes or no."

"They got semen in the rape kit. The crime lab sent us an email this morning, *mister all business, all the time*."

"No shit, huh?"

"No shit, Dickie."

I thought about it for a moment.

"Doesn't mean much, given she's a working girl."

"See? Nothing makes you happy when you're like this. Not even finding out we have evidence."

I started to respond when Floyd suddenly smiled, his eyes brightening as his attention was drawn past me, over my shoulder. He said, "Hey sweetheart, how are you?"

Detective Lacy Jones placed a hand on my shoulder, now standing behind me. I looked up and said, "Good morning, sis."

With the same last names but very different complexions, we always joked that our daddy was a rambling man.

"You guys okay?" she asked, very sincere.

Floyd said, "Dickie here saved my life."

I said, "I need to stop doing that."

Lacy patted my shoulder, smiled and said, "Glad you guys are okay. I love you guys." Then she walked away.

Floyd called out, "Love you too, Lace."

I said, "Thanks, sis."

My partner and I faced each other but neither said anything for a moment. Then Floyd picked up his notebook, flipped through a few pages and stopped when he apparently found what he had been looking for. "Okay, so you aren't thrilled with semen, what about fingernail scrapings?"

"Hell yes. Did we get DNA?"

"Haven't hear back yet, but the coroner said we have tissue. I'll give them a call after a bit."

"Consistent with strangulation," I said. "Good, she got a little of him while he had his hands wrapped around her throat. Let's find out about that. Put it at the top of your list."

"Don't get bossy with me."

"Then let's talk to Sandy's little gangster."

"He lawyered up, remember?" Floyd spat into a metal trash can between our desks. "Seems everyone's got a lawyer around here, except me. Charlie Wright's got one, Sandy's gangster has one, your ex-wife has one . . . I think I need one too, Dickie, paternity suits being on the rise and all."

"Sandy said she tried to talk to her suspect based on what an informant gave her, and the suspect lawyered up. I don't know I blame him. Bottom line is, if we don't think he did it, we need to clear him. I say we get his attorney lined up and give it a whirl. Go at him like that."

"Make it happen, Dickie. That'll give you something to do while I enjoy my soda. Keep you off my jock for a bit."

I picked up my phone. "I'll set it up."

Before we left the office, Sandy Landers stopped by our desks and viewed the photographs that were seized at James Scott's house. She said yes, she was certain the guy in the skirt walking behind our victim was Steven Dubois, the victim in her case who goes by the name Stephanie. Then she said she wondered what he was doing there, but didn't seem to give it much more thought than that before walking away.

"Do we have time to grab lunch?" Floyd asked as we crossed the parking lot later that afternoon.

We crammed ourselves into the Ford Tempo the captain had assigned as a loaner until my bullet-riddled Crown Vic was out of the shop. I sensed it was meant as a form of punishment.

"Sure," I replied, "what do you feel like?"

"I don't care. Manny's?"

"I could do Manny's. Steak burrito sounds good, chips and salsa. Shit I might have a shot of tequila too."

"Now you're talking, Dickie. A little something to take the edge off."

I turned out of the parking lot and headed north on Eastern Avenue while playing with the A/C and vents. Floyd tuned the radio. He settled on a country station and said, "So, they still haven't found Fudd?"

"I guess not. I don't get how a guy disappears in broad daylight after blasting the shit out of two cops for an hour and a half."

"Guess he had it all planned out, including his escape route. But I think it was actually only about ten minutes, Dickie."

"Makes me feel a bit uneasy, knowing he's out there."

"With a rifle."

"I hope he turns up somewhere. Preferably alive. I'd like to have some answers on this case."

Floyd said, "I hope the fat bastard's dead."

WITH BELLIES FULL OF STEAK BURRITOS AND DIET COKE, FLOYD AND I walked from the parking structure at the Los Angeles County Men's Central Jail to Main Control. There, we signed in and told a young lady in uniform we had an interview scheduled with an inmate and his attorney. We were issued visitor badges and directed to the Attorney Room.

"Ms. Freeman," she said, introducing herself as we stepped inside the small room. It was a concrete box, really, with a polished metal table bolted to the wall and four plastic chairs, two yellow and two orange. Romper room for adults. Bad ones.

She offered a hand to Floyd, her flowing blonde hair framing a narrow face that held a pleasant smile.

Floyd put on the Baldwin charm: "Pleasure to meet you, Counselor. I'm Matt Tyler, this here's my partner, Dickie Jones."

"Dickie?" she asked and smiled.

"It's actually Richard, ma'am," I said.

"Oh, well it is nice to meet you both." She glanced back at Floyd but then directed her question to me. "I understand you have an offer for my client?"

I glanced at Floyd and caught his gaze returning from the counselor's short, blue skirt.

"Not so much an offer," I said, "really more like a request."

"Well, I may have been misinformed," she said, sliding into a chair, careful of her skirt. She sat next to her client who had remained seated at the table. Floyd and I followed suit, sitting in the two available chairs across from her.

She said, "What would be your request?"

"He refused to give a statement to one of the other detectives in our unit, Sandy Landers," I told her. "We would like him to consider speaking with us about the murder he was arrested for, and another case that may be related."

"Those murder charges were dropped," she said, glancing toward Floyd and smiling. "Surely you know that. The D.A. rejected the case so my client only remains in custody on a probation violation."

"I realize that," I said. "However, it was rejected with a request for further investigation. That means technically, he isn't completely off the hook."

"What could he gain by speaking with you?"

"We don't think he did it."

Her brows lifted. "Oh?"

"That's right, ma'am," Floyd said, "and we'd like the opportunity to eliminate him from our list of suspects. It would be helpful to our investigation."

"Interesting," she said, holding her gaze on Floyd. After a moment she said, "I don't think I've had a detective ever make such a request before."

Floyd smiled. "You'd be surprised the things we come up with."

"I bet," she said, and returned the smile. She turned to her client and for the first time since we had entered, acknowledged his presence. "I am curious to see where this is going. Do you have any objections?"

The man in the orange jumpsuit replied, "Huh?"

"I would like to hear the detectives' questions of you. Are you willing to speak with them? I'll be right here, and if there's anything I think you shouldn't say, I'll let you know."

"I don't really care," he said, slouching further into his seat. "I ain't got nuttin' to say anyway."

I glanced in my notebook to refresh my memory. *Cedric Mayfield.* "Cedric, they're holding you on a violation, right?"

"Yup."

"No other charges?"

"Nope."

"We clear this up, I'll call your probation officer, see if we can take care of this violation."

"He said it's 'cause when y'all busted me on this humbug, I had dat weed in my pocket. I told him the po-po planted it, and he say dat what everyone say."

Cedric sat back a little, curled one nostril and snorted loudly. The nostril stayed put, a permanent smirk now on his face.

"C'mon now, Cedric," I said, "you know the po-lice don't plant no marijuana. If we're gonna put something on you, it'd be something good, like a bag of crack, or maybe the knife that was used to kill them girls."

"A knife? I don't even carry a knife, man. How am I supposed to kill a bitch with a knife if I ain't got one. Y'alls been hittin' the pipe, man. I ain't stabbed no bitches."

"Why'd you tell someone you killed that prostitute?"

"Wait," Ms. Freeman insisted, holding a hand up to stop him from answering.

She then leaned over and whispered something in his ear. He looked at her and said, "Huh?" She whispered again, and he just looked away. Then he looked at us and began.

"My homie caught me leavin' there. He say to me, 'Man, whatchya doin' up in dat room, with them dudes that dress like bitches?' See, he been knowin' dat nigga was a dude, and now I'm over here on front street wit my niggas over this bullshit. So next mornin', I hear what happen up in there, that that faggot got killed, and I just said I did it. Told my homie soon as I found out it was a dude, I went back up in there and took care of bidness. Man, I got a reputation to protect."

"How'd you tell him you did it?"

"Just said it to him like that. I said, 'I kilt dat nigga.'"

"No, I mean, what did you say you did, like, how did you kill him?"

"Oh," he said, sitting up straight now, "I said I beat the nigga to death with my bare hands. I don't carry a knife—I done told y'all that. So I never even thought to say I stabbed the bitch. But I didn't know how she was kilt."

Cedric smiled for the first time, looking straight at me and then over to Floyd.

Floyd sat back and crossed his legs in front of the table. "We know you didn't kill him, Cedric. Your story makes sense and I think we'll be able to clear you. Only other thing we need is a few pictures, a couple with your shirt off."

"Why is that, Detective?" Ms. Freeman asked.

"Our killer will likely have some scratches. Probably on the arms, maybe around the neck or on his face. From what we can see, your client doesn't have any marks or scratches. I'd like to document the absence of injuries."

She nodded and Cedric rose to his feet. He dropped the top half of his jumpsuit and pulled the county jail t-shirt off, revealing a lean and muscular frame. His light brown skin was blanketed with jail and prison tattoos, black and gray shades of ink portraying gangsters and women and marijuana leaves. On his chest was a hard looking dude wearing shades and a bandana pointing a shotgun, a jailhouse with barred windows behind him.

Floyd pulled a camera from his brief case and stepped over, guiding Cedric to the wall. Stand like this, now turn that way . . .

He took several photos from different angles and when he finished, Floyd said, "Thanks, man." He then turned to the counselor and extended a business card between two fingers and said, "And thank you, Counselor."

She followed us into the hall. "So, this person, your victim, she was stabbed to death?"

I waited for the door to click shut behind us. "No ma'am. Your client didn't have any of it right, he wasn't beaten or stabbed."

"We just cleared your client, Counselor," Floyd said and smiled, "at least on this one."

12

THE CLOCK DISPLAYED 6:37 when the doorbell rang the first time. Seconds later, it rang a second time, and then a third. I grabbed my pistol and hurried down the hall thinking, this had better be an emergency.

My neighbor, Virgil Chamberlain, stood wrapped in a blue terrycloth robe over checked pajamas. His gray hair was disheveled, and tears welled up in his eyes. "May's gone to see the Lord," he said.

She'd been battling cancer for a couple of years, had one lung removed a few months prior and recently learned the cancer had spread to the other. In spite of her condition, she and Virgil spent most of their time sitting in their open garage, smoking cigarettes and sipping black coffee as they watched the world go by. Seeing it had made me cringe at the thought of retirement.

They were both going to quit smoking, Virgil had said.

I said to him, "Come in, Virgil, let me throw on some clothes."

He declined, saying he needed to be with her.

"Where is she?"

"Right over there, in the garage," he said, turning partly that direction and nodding his head.

"In the garage?"

"Well yeah, where I found her. Right over there in her chair."

I discreetly placed my gun on a shelf near the door and stepped onto the porch alongside Virgil. I squinted across the street and saw her sitting there in her chair, her normal position and pose, looking this way.

"Are you sure she's dead?"

"She ain't saying nothin', or doin' nothin'. She would've at least made the coffee by now, if she wasn't dead."

"I better have a look," I said.

This was payback, in a sense. Virgil, the retired electrician, had wired my shop, installed security lights, even ran the wiring for my Jacuzzi tub when I put it in, saving me a couple bills. Other than memorizing the license number of the occasional suspicious vehicle, or talking to the kid who races that damn motorcycle around the neighborhood, my skills are generally useless in a crime-free community like ours. But now I could assist Virgil at a time of grief, march over there and confirm May was dead. Tell Virgil, yep, she's a goner, putting my skills to use.

"I'm sorry to bother you," he said, as we crossed the street together, headed toward May, "but I really didn't know what else to do. I couldn't see no sense calling for an ambulance, what that would cost and all."

"No bother, really, Virgil."

"I knew you'd know what to do," he said, his words coming out slowly. "You dealing with this stuff all the time."

We stopped at the threshold of the garage. There she sat, posed in her chair, her mouth partly open. Her eyes were mostly closed, though the left one remained slightly open, peeking toward us. I stepped inside and checked her pulse, just to be certain. After all, she didn't appear all that different than the last time I had seen her alive. There was no pulse, of course, and her skin was cold to the touch.

"We should go inside, Virgil, make a couple phone calls."

"Who we gonna call?"

"We'll have to call the sheriff's station to have a deputy come out. He'll contact her doctor to see if he'd be willing to sign a death certificate, so you'll want to have that information available. Probably get it from a pill bottle if you don't know it offhand. You'll also need to choose a mortuary, someone to give May a proper burial, or do whatever it is you two have decided to do when the time comes. You're probably going to want to call some family, or maybe friends, let people know what's happened. Maybe have someone come and stay with you a couple days, help out around the house, if it suits you. Of course, Val and I will be here for you too."

"Ah damn it!" he said, pulling a wad of tissue from his robe pocket to catch the tears now rolling down his cheeks. "I can't believe she's gone."

"I'm sorry, Virgil."

"Are you—do you know for sure she's gone? Don't you have to check her with one of them machines or something?"

I told Virgil I had checked her pulse and explained how that worked, though I did not mention the rigor mortis and postmortem lividity, indicators she had been dead since sometime last night. Probably since he had gone to bed, May staying for that one last smoke. A cigarette remained between cold, nicotine-stained fingers. Virgil seemed to accept it better once I told him, yes, I'm sure she's gone, and no, she wouldn't have suffered.

The deputy who responded to Virgil's home looked familiar to me, probably someone I had run across at a crime scene. The homicide cases spread us throughout the various substations around the county, which meant a lot of new faces and names on every assignment. I always struggled to remember the names, but recalled faces with ease. The uniformed deputy left his car running, parked on the street across the driveway, not far from the upright remains of May Chamberlain.

"Little casual today, Detective?"

He obviously recognized me. I glanced down at my gray sweats and flip-flops under bare feet. "Off-duty."

"Yeah, I figured," he said with a grin. "Relative?"

"Neighbors," I said, nodding toward the yellow house across the street, the one with the American Flag and a beat-up Ford Tempo in the driveway. "Virgil came and got me this morning."

"It's a natural?"

"Trust me on that," I said. "Nothing more than a log entry for you. We've already called a mortuary."

He studied the remains for a moment, then turned back to me, apparently satisfied with the assessment. "Whatever happened on that murder you handled, the one at the motel out on Sierra Highway? I think that's the last time I saw you."

"Sierra Highway?" I thought about it, trying to recall the case. "When are we talking, partner?"

"Six months ago, maybe. Guy was found dead in a car, shot in the head."

I thought for a moment, then asked, "The Highway Inn?"

"Yep, has the blinking sign out front, the arrow pointing toward the place."

"Yeah," I said, now recalling the scene, "the motel owner was a hunched over little gal with long stringy hair, one eye bigger than the other, her glasses all cockeyed all the time."

"Yep, dead guy was a Mexican, sitting in a Mustang."

"I remember," I said, thinking, Jesus, has it only been six months?

"What happened on that one?"

"I have no idea."

He grinned, giving the impression he thought I was putting him on. After an awkward moment, he said, "What do you mean, you have no idea?"

"The guy I caught the case with, Hispanic guy, Martinez? It was his case. I was just out there while his partner was in court. I assisted him with the scene, helped out with a few interviews, and that was about it. I personally didn't have much to do with it after that and haven't heard any more about it."

"It was a wicked hole," he said, his eyes wide now, "side of his head."

Virgil listened, taking it all in. Two cops casually speaking about a guy who'd been whacked in a parking lot, a gunshot to the head in his Ford Mustang. Just another statistic in the county, another coroner's case number issued. Virgil seemed to forget, if only for a few moments, his wife of forty-five years sat nearby, having a cigarette in the afterlife.

It occurred to me to change the subject.

"You need anything," I said to the deputy, "I'll be home another hour or so."

The leather creaked when he stuffed his thumbs into his police belt holding a 9mm pistol, ammo pouches, two sets of handcuffs, and a police radio. "We've got it here, Detective," he said, rocking on his toes.

"Virgil, I'm real sorry about May. I'll be working today, but you have my pager. Don't hesitate to call if you need anything."

"Thanks, uh, Rich," he said, fumbling with the words. "I appreciate you taking care of all this."

I nodded and stepped out of the garage, headed home. I glanced at the sun rising over my left shoulder as I crossed the street, thinking here we go, another hot one in Southern California. Thinking about the busy day ahead of me, how I'd better get moving. I'd already lost an hour spending the morning with Virgil and having my final visit with May. Then thinking maybe Virgil could have her stuffed, keep her sitting there in the garage, and we could continue to visit from time to time, her and Virgil memorialized in time. Put a cigarette in her hand and prop her up right there with a view of the street.

And then right away thinking, *Jesus, there I go.*

"MAY'S GONE TO SEE THE LORD," I TOLD FLOYD WHEN HE ANSWERED HIS cell phone.

"Who's May?"

"Neighbor lady."

"Not the hot one, two doors down?"

"No, dipshit, Virgil's wife. Virgil's the old guy across the street, helps me with electrical work. You've met them."

"Thank God. I thought you meant—"

"Katie, the soccer mom."

"Yeah," Floyd said, "you had me worried."

"Nope, the old couple right across the road, blue house. I feel bad for him, poor old bastard."

"Well, God bless Virgil and May," Floyd said, "and the 82nd Airborne Division and Miss America too while you're at it."

"My sentiments exactly. What are you doing?"

"Fighting traffic, headed to the office. About ready to kill this asshole behind me." Floyd yelled, "Get off my ass, dickhead!"

"I'm not on your ass," I said.

"Not you, dickhead, the dickhead behind me."

"You're headed to the office?"

"Yeah, aren't you?"

"You forget we have court today?" I asked.

"On what?"

"Prelim on the Grover case, Compton Court."

"Ah, Christ. Yeah, I forgot. I'll see you there, Dickie."

WAITING FOR OUR CASE TO BE CALLED, FLOYD AND I SAT IN A VACANT jury room dictating the case of Shane Clayton Wright, managing our time in a futile effort to keep from falling further behind on reports. We passed the recorder back and forth to maintain the chronological order of events memorialized in our respective notebooks. We preferred that method over the cut-and-paste method some detectives used to organize a dictated report. We felt it was a more proficient way to prepare our reports, plus dictating together seemed more enjoyable than apart. After all, we were partners.

Floyd paused the recorder and handed it to me. "So what happened to May?"

"Well . . ."

Floyd grinned, my expression probably telling him this would be one of those stories.

"Virgil left her out in the garage last night, smoking—"

Floyd chuckled. "Ah Je-*sus* . . . here we go."

"This morning, he can't find her cause she isn't in the kitchen, making coffee, cooking breakfast, whatever—"

"She's in the garage," Floyd guessed, his face now wrinkled, his eyes beginning to water.

"Still smoking."

Floyd let out a burst of laughter.

"Serious, man."

"She's dead?" he asked.

"Yeah, but she's smoking."

"Ah Jesus, Dickie," Floyd said, wiping his eyes. "You're killing me. You know, only you can have all this weird shit in your life. You do realize that, right? Well, me and you. No one else though, I'm convinced of it. This kind of shit doesn't happen to normal people."

"She still had the cigarette in her hand, burned out at the filter."

"See," he said, "that's what I'm talking about. That's exactly what I'm talking about!"

"I could hardly believe it."

"No," Floyd said, "I mean, that's the way to do it. You have to go out enjoying life."

"Smoking cigarettes?"

"Whatever, Dickie. Smoking, skydiving, snorkeling, dancing on tables. Anything that floats your skirt."

"Your boat."

"You might find me buried under three dozen empty beer cans in my garage, an empty beer box on my head for a hat."

"Cell phone in your hand—"

"Hell, yeah."

"—cause you always call me when you're drunk."

"That'd be cool," Floyd said. "I'd make the call, then stiffen up. Flatline right there between my Jeep and the fridge with you on the line going, 'Are you there, asshole?' . . . all pissed off cause I'm not answering you."

"Shades on."

"Exactly. That's the way to go."

We had almost finished dictating when they called our case. The district attorney decided he would only need Floyd to testify. I would be his Investigating Officer, meaning I would sit at the counsel table with the D.A., there to answer any questions he might have of the investigation. This was a common practice in murder trials, less common in preliminary hearings. I got the feeling the D.A. just wanted an additional buffer from the lunatic in chains.

The defendant, Nathaniel Grover, had killed his mother, two sisters, a niece, and a nephew, just days after being released from the California Department of Corrections. He had been rehabilitated.

The fact we were even having the hearing astounded me. The defendant had confessed to the murders during a two-hour interrogation that had been videotaped and submitted as evidence. Then he pled not guilty at the time of his arraignment. Floyd had said we should have shot him when we had the chance. I reminded him we hadn't actually had the chance, the guy being handcuffed and in the back of a patrol car when we arrived at the scene. That wasn't the point, he had said.

The hearing went without a hitch and the defendant was held to answer. Walking to the parking structure after the hearing, Floyd said, "Ought to be a fun trial."

"I'm looking forward to it," I said. "Maybe he'll get killed before then. The asshole's not likely real popular at the county jail."

We reached the entrance to the structure and stopped near the guard shack. There was a staircase on our left and elevators beyond it. I nodded toward the stairs. "Up on three. You?"

"Right here," he said, nodding into the dark garage. "I meant to tell you, the trace on the implants?"

"Yeah?"

"Came back to a medical distribution company in Dallas. Their number one product? Breast implants."

"They give us the name of a doctor?"

"Still working on it," Floyd said, as he brought a can of Copenhagen out of his suit pocket.

The two of us stood comfortably in suits and shades, two white guys at home in the City of Compton. Floyd packed a pinch of snuff and brushed his hands together. "You ever wonder if we're in the wrong business, Dickie?"

"No."

THE EVENING L.A. TRAFFIC STOOD STILL AS I HIT THE HARBOR FREEWAY in the Ford Tempo with its broken air-conditioner. I merged into traffic while wiping the sweat from my forehead, seeing miles of brake lights ahead of me. I decided to check in with the office, see if my car was back from the shop or if there had been any news on the search for Elmer Fudd.

"Not a word," Lieutenant Jordan said. "But you might be interested in a murder Team Four is handling out in Hollywood."

"Oh?"

"Yeah, they picked up a case involving a cross-dresser, or drag queen, whatever you call it."

"Transsexual?"

"Whatever. All I know is it's at a club on the strip, apparently known for that type of thing."

Jesus.

"All right, LT, give me the address."

13

AFTER SIGNING IN on the crime scene log maintained by a deputy at the edge of the parking lot, I ducked under the yellow tape and made my way to the front door of Club Cabo on the corner of Sunset and La Cienega. The putrid smell of urine and beer wafted from sticky asphalt as I walked across the lot. I noticed about six low-budget economy cars and a black convertible Corvette parked outside the building.

The front door of the lounge flew open as I reached for the handle, and Kenny Hollis charged through it, his latex-gloved hands holding large paper bags away from his body.

"Whoa, sorry, dude," he said, catching the door with an elbow.

"No problem, Kenny. You in a hurry?"

"Little bit. I'd like to get home before midnight. Got a fishin' trip planned for tomorrow. What brings you here, Dickie?"

"Just wanted to have a look, see what you guys picked up. Where're you going fishing?"

"We're going out of Long Beach, headed toward Catalina. Just a one-day gig. Let me throw this shit in my trunk," he said, lifting the bags of evidence for clarification, "and I'll give you a tour inside."

I stepped aside, holding the door as Kenny crossed the parking lot to a dark brown Caprice parked outside the yellow tape, half in the driveway, half on the sidewalk. He dropped the collection of evidence into the trunk, along with his gloves, and then closed the lid and ducked back under the tape. He was wiping the sweat from his head as he made his way back to the front door where I stood waiting.

"It's still hot out here," he said, arriving back at the door. "I'm sweating like a pig."

"Did you know that pigs don't actually sweat?"

"I didn't."

"True story. I don't remember where I heard it, but it's true. Now, when someone says that, *sweating like a pig*, it seems funny to me."

"No shit, uh?"

"Yep. Apparently, it's why they wallow in mud to cool themselves. So really, when you say, '*sweating like a pig*,' you're actually saying you're not sweating at all. You'd be better off saying you were sweating like a borrowed mule—that's one I like—or you can say a rented mule. You could also say you were sweating like a whore in church, or you could say sweating like a brotha at a free dance. That one's pretty funny too, I'm not going to lie."

Kenny grinned. "Now, do you actually say, *brotha*, when there ain't no *brothas* around?"

I grinned and said, "I try to, Kenny."

He chuckled and said, "I bet."

"It is warm this evening though, I'll give you that."

"Not much better inside either, *brotha*," Kenny said, grinning a bit.

We both chuckled, comfortable in the absence of political correctness.

Kenny wiped the sweat from his head again.

"You need a cover," I said.

"I can't hide this bald head, man, all this beautiful brown skin."

"Looks good too," I told him. "You've got that shine going on. It never looks as good on us white guys, the bald and beautiful look. Now a hat, on the other hand . . ."

Kenny smiled. "Yeah, you could stand to get your dome tanned a little bit, get that glare off it. Maybe you could get out and do some fishin', play some golf or something. For Christ's sake, man, all you do is work."

"My head would fry, Kenny, if I didn't wear a hat. I'd have to lather it up in sunscreen. Some hardcore shit, Peckerwood-99."

Kenny chuckled. Then he grabbed the door and gestured for me to step inside.

"Scene's in a dressing room in the back. Nothing to worry about up front here."

"What will you guys be fishing for?" I asked, pausing after I stepped into the dimly lit room. There were black leather chairs and wood tables scattered over the red-carpeted floor. A raised, half-circle shaped stage with two brass poles sat along the back wall. Just off the stage was a doorway covered by a red velvet curtain. The entire building reeked of cigarettes, stale beer, and cheap perfume.

"Calico bass, white sea bass, yellowfins, anything that gets on my hook, really." Kenny was now at my side, two big guys standing shoulder to shoulder in the narrow entry.

Kenny's partner, Ignacio Ramirez, stood just this side of the curtain next to the stage, his back to the main room. Kenny began walking that way and I followed, Kenny saying, "Last time out, I brought home about fifty pounds of tuna filets."

"That's a lot of fish," I replied.

"Guy across the street traded me some of his elk, and that worked out just right. The wife loves fish, but I am more of a red meat kind of guy. Elk is good, if you've never tried it."

"I have," I said, "couple of times."

Kenny said, "I'm thinking of taking up hunting."

"In all our spare time."

We were just behind Ignacio now, having moved slowly through the main room. Kenny was back to telling fish tales, mentioning the name of the boat they had chartered and what time they were leaving, obviously excited about the trip. I had barely paid attention, too busy in my head wondering what kind of freaks came to this joint and paid to see ugly men dressed as uglier women. I pictured the action in my head, some hairy-legged dude in a red mini, on stage, blowing kisses to some weirdo wearing women's underwear beneath his Dockers, the wife at home thinking he worked late again.

Kenny stopped, held a hand across my chest, and said, "You ever go?"

"Deep sea fishing?"

"Yeah."

"Never have," I said, "though I wouldn't mind trying it. I've got a buddy who—"

"Take the day off, come along. You know Jake Helmouth, Bobby Bryant, both from Narco, right?"

"I know who they are."

"Good guys. Them and a couple buddies of theirs from DEA are all going. Seriously, man, it'll be a good trip, you really should come along."

"I appreciate the offer, Kenny, but man, I'm buried."

"Gotta make time for the good stuff, my man. Life's too damn short to be killing yourself over this job."

"Maybe next time," I said.

I stepped alongside his partner. "Hey, Iggy."

"Hey man, what brings you here?"

I tilted my head and peeked around the curtain. "I was telling Kenny, I heard about your murder, thought I'd better have a look at your victim. We've got a dead prostitute who turned out to be a transsexual. It's probably related to a case Sandy Landers and that new guy have, the guy that came here from Lancaster. They handled a dead prostitute who shared a motel room with our victim, a murder me and Floyd stumbled onto while working our case."

"Where's that asshole, Floyd?" Kenny asked and chuckled.

"I fired him," I said, "conduct unbecoming."

Iggy smiled and said, "Seems reasonable enough to me. He is definitely *unbecoming* at times."

"So your victim and Sandy's," Kenny chimed in, "they were actual transsexuals, had the operations and everything?"

"The case Sandy and the new guy picked up, the hooker in the motel room, she was only half done, just the breasts. Ours had the entire package."

"You're shittin' me?" Iggy said. "Like, everything?"

"Complete retrofit. I saw it with my own two eyes."

"I'm not sure I'd want to see that," Iggy said, then seemed to think about it for a moment. "Maybe just out of morbid curiosity."

"Kind of wish I hadn't seen it myself," I admitted. "Anyway, our case and Sandy's case are likely connected, so when I heard about this one, with the similar theme of this joint, I figured I'd better see if anything connects up."

Ignacio asked, "Yours happened down in Lynwood?"

I nodded. "Long Beach Boulevard."

"I thought you guys solved that one, had a big shootout with the suspect?"

"He got away. Broke containment or maybe he was gone before the troops arrived. Either way, we don't know if that shooting has any connection to our case or not. Maybe just a nut job gone off the deep end."

"Why else is a guy going to take shots at the police?" Kenny asked. "It's got to have something to do with it, you'd think."

I shrugged, "Unless he's just crazy."

Kenny shook his head. "Neighborhood where I grew up, you'd have to be insane to shoot at the cops. I mean, it happened, but only when a guy was cornered hard, didn't want to go back to the joint. You didn't just shoot at the po-lice for shits and giggles. Of course, back then, a brother shoots at the cops, he didn't ever make it to court. There would always be some kind of furtive movement or some other shit to justify killing the asshole, or so it seemed."

I thought about Fudd getting gunned down by the surveillance guys, thinking it wouldn't be a bad thing.

"I don't know, Kenny, none of this makes any sense to me. It's not like we put any pressure on the guy, never even questioned him. We spoke to him one time on the sidewalk, asked him what he knew about some people living in this house, a place we later find out our victim had been to the night before she was killed. This guy—Floyd named him Elmer Fudd—goes off, talking trash about all of them. The girl we're looking for because she's black, her friends because they're Mexican, the lot of them screwing up his neighborhood, blah, blah, blah."

Iggy, grinning again, said, "The same guy blasting at cops from his window is worried about the neighborhood going to shit?"

"Can you believe it? And we didn't do anything but listen to what he had to say, thanked him for being a concerned citizen, and left him standing there rubbing his belly."

"Good thing me and Iggy didn't get that case," Kenny said. "He might have shot our asses the first night, Mexican and a brother snoopin' around the neighborhood."

"Maybe he is a nut job," Ignacio said. "One of them guys that just decides he hates the cops, and there you were."

Kenny shrugged. "Who knows?"

I shrugged also, nothing to add.

After a moment, Kenny said, "I have a question for you though. What do you call them?"

"Who?"

"These transformers. Do you call them *he*, or *she?*"

"It's confusing."

"I mean like on the reports," Kenny clarified. "You refer to them as male, or female?"

"We listed ours as Shane Clayton Wright, Susie as an alias. Sex? Female. Born male, died female. Probably setting a precedent here, not entirely sure it's the right way to do it."

"It's crazy," Kenny said.

I agreed. "Something Joe Friday never had to deal with; that's for sure."

I stepped inside the curtain and scanned the dressing room, making slow visual circles, beginning on the outside and spiraling my way to the victim. A seasoned investigator will try to see not only that which is present, but also that which might be missing, something that should be present in the scene but isn't.

While continuing my study of the dressing room, I asked, "Did you guys get him ID'd yet?"

"Not yet," Ignacio said. "Definitely a man, though. See his hands, feet?"

"Hairy-assed legs," Kenny added.

"Any witnesses?"

"Just two. The owner, and a doorman," Kenny said. "The patrons made it out before the cops got here, as shocking as that may seem."

"Looks like some of them left their cars," I said. "Maybe you guys will ID a couple wits from the cars?"

Kenny nodded. "I would think so."

"That's the plan, anyway," Iggy added.

"Don't reckon you'd be lucky enough that one of the cars belongs to your suspect."

"Not likely," Kenny said. "We aren't that lucky."

The victim lay sprawled on the floor, face down next to an overturned vanity chair. Assorted makeup containers and lipsticks littered the vanity and the floor beneath it, scattered around the victim's body along with cigarette butts from a spilled ashtray.

He—or maybe, she—wore a long black sheer dress, black nylons, and black pumps. The hair, presumably a wig, was long, thick, and black; it would be perfect for Halloween. I stepped closer and squatted next to him. There were bruises on the side of his neck, his head turned slightly to one side. His brown eyes were dull and clouded, holding the familiar stare of sudden death.

"You guys ask for a coroner yet?" I asked, still squatted, studying the victim.

"Should be here any time," Kenny said, "if you want to stick around."

I stepped back alongside Kenny and Iggy, and the three of us stood there in silence. Three veteran homicide detectives visually processing the scene through practiced, weathered eyes, and taking our time with it. Allowing it to marinate in the silence, no place for urgency in the practice of crime scene investigation. Three cops—black, white and Hispanic—and a dead man dressed as a woman, gathered in a plush room with mirrored vanities and racks of exotic clothing and lipsticks for the boys. It occurred to me there were few circumstances that could bring the four of us together, this gathering the most likely of scenarios.

"At this point," I said, "I primarily want to know how much work he's had done, what kind of aftermarket equipment he's got going on in them designer panties."

"That'll make a difference?" Kenny asked.

"I don't know. It might."

Ignacio folded his notebook and stuffed it in his rear pants pocket. "You think we've got a serial killer?"

"It's what I'm wondering."

WHEN THE CORONER'S INVESTIGATOR ARRIVED AND EXAMINED THE remains of the victim, he determined the sex to be male, though he appeared to have had breast augmentation surgery. I asked Ignacio to keep me posted with his case, let me know if anything interesting happens. I also told him what we learned about serial numbers on breast implants and asked him to be sure to check into that at the autopsy. I wished Kenny the best of luck on his fishing trip and departed the scene in style, the Ford Tempo an excellent choice to motor through the city of the rich and famous.

The Hollywood Freeway flowed nicely now. The rush-hour crowd had been replaced by those who worked late and those who had waited out traffic by doing happy hour or hitting the gym, and the few of us who hung out at drag queen bars with dead entertainers. I rolled the windows down and took in the sights, sounds, and smells of the big city as I motored south through Downtown Los Angeles.

South, the opposite direction of home.

14

STRUGGLING WITH WHETHER or not to call my partner, I continued toward Donna Edwards's house thinking I could pull this off with no trouble, without a chance encounter with Fudd or any other catastrophic event. Fudd wouldn't be home, I reasoned, not after shooting it out with the cops. Every detail of the incident had been broadcast on the five and eleven o'clock news, two days in a row now.

No way he would be stupid enough to come back here, I thought. At least not yet.

I hoped.

Besides, I thought, Floyd would probably be in bed by now, nearly 11pm. We had both been buried lately, the cases coming steadily, and it had kept us working long hours. Floyd tried hard to balance work with the family life, having three kids, all involved in sports. I pictured him coming home in the Suburban, unloading football and soccer gear from the back hatch while telling the kids to get started on their homework, maybe saying to Cindy, *Yell when it's time for dinner, I'll be out in the garage.* The garage being Floyd's happy place, complete with weights, a heavy bag, a speed bag, and miscellaneous workout equipment. Also, a refrigerator full of beer. And by now he'd have the kids in bed, a belly full of beer, and likely be passed out.

Everything would be fine, I reasoned. I'd just drive by, have a look at the house—*what would be the harm in that?*—and be on my way, headed home. Thinking about this as I drove south on the Hollywood Freeway, south on the Santa Ana Freeway, and off at Paramount Boulevard. Still confident it would do no harm as I turned the corner onto Third Street and saw Floyd's car parked two houses down from Elmer Fudd's.

What the hell?

Probably doing the same as me, I reasoned, as I coasted to the curb with my headlights off, pulling in behind his car in stealth mode. Maybe Floyd and I were on the same page, each thinking to swing by and have a look, check Donna's house, no need to bother your partner, no reason to make a big deal of it. See if Donna had made an appearance yet, or if the bodies had mysteriously surfaced. Maybe they'd been dug up by cats.

I could see the front of Fudd's house, the dark, bullet-riddled, two-story that now sat boarded up and garnished with crime scene tape and evidence markers.

A light flickered inside Donna's house, which I caught with my peripheral vision. I watched for a minute but didn't see any other light or movement. I began second-guessing what I had seen, and wondering if I had seen anything at all.

The interior light of my loaner vehicle came on as I opened the squeaking car door. I quickly reached to cover the light with the palm of my hand and cursed the loaner. I needed my cop car back, the Crown Victoria. A vehicle properly equipped for police work: big engine, heavy-duty suspension, hardwired police radio in the glove box, red light for the front, a blue and amber for the rear, and a siren to assist in commuting through the congested city. But most importantly, quiet doors and adjustable interior lights, the small things cops truly appreciate.

I glanced at Fudd's house again as I stepped from the car, the memory of Floyd and me being pinned down by gunfire flashing through my head. I crossed the street and paused beneath a tree in Donna's yard, feeling slightly more secure in the dark shadow. I scanned Donna's house again and it occurred to me that the front blinds were now open. Someone had been in the house since my last visit.

I looked over at Fudd's house, then again to my partner's vehicle. I lifted my H&K 9mm from its holster and tucked it along my leg. I moved further onto the property, silently following shadows cast from trees and rooftops as I listened for any sounds. I heard nothing beyond the distant traffic and crickets in the night.

Moments later an explosion pierced the silence. I hit the ground—falling partially into the hedges along the garage—and scurried through the dirt and foliage to the corner of the house. I looked up to see a couple kids speeding past in a lowered Honda car, its tires squealing and stereo thumping as the occupants laughed, enjoying the moment. I stood and brushed myself as the taillights faded into the night, realizing the loud report had been a backfire. My heart pounded as I poked at the inside of my hat, reshaping its crushed dome and brushing away the dirt.

A female voice startled me. “May I help you?”

Donna Edwards. I recognized her in an instant as I turned. She appeared just as she had in her photo: straight brown hair framing soft brown skin and defined cheekbones. Her jawline tapered to a small chin, accentuated by a dimple. Her narrow eyes studied me, her head cocked slightly to one side as her brows crowded together, indicating question or maybe concern about the man in her yard fixing up a dirty fedora.

I brushed myself again and straightened my tie. “Yes, ma’am,” I said, pulling the gold star from my belt to display. “My name’s Richard Jones. I’m a detective with the sheriff’s department, and I’ve been looking for you.”

“Looking for me?”

“You’re Donna Edwards, right?”

“Yes.”

“There’s some things—”

“Is this about that crazy man across the street?”

“No—well, not exactly. Why do you ask?”

She nodded that way. “Looks like something happened.”

I glanced over and realized the yellow tape made it obvious.

“Maybe we should step inside, if you wouldn’t mind too much. I’d like a few minutes to speak with you.”

“Fine, come in,” she said.

I followed her to the front door.

“By any chance, have you met my partner?”

“Um, no,” she replied, “not to my knowledge.”

She reached inside and flipped a switch and the living room lights came on. She held the door open and stood to the side, inviting me in with a nod of her head.

"Nobody's been here to see you?" As I stepped past her through the entryway, I smelled the distinct odor of burned marijuana.

"Not tonight," she said.

Donna closed the front door behind her and walked past me, leading us into the living room where she gestured for me to have a seat on a leather sofa. She sat at the edge of an adjacent chair and pulled a cigarette from a brown snakeskin cigarette pouch. Her red, manicured nails accentuated her delicate hands as she lifted the cigarette in one hand, a butane lighter in the other. It was the type of lighter most often used for lighting cigars. Or to burn a spoon full of heroin, or heat the end of a crack pipe.

I took the seat, still smoothing out my hat, turning it this way and that, checking the shape while thinking of where to begin with the young lady, the childhood friend of Shane Wright. Get right to it and tell her about his death? Or maybe start off by talking about the whack-job across the street?

But something bothered me and gave me pause. And it was more than just the smell of marijuana or the image of Donna Edwards burning a glass cocaine pipe. It was something else.

I thought about Floyd's car parked across the street. I had glanced inside and saw his raincoat—a black London Fog with an American flag on the lapel—neatly folded across the back seat. He always kept a coat in his car year around. His tan London Fog had burned up with the other car, and I remembered him replacing it with the black one. It left me no doubt this was the car assigned to my partner. But why was it here and where the hell could my partner be in this neighborhood? I had left him at court several hours earlier, splitting up for the day as he needed to head home and get the kids off to their games. He had said maybe he would barbecue some steaks tonight, have a few drinks, and he seemed happy to be ending the day early. So why the hell was his car parked across the street?

"Well?" she said, breaking the silence, "what did you want to talk about?"

Her light-brown eyes beneath long narrow brows studied me as I sat in silence, hearing her say it again, her voice calm, quiet, and cool as she waited impatiently to find out what I wanted to talk about. She sat perched on the edge of her seat, her posture perfect, the light-blue t-shirt draping over her shoulders and nearly covering her gray shorts. A confident young lady but with questions, not unexpected from someone who received a surprise visit from a homicide detective.

Had she been sleeping, maybe awakened by the backfire of the speeding car? All of the lights in her home were off when I arrived and had remained so until she and I entered the home. Why were the lights off? There had been a flicker of light; was it from inside, a television maybe, or could it have reflected from somewhere outside the home? Was someone else in the house? Had she been in the Jacuzzi tonight? Maybe, I thought, I should take a break, tell her I'd be back and go have a chat with my friend, Lanh Hoang. See if he had anything to report, find out if he had enjoyed a peep show tonight.

I glanced at my watch, aware of her watchful eyes. It was now 11:22 p.m. Where the hell was Floyd?

15

FLOYD ANSWERED HIS cell phone on the fourth ring asking what the hell was my problem, calling him at 11:30 at night. He said, "Of course I'm home, where the hell else would I be?" Then he said, "Yes, I drove my county car home tonight. Did you think I took the train?" A moment later he yelled through my earpiece, "What the hell do you mean my car's been stolen?"

It sat in front of me, plain as day. I leaned on the hood of my Ford Tempo, looking at the license plate with the December registration tag—one of several indicators of a government vehicle—and said, "How else do you suppose it ended up at Elmer Fudd's house?"

"It's where?"

"You know what, hold on, let me take a better look. See if the ignition's punched or maybe you left your keys in it."

"I'm going outside," Floyd said, "check for myself. I think you're screwing with me."

Floyd grunted and groaned into my earpiece as I walked to the passenger side of his vehicle. I could see him in my mind, Floyd sitting up, paused at the edge of his bed, his eyes squinted and nose wrinkled, looking for a pair of shorts or something to throw on, no doubt sleeping in the nude. Probably looking at the clock now, then over at his sleeping wife. Rolling his eyes and shaking his head, pissed off. At me or her? All these images from too many business trips, too many shared hotel rooms, too much information about my twisted sister's personal life. I looked through the passenger's window but saw nothing unusual, no stripped steering column, no punched ignition, none of the usual signs of a stolen car.

"Son-of-a-bitch!" he said through my earpiece.

"Not where you left it?"

"Captain's going to kill me," Floyd said. "What's this, three cars in a week between the two of us? This isn't a joke, right?"

"Lucky for you, I've recovered it."

"You're serious?"

"Dead."

"Jesus. What's the damage?"

"None that I can see. Ignition is even intact. Probably jimmied the door, I don't see any damage to the locks or windows."

"Wait a minute, Dickie, are you telling me Elmer Fudd stole my car?"

"More likely than Donna Edwards."

"She's probably dead."

"Well, actually, I have some more news for you, slick. Donna Edwards is home now."

"What?"

"I just had a little visit with her—"

"What the hell are you doing out there by yourself, anyway?"

"Something told me to come by."

"Great," Floyd said, his voice suddenly calm again, "you're having visions and hearing voices. I knew it would come to this eventually."

"It's like a sixth sense. Woman's intuition."

"I'll be there in twenty," Floyd said, disconnecting without saying goodbye.

I stood pondering the situation, knowing someone other than Floyd drove his car here, to a place we were investigating a murder, this place where Elmer Fudd resides and a scene of mayhem where bullets from a high-powered rifle destroyed my Crown Vic just two days earlier. It didn't make any sense. The options were either Elmer Fudd did it, or it's a bizarre coincidence. I don't believe in bizarre coincidences.

It occurred to me we should have kept a surveillance going of the house. After the shooting, they searched the house and surrounding area for Fudd but never found him. Why didn't we keep surveillance of the house for a few days? They probably wouldn't have wanted to pay for the man hours, I reasoned, the captain would have argued that there's no way the guy would show up after that.

I phoned the Downey Police Department and asked for backup. I told the lady on the other end of the line we needed to establish a containment of the residence of James Scott, the guy wanted for shooting up their city a couple days ago, as he may have returned to the scene of the crime. The dispatcher said she'd get some units rolling. In the meantime, I'd better speak to the watch commander.

I know it sounds crazy, I told him, this watch commander who seemed a little uncertain about the information I provided, but there really is no other way to look at it. Yes, I have confirmed my partner is home and accounted for. No, his car was not stolen from a bar or motel and we are not trying to clean up some sticky mess my partner got himself into. Not that Floyd isn't capable of any such mischief, I thought, but this time he seemed to be squeaky-clean. *Seemed to be.*

The mysterious house across the street sat still in the quiet darkness. Yellow crime scene tape decorated the front porch and yard, a red evidence sticker sealed the door. I thought about the serial killer who previously occupied this place and wondered what type of man would shoot it out with the cops, get away, and then steal the same cop's car—from the cop's house, apparently—and drive it back to the crime scene. Every cop in the county looking for him, and he boosts a cop car and drives it home?

It made no sense. Maybe I needed to rethink this, make sure I hadn't been completely fooled by my partner, or that I wasn't missing something even bigger than that.

Or maybe I just needed a drink.

Floyd lived just close enough to the edge that a situation like this gave me pause. I had to consider the possibility that he went bat-shit crazy on me, off the deep end, over the top. I always knew it could happen. After all, it had been his idea the time I had dinged up a county car during an unauthorized pursuit, to *clean it up* without a report. I had tried to stop abruptly at the end of a pursuit and slid into a clothesline, creasing the bumper and bending the clothesline nearly in half. When chasing bad guys, it was easy to get caught up in the moment. But we weren't supposed to be in the projects, which were outside our jurisdiction, and the department generally frowned on driving across sidewalks and lawns. For that matter, we shouldn't have been in pursuit in an unmarked vehicle. So with all of these factors, doing the *right* thing took a backseat to career survival. Rather than reporting the damage, the two of us muscled the pole back into a nearly vertical position, and then we took the damaged county car to a shady body shop where cash bought us a quick but doable fix, and most importantly, no paper trail.

Sometimes you had to be creative, clean up your mess.

Which left me with doubt. Maybe Floyd's car had been stolen, but maybe from somewhere else, I thought. Somewhere he maybe shouldn't have been. Just one of the many possibilities.

I'd know soon enough, I thought. As soon as I could look him in his eyes and continue the conversation face to face. He wouldn't be able to lie to me, any easier than I could lie to him.

The police arrived and established a perimeter of Fudd's house, covering the back from the next street over and making the front look like a donut house parking lot. They had just started evacuating neighboring houses when Floyd pulled in behind me, the narrow Jeep headlights leaving no doubt it was him. He hopped out—the top and doors almost always removed from his weekend toy—and met me between our vehicles.

"What kind of shit have you gotten me into now, dickhead?"

"Comfortable?"

He looked down at his jeans and Rockports beneath a V-necked pullover sweater. "What did you expect, I'd put on a suit to come out here and kick your ass—yours and Elmer's?"

"Why would you kick my ass?"

Floyd started counting on his left pinkie, working his way toward the thumb: "One: you shouldn't be here without me. Two: what the hell is my car doing here? Three: you just need your ass kicked."

"I'm not going to argue with you on three; I definitely could use a good ass-kicking."

"Oh, and five—"

"Four."

"—now you're giving me shit about my outfit."

"Yeah, well, I'm not as G.Q. as you, obviously."

"Obviously," he agreed.

"We have a witness to talk to," I said, "once we resolve this other mess. I would have thought you'd wear something a little more professional, or at least something that wouldn't get you beat up, have your lunch money taken."

"You're an asshole," he said. Then he looked toward the conglomeration of police vehicles casting beams of red, blue, and amber-colored lights throughout the neighborhood. "You got SWAT rolling?"

"I was stalling."

"Why?"

"I wanted to talk to you first, face to face."

"What for, Dickie?"

I glanced over my shoulder and back. "This lieutenant out here from Downey seems like a real hard-on. So far, this isn't much of a deal, but before we make it a big one, I felt the need to make sure you're clean on this."

"Dude, I swear to God . . . Wait, you think I pulled this shit? Why would I do something this bizarre?"

"I don't know, you're just funny that way."

"Yeah, I'm hysterical that way, sometimes. But I had no part of *this*, that I can assure you. I'm a victim."

"You went straight home, parked the car out front, right?"

He rolled his eyes. "Yes, Dickie, I did. Do you need a note from my mother?"

"Just tell me there's nothing bizarre going on here, nothing at all."

"I'd tell you. You know that."

"I know." I looked off for a moment. I turned back to him, pushed the brim of my hat up in front and said, "I'll notify the desk, tell them we need

SWAT and they better notify the captain. You call Norwalk Station, ask them to check your street—probably your whole neighborhood—see if there's any suspicious vehicles around there. Make sure they look for that brown van."

"So, if it was Fudd, how the hell would he know where I live?"

"Good question, but I don't have an answer. Better have Norwalk check in on your family too, maybe leave a couple guys at the house until we sort this out."

"Jesus, Dickie."

Floyd appeared concerned, worried. Not a common reaction from the man who welcomed challenge and danger. I put my hand on his shoulder as if telling him it would be fine. There were no words necessary, both of us knew that whatever we went through, we went through it together. Professionally or personally, that's just the way it had always been.

Floyd took a deep breath and let it out slowly. Likely getting himself back in his zone: focused, driven, in complete control, and prepared to prevail under any circumstance, against any challenge. Floyd had always prepared for the ultimate confrontation, mentally and physically. On the rare occasion of insecurity, he would reach into that treasure chest of confidence, compiled from all the years of training and preparation, to quickly regain his edge.

I recalled an occasion when Floyd had a problem that involved a family member and a rather aggressive adversary. He called, and I heard it in his voice, that same but very rare uncertainty. I told him I'd be there with him, and when I arrived, he explained that the person he had to deal with was a violent one, the type who'd probably look for a fight. He also worried the guy would show up with friends, as he always seemed to be in the company of other thugs. I had lightened it up, saying, yeah, and he probably runs ten miles a day and lifts weights and trains in the kickboxing gym and spars with professional fighters too. Floyd nodded as I finished making the point. I said, "I'm just here to watch this guy either bitch up or get pummeled, that's it. You won't need me for anything else, unless his friends get involved, and then I guess we'll both be busy." He realized he had no real need for concern, and in that instance too, he gathered himself, focused, and mentally prepared for the event. Which interestingly, never happened; the guy never showed up and was never heard from again. Likely a sign of intelligence.

With SWAT having an estimated arrival time of whenever the hell they got there, I told the Downey lieutenant we would be over there, pointing toward Donna's house, if anyone needed anything from us. I explained we might have someone who could provide some insight into all this crazy shit, and we needed to talk to her sooner rather than later.

Donna answered the door with a puzzled look about her. "What's going on now? It's getting crazy around here."

"Donna," I said, "this is my partner, Matt Tyler."

Floyd smiled and offered a hand. "Nice to meet you, Donna."

She opened the door and stepped aside. "Come in."

I led the way to the living room and returned to the sofa. Floyd plopped down in the adjacent chair and Donna took a seat next to me. I opened my notebook and jotted the date and time, her name, the location of the interview and then asked, "What is your birth date, Donna?"

"Um, January tenth, nineteen-eighty-two."

"You're what, twenty-three?" Floyd asked.

"Yes."

"Damn," he said.

"What?" she asked, as she and I both glanced at Floyd.

His expression seemed to say, Did I say that out loud?

"Nothing, sorry . . . I was just thinking, you're really young."

I stepped in. "Donna, when's the last time you spoke with Shane Wright?"

She tilted her head and studied each of us for a moment before answering. "Last week sometime. Why?"

"Can you remember the day?"

"I don't know. Why? Is something wrong?"

"It's important that you think of when you last saw him."

"Okay, let's see . . . I left for Cabo Saturday morning, so it must've been Friday. Yes, she was here Friday night. You know, it's actually Susie, she's had a complete sex change and prefers to be called Susie, not Shane."

She remained posed, relaxed, comfortable in the shorts and loose-fitting t-shirt. No concern, worry, or deceit, or so it seemed.

I asked, "When did you return?"

"Just got home a few hours ago."

"Do you mind saying who you went with?"

"Is there something going on?" she asked, now showing some concern, maybe irritation at the questioning. "Am I suspected of something?"

"No ma'am," I told her, "something's happened to Susie."

She didn't show the emotion I would expect if this were a surprise. "What's happened?"

"She's been killed, Donna. Last weekend."

"Oh my God!" she said, her hand rising to cover her mouth.

She looked at Floyd, then back at me, shaking her head and fighting back tears.

"I'm sorry," I said.

I studied her to see if anything in her response seemed inappropriate for the emotion she displayed. There was nothing that concerned me. Although her initial reaction had puzzled me slightly, I dismissed it as she probably never dreamed the news would be this bad. People reacted differently when they learned that a friend or loved one had been killed.

Donna took her time, stifling emotions as she dabbed her eyes with the backs of her hands. "What happened?"

"She was murdered," I said.

"Oh, my God! Does the man in that house have something to do with this?" she asked, nodding across the street.

Floyd said, "Why do you ask?"

"It only makes sense. With everything going on over there, the cops out front and all, you guys here . . . What else could it be?"

"Do you know the man who owns it?" he asked.

"No, I don't know him. I know who he is, what he looks like. He seemed nice enough, but I've never spoken with him. Waved to him once in a while is all. His wife—"

"His wife?" I interrupted.

"Well, I assume she's his wife, they're an older couple, you know. Anyway, she seems pleasant enough, says hello when she sees me, always has a smile."

Floyd and I exchanged glances.

"When's the last time you saw her?" I asked.

"Month or so, maybe. Him, too. I think they went on vacation or something. The guy in the van started staying there. He let the lawn die, made the place look trashy."

"Is that who you meant, when you asked earlier if this was about the crazy man across the street?"

"Yeah, he seems crazy to me. Just stares at everyone, frowns all the time. The night Susie left—she had a friend with her—they were getting in their car and he said something nasty to them."

"You heard this?"

"I heard him say something, but I couldn't hear what he said. You could tell it was mean, or nasty or something."

"Did they say anything back?"

"Susie's friend—I think her name is Stephanie—she's kind of obnoxious, you know the type? She smarted off, told him something. I don't know what she said, but he didn't look happy."

"Then what happened?" I asked.

"They had just got into the car as he started walking that way, like going toward them, so they drove off real quick. You could hear them laughing at him. After they were gone, he glared over here at me. It was real creepy, to be honest. So, he does have something to do with this?"

I turned to Floyd. "I need to get the case file out of my car, get that photo. You want to entertain Donna for a minute?"

"It would be my pleasure," he said.

I stood and excused myself, stepping across Donna's thin, bare legs on my way to the door.

When I returned, Floyd was saying to her, ". . . never to Cabo, but I've been to Cozumel and Cancun."

"Oh," she replied, both of them smiling now, "I'd love to go to Cozumel."

Floyd glanced at me but disregarded my presence, looking back at Donna now, batting his eyes as he talked to her.

"I actually like Mexico more than Hawaii. You get a lot more bang for your buck. But I like them both, really. Hawaii, you have the nicest beaches, great snorkeling—"

"You two planning a vacation now?" I asked as I sat back down on the couch.

"What?" Floyd asked.

"Just asking if you were planning a vacation with Donna."

"We were talking about something other than work. You wouldn't be interested."

I shrugged.

"You should lighten up a bit, Dickie, think about something other than police work for a change. Take a vacation some time, go suck up some rays, enjoy life, you know? Did you get the photo?"

I sat down and opened the file, thumbing through it until I found the Wanted Poster with the photo of Elmer Fudd. I put it in front of her. "Is this the guy you're talking about, the guy who's been staying across the street?"

She studied it for a moment before answering. "No, this is the man who owns the house. He's gone."

Floyd and I exchanged glances.

"You're sure?" I asked.

"Yeah," she said, "I'm sure."

Floyd said, "Not the asshole with the van, the guy who yelled at Susie and her friend?"

"No," Donna Edwards said, her back arched as she posed on the edge of her seat, "though they do look similar, in some ways."

FLOYD AND I STOOD ON THE EDGE OF DONNA'S DRIVEWAY TAKING IN THE action across the street on a warm spring night. There were SWAT vehicles now, an armored transport, four black and white patrol cars, and the tactical van that folds out to create a mini-command post. The sound of helicopter blades chopping through the air faded in and out as the bird circled above us, its spotlight illuminating the house across the street.

"So I wonder what happened to James Scott?"

Floyd stuffed a pinch of Copenhagen behind his lower lip, brushed his hand on his jeans, and spit a stream of brown fluid toward the gutter. Putting the can back in his pocket before he responded, "And the lovely Mrs. Scott."

"The little woman."

He packed the snuff with his tongue and spat again, leaving a brown stain on the driveway. "I sure hope he's in there, and I hope SWAT lights that place up like it's Independence Day. Dead or alive, I don't care at this point. This is nuts."

"We're off somewhere on this, partner," I said "I really feel we're missing something big."

16

THE PAGER WENT off, piercing my deep slumber beneath an open window, the cool nighttime breeze a welcome change from the daytime heat. The alarm clock displayed 3:22, and the code in my pager told me to call the office.

My house phone rang before I could make the call.

"Hello?"

"Did you talk to the office yet?" Floyd asked, his voice sounding wide awake, excited.

"No, I was just getting ready to call. What's up?"

Floyd said, "The fugitive task force has a lead on James Scott."

"What do you mean?"

"They've tracked his credit card. Looks like he's alive and well, spending plastic money on a daily basis."

"Where?"

"That's the best part, Dickie, we're headed to Texas!"

"Great."

"They love us there," Floyd said.

WE WALKED BRISKLY THROUGH TERMINAL 4, PAST THE COFFEE SHOP, PAST the newsstand, past a stand of cinnamon rolls that filled the halls with the smell of pastry and sugar and spice. We might have stopped but we were running late, thanks to the trainee at the ticketing counter, the kid who had stood with a blank stare when Floyd badged him saying, *We're LEO's . . .*

LEO's? he had asked, and that was the beginning of a long morning at the Los Angeles International Airport.

"Law Enforcement Officers," I had said, shrugging my carry-on bag from my shoulder and dropping it to the floor, "means we have lots of paperwork to complete. You might want to ask for some help, if you're new at this."

The young man with strawberry-blond hair and an American Airlines ID with a photograph of his freckled face, the name John Walker beneath it, turned to the lady next to him and asked for help. She didn't help much, as it turned out, but not because she was new and inexperienced like the kid. She came with an attitude and a look on her face that said she was unappreciated and underpaid, and the last thing she needed was to have to help the freckle-faced kid fill out all those damn forms, the ones we needed to get on the plane with our guns. She took a deep breath, rolled her eyes and pursed her lips, just enough to show her disgust. As if we were doing this *to* her.

When we finally reached the gate, the attendant smiled, said she would pre-board us and asked that we stop in at the cockpit and introduce ourselves, let the captain know there'd be a couple cops on board. Sure we can, is what we told her, having grown accustomed to post 9-11 travel protocols.

"I always check the cockpit anyway," Floyd mumbled after we thanked her and headed down the ramp, "make sure Jimbo isn't driving."

"I thought he worked for Federal Express?" I said across my shoulder, feeling the ramp bounce beneath every step.

"When he first quit the department, he did. Then he got on with American or Delta, one of these commercial outfits."

I pictured Jimbo sitting at the helm, looking over his shoulder, smiling at the sight of his old friends. Saying he's sure glad to see us, hope we'd enjoy the flight. Then a demented laugh, a *Welcome to Hell* smirk on his face. It took a minute to remember the name. James Garland. A short, stocky, former Air Force pilot who had seemed to lose a couple marbles somewhere along the way. He had worked patrol with us in South Los Angeles and was a good cop, but he definitely marched to a different drummer. Floyd had something there, I thought, making sure ol' Jimbo wasn't our pilot.

After a brief introduction at the cabin, we made our way to the rear of the plane near the restrooms and took two of the three empty seats of an exit aisle.

"No Jimbo," Floyd said, picking through magazines in the seat pockets in front of us. "Not so sure I like the idea of a broad up there though."

"Hopefully, she's the copilot. She was on the right. Does the copilot sit on the left or right?"

"I don't know," he said. "Does it matter?"

"Long as she keeps her eyes forward, I guess not."

"Right, cause we don't want any hanky-panky going on up there," Floyd said.

I leaned to my left and pulled the seatbelt from beneath me. The flight attendant was making her way down the aisle, checking seatbelts and overhead compartment doors. I glanced to see Floyd flipping through the pages of a Cosmopolitan magazine, his right leg crossed over his left, shoulder against the window.

"Better buckle up there, slick," I said.

"We haven't even left the ground and here you are, all over my jock."

"What the hell are you reading?"

"Cosmo," Floyd said, dropping the magazine to his lap. "You don't read Cosmo?"

"Are you shitting me?"

"Jesus, Dickie, you are so short-sighted at times. This is like having a look at the rival team's playbook, or having your enemy's war plan."

"Yeah?"

"All the plays," he said, tapping the cover with his index finger, "right here."

"The plays?"

"What women like in men, what turns them on, what they're looking for in a relationship—which is really unbelievable when you see some of this shit. Some of these broads in here are trying to say it's not so much the physical attraction, but an intellectual connection. I call bullshit on that. There was one issue, had all these interviews, tramps from all over the country revealing how they cheat on their husbands. Didn't give their real names, of course, but would give the particulars. You know, age, how long married, profession—if they were employed—the whole bit. Do you have any idea how interesting that was?"

"How interesting was it?"

"Very. Let me tell you what I learned from that little gem—"

"Tell me."

"Tupperware," Floyd said and paused, "biggest scam they've got running. Know why?"

"Why?"

He waited as the flight attendant passed. "Because, Dickie, what kind of asshole wouldn't let his wife go to a Tupperware party? They say, 'Hey babe, Shelley's taking me to a Tupperware party tonight. I won't buy anything, promise.' At the most you say, 'Why go, if you're not going to buy something?' She comes back with, 'It's like your poker night, you know, just a night out with the girls, have some hors d'oeuvres, a few drinks, dessert.'

"That's their tactic, all planned out. They know you don't want to go there, jeopardize poker night, so you're up against the ropes. And after all, it's just a Tupperware party, right? So you think, what the hell, there's a ball game on television, what do I care if she's out of the house for a few hours. Give me a night of peace and quiet, right?"

"Okay?"

"What you don't know is she's down at the Holiday Inn swinging from the chandeliers with Charlie the bug guy or some other asshole while you're watching the Dodgers blow another lead in the ninth, what's his name out for the season, guy with the glasses and hair on his chin."

"Gagne," I said, looking past him now through the rectangular window, seeing a blonde woman with earmuffs and an orange vest drive a cart under the wing of our plane, "Eric Gagne."

"They suck now anyway. You been to a game yet this year?"

"That's what the article said?"

"What article?"

"The one on cheating spouses."

"Lays it all out, Dickie. Everything right there in black and white. Problem with it is that only women read this stuff—"

"And Floyd."

"—so actually, they learn to be smarter sluts. Men just keep watching their ballgames, drinking their beers with not a clue this shit's going on. Also, there's always hot babes in there. Seriously, you've never seen one?"

"You never cease to amaze me," I said.

"Dickie, I amaze myself at times."

TURNING INTO THE PARKING LOT OF THE MARRIOTT HOTEL AT DALLAS-Fort Worth, I asked Floyd what he felt like for dinner, and wasn't it his turn to buy.

"I wouldn't doubt it," he said. "It always seems to be my turn to buy when we're spending more money. Let's see, you picked it up at that Mexican joint the other night, spent what, fifty bucks?"

"Exactly that, including the tip."

"Yeah, well, you may recall, Dickie, this place will run us a couple bills, at least a buck and a half, if we do it right."

"It all works out in the long run," I told him. "Besides, when's the last time we popped for a really good meal?"

"When we were here last, probably."

"Yeah, and that's been what, two years?"

"Wait, New York, Dickie, last year. We spent a fortune in that Italian joint in the Bronx, the place the Cold Case Squad took us when you said you wanted to see a mob joint. That crazy lieutenant from Brooklyn, Jim Dover, said he'd take us to a joint where they hung out, remember? We get there and see a couple old Italians with shoe leather for skin, looked the part, and your dumb ass kept looking over there, sizing them up. My Dickie, always on the J-O-B. The lieutenant finally told you to quit staring before we had a problem."

"I'd never met any real mob guys, you know? Not that kind, anyway. Something different than our local street thugs who call themselves gangsters. I mean, what do we have for organized crime, the Russians? That's about it, really. Personally, I'd like to have some real mobs in L.A. Al

Capone, Bugsy Malone, that *Godfather* shit. Something to make our murders more interesting. Dude in a suit steps into a room and finds himself standing on a sheet of plastic and realizes he's done. Some fat dude with a .22 behind him, used to be his best friend, puts a bullet in the back of his head. Then he gets dumped in the river or chopped up and put in sausage, shit like that."

"Jesus, dude . . . sausage?"

"I'm just saying, there's different ways to dispose of bodies than just dumping them in an alley or up in the Angeles National Forest. Mobsters are more creative than that. Of course, maybe that's why they aren't out here, now that I think about it. The L.A. river never has any water in it, so there's no place other than alleys to drop the stiffs. Other than maybe the butcher's shop."

"Mobsters like the east coast, Dickie, that and Vegas. L.A.'s not real mobster friendly." Floyd paused and said, "I heard back in the fifties, they tried moving in on Hollywood, tried to get in on that racket but LAPD ran them off. That was back when the boys in blue had some balls, didn't have a pussy for a chief. They apparently roughed them up pretty good, maybe even killed a few in shootouts, and basically shut them down and shipped their asses back to the east coast. Probably disappeared a couple of them too, now that I think about it. There's books about it, movies too."

"*Mulholland Falls*," I said.

"Exactly."

"Well, seems to me I bought in the Bronx, so it's your turn."

"Fine," he said, "I'll buy, but that means I pick the wine."

"Whatever."

"There's a spot," he said, pointing across my chest, "next row over."

WE EMPTIED THE BOTTLE AND FLOYD TOLD STANLEY, THE TALL, THIN waiter with dark hair but only on the sides of his head, that we'd each have an Espresso Cappuccino. Stanley glided away like a leaf blown by a fledgling breeze before I could object.

"Regular coffee works for me."

"Trust me on this, Dickie, you've got to try it. Espresso is like supreme, ethyl, high test, that shit they put in race cars."

"Nitrous oxide?"

"Yeah, that," he said. "What time are we heading over to the Holiday Inn, have a visit with Mr. Scott, or maybe Elmer Fudd? Whoever the son-of-a-bitch is that stays in that house now and shot the shit out of your car and stole mine. The way I figure it," Floyd said looking up at our waiter, Stanley, who had drifted back to the table with a tray holding two Espressos, "there's no way this guy's here in the great state of Texas. Whoever is using James Scott's credit card rented a room here three days ago, paid for a rental car and bought dinner at the Outback two nights ago. He can't be in two places at once, right?"

I nodded after a sip of the Espresso, then had another sip. Floyd had it right on the fancy coffee, though I wondered why it didn't come in a regular-sized mug, as much as they probably charged us for it.

Floyd took a sip of his, then lowered it half way and said, "Not only that, but did you notice the total on that meal, the Outback? Sixty-two bucks. That had to be for two, even if you factor in drinks. My guess is we'll find the real James Scott here, him and his wife. Alive, on vacation, enjoying Texas like good Americans."

"I hope you're right."

Floyd said, "Damned right I'm right, dickhead."

Stanley had reappeared with the check as Floyd said it. He placed it on the table and disappeared, probably thinking we were the most uncivilized men to whom he'd ever served sixty-dollar steaks and eighty-dollar bottles of wine.

"What are we, two hours ahead here?" I said, and glanced at my watch. "It's almost eight now, we could check it out tonight, if you want."

"Tomorrow, Dickie. We're on overtime now."

ROOM #114, THE YOUNG LADY AT THE COUNTER TOLD FLOYD ONCE HE explained that in Los Angeles, we don't need a warrant to get registry information, being law enforcement professionals and all. He explained that all public information is to be released upon request, hereto and forthwith, as set forth by the Public Information Act of 1986. And since Texas had not actually seceded from the Union—*though we applaud both their effort and enthusiasm*—there would be no reason the laws would differ here. Then he told her we could call up a tall Texas Ranger, have him come down to explain the whole process if she insisted, but why make such a bother?

As we turned from the counter and made our way to the room, Floyd looked over and smiled. "How was that, Dickie?"

"You should be ashamed."

"It worked."

"Poor little girl, you had her all stressed out. She didn't know what to think."

We stood to the sides of the door now, brass numbers 114 above a peep hole. We listened for a moment and shrugged, telling one another we didn't hear anything, might as well knock and see how it goes.

I asked, "You don't suppose he requested a ground-level room for a reason, do you?"

"What are you thinking?"

"Gives him a rear exit," I said, "is what I'm thinking. The question is, what was he thinking?"

"I'll go around the back," Floyd said, "just to be safe, and to make you feel better. Give me five minutes, then do your little knock and talk routine. Call me on the cell if you're getting your ass kicked, and I'll get back here as soon as I can. As long as I don't get distracted."

"Hopefully there's not a pool."

"You did bring your phone, right?" he asked.

I pulled it from the inside of my jacket and held it up. "It's even turned on."

"I'm proud of you, Dickie. You're coming right along."

When I figured it had been five minutes, having forgotten what time it was the last time I looked at my watch, I brushed my elbow against the pistol beneath my suit jacket to reassure myself of its presence. Then I reached over from the side of the door, careful not to stand in front of it, and rapped my knuckles three times against the wood.

After a moment of no response or movement detected inside, I knocked again. Still, I heard nothing. Just when I started to think it had been a dry run and thinking maybe we should have come last night like I had suggested, my cell phone rang.

"Hey, Dickie."

"Yes, dear."

"When you get done screwing around up there," Floyd said, his cocky attitude coming through loud and clear, "come on around back. There's someone here you're going to want to meet."

17

THE POOL AREA gate slammed behind me, causing a metallic sound to reverberate through the iron fence surrounding a kidney-shaped pool. Two men sat at a table beneath an umbrella: my partner, dressed in a cream-colored Armani suit with a light blue shirt and matching tie, and a rough-looking Hispanic man with tattoos and dark shades. Floyd sat crowding the tattooed man in his tan, baggy shorts and loose-fitting tank top, the Mexican leaning back in his chair trying to have his personal space.

The tattooed man showed no interest in the continental breakfast in front of him, and barely glanced at me as I pulled out a chair next to him, placing myself on the opposite side from my partner. The stranger between us seemed uncomfortable, or maybe he didn't like Floyd.

Looking at me through mirrored Ray-Bans, the bright morning sun reflecting off of the lenses, Floyd said, "Remember that photo, the one with Susie, Donna, and the dude?"

"The tattooed Mexican . . ."

Floyd nodded, then scooted even closer, now close enough the man likely felt Floyd's breath on his cheek. Floyd, his chiseled jaw tightened, said to him, "Introduce yourself to my partner, Gilbert."

The man looked at me through cheap sunglasses with thick, black plastic frames, and green lenses. "How ya doin', Officer?"

I nodded.

"Tell my partner your name," Floyd said, putting a little more pressure on him.

"Gilbert, sir. Gilbert Regalado."

"Good, Gilbert, now tell my partner what room you're staying in."

He stuck his thumb over his shoulder and motioned toward the patio area behind him. "One fourteen."

Floyd said, "What do you think of my partner so far, Gilbert?"

Gilbert nodded. "He's cool."

"No, Gilbert, he's not cool. He's not cool at all. In fact, if you think I'm a dick, you just wait till you get a load of this asshole."

Gilbert glanced over at me and then looked down.

"Want to talk to him here," Floyd asked, "or inside where we can have some privacy?"

"How's his attitude?" Talking about him like he wasn't there.

"Shitty," Floyd said, "may need some adjustments. He started out lying when I sat down, and then he wouldn't give me a bite of his English muffin."

"Maybe inside, he'll be friendlier, more accommodating."

"That's what I was thinking."

"What are you guys, feds?" Gilbert asked, his tone humble now, a hint of fear.

Gilbert flinched as Floyd quickly stood, his chair scraping across the concrete.

His six-foot muscular frame showed through his suit as he stood posed, his hands clenched to his hips, the suit jacket pushed back to reveal a gold star. Floyd said: "Feds? Hell no we ain't feds! I'm Captain Floyd T. McCray of the Texas Rangers—"

Gilbert nodded as if he understood, squinting now as he looked up toward Floyd.

"—this here's Dickie Jones. He's with the Number One Posse from El Puso. You ever heard of them?"

"I don't think so, sir, but I'm not from around here."

"Neither are we," Floyd said, "but you *have* heard of the Texas Rangers, right?"

"Yes sir."

Floyd looked at me. "See, Dickie, I'm famous. Nobody's even heard of you, or *El Puso*." Then he nudged Gilbert's shoulder. "Get up, Gilbert, we're going to go have a nice little chat about who's paying for the bed and breakfast."

Gilbert and I stood at the same time and paused there, sizing one another up. Gilbert probably wondering could he take this guy in the suit. I pictured myself dropping him with an elbow across the bridge of his nose, previously broken, no doubt, by the shape of it. No sense in playing games, rolling around in a suit, is the way I looked at it. Floyd would be thinking *mano a mano*. Being the pugilist, he would no doubt enjoy making sport of it. I'd just as soon get it done and over with. Either way, we both would have a plan to take him out, if need be; there was no doubt about that.

Floyd nudged Gilbert and said, "Walk, asshole."

Walking to the room, Gilbert looked at me on his left flank and asked, "Did he say, 'El Paso?'"

I shook my head. "El Puso."

"I ain't never heard of El Puso, I don't think. I got family in El Paso."

Floyd said, "It's more of a state of mind, Gilbert, like reverse osmosis."

"Oh."

We were now at the door to Room 114, all of us stopped, Gilbert in the middle, a look of confusion on his face. Maybe it was fear. Floyd continuing to mess with his head, telling him anything but the truth until he answered some questions.

Gilbert looked from the guy in shades to the one with the hat as he searched his pocket for the keycard. Finally, and maybe only to break the silence, but more likely because Gilbert was now very concerned about his future, he said, "You guys *are* feds, right?"

"We're actually commissioned officers of the East Westchester Northstars of the Southern Division. It's a secret cavalry unit, though we've lost all of our horses, the Indians damn near wiping us out back in the day. Me and Dickie here jumped a train from Tucson."

As Gilbert stood listening, frowning a bit, perhaps from confusion, Floyd took the keycard from his hand. He keyed the door open, a red light giving way to a flashing green one.

Floyd stepped inside, saying, "But I really am a captain."

I stepped in behind Gilbert, letting the door fall closed on its own.

"Where's your girlfriend?" Floyd asked as he pulled a chair from the round table near the window and nodded for Gilbert to sit down.

Gilbert stepped over and lowered himself into it, slowly, watching us carefully. "What girlfriend?"

Floyd slipped out of his suit jacket and rolled up his sleeves. Standing in front of Gilbert but talking to me, he said, "See what I mean about this guy? *What girlfriend?*"

I stepped back and bolted the door for effect.

"You're not here alone, Gilbert," Floyd said. "Do you think we're stupid?"

Floyd pulled out the chair next to Gilbert and squatted down, placing himself on the edge but still on his toes, easy to come to life. The two of them on this side of the table, their knees nearly touching, Gilbert leaning back and Floyd leaning into him again. Gilbert glanced back and forth from the cop in his face to the cop by the door, a look of fear now clearly present.

I began looking around, making myself at home.

"I asked you a question, Gilbert," Floyd said, "and I get the feeling I'm being ignored. If there's one thing I hate, Gilbert, it's being ignored."

"Sir?"

"Do you think we're stupid?"

Gilbert said, "No sir, I don't think you're stupid."

"Then?"

He said, "Sir," and held it there, as he watched me going through the drawers, the closet, the suitcase . . .

"Don't you guys need a warrant or something?" he asked, cautiously, the question directed toward me.

"Tell him, Floyd, about the Public Information Act of 1943."

"1986 for Christ's sake, Dickie. What he's saying, Gilbert," Floyd said, "is we don't need a warrant or anything else. You may be needing a lawyer when this is all over though, or maybe a doctor, depending on your level of cooperation."

"I want to cooperate, sir."

"Good. Your girlfriend?"

Gilbert's eyes shifted away as he answered, "Her name is Maria. I don't know her last name. She was here a couple days, then she left. It was her paid for the room, I don't even know how."

Floyd slapped Gilbert across the side of his head and crawled into his lap, his hand cocked for another. Gilbert sank into the chair shielding his head with two hands, a rosary tattooed on the back of one.

"Try again, Gilbert!"

"Okay, okay . . ."

Floyd backed off but not too much, and Gilbert slowly lowered his hands, his bulging eyes now fixed on Floyd. I stood to the side, casually lifting women's clothing from a suitcase, displaying the items as conversation pieces.

"Well?" Floyd said.

"Some girl I know in California."

"Go on."

"We just came out here for a visit, you know, a vacation."

Floyd drove a knee into Gilbert's rib cage and clamped his hand around his neck. He leaned into him again, Floyd's face now red with anger. It seemed a good time to intervene, before it was too late.

"We know you're not here on vacation, Gilbert," I said, sliding into the third chair.

Floyd released his grasp and sat back a little.

"Let me talk to him a minute, partner," I said. "Maybe he and I can get along better. What do you think, Gilbert, you wanna get along?"

"Yeah, sure, I don't want no problem." He watched as Floyd sat back in his chair now, but not too much.

"Listen, Gilbert," I said, "you may be in some trouble here, the business you guys are in, but I'll let you in on a secret. We're homicide cops from L.A. We don't care about anything other than a couple murders we're looking at. Not the dope, nothing else."

"Murders?"

"Yeah, some friends of yours. What do you want to tell me about that?"

"Nah, man, I didn't have nothing to do with no murders."

"Gilbert, I'd like to believe you, but you've not been real truthful so far. How about let's talk about the players, for starters, see how truthful you're going to be. First, we've got Gilbert," I said, touching the tip of my left pinky with my right index finger, "and Gilbert doesn't want to take a fall all by himself. Then we have this girl, what was her name?"

Gilbert sighed and looked down. Then he raised his eyes and said, "Donna."

I continued as if the name hadn't fazed me. "Okay, Donna . . . who else?"

"I don't know the ones out here, the two guys we met for the stuff. That's all Donna's deal. Just me and her came out though. Man, I'm not even really into the dope thing, just more helping her out, you know, kind of just hanging with her and shit while she's making some green. She's not really even my girlfriend, just more like a piece of ass sometimes."

Floyd still appeared wound tight, waiting for a reason to pounce.

"Where's the stuff you picked up?"

"That's the thing, we got ripped off. Donna went back, see if she could put together another plan. Told me hang out, be cool. That worked for me," he said, now grinning, showing his crooked teeth, yellow with brown stains. "It's cool here."

"How much did you guys get ripped for?"

"Twenty K."

"Damn," I said, studying him for a minute. "Where'd she come up with that kind of money?"

He looked away, ready to lie. The look, I'd seen it a thousand times. Floyd too, and he moved in ready for it, pushing his sleeves up a little, ready to respond. We were getting close now with this guy; we weren't about to let him off the ropes.

I said, "The truth, Gilbert."

"She'll kill me, she ever finds out I said this."

Floyd inched closer. "*We* might kill you, if you don't."

He paused, dropped his head in his hand, looking between his bony knees.

"Gilbert?"

"Yeah?"

I said in a low tone, "I'd like to leave here, get out of your life for a while. You want me to leave, take this asshole with me, or do you want me to leave him here, let the two of you get better acquainted, maybe see who's tougher?"

He glanced at Floyd but returned his gaze to the ground.

"Where's Donna get twenty K?"

"Started out," he said, "she had a couple whores pimped out, plus had 'em running some dope. Then she started doing some weird shit."

"Go on," I said, seeing we'd hit pay dirt but keeping it low, playing it cool.

"I don't know a lot, but there were some pictures, a few clients she tried to scam for money."

"Extortion," I said.

Gilbert nodded. "Something like that."

Floyd said, "Who's these whores you're talking about, Gilbert?"

"Couple drag queens," Gilbert said. "She's got 'em put up in their own place, down in the ghetto, somewhere on the boulevard—"

"Long Beach?"

"Yeah, at a motel. But they're cool with that, like it's good enough for them. Then she's got this hookup with some kinky place in Hollywood, gets some clients looking for that type of thing and sends her queens out for business. Big dollar business, like executives, lawyers, shit like that."

"How's she send them?"

"Hires a driver."

"You?"

"And others. Anyone looks tough enough to scare these guys, keep 'em from hurting the girls . . . guys, whatever."

THE HOTEL'S AUTOMATIC DOORS SLID OPEN, AND FLOYD AND I WALKED through them, passing a pair of businessmen with attaches and overnight bags. They nodded as if we were in the same club, medical supplies or maybe vacuum cleaner salesmen, four white guys wearing suits in Texas.

They had no idea we were packing heat, that we'd roughed up a gangster in Room 114, or that we were thinking only of Susie, ligature marks criss-crossing her delicate neck, a man-made woman now lying still on a metal slab in Los Angeles. The two businessmen wouldn't know any of this, nor that we could never share a drink with them; our worlds were just too far apart.

18

ARRANGING AN EARLY flight became my problem, Floyd saying if he didn't get a run in this week he'd surely blimp up like a whale, all the great Texas food we had eaten: filet mignon and huge potatoes last night, shrimp cocktail appetizers and then cheesecake for dessert; Texas-styled breakfast skillets with sides of biscuits and gravy this morning, cheeseburgers and fries at Hooters for lunch. Texas-sized portions, *yessir*, and we did not weaken. Man, this traveling was going to kill us, he had said. Of course, he didn't mention the dozen or more beers, wine with dinner, those two gin and tonics in the lounge . . .

I sat at the edge of a floral-patterned bedspread doodling on hotel stationary as Carmen from Delta checked afternoon flights. There was room on the 3:52 departure out of Dallas-Fort Worth, nonstop into Los Angeles International, she said. I glanced at the clock displaying 2:18 and told her we'd take it, thinking, we're going to have to haul ass. Also wondering just how long my partner would be gone working on his cardio and suntan, thinking it might be a little tight unless he returned soon.

I packed my bag, throwing everything together with little concern for organization, periodically glancing out the window hoping to see my partner jogging back toward the hotel. No sign of Floyd, and the clock seemed to move quickly now. At 2:55 p.m. I shrugged into my suit jacket, stuffed Floyd's gun, badge, cell phone, shaving kit, and dirty clothes into the outside pocket of his garment bag, zipped it closed, and slung it over my shoulder. I glanced outside again but finding Floyd at times could be like spotting Big Foot, and I didn't see either of them. I flipped my gray felt onto my head, grabbed my garment bag, and squeezed through the door into the hallway.

When I stepped into the elevator, I dropped Floyd's bag to the floor, cursing its weight. I pictured the hotel laundry bag inside, no doubt filled with hotel shampoos, conditioners, soaps, packages of coffee . . . Floyd telling the maid we needed extra everything as he had walked a perimeter around her cart: *Yeah, sure, a few extra pens too, maybe some tissues . . . What else do you have?* Floyd smiling and thanking her in Spanish.

When I finished my business at the checkout counter, I turned to catch Floyd pacing in front of the hotel, his hands on his hips and his head tilted back, searching for air. People passing by seemed to notice the man in black nylon shorts and white running shoes with no socks, his t-shirt wadded in his hand. His bare chest and shoulders were wet with perspiration, glistening in the sunshine.

I trudged through the automatic doors, catching Floyd's attention just as he bent at the waist to stretch it out.

"Good timing, asshole."

Floyd looked up and instantly frowned. "The hell you doing?"

"We're checked out, got a plane to catch."

"Dude, I need a shower, change of clothes."

"Don't know what to tell you about the shower; you can change in the car."

"You're kidding, right?" he said, now following me to the rental, maybe a little pissed.

I dropped the two garment bags next to the trunk. "We've got forty-five minutes to catch the next flight, which is the only flight until seven-something. Better grab what you need, you can purty up on the way to the airport."

"You're an asshole," Floyd said, wiping sweat from his face, his chest, his underarms and then draping the sweaty t-shirt around his neck.

"You said get us on the next flight, that's what I did. The goal, you may recall, is to get back and find Donna before she disappears or does something really stupid."

"You're killing me." He picked up his bag and laid it across the hood. "You want me to put on a suit in a Taurus while sweating my ass off and listening to you bitch about Texas drivers and traffic and the sun and whatever else, all the way to the airport?"

"Like it'll be the first time you dressed or undressed in a rental car."

"You ever wonder why you don't have any friends?" he asked.

I dropped my bag into the trunk, left the lid open, and walked to the driver's door.

"Hurry up," I said, as I slid in behind the wheel, "if you're riding with me."

I CALLED THE OFFICE JUST BEFORE THE ANNOUNCEMENT TO TURN OFF ALL portable electronic devices. When Lieutenant Jordan answered, I went straight to the point, asking if he had anything new to report as to the whereabouts of Elmer Fudd. No, he said, without elaboration. Then he asked how it went in Texas. It was a long story, I told him, but the bottom line is we have not found James Scott, Donna Edwards is a dirty little lying bitch, and my partner is still an idiot. Then I asked, "Any questions?"

Jordan chuckled and said, "Well, you and that partner of yours will be first up in the rotation for murders come Monday morning; better get some rest."

After pushing end, I turned off the power and slid the cell phone into my inside jacket pocket to the side of a ballpoint pen and mechanical pencil.

"Well?" Floyd asked.

"Lieutenant has us first up Monday."

"You've got to be kidding."

"It's what he said. And as far as your buddy, Fudd, they've got nothing."

Floyd stared out the window. "I'm not so convinced Elmer and James Scott are two different people."

"Thinking she steered us off the path?"

"It crossed my mind," Floyd said, and then turned to face me. "What do you think? And how the hell are we first up again, all the shit we've got going on?"

"I was thinking the same thing as far as Donna," I said. "Makes you wonder, Gilbert having his credit cards. We should have had him busted, called the Rangers. And the reason we're always first up is because you piss off the lieutenant. He hates us."

"Nah, he loves us, Dickie. Always playing his big hitters is what I think. Anyway, Donna's too important to put on ice right now. First up or not, we have to get at her."

I pulled my hat off, set it on my lap and leaned my head back, waiting for takeoff. "Why would she want us thinking Elmer Fudd isn't James Scott, if he is? She looked at the picture and said, no way, that's not our boy. You think maybe she's keeping us distracted while they do their thing? Running around the country making dope deals, using Scott's credit cards?"

"What about the story of his wife? Remember," Floyd said, "nice little lady always speaks to her, says hi."

"We better look into it, see if there even is a Mrs. Fudd."

"Neighborly type, always waves to the dope dealer across the street," Floyd said.

I looked past him now, stealing a view through his window as we taxied to the runway, planes coming in and taking off in the distance. I couldn't help but think of the last time we left Texas, only to turn around and come in for an emergency landing. The runway lined by fluorescent green fire trucks, ambulances, Dallas-Fort Worth Airport police, and a couple trucks loaded with foam, all awaiting our unexpected arrival, none of them praying the way we were with our birds-eye view of the action below.

It had been one of those trips from hell, the kind not easily forgotten. I figured Floyd was thinking about it too, feeling a little apprehensive like myself maybe.

"I always miss this place, every time we leave."

"Yeah?"

Floyd chuckled. "Except the times we come right back."

"Right."

We both sat back and snugged our belts as the jet engines wound to a powerful roar. I started thinking of the case, most likely to get my mind off the flight, or more likely the prior departure from Texas.

"No wonder that asshole hates his neighbors," I said.

"Who?"

"Your buddy, Elmer. I'm starting to see his reason for hating Donna Edwards and her asshole friends."

"Gilbert."

"Yeah, the little prick."

Floyd glanced back at me and paused. "Doesn't explain why he shot at us though, Dickie."

"That's the part that doesn't make sense," I admitted.

"Then he's got the balls to steal my car. How's he even know where I live? Did you figure that part out yet?"

"We're missing something; that's for sure."

Floyd said, "Yeah, like who the hell is doing all this crazy shit? We might be off on the whole thing, Dickie."

The acceleration silenced us both and we looked straight ahead as the 727 roared down the runway and lifted slowly from the ground with a couple bumps and a little shaking. Moments later we were banking to the right, still climbing, and I looked across Floyd again to see the ground fading away.

Floyd looked at me, just a corner of his mouth turned up in a grin, and he said, "*You may all go to hell and I will go to Texas*."

I frowned at him.

"Davey Crockett, Dickie . . . a legend like ourselves."

WE ARRIVED JUST AN HOUR AFTER DEPARTING TEXAS, ACCORDING TO MY watch, having gained two hours with the change of time zone. The two of us walked down the center of a wide terminal hallway, each with a carry-on slung over a shoulder, each scanning the opposing foot traffic the way cops do, and each noticing a brunette flight attendant with long legs and getting just a hint of a smile in return. Just enough to say she noticed us noticing.

Probably headed for Texas.

Floyd brought his head around just in time to steer us to the right, avoiding an oncoming cart. The Cushman pilot, a gray-haired black man with bulging forearms, his huge hands wrapped around the steering wheel, swept by without slowing or swerving to avoid us. His eye contact told me he wasn't all that impressed with our swagger.

We picked up our bags and were able to navigate through the airport quickly and find our county car awaiting us in the concrete maze called a parking structure. We loaded up and hit the road but our rapid pace quickly came to a stop.

"Rush-hour," Floyd said, glancing at his Rolex Submariner. "With this traffic, it'll take us two hours to get to Donna's."

"You got a better idea?"

"Yeah, you can buy us dinner, let traffic die down."

A cold beer sounded good and my stomach growled from hunger. One or two beers wouldn't kill us before finding Donna, maybe put us in a better mood after a long couple of days. I started to agree it might be a good idea, but also thinking maybe I'd ask whose turn it was to buy, just to give us something to argue about.

My thoughts were interrupted by a page to call the office. When I did, Floyd and I learned our team had been called up early, meaning we were now officially on call, ahead of schedule.

It also meant we shared a destiny with an unsuspecting, maybe yet-to-be-determined soul. A chance meeting wherein someone, somewhere, would soon come to the ultimate realization—if only for an instant—of his or her mortality. Or maybe their life would flash before them in their final moment, a transition into the afterlife, and they would recognize it as Karma. I would ponder this at times and then wonder what he or she was doing right now that was about to get them killed.

19

FLOYD LOOKED UP as he bit into a juicy cheeseburger, his eyes wide with anticipation. I set down a frosted mug of Coors Light and watched an icicle slide down its side and soak into a coaster advertising Corona beer. I stared at the amber-colored liquid, frustrated, thinking of the hours we had put into this case that seemed to be running off course. It didn't help to think of my phone conversation with the lieutenant, the notice that we were up early for murders. Knowing the cases never stopped coming, that you were never caught up or finished, that there would always be more work than you could manage no matter how devoted you were, brought a level of stress, pressure, fatigue, and eventual burnout that only those who worked the assignment could ever understand.

I lifted the mug for another gulp and glanced at Floyd, watching him cock his head to the side as he chomped into the now half-eaten burger.

"What?" he said through a mouthful of meat, cheese, and bread.

I lowered the mug and reached for the untouched burger in front of me. "Just thinking."

"About?"

I retreated from the burger, leaving it on the plate. "About how ridiculous this job is at times. How the hell do they expect us to solve any of these murders when they pile new ones on us every seven, eight days? When's the last time we had a day off anyway?"

Floyd picked up an onion ring, dragged it through some ketchup at the edge of his plate, then paused just before it reached his mouth. "Since when do you care about days off? It's not like you have a life, Dickie."

I looked away, the untouched burger resting on the plate next to a pile of fries. A blonde-haired child hung over the back of an adjacent booth, looking over Floyd's shoulder. Her chocolate-covered smile and sparkling eyes revealed the playful innocence of her youth. Her mother pulled her back, and told her to behave.

"Maybe that's my problem," I said, looking back at Floyd now. "Maybe I've cared too much for too many years, too many victims. The families are taking a toll. I get one more call from Bethel Casey, I swear I'll eat my gun."

"She's still calling?"

"Every couple of weeks. To keep me on my toes, make sure I'm still working the case. Then on Tawny's birthday, just a couple weeks ago—"

"March 30th, same day Jenkins was killed."

How could I forget? I reached for my beer, the appetite still not there and the thirst seemingly unquenchable. Jenkins was yet another toll-taking memory, the 28-year-old patrol deputy getting shot by a gang-banger on a routine stop. Jenkins had seen the gangster exiting a vehicle and noticed he appeared nervous when he looked toward the patrol car. As Jenkins exited his vehicle, the gang-banger spun toward him with a gun in his hand, the muzzle coming up on the deputy. Jenkins had bent at the waist, trying to get low as he drew his gun from its holster, but before he could get a round off he was struck just above the vest by a .357 Magnum hollow-point round. The round missed the Kevlar protective vest by millimeters, and due to Jenkins' body position when struck, the bullet traveled in a downward trajectory, essentially traversing his entire torso before coming to stop against his hip. It had penetrated a lung, the heart, and the young deputy's liver. He died quickly, bleeding out on the filthy pavement of a filthy, gang-infested street, in a filthy, gang-infested neighborhood, of a filthy, gang-infested city. And for what?

I took a long pull from the frosty mug, the cold liquid going down nicely and having just the right effect. Anything to help drown the laughing kids in the adjacent booth and dull the memory of Jenkins' autopsy, the first I had attended where I personally knew the decedent.

"We're never going to solve that one, Dickie," Floyd had continued. "You have to move on, worry about what's in front of us. Don't let those unsolved cases get you down."

"That's the problem with dead kids," I said. "They tend to do just that, get you down."

While finishing his last bite, chewing around the words, Floyd said, "Change your pager. Stop returning her calls. What's the worst that can happen, she starts calling Jordan? Let him deal with her; that's why they pay him the big bucks."

I glanced back at the little girl as she peeked over again. I guessed her to be about the same age as was Tawny Casey at the time of her death, probably three or four. Innocent, sweet, vulnerable.

"You still have that case file under your desk?" Floyd asked.

"Yeah, I've got it."

"Get rid of it. Send it up to the library and put it behind you. You don't, Dickie, I will. I'm not kidding either."

"I'm not ready to give up."

"Big surprise," he said. "What the hell more can we do with it? Everything's been a dead end. We just about killed ourselves working that case. Something comes up, a new lead, we'll bring it back from the library. Meantime, we move on. Nothing else we can do. You're not going to last, buddy, you don't start letting some of this shit go."

I nodded, knowing he was right, but thinking, not yet . . .

Floyd took a gulp of beer. "You gonna eat that burger?"

"JESUS," FLOYD SAID AS HE PULLED HIS CELL PHONE FROM HIS EAR, looked at it, and then pushed a button to disconnect. "They're giving us an officer-involved shooting in Hawthorne."

"We've got the handle on it?"

"Yep."

I glanced in the rearview mirror. "Who's assisting?"

"No idea. I didn't bother to ask. I'm not even sure I care."

"Maybe we should have stayed for that seven o'clock flight," I said.

I glanced over my shoulder and then changed lanes, veering toward the next off-ramp to turn around and head west toward Hawthorne. Floyd sat silent. Once we were safely turned around and headed for the South Bay, I continued: "We could've hung out in the airport bar all day drinking gin and tonics, lying to barmaids and flight attendants about what we do for a living. What's the story on this piece of shit, anyway?"

"And I could have had a shower. That would have been nice. I don't know much, sounds like another suicide by cop. Those seem to be all the rage now."

"That's it? That's all you know?"

"I guess some asshole tried to rob a bank and got smoked when he walked out, the cops outside waiting for him. What else do you need to know?"

"Jesus."

"That's what I said."

WE DIDN'T NEED ANOTHER CASE, BUT IT SEEMED THAT WAS NEVER PART OF the equation that equaled more cases. And since it seemed to be the norm, not the exception, that the cases stacked up faster than we could handle them, we had become accustomed to allocating tasks and utilizing available resources whenever possible.

In this instance, we decided to put Donna Edwards under surveillance until we had an opportunity to get back on track with the Susie Q investigation. This would allow us to know where to find her when we did have the chance to call on her again, and more importantly, it might provide evidence to corroborate Gilbert's statement about her illegal activities.

The sheriff's department consists of various divisions such as Patrol, Custody, Court Services, Administrative and Detective Divisions, for the purposes of command. Such structure is necessary in a department of more than 10,000 sworn personnel and another 5,000 civilian professional staff. Each of these divisions is commanded by a chief, who is only outranked by the sheriff, his undersheriff, and two assistant sheriffs. Each division has its own budget, and throughout the history of the department, the

Detective Division has always been the stepchild when it came to allocated funds. Homicide Bureau is in the Detective Division, as is Major Crimes Bureau, which among other responsibilities maintains several highly trained, experienced, and properly equipped surveillance teams. Homicide Bureau utilizes the surveillance teams on a regular basis, which of course results in administrative disagreements about funding, and Homicide usually picks up the tab. Especially when the investigation requires overtime. Of course, the detectives assigned to these respective units couldn't care less about any of the financial considerations or woes of the administrators, and we were no exception.

Floyd called Dwight Campbell, a sergeant in charge of one of the two Detective Division surveillance teams, bypassing the standard protocol for requesting their services. He told Sergeant Campbell we were working a fresh murder and asked if his team was available to set up on a possible suspect. Floyd told him the suspect, Donna Edwards, was not only a person of interest in our murder investigation, but that we believe she is trafficking cocaine. Then he thanked the sergeant and told him we'd be in touch.

"He said no problem," Floyd said when he finished the call, "they're available and can set up on her within the hour, if they're able to locate her. I told him to keep us posted, we'd be out all night on this officer-involved shooting case. I'd like to give a course, maybe even set up a hotline, *How to Kill Yourself Without Involving the Cops*. What's this, the third one this year?"

"Something like that," I answered, but still thinking about Donna and the surveillance. "What'd you tell him about Lieutenant Jordan? You mentioned his name."

"Dwight said his team was out of hours—"

"Seems they always are."

"—asked who'd pay the overtime. So I took the liberty of telling him Homicide would pick up the tab. Told him Jordan had already approved it."

"He'll never know the difference."

The only officer on scene who hadn't shot the would-be bank robber gave us a synopsis of the events, the best he could from what he had gathered from the involved officers and civilian witnesses. I copied the information into a new notebook:

> *At 4:55 p.m., just minutes before the bank was due to close, the suspect/decedent entered through the doors located on the south side of the building, adjacent to the parking lot. He appeared to be of Asian descent, wearing a black windbreaker, blue jeans, and dark-framed sunglasses with green lenses. He approached the first teller on the left, stepping in front of a female customer at the counter, and brandished a pistol as he announced it was a robbery. He then moved to the next teller, and the one after that, repeating his intent to rob the bank.*
>
> *The manager, who has personally been present during seven robbery attempts during her twelve-year banking career, said there was something very different about this robbery. The man never actually demanded money; he seemed more interested in the activity outside.*
>
> *When the cops arrived, the sirens announcing their presence, the Asian man walked to the glass doors and paused. He turned to face the tellers and customers and said, "Have a nice day." Then he walked outside and pointed his gun toward the cops.*

"Anything else?" I asked, hovering a pen over the opened notebook.

"It's all on video."

Having finished the crime scene walkthrough, we relinquished the task of documenting and collecting evidence to one of our assisting teams. We departed and drove to the Hawthorne Police Station where four officers, six bank employees, and four civilian witnesses waited to be interviewed.

We arrived and met with four additional detectives from our bureau, each assigned to assist in the interviews. I told them Floyd and I would handle the cops, they could divide up the employees and civilians.

Floyd's cell phone rang as we walked into an interview room where the first of the four cops we intended to interview waited.

"Hello?" he said into the phone. "Yeah? . . . Really? . . . Okay, hold on a second."

Floyd covered the mouthpiece and said to me, "They've got Donna on the move, just left Downey and heading west." Then he thanked the sergeant on the other end of the conversation and asked that he continue to keep us posted.

I waited for him to slide the phone into his suit pocket. "You ready?"

"Sure."

We sat at the table across from the officer and I pushed the record button on the digital recorder. "I'm Detective Richard Jones, my partner here is Matthew Tyler. We're from Sheriff's Homicide Bureau, investigating the officer-involved shooting incident occurring at the First National Bank in the city of Hawthorne. Officer, would you please state your name for the record?"

The young man dressed in a dark blue uniform leaned toward the recorder and said, "I would like to have an attorney present."

DOWN THE HALL, PAST THE SECRETARIAT, PAST THE LOCKER ROOMS, restrooms and an old gray metal drinking fountain, Floyd and I stood next to a coffee vending machine. Almost nothing surprised us anymore, we agreed, waiting for the paper cup to fill with fresh brewed coffee. Certainly not an asshole pointing a pellet gun at four cops armed with forty-fives and shotguns, and not even cops asking for attorneys before providing statements when they killed some dipshit who pointed a pellet gun at them. But homicide detectives having to *buy* a cup of coffee from a vending machine at a police station, while assisting them on *their* case, seemed to put Floyd over the edge.

"They can take their shooting and their coffee and shove both up their asses," he said, facing the vending machine with his hands on his hips, ready to fight it should the opportunity present itself.

I pulled a cup with playing cards printed on the side from the metal rack and handed it to my disgruntled partner. Then I dropped two more quarters in the machine and waited while the fresh brew slowly dripped into a second cup.

I said, "Doesn't smell too bad, how's it taste?"

"This punk and his lawyer—"

"It's a new breed, partner. It's just the way these kids are now."

"Back in our day, you dropped the hammer on someone, you pulled up your big-girl panties, sat down with Homicide and told them what happened."

"We could fire up a Grand Jury, see how they like that. Maybe that's something the bureau needs to consider in these changing times. I think they'd see before long, it was better the old way."

I watched as the second cup finished filling, steam rising from the paper cup with a pair of jacks on the side. I glanced at Floyd's cup: king of clubs, seven of hearts.

Floyd jerked his cell phone from his pocket and barked into the mouthpiece: "Hello?"

I could hear Dwight's voice coming through the speaker, but not clear enough to understand the words.

Floyd's eyes narrowed. "The airport?"

"They're at the airport?" I asked.

He held his hand up for me to wait, saying into the phone now, "Hang on . . . hold on a second, D, let me see what my partner thinks."

Floyd lowered the phone and said, "She's at the airport, checking in. No luggage, just a carry-on. What do we want them to do?"

"Get a ticket and get on that plane with her."

"You don't think we should just grab her?"

I stood thinking about it for a moment. Dwight waited on the line. The Hawthorne Police watch commander appeared in the hallway, not far from where we stood, and said, "They're ready for you guys in the interview room."

"No problem," I said, "we'll be there in a minute."

Floyd rolled his eyes. "Jesus, like we need this shit. What do you want to do?"

"Tell them to wait until she leaves ticketing," I said. "Badge the agent and find out where she's going. Then get back to us, and fast. We can interrupt an interview for a murder suspect boarding a flight, I would think. But let's see what she's up to before deciding."

The lieutenant stood fidgeting in his dark blue, long-sleeved uniform complete with a tie, watching impatiently.

Floyd spoke into the phone, "D, can you guys—"

The watch commander glanced at his watch and said, "These guys are all on overtime now."

Floyd lowered the mouthpiece, "Are you fucking kidding me, man?"

The lieutenant, who had just begun to turn away when Floyd let loose, snapped back around, his brows furrowed, and eyes narrowed, his olive complexion having instantly turned red.

Before he could respond, I said, "We've got a lot going on right now, lieutenant. We'll be right there."

The lieutenant turned away slowly, his eyes shooting daggers at my partner.

Floyd flipped his middle finger at the lieutenant's back and said to nobody in particular, just his partner standing there with a cup of coffee, winning with the pair of jacks, "Pussy."

I could hear Dwight's voice from the phone, so I nodded my head at it, redirecting Floyd.

Floyd said into the phone: "Sorry, man, we've got this dickhead lieutenant down here who won't get off our balls. Did you hear what my partner said about checking with the clerk, see where Donna's heading and then get back to us?"

Dwight's voice again, the words *right on* and *brother* was all I could make out.

"Thanks, man," Floyd said, and then added, "and get back to us soon as you can."

When Floyd put the phone away I asked, "They're at LAX?"

"Probably headed back to Texas, would be my guess" he said. "Which is where I'm going after I beat someone's ass, probably that pussy lieutenant if he gets in my face again."

"Gentlemen?"

We looked up to see the same watch commander now standing side by side with a short, chubby-cheeked man in a cheap suit and comb-over. "What?!" Floyd snapped.

"We'd like to get started," the man in the suit said.

The lieutenant just glared.

I cringed, not sure at this point what to expect of my partner.

"Well by all means," Floyd bellowed, "let's get to it!"

He sounded like a drunken sailor about to throw the first punch at a soldier who sat next to his gal.

The lieutenant and the attorney stood silent.

Floyd continued, "Or maybe you could make sure junior's found his nuts, then let us know when you're sure he's ready to give a statement. Tell him to take his time, think it over, because we sure as hell don't have anything better to do than sit around this goddamned place drinking shit coffee that costs us a buck a fucking pop."

They stood dumbfounded.

I mumbled, "Fifty cents."

Floyd's phone broke the standoff.

"What?" he snapped into his cell . . . "Great, hold on." He moved the phone away from his cheek, glanced at the watch commander and attorney who watched in disbelief, and then back to me. "She just boarded a plane, headed for Cancun."

20

SURVEILLANCE TEAM SERGEANT Dwight Campbell rocked back and forth on a pair of black Reebok tennis shoes, his hands shoved into the front pockets of baggy jeans. His six-point sheriff's star hung around his neck on a chain outside a black Harley Davidson t-shirt. We stood in the parking lot of the Hawthorne Police Station, the type of place where a black man with a shaved head, a soul patch, two gold earrings, and a Glock 9mm stuffed in the front of his jeans needed to make certain the locals knew who he was.

"You should've seen the flight attendant when we boarded the plane, my whole damn team coming on, looking like a bunch of renegade commandos."

"Or a prison break in progress," Floyd said.

Dwight rolled his shoulders back, straightening his posture next to Floyd who stood erect, his feet planted shoulder-width apart, a fighter's stance. Dwight looked him over and said, "Shee-it."

"So, no problems?" I asked.

"Homegirl looked like she was about to shit a brick," he said. "But no, as far as getting on the plane and taking her off, it went smooth. Buddy of mine who works the LAX dope crew walked us through security."

We all paused to watch a young officer in a tailored blue uniform pass by, strutting with that young cop machismo, maybe each of us having seen it somewhere before.

I looked up as a jet buzzed overhead, inbound LAX, and after it passed, I said, "She know why you snatched her up yet, D?"

"Nah, man" he said, also glancing up at the plane. "She kept asking, but we just kept our mouths shut. Told her she'd find out what it was all about soon enough. She kept saying, 'I've got a right to know why you're arresting me!' I says—check it out—'Ain't nobody arrested you yet, baby, but you keep talking smack, and see what happens.' Then baby comes back with, 'What do you call this shit, sitting here in handcuffs?'"—Dwight let out a big chuckle—"We were on our way to Lennox, right? Had her in the back of Jake's ride. I said, 'Baby, you call it what you want. You can call it arrested, or you can call it kinky, or you can call it a righteous kidnapping, all I care.'"

I grinned and said, "Yeah, what'd she say to that?"

"She says, 'I ain't yo baby, asshole.' So I don't say another thing to her the rest of the way there, if that's how the bitch is gonna act. But Jake, he tries to be all smooth, the big-assed white boy gonna talk some shit to the little sista, right? He says, 'Honey,'—some shit, and she gives him the same thing, 'I ain't yo honey.' Bitch has got attitude, I'll give her that."

Dwight grinned, his arms now folded across his chest as he leaned against a black and white. "We get to Lennox and lock her ass up in the holding cell. I tell her, 'Be cool now, baby.'"—Dwight now laughing—"Bitch about comes unglued. Anyway, we told the watch commander she was there for Homicide, in the event she starts pitching a bitch."

"Hope they can hold her for a while," Floyd said. "We just finished our second interview here, got some two-bit lawyer slowing things up. Two more to go before we can break away, go see our girl."

"My baby," Dwight said, grinning.

I glanced at my watch and shook my head at the time, now past midnight. "Wonder if I'm still married."

"Married?" Dwight said. "Shit, who's still married? Only cops I know still married are dudes smart enough to take a war bride, maybe one of these little Latinas that don't speak no English, ain't got no driver's license or checkbook. Got them dirt-sweeping mamas, make homemade tamales for their little girl's man. I done messed up twice, got my pension divided up between two bitches I can't stand. Never again, man, not this brotha."

I said, "You're right about that, man."

"Hey, listen, Bobby Ross is the watch commander over at Lennox tonight. You want," Dwight said, "I'll call him up, tell him it'll be a while 'fore y'all make it over there, maybe buy you a little time."

"You wouldn't mind?"

"Hell no, man, I don't mind. Bobby won't give me no shit, neither. I still got dirt on his ass from when we worked a radio car in Willowbrook, back in the day. Some shit ain't got no statute of limitations, if you know what I mean."

"I've heard stories," I said, "about both of you from back then, back in *the brook*."

"Shit," Dwight said, "you ain't heard half of it."

He seemed to be enjoying the moment, looking away for a minute with a smile on his face, still leaned back against the car, his arms folded. He glanced over at Floyd then locked his eyes on me again as he continued. "This one time, we were back in the gang office talking to this chump from Watts, this little boy who thought he was the shit, a real tough guy. We'd taken him down for some dope, him and another little nigga trying to make it back into the projects before the po-lice snatched them up. Well his little homie got away, bailed out of the ride and beat feet, so of course we stayed with the driver, let the other run. Brought this little shit into the office and Bobby asks who's his homeboy, the little nigga got away from the car. He says he can't remember his name. Bobby asks him a couple times, but the little asshole just kept lying through his lips. Check this out, Bobby picks up a phone book, one of those L.A. books 'bout four inches thick, says to homeboy, 'You suppose his name's in here?' The little bad-ass sucks his teeth a little, then says, 'Maybe.'

"Bobby opens it up, points to a name and reads it. 'Was it Fernando Diaz jumped outta your ride?' Kid says, 'Huh?' Bobby says it again. 'Was it Diaz, is that the nigga jumped out of your hoop? The kid says, 'No.' *Whack!* Bobby hits him across the head with the book, knocks him sideways in his chair. The kid now holding his hand up to the side of his head, looking at Bobby like that nigga crazy. Bobby opens the phone book up again, points to another name and calls it out, same thing, some shit like,

'What about John Smith?' Kid shakes his head. Same thing, whacks the kid across the head with the phone book. Little bastard about comes out of his chair this time, slumped over now holding his head with both hands. Bobby tells homeboy, 'We ain't stopping 'til I get that nigga's name.'"

Dwight stared off, recounting the good ol' days, his grin starting to fade a bit. "He gave up the name after about four of those smacks across his nappy little head. Can you imagine doing some shit like that today? Shee-it."

"They'd have your ass," I said.

Floyd nodded toward the back door to the station. "We better get at it, Dickie, two more to go."

I said to Dwight, "D, we appreciate all your hard work, man."

"Ain't nothin' to it, man. You want me to give Bobby a call?"

"Yeah, might as well. Tell him we'll owe him one if he can hold onto her a few hours without being booked. I don't know what the hell we're going to do with her, but I don't want her booked for anything yet."

"All right then, fellas, we'll catch up with y'all later."

"Thanks, D."

"No problem, brother."

"Take care, man," Floyd said.

Dwight nodded, turned, and disappeared between a row of black and white cars with parking lot lights reflecting off their hoods and windshields.

It was nearly three A.M. when we finished our final interview of the officers who had been involved in the bank shooting incident. We had unknowingly saved the worst for last: Donald Platt, a rookie officer with six months on the street. His body had trembled when Floyd answered his question, telling him yes, it's true, the guy you killed was armed with a pellet gun. That spun us into another break and another conversation over fifty-cent vending machine coffee while the Police Protective League's attorney worked on getting the kid under control.

Pulling out of the lot, I asked Floyd, "You wanna stop for a cup?"

"Whatever you think, Dickie. You got a plan for talking to Donna?"

"No."

"Then let's stop, come up with a plan. Not like we can just walk in and tell her we know she's a lying bitch."

FLOYD STARTED OFF THE INTERVIEW BY ASKING DONNA EDWARDS A FEW simple questions: where's she been lately, how was Texas, has she heard from Gilbert since we visited with her at her home the other night . . .

Donna, sitting in the small, cold room, her arms folded across her chest, said, "I don't have any idea what you're even talking about."

And that's when Floyd called her a lying bitch.

Though briefly stunned by the change of plans, I said, "He gets a bit cranky when we've been up for two days straight."

I slid a metal chair from the table and sat next to her.

Her glare did not soften as her eyes shifted to mine. She glanced back at Floyd while drumming the table with red fingernails. "I'm not saying anything else to *Joe Cool* here. He can kiss my ass."

"You know what—" Floyd began.

"Give us a second, partner," I said, interrupting him.

Floyd turned and walked out, slamming the door behind him. Probably just playing the good cop, bad cop routine to its fullest. We never planned it, it just came naturally, the two of us knowing how to play off each other without a script. Usually, I played the bad cop, especially with the women, Floyd figuring he could flirt a confession out of anything with estrogen. Usually telling me after—if we did happen to get a confession—that he had softened her up just right for us, the Floyd charm hard at work.

But not tonight, for some reason. Maybe my partner had been off his game since the Hawthorne lieutenant had pissed him off. No matter, tonight I'd be the good guy, to the best of my ability. The trick would be not having this turn into bad cop, worse cop.

"See Donna," I said, "here's the thing. We have enough right now to put a twenty-year trafficking case on you, no questions asked."

"What?!"

"Gilbert gave you up, the whole thing with the cocaine deal in Texas, getting ripped off, everything."

"Gilbert?" As if she didn't know him.

"We just got in from Dallas-Fort Worth, Donna, haven't even been home to change clothes yet. Visited Gilbert at the hotel the two of you were enjoying on your neighbor's tab."

"I don't know—"

"James Scott, the guy across the street. The one you said has been gone for a while? Him and his wife, the nice little woman who always says hello? Yeah, well, we know his credit card's been paying for you and your Mexican friend to live it up in Texas the last few days, and that's the least of your worries at this point."

Floyd opened the door, poked his head in. "I'm on the phone with DEA. You want them to come down tonight? The guy wants to know."

"Not yet."

He shot her a look and closed the door. I waited a moment listening to Floyd's footsteps on the tile floor fading behind him.

"I don't know why he's on your ass like this, what you did to piss him off. I'll tell you though, he's hard to please once he gets this way. I can barely live with the guy."

"He's a pompous ass. I thought he was nice, that night at the house, but now I think he's a dick."

"He is a little grumpy tonight," I conceded, "but I've got just as much say in what happens to you as far as the dope business goes. Truth is, we don't really care about all that shit anyway, Donna. What we want is to get some answers about this other stuff, your friends getting killed, the head-case across the street from you, the business you and the Mexican run. But you need to be truthful and up front about everything, or all bets are off."

"ONE MORE PERSON TELLS ME THEY WANT A LAWYER THIS WEEK, I'M going to rip his eyelids off with pliers and staple them to his forehead—or hers. Swear to God. What the hell are we going to do now?"

Floyd grinned, the two of us standing in the hallway just outside the interview room. He had that *I could have told you so* look about him, but he didn't actually say it. What he actually said was, "I say we book the bitch for trafficking, see if she softens up after a couple days of fighting dykes at the county jail. Unless she actually likes that type of thing, and goes both ways. That actually makes more sense, now that I think about it. The bitch is probably a lesbian."

"You don't think that case is a little thin? No dope, no money, just the word of Gilbert, the confession you beat out of him?"

Floyd thought for a moment. I could see the wheels spinning inside his head.

He said, "That or we put a surveillance team back on her and let her go. Maybe get more on the dope case, or maybe she leads us to more whores and their clientele. Either way, I like having someone on her ass."

"Sounds like a better idea, partner. I'll give Dwight a call, if you want to let the watch commander know the plan."

"Deal, Dickie."

21

FLOYD AND I parted ways vowing to get home and get some rest, get showered, and change our clothes before the next disaster found us. I spoke into my cell phone over the cool wind whirling through an open window. "D, I hate to do this to you, but—"

He laughed, asked what happened, and said he thought we were the experts on getting folks to talk.

I said, "My partner screwed it up."

"Not as cool as ol' boy thinks he is, huh?"

Not knowing quite how to take the comment, I let it pass through my earpiece and out the window. I told him his buddy, Bobby Ross, said he'd hold Donna Edwards overnight without her being charged, Floyd had worked it out with him. That would give Dwight and his team a chance to get some rest and be ready to start fresh in the morning.

Dwight said, "Not a problem, we'll be on her. You boys just relax, play a little golf, we'll let ya know if we get something going with your girl."

I didn't bother telling him I'd played exactly four rounds of golf in the last eight years since promoting to Homicide Bureau. I didn't tell him what I wanted to say, that if I worked surveillance, I'd get in two or three rounds a week, then lie my ass off about being out of hours and needing overtime when Homicide wanted someone tailed. What I said was, "Thanks, D, you're the man."

Then I turned off my cell phone and adjusted myself in the seat, stretching and scooting, leaning into the wind like a thirsty dog. My eyelids were heavy—dropping slowly and rebounding quickly—the radio news my only companion as I navigated north through the county. The reporter spoke of a police shooting in the evening hours yesterday, stating the cops executed an Asian man armed with only a pellet gun. I switched to FM as the reporter said the detectives investigating the shooting had refused to provide details on the incident.

FOUR HOURS OF SLEEP FELT LIKE TWELVE AS I WOKE TO A QUIET HOUSE, the patter of rain against windowpanes, the only sound at all. I made my way to the kitchen, my usual routine, to find a note and mug next to a readied coffee pot. I switched it on and read the note as the brew dripped into the carafe.

Hi honey,

You must be exhausted! Your snoring gives it away. Any chance you can get a break, take some time off? Call me at the office when you have a chance, I have an idea about this weekend if you think you can swing it.

Val

I WALKED BRISKLY THROUGH THE HALLWAY OF OUR OFFICE TOWARD THE kitchen where coffee brews twenty-four hours a day, supplying caffeine to the weary and worn out detectives of Homicide Bureau, the support staff, and all of our guests. Before I could make it there, Captain Stover intercepted me, calling out from behind his desk as I passed his office. I cringed, knowing this would likely be just another bitch session. He would ask why we were spending all this time—not to mention money—on a *piece of shit* prostitute murder, or maybe he would ask if I knew how much it cost him to repair the cars me and that idiot I work with destroyed in the last ten days. It could be anything other than to say he appreciated our hard work, or to ask how our case was going, or to see if there was anything we needed, anything that would maybe improve the overall morale of the troops or functionality of the bureau. No, it wouldn't be any of those inquiries because this captain had the leadership skills of a caboose.

"What's up, Captain?" I said, stepping into his office.

He sat behind a cherry-wood desk with a blotter framing photographs of the captain posing with various department executives. Then there were the executive portraits hanging on the wall behind him: the sheriff with five gold stars on each collar, a big smile for the camera; the undersheriff with his comb-over job; both assistant sheriffs appearing bored. And, as with all department executives and Mexican generals, no office would be complete without the display of various awards routinely bestowed to one another for any absurd so-called accomplishment one could claim. On Captain Stover's wall hung the Exemplary Service Award, this particular one awarded for implementing an inmate feeding procedure while commanding the men's jail, an Award of Meritorious Conduct, received for "overseeing" the investigation of a murdered deputy—meaning he occupied the position of captain at the time the unfortunate homicide occurred, and as captain he would occasionally ask the hard-working detectives to brief him on their progress so he could inform the sheriff—and the Community Service Award, given to him for his dedicated attendance of community meetings. And there were others, all framed and encased with blue and gold ribbons, all paid for through the department's budget, or rather, taxpayer money.

He said, "Sit down, Richard."

I slid one of two dark leather chairs on rollers from the front of his desk and took a seat with a view of his *I love me* wall. I glanced at my watch, wondering if he had any idea how many hours we'd put in, how busy we were, how many other things I could be doing rather than having this little chat with arguably the worst captain for whom I had ever worked. Then I braced for the lecture, reminding myself to just listen, don't argue. Hear him out, let him rant, agree, thank him, and leave. Try not to shoot him or flip his cherry-wood desk over on his skinny ass.

He leaned back and gently rocked his chair, studying me while holding a gold pen to his chin, the pen matching his cufflinks accentuating a crisp white shirt. He glanced toward the interior office window with a view of the hallway where a steady stream of detectives passed by, the faint sounds of greetings and laughter muffled from inside. The captain leaned forward to address me and said, "I'm moving you to another team."

"What?"

"I need you on Team Three. They're short on bodies right now, and they're weak."

"Splitting me and Floyd up?"

"You can take a new guy," he said, "break him in. We're getting four new bodies the first of the month. It'd be good for everyone, good for the bureau."

"No."

"What do you mean, *no?* It's not a request."

I thought for a moment, my head spinning as I replayed his words in my head, thinking this seemed surreal, it couldn't be the case. Why would he move me? Homicide partners didn't get split up for no reason, and without good cause. We weren't the type to put up with it. We were all seasoned veterans who had worked hard to get to where we were. We were also almost all A-type personalities, the type to fight when it was time and not put up with much bullshit. In the academy and throughout the first few stages of one's career there remained a regimented rank structure and its attendant expectation of respect and protocols. But at this level, the rules were very different, and the relationships much more casual. Lieutenants and captains were addressed by first names by most of the detectives, for the most part. Very seldom did a detective receive discipline, nor did he expect to be treated like a child. Most would simply not tolerate it, and I certainly topped that list of the intolerant.

"Just what I said, no. I'm not going to do it. You split me and Floyd up, I'm out of here. I'm tired of busting my balls around here for nothing anyway. I'm sure as hell not breaking in a new guy." I pushed the chair back and rose to my feet. "I'm serious, Captain. I'll put the transfer in today if you move me to another team. This is bullshit and you know it."

"Where're you going to go?" he asked, rhetorically. "Patrol? You couldn't afford the cut in pay, not to mention you're too damned old to be pushing a radio car."

"Maybe I'll go to Surveillance," I said, "make some of that overtime, not deal with all this bullshit. I'm pretty sure I can move anywhere I want in Detective Division without too much trouble. Maybe I'll go to Arson-Explosives, investigate burned up cars and buildings for a living, occasionally put the bomb suit on and cut a wire or two."

"Good luck with that."

Just like that, the captain called my bluff. Or maybe he was trying to see how far I'd take it before giving in, saying okay, whatever's best for the bureau.

We sat staring at each other like the only two poker players left in a hand, one of the two bluffing, the other holding aces. Did he have all the cards? I knew I didn't, but I also felt the need to push back. I was tired of folding hands to this man with the awards on his wall.

The captain before him had the respect of the troops by and large. He had earned that respect by being a great cop before promoting, and then as a captain, he was thought of as an advocate for the men and women who served under his command. All too often executives were promoted for reasons other than that they had been good cops, or that they would make good leaders, and the department had suffered greatly for it.

If it were almost anyone other than Stover, my tone would have been very different, and I would have been more reasonable. But if it had been anyone other than Stover, I wouldn't have been sitting in his office having this conversation. The truth of it is, I just had no respect for the man, and that set the tone of all of our interaction.

"You're serious?"

"My mind is made up," he said. "Effective first of next month."

"That's two weeks."

"Yeah."

"We have cases—"

"Split them up. He keeps half, you keep half. Happens all the time. Partners promote, transfer, retire, die . . . You'll figure it out."

With that I turned and walked to the door, paused for a moment, but reminded myself to stick to the game plan. *Be cool, don't let him get under your skin.* So all of the thoughts running through my head, the things I wanted to say, the fight I felt compelled to continue or maybe finish, went by the wayside. I stepped through the threshold without looking back and rejoined the men and women who made this place work in spite of these executive types. Men and women who worked tirelessly to solve their cases and bring justice to the loved ones of our victims, and not for the captain or the sheriff or the awards on the wall.

"I SWEAR TO GOD THAT ASSHOLE'S GOING TO WISH HE NEVER KNEW ME," I said to Floyd at the coffee pot.

Floyd stood with his cup out as I poured him the bottom of a pot. I pulled the filter out and dumped it in the trash. Floyd stepped over and began filling the plastic water container as I scooped fresh grounds into a new filter, stepping right in with the team work. Best partner I ever had, and we were about to be divorced against our wills.

Floyd said, "What're you going to do, Dickie?"

I sighed. "I don't know, but I'll think of something."

"He can move you around in the bureau however he wants, nothing you can do about it. Nothing the union can do about it. It's not a demotion or discipline. It's his discretion to put you where he wants, partner you with whoever he feels like partnering you with."

"I'll make life hell for him."

"How?" he asked.

"You don't care?"

"Hell yes I care, Dickie. I just don't see how we can do anything about it. And I don't want you blowing a gasket over it, stroking out in the kitchen for Christ's sake."

"Maybe I'll get him dirty, bust his balls for him."

"How're you going to do that?"

"He's a drunk," I said. "That son-of-a-bitch has gotten away with lots of shit. When he wrecked his county car a while back, he was drunk off his ass. Everyone here knew it but of course that was swept under the rug. Then that time he shot at the guy breaking into his car behind a bar. I'm sure he was drunk then too, the idiot. Turned out the poor bastard was just taking a leak, ended up losing a kidney in the deal. My point is, he'll screw up again, and when he does, we'll make it our business, get some dirt on the bastard."

Floyd shook his head. "If you or I did any of that shit, they'd give us a month on the bricks and take away our cars for good. Probably send us to Sex Crimes or Fraud."

The two of us stood griping, conspiring, watching a fresh pot fill to the brim. We waited patiently though in piss-poor moods now. One of the very few simple pleasures and perks of the job, the endless supply of coffee, ruined this morning by an administrative power play.

"Who do we know that drinks at Nichol's?"

Floyd thought for a moment. "Few guys: Davey, Steve, sometimes Rudy . . . Why?"

"He goes there three, four times a week. I bet those guys have some shit on him."

"Like that waitress he's supposed to be sweet on? You heard about that, right?"

"No! Are you shitting me?"

"See, that's your problem, Dickie. You don't socialize enough, always too busy working. Yeah, dickhead, he's got a little something on the side, from what I hear. A chubby little Mexican girl who works at the lounge."

"That's exactly what we need," I said, excited now with the new information.

I picked up the fresh pot in one hand, my cup in the other. Floyd thrust his cup ahead of mine, expecting a refill first.

"Only we get it on tape," I continued. "The jackwad and his plump little Mexican girl in the county car, or maybe checking into a motel room somewhere."

"You're serious."

"Hell yeah, I'm serious. I'm pissed! I'm tired of laying down for that asshole just because he's the captain. That prick talked to me like that in a bar—if we were just a couple construction workers, not cops—I'd hand him his ass. You hear from Dwight yet today?"

"No," Floyd said over his shoulder, now leading the way back down the hall. "You?"

"No. Hey, what's the deal with you and him anyway? Seems to be a bit of tension."

Floyd stopped and turned to face me, the grin coming back. "You don't remember?"

"No."

"Dwight used to work the training bureau back when you and I worked patrol. There was that training class, the one they were going to teach us how to box, remember?"

"Vaguely."

"I'd made some smart-assed comment—"

"How rare."

"—and he decides to choose me for his demonstration, make an example of me. Tried to nail me a few times with a weak jab, slow hook, but doing it like he wanted to make a point. I mean, he tried to hit me, but he just didn't have the speed."

"Yeah?"

"So I knocked him on his ass in front of the class. You don't remember that? Jesus, he was pissed."

"I think I remember hearing about it, don't think I was in that class. I'd probably remember that."

"He came back up and another instructor stepped in, seeing he was out of control. I just grinned, which really pissed him off. Few years later, we get to talking during a search warrant operation, standing around a command post and he hits me up. Before, I'd see him and we'd just give each other the eye. This time, he comes up, acts all cool and says, 'Hey Floyd, I hear you're into martial arts.' Which is funny, you know, that he's been asking around about me ever since. I mean, this is what, two, three years later? Well, you know me, how I can be a dick—"

"Do I."

"—I say, 'I used to mess around a little bit,' left it at that," Floyd said and paused, maybe waiting for a reaction. He continued, "Then Dwight tells me he studies Tae Kwon Do, like that's going to impress me. Jesus, everyone knows Tae Kwon Do's for girls. Anyway, so then he starts telling me how important the elements of discipline and control are, in this art he practices, how you stay centered, focused, never lose your cool. You know, all that grasshopper shit. My take on it is he's trying to justify not getting up that day and stomping my ass, or pussing out. So I say, 'Most of my training is in Muay Thai kickboxing. You've heard of it, right? Very combative,' I said. 'Our idea of control is putting your opponent on his ass.'"

I shook my head and chuckled, then we started walking again, past the captain's office and into the squad room. I said, "So what'd he say to that?"

"Not much," Floyd said, grinning now, enjoying the memory more than likely. "We're okay though, me and D. I don't think he wants to mix it up again. Shit, he acts like we're old homeboys every time I see him."

"Did ya see that prick in there, giving us the eye as we passed?"

"I saw it," Floyd said. "In fact, I smiled at him."

"You had any hair on your ass," I told him, "you'd walk in there and knock him out of his chair, show me how tough you are."

"Don't tempt me."

"Tempt you? Hell, I'd pay you."

I SAT AT MY DESK WITH A HEADACHE AFTER LESS THAN AN HOUR OR SO AT the office, sipping coffee while listening to voicemail messages. Floyd sat next to me, looking at the screen of his notebook computer, his shirt already darkened by sweat beneath the arms. I half-listened to the attorney on my voicemail asking about his discovery motion, wondering when he could expect to receive the requested material. Saying it had been over a week and he hoped to hear from me soon. Saying it in that lawyerly tone I had quickly grown to despise. I jotted a note to look into it as I thought about my impending transfer.

The next message took my mind off of the transfer, the captain, and my partner sitting next to me sweating. It was a message from the fugitive task force saying they had located James Scott in Phoenix, Arizona.

When I shared the message with Floyd, he broke into an ear to ear grin. He loved to travel and always had a bag packed and ready to go. He'd leave on a moment's notice without a second thought or care in the world, and with the excitement and intensity of a puppy with its head out the window. The destination mattered not; Floyd loved everywhere. He loved going. He especially loved going on the county dime.

Floyd said, "Jesus, Dickie, that's great news. We love Phoenix."

22

WE WERE TOLD James Scott had been picked up in Phoenix just before boarding an airplane that would have brought him to Los Angeles via Las Vegas. I wondered why they hadn't held off arresting him until he landed at LAX; it wasn't like he could pull a D.B. Cooper and disappear mid-flight. Or at least it wasn't likely. Then I thought about how it would irritate the captain to see us spending *his* money, traveling on this *damned prostitute* murder case again, and thought, *What the hell?* I grinned at the idea of pissing him off.

It was this newfound contempt for the captain and the bureau that spurred me to call a contact at Arson/Explosives to see if they were taking applications. In addition to blowing things up, the bomb squad investigates fires, hence the title. As is the case with homicide detectives, Arson/Explosives detectives receive Bonus II pay, the highest salary of detectives on the sheriff's department. Plus they get hazard pay for playing with bombs, which is good unless they cut the wrong wire, and then it doesn't really matter. Maybe to the widow.

My contact at Arson asked if I was claustrophobic, telling me it isn't easy moving around in an eighty-pound bomb suit. Some guys, he said, panic when the final piece of equipment, the helmet, is applied to the suit. I told him I could handle it, the protection from accidental detonations would be worth the discomfort, I supposed. A bomb goes off, he said, the suit keeps the parts together, but that's about it. Makes it easier for cleanup and probably burial, he said.

They weren't taking applications at Arson at the moment, but he could let me know if anything changed. I told him it was okay, he didn't have to worry about it.

Next, I phoned Dwight Campbell and asked if he had a minute. He said, "Anything for you, my man, I ain't doing nuttin' but following some sexy little dope dealer 'round town, making me some overtime, courtesy of my friends at the Homicide Bureau. Whatchya got, dawg?"

"I meant to ask about her. How's that going?"

"Nothing happening right now. When they cut her loose from Lennox this morning, she waited out front for damn near two hours before some dude in a white Tahoe with rims picked her up. They went to the Tony Roma's in Carson and had lunch. The dude had baby backs and corn on the cob, looked like some baked beans and a Coke. Your girl, Donna, had a salad. Might have been chicken on there, or maybe shrimp. White dressing, probably ranch. Only white folks eat blue cheese. Oh, and she had an iced tea with a wedge of lemon. Maybe it could have been blue cheese, now that I think about it.

"Currently, we're sitting outside the Foxy Lady Hair and Nail Salon in beautiful downtown Compton, watching homeboy take a nap in his Tahoe while baby-girl's inside getting a 'do. This nigga's got his head all laid back on his leather seat, got his shades on his head doin' a Stevie Wonder impression in his sleep. I'm praying he wakes up with a nine against his temple, gets jacked for his ride. He's got them fancy spinners on there some of these Compton niggas be killin' for.

"Anyway, looks like we're here for a while," Dwight said, "now tell me what can I do you for?"

"First," I said, "who's this guy in the Tahoe?"

"The ride comes back to a Lamont Porter out of Inglewood," he said. "Don't know anything more than that."

I paused, running the name through my head along all the others. "I don't think I know the name."

"We'll do a work-up later on," Dwight said over the sounds of traffic in the background, "and if we get the dude ID'd, I'll give you a shout."

"Thanks, D," I said. "Oh, the reason I called?"

"Yeah?"

"You guys taking any bodies over there?"

"You know someone wants to work Surveillance?"

"Yeah, me."

Dwight laughed.

"Why not?"

He apologized for the outburst and said, "Brother, they'd make you for the po-lice if you was dressed like a bitch, complete with a skirt and wig. Plus, you ain't got the patience for this gig neither. When's the last time you spent twelve hours in a car, pissin' in a bottle?"

I thought about that for a moment. "It's been a while."

"And you'd take a hit on the paycheck too," he said. "I know you don't want to give up that bonus pay just to get out of that suit."

"You're probably right," I said, now looking over each shoulder, checking my surroundings in the office. "I'm just grasping at straws here, D. I don't get away from this idiot captain of mine, I might end up doing time."

Dwight chuckled. "You don't like ol' Stove-pipe?"

"Guy's a prick," I said. "You know, I've worked for some bad captains—"

"You'll outlast him."

"Ya think?"

"I know it, homeboy."

I perked up. "You know something we don't know over here?"

"They're looking at making him a commander," Dwight said, "from what I hear. That's if he can keep from stepping on his dick another couple of months 'til Commander Bowman retires. That's the spot opening up."

"No shit?"

"No shit," he said. "Hey, gotta run homeslice, looks like we're on the move. Check witchya later."

Floyd held his stare as I reached over and placed the phone back in its cradle. His eyebrows crowded together letting me know he knew I had been up to something.

"What?"

"Don't you *what* me, dickhead, I heard the call. What the hell are you up to now? And what was all that shit about with Dwight knowing something we don't know?"

"It's hard getting a little privacy around you. Do you know that?"

"No secrets between married couples, Dickie. That's in the rule book."

"Yeah, well, we're apparently going through a divorce."

"Now that you bring it up, I'm going to be needing alimony so I can stay in my accustomed lifestyle."

"Yeah, I figured. Anyway, that was just Dwight, updating me on the surveillance."

"Don't lie to me, Dickie. What'd he say about you getting a job over there, and what about the captain?"

"You were eavesdropping?"

"What'd he say?"

"He said I'd hate surveillance work—"

"Yeah we already know that. What else?"

"And that Stover may not be here long."

"Really?" Floyd said, a bit of a grin on just one side of his mouth. "That's interesting."

"Dwight said he'd heard they're grooming the asshole for commander, if you can believe that shit."

"Well yeah, man, promote the most incompetent."

"If he don't step on his dick first, D said. You get our reservations squared away?"

"Yep. We leave tomorrow morning, seven-something. Flying Delta. I figure we'll need to leave here by five-thirty, get to LAX by six. You got anything else to do today?"

"I was thinking maybe see my wife before she also reassigns my dumb ass."

"Good plan," Floyd said. "Go home. I'm heading for the gym and then I'll be headed home too. I'll see you tomorrow at zero-dark-hundred." Floyd pushed his chair under his desk and swung his suit jacket over a shoulder, pausing for a minute with his shades on inside the office, ready to go. "And don't worry about him splitting us up, Dickie, I've got a plan."

"What?"

"Don't worry about it. I'll let you know when you need to know."

I STEPPED INTO MY LIVING ROOM CARRYING MY JACKET AND BRIEFCASE IN one hand, my hat in the other, to find Valerie waiting as if she had something to say. I said, "Hi honey, everything okay?"

"Fine."

"What's wrong?"

"Would it kill you to call once in a while?"

I didn't even realize that I hadn't.

Valerie turned and began busying herself by polishing the living room furniture, not available for a hug, apparently.

I said, "Sorry, honey, it was a hard day at the office."

Still facing away, she said: "Do you have any idea how little we see of each other?" Not waiting for a reply, she turned toward me, her hands now clutching her hips and said, "Or for that matter, even talk to one another? Do you realize or even care how much of a toll that job is taking on our relationship?"

I stood there, aware of the fresh lemon scent drifting past me, a breeze sneaking through the windows and out the door I left open behind me. I searched but found nothing in my head that sounded right as a response, so I remained silent.

She continued, "A simple phone call at some point during the day would mean a lot, you know. It's what normal husbands do, men who don't go to work to hang out with their best friend and dead people all day."

"Babe," I began to plead, "I'm sorry. Honestly, today was a very tough day. Between the captain busting my balls, the phone ringing off the hook, the surveillance we've got running, trying to plan a trip—"

"And you're leaving again?"

"It'll be a short one, just a one night turnaround to Phoenix."

She turned away and spoke toward the rag she slid back and forth on a coffee table with plenty of vigor. "I swear you two love each other more than your wives."

She walked away saying maybe I should find another place to stay for a while. Maybe move in with Floyd, since we seemed to enjoy spending so much time together.

"She'll cool off and come to her senses," Floyd said, pulling out of the lot on the way to the airport early the next morning. It was still dark outside, just beginning to show signs of a cloudless day in Los Angeles.

"I've never seen her like this. Now the ex? Sure, all the time. She hated the job, hated you, hated me—"

"Hated me? I can see her hating you," Floyd said, "but I don't get her hating me. What the hell did I ever do to her? Other than that one time I accidentally grabbed her girlfriend's ass in the kitchen. And that was an accident, I don't care what anyone says."

"This is serious, though. Val doesn't usually have these moments, the way the ex would. Maybe you should go without me," I said, but didn't mean it. "I could stay here, patch things up."

"You're better off letting her have a couple of days to cool off, think things through. She'll be fine," Floyd said, "trust me. I ever tell you about that article I read, the one that says women look for conflict in their relationships when they're angry with themselves?"

Jesus, this guy, Floyd the marriage counselor now. I stared out the window without responding, watching a graffiti-covered city bus slow and veer to the curb. Blue-collar men and women stood nearby, waiting to board, prepared for another grueling day of dealing with asshole bosses. The brakes squealed as the bus came to a stop, dust bellowing from beneath the modern-day urban beast.

Floyd continued, "Probably not even you she's pissed at. More than likely it's some kind of hormonal eruption messing with her system, causing a complete imbalance or something. That shit makes women eat their young, Dickie. You do realize that, right?"

The turn signal indicator ticked an easy rhythm as we waited to enter the Long Beach Freeway south.

"You come home tomorrow night," Floyd said, now looking back and forth from the road, "she'll have things all sorted out, good as new. I'm so sure of it, that if I was you, I'd pick up a bottle of wine on the way home, walk in and slap her on the ass."

"Just what I need, Floyd as my marriage counselor."

"Fine, Dickie, you don't want to listen to me, I'll keep the guest room open. But you're not getting out of this trip. I'm not dealing with that asshole Elmer Fudd without you."

WE WALKED AWAY FROM THE RENTAL CAR COUNTER, FLOYD HOLDING A contract in one hand, a set of keys to a Mercury Sable in the other, saying, "Isn't this where they've got that sheriff who makes the inmates wear pink and sleep in tents?"

"Sheriff Joe Arpaio," I said, "my law enforcement hero. Makes the inmates watch CNN, Fox news, and a religious channel. None of that Soul Train crap, MTV. Guys act tough, he puts them in pink jump suits. No coffee or cigarettes. Bologna sandwiches for lunch. He said in an interview once—I saw it on Fox—'Our troops in Iraq sleep in tents, when they're lucky, not sleeping under a tank. It's a hell of a lot hotter there, and those brave men and women haven't committed any crimes.' The ACLU goes crazy over him, file new lawsuits every day. Joe says they can kiss his ass, pretty much. Kind of boss we need, guy with some nuts."

Floyd and I walked down an aisle of mid-sized sedans, Floyd pushing the trunk release on the remote until we found our rental. "We should see if we can get a tour," he said, dropping his bag in the trunk, "get our picture with the sheriff. He could wear that cowboy hat, and your dumb ass could pose there next to him in your fedora. I'll get in there with you, just to spice things up."

I tossed my bag in the trunk and closed it. "Tell him we're looking for a new boss, if he's interested."

"That'd be cool," Floyd agreed.

"Arizona's one thing," I said, "but I think we'd have riots for a year if he was elected sheriff in L.A. Can you imagine? The guy makes Daryl Gates look like a liberal."

I folded myself into the passenger's seat, found the lever that moves it back, and rolled it to a clunking stop. "Damned midgets riding in this thing," I mumbled.

Floyd checked the instruments, adjusted the mirrors, and tuned the radio to a rock station in preparation of takeoff. Then he looked over and asked, "Get checked in or head straight for the jail?"

"Might as well get this over with," I said, reaching for the air-conditioner controls. "I'm sure this asshole's going to ask for an attorney, just to make my week complete."

WE ENTERED THE MARICOPA COUNTY SHERIFF'S OFFICE, DURANGO JAIL facility on West Gibson Lane in Phoenix, and approached the desk officer with our badges displayed. After identifying ourselves, Floyd explained he had arranged for us to interview Inmate James Scott today, and then asked, "Is Sheriff Joe here?"

The thin, pale-complexioned deputy with wavy brown hair and thick eyeglasses rose from his chair without comment and stepped over to an operation panel with red and green lights and black buttons. He pressed something and the gray, heavy metal door to our right clunked. The familiar sound told me we could enter, and also hinted that the young man had no intention of entertaining Floyd. Perhaps he had no sense of humor.

Floyd seemed less perceptive, or maybe more persistent. "We were hoping to meet him, get a picture with him. Maybe have a tour of that place with the inmates wearing chains and pink jump suits."

"Gentlemen," the subdued deputy said, continuing to ignore Floyd, "you'll have to check your weapons before you proceed."

"Guns and knives on the table, Dickie, is what the young man's telling you," Floyd said, continuing to have fun with the young man. "And don't forget that switchblade in your boot."

Guns, extra ammunition, knives, and handcuff keys secured in the small metal lockers, the deputy escorted us to Interview Room One, the black plaque on the gray door identifying it for us. The figure of a man wearing an orange jumpsuit sat in a chair near the center of the room. He turned to face us as we entered and the heavy door closed behind us.

I studied the man for a moment, a bit perplexed. "James Scott?"

"Yes sir?"

Floyd frowned and said, "Where the hell is Elmer Fudd?"

23

FLOYD PULLED OUT a chair opposite the man in his orange jumpsuit. He appeared to be in his sixties, and was fit, thin with a straight posture. His complexion was clear, his eyes a soft blue surrounded by brilliant white, and he was neatly groomed and clean shaven though showing a day's shadow. He was a perfect match to the DMV photo of James Scott.

I paced the length of the wall in front of a two-way mirror, thinking, who is this James Scott, how is he related to Elmer Fudd—or is he?—and is anyone watching through the glass as the mystery man sat silent.

He appeared slightly nervous, his hands buried in the pockets of his jail-issued clothing, fidgeting. His eyes darted from me to Floyd; he was probably anxious to find out who we were and why we were there. Everyone in the room seemed a little unsure of the situation.

I stopped in a corner with a ringside view of the action, Floyd now seated at the table across from the man in the county jail jumpsuit. Floyd opened his case file and pulled out a pen and paper. The two of them studied one another, not quite ready for the bell, and also not willing to touch gloves.

"You're James Scott?" Floyd finally asked.

"Yes sir."

Floyd paused for a moment, looked over to me, his corner man, but I had nothing to offer. Though I wasn't ready to throw in the towel either. He turned back to face his opponent.

"Mr. Scott, I'm Detective Tyler with the Los Angeles County Sheriff's Department,"—he nodded toward me—"this is my partner, Detective Jones."

The man glanced over, nodded, and returned his attention to Floyd.

"Do you own a home in Downey, California?"

"Yes sir, I do."

"Do you currently live at the Downey residence?"

"Kind of," he said and paused, "what is this about, Detective?"

"Kind of?"

"My wife and I moved out here to Phoenix—temporarily, I hope—to be with her mother. She, my mother-in-law, has had some problems with her health."

"Is anyone supposed to be staying at your house, the one in Downey?"

"Sometimes my brother stays there," he said, "that should be it."

Floyd glanced at me and then back. "Tell me about your brother, Mr. Scott."

"I'm not sure I understand your question. What is it you want to know?"

"Let's start with his name," Floyd said. "What's your brother's name, Mr. Scott?"

"Randy . . . Randall Scott," he said, his eyes now squinting, deep in thought.

"Tell us about him?"

"What do you mean?"

Floyd, patient with the man but maybe frustrated. "I mean tell me about your brother. Is that a difficult question? What is he like? Does he work? Is he a drunk? Has he been to jail? What's he look like?"

"Randy," he said and let a breath out, giving it a moment, "is a good man, honestly. He may be a little unsettled, or maybe troubled would be a better way to say it." He pulled his hands from his pockets and folded them on the metal table before him. He seemed to relax a bit, probably seeing where this was headed. "The last ten years or so have been challenging for him. He's had some trouble holding down a job, maybe drinks more than he should. I'd say he's been down on his luck. He's been in and out of the V.A. for depression over the last couple years, and now, finally, they have him taking some medication that is supposed to help."

"So, he's a veteran?"

The man nodded.

"As for jail," he continued, "he's had a couple minor brushes with the law, nothing major."

"Tell us about that."

"Well, just minor incidents, as I said. He had a fist fight outside a bar one night that landed him in jail—he and the other guy both. But it was only a disturbance charge or something, maybe public drunkenness, I'm not sure. He was out the next day and I don't think anything else ever came of it. He's had a few tickets I know, but honestly, I think that's about it."

Floyd with his arms crossed: "You indicated he's a vet."

"Both of us were in 'Nam."

Mr. Scott paused for a moment, apparently in thought. He said, "Funny thing about that war, the way some of us came back okay, others were never the same. I saw some combat with my outfit, but not to the extent he did. Randy was with the 101st, and those boys were always into something. He fought in three major battles, God only knows how much unsanctioned action he saw. That's the way it was over there."

"So, he was Airborne?"

"Yes, he was," James Scott said, "a sniper. He doesn't talk much about his time overseas, never has. Can I ask what this is about? I've answered a lot of questions for you gentlemen. I don't mind helping out, but it'd be nice to have an idea what's going on, know what kind of trouble he's in or if he's okay. I also like to know what this has to do with me, and why I'm locked up."

"We had a bit of a problem out there at your place," Floyd said, "that might have involved your brother. Is he a big fella, kind of sloppy, out of shape?"

James frowned for a second and glanced in my direction. He turned back to Floyd, leaned forward and said, "He's been a pretty bad drunk over the past few years. Probably doesn't help his depression much, and to your question, it hasn't been good for his overall health either."

"So, yeah, he's a big guy?"

"I would say yes, he is overweight."

Floyd nodded. "What does he do for a living?"

"Last I knew, he was driving a tow truck. That and he receives a disability check from the government."

"Who's he drive for?"

"He was driving for a company in Inglewood, or Compton, one of those neighborhoods down there. He complained quite a bit about having to work around blacks and Mexicans, to be real honest with you."

Floyd sat silent for a moment, then looked at me and nodded. It was my cue to jump in if I had any questions.

"Sir," I said, coming away from the wall, lingering near the table now, "have you had anything stolen, your wallet or anything? Maybe lost your credit cards?"

"Someone broke into our house the first time we came out here to Phoenix. We'd been gone a couple of weeks and went back to a ransacked mess. They got in through the back door. Broke the glass, and reached through to unlock the bolt. Since then, we've had Randy keeping an eye on the place. He stays there off and on and takes care of things for us, or at least that's what we hope."

I pulled out a chair and sat next to Floyd.

"What was taken?"

"A pistol, some jewelry . . ."

"What about anything with your identity, or maybe credit cards?"

"Not that I know of," he said.

I paused in thought. "You haven't had any problems with your credit, noticed anything unusual in your statements?"

"No, nothing I know of. Is Randy using my credit cards?"

"I don't think so," I replied. "Does he have access to any?"

"He collects my mail and forwards it here. I guess he could have access to the statements, maybe new cards. He could call and have them activated, I suppose. That would surprise me though. Randy isn't like that."

I thought about the credit card used by Donna Edwards and her boyfriend, Gilbert, at the hotel in Texas. Then I wondered about the burglary of James Scott's home, thinking of how some of Donna's friends

—Gilbert Regalado and the dude in the Tahoe, to name a couple—seem like the breaking and entering type, especially if they knew for sure a house sat vacant, the owners out of town. The conversation with Donna replayed in my head, her telling me about Mrs. Scott, how she'd see her in the mornings. Maybe she noticed Mrs. Scott's absence, or newspapers collecting in the driveway.

I asked, "What do you know about the young lady who lives across the street from your place there in Downey?"

"Donna?" he asked.

"Yeah," I said, a bit surprised by his response. "Do you know her?"

"Sure, we know her. The wife knows her better than I do. I'm not too fond of the amount of company she has, in and out all hours of the day and night. But other than that, she seems to be a real nice girl."

"Does your brother know her, as far as you know?"

"I wouldn't think so. Even if he's seen her since he's stayed there at my place, I wouldn't think he'd know her. He isn't real sociable, and again, he seems to have a chip on his shoulder about minorities."

Floyd chimed in, "I believe you are right about that."

"You guys have met him?" he asked, glancing at Floyd but directing his question to me.

"Briefly," I said. "Did Donna know you and the wife were out of town?"

"She picked up the mail and newspapers for us the first time we came out here to Phoenix. The wife had thought it'd be a good idea, and thought her trustworthy. I was a little concerned, honestly, not so much because of Donna, but the company she keeps. When we went back home and discovered the break-in, I decided to have my brother take care of the place the next time we left. My wife wasn't crazy about that idea, but we didn't have other options.

"With all due respect, Detective, I really would like to know what's going on here. I've been arrested and held, and I have no idea what any of this is about. Now they tell me I have an extradition hearing, something about whether or not I'll go to California to face charges? This's crazy, and I haven't even had a phone call."

"Mr. Scott, we'll see to it all of this is sorted out as soon as we finish with this interview. You'll be released, and I can assure you there won't be any charges."

He nodded.

"So how long have you been here in Phoenix this time, Mr. Scott?" I asked.

"Couple of weeks, maybe more."

"I assume you can prove that? Dinner receipts, hotel, gas? Someone who can vouch for you being here?"

"My wife, her mother . . . I'm sure we have some receipts."

"Okay, good. So I think that wraps it up for us, sir, but we're going to need your help."

"With what?"

"Finding your brother."

"What did he do?"

"We think he tried to kill me and my partner," I said. "Someone shot up our car with a high-powered rifle, turned your nice little neighborhood into a Mogadishu with streetlights."

"You two?" he asked, glancing at me and then Floyd.

"Yep," Floyd said, "right there in front of your house. Had us pinned down for a while."

He took a deep breath, paused, and let it out with a sigh. Then he grinned. "Either you got the wrong man, or he didn't have any intention of hurting you. Neither of you would be here talking to me if he wanted you dead."

"That sure was a relief," Floyd said, steering the rental out of the jail parking lot and onto a crowded Arizona street, "knowing if he wanted us dead, we'd be dead. *Army Ranger, sniper. One shot, one kill, blah, blah, blah*. Jesus."

"Hundred and first."

"Ranger, hundred and first, whatever. Who're you calling?"

I closed my cell phone and slid it into my pocket. "I was trying to get ahold of Val."

"Not home?"

"Guess not."

"Try her cell?"

"Went to voicemail," I said. "So you think it's true, what he said about Elmer, he would've killed us if he was trying?"

Floyd shook his head. "I don't know, Dickie. Shooting is like fighting, running, drinking beer, whatever. You don't do it for a while, you lose your edge. He may have been a badass in 'Nam, but that was a long time ago. You've seen him."

"Yeah, good point. None of this makes any sense though. By the way, do you still have someone sitting on your house, watching out for the family?"

"Around the clock. Two Metro dicks in a slick parked out front, right in my driveway."

"Like no one knows they're cops?"

"Right," Floyd said. "But at least someone's there. That's all I care about at this point. It's a deterrent, if nothing else."

I thought about Valerie, the possibility of another marriage falling victim to the job as we drove across the desert-turned-city. Thinking about things at home when Floyd interrupted the silence, no doubt knowing I had a lot on my mind, probably knowing exactly what it was.

He said, "You all right, partner?"

"Yeah, I'm fine. Just thinking."

"You guys will be fine, trust me."

I looked over at my new marriage counselor. The guy had it all figured out, everything from hormonal imbalances to Tupperware parties. What else did you need to know?

He glanced over, grinned, and repeated, "Trust me."

He probably had a point, it would most likely work out. Why dwell on it at this point? Nothing could be done until I went home, and until then, Floyd and I had a lot on our plate.

First, we needed to find Fudd, Mr. Randall Scott, the *Army sniper*. Find him and get some answers about that shootout, about Floyd's car, about a lot of things that didn't make sense. Little things like how the people across the street were dealing dope, and now two of them have ended up dead, our boy Fudd the prime suspect at this point.

"What're we going to do about finding Fudd?" I asked.

"You come up with anything?"

"Not yet, you?"

"I actually had a thought," he said. "Let's find the tow company he's working for, see if we can get our hands on him there. What if he isn't the one who shot at us? That's something we need to know in a hurry. If he is, we'll probably know as soon as he sees us coming. If he isn't, we need to rethink all of this. If he no longer works there, maybe we can talk to someone there who knows more about him, where he might be."

"Who else could it have been, if it wasn't Fudd?" I asked. "I mean, there's no doubt it came from his house, right? And it's probably no coincidence he's nowhere to be found ever since."

"No doubt about it."

"You saw the same thing as me, right? Muzzle flashes from the windows?"

"Yeah, I saw it. The thing is, maybe it was someone else in there. Gilbert? The dude in the Tahoe? One of Donna's other boyfriends? It's not like they haven't been in that house before. You know they're the ones who ripped off James, the first time he left town. I'd bet on that. How else are they using James Scott's credit cards?"

"What's the motive? Why the hell would any of them be shooting at *us?*"

He thought about that for a moment. "Frame Fudd, maybe? Get his dumb ass out of the neighborhood? Remember how he always watched them, kept an eye on them? Well, if you're dealing dope, you don't want some asshole redneck putting the heat on you."

"Maybe," I said, seeing the possibility.

"Or to distract us on the murder," Floyd said, "which has certainly worked wonders. Shit, we've been all over the board on this one, not to mention the country. Haven't gotten any closer to figuring out who whacked our little Susie, or her buddy. Been too busy chasing our tails in circles."

"True," I said. Then after thinking about it, I asked, "How's that work with your car being stolen from your house?"

"Got me, Dickie. We're still missing something, I'll give you that. What we need to do is expand our thinking on this, get creative. Start with finding Elmer Fudd. Why don't you give Dwight a call, see what's up with Donna?"

"Sounds like a plan."

Then he looked over, studied me for a moment longer than maybe he should have while driving, and shifted his eyes back to the road. The look on his face told me he had something cooking up there, in spite of his eyes being hidden behind dark glasses. Something cooking when Floyd was in the kitchen could be disastrous.

"What the hell are you thinking, asshole?"

"You don't think there's a chance . . . that maybe . . . Ah, never mind."

"Let's hear it," I said. "It's not often you have a thought that isn't related to sex."

"I was just thinking—"

"Yeah?"

"Well, it occurs to me, we took for granted my car was totally burned up when you started that fight with Charlie Wright. We never actually went to look at it, checked to see if anything could be salvaged."

"Yeah?"

"A lot of my personal shit was in that car, including stuff with my address, I'm sure."

"What's your point?"

"Well, we never could figure how Elmer Fudd could have known where I live, right?"

I just looked at him.

Floyd continued, "What if he works for the company that towed my car? Remember, his brother says he works in Inglewood, or Compton."

"It's a long shot," I said, "but you might be onto something."

"Maybe, maybe not. Let's call Dwight."

24

AND A COSMOPOLITAN for my nineteen-year-old friend," Floyd said to the back of a bartender who stood collecting beer into a frozen mug from the tap. We sat passing the time in an airport bar, checked in and ready for our return flight to Los Angeles.

He glanced back at Floyd as he replaced one mug with another, the tap still open, beer cascading over the top and down the side of the first mug and into a tray.

Floyd nodded toward the blonde sitting a few stools away and continued: "Or whatever it is she's drinking."

The young lady, sipping something pink from a martini glass, proffered a smile with a simple, yet meaningful, "No, thank you."

Floyd turned toward me and grumbled, "Just trying to be neighborly."

"So, two Coors Lights, eleven dollars," the bartender said, setting the mugs in front of us, his contempt for the two of us, or at least Floyd, not disguised.

Floyd didn't disappoint him. "Jesus, eleven dollars?"

The portly man stood, watching, waiting, his robust forearms protruding from white sleeves rolled up to his elbows. He leaned into his thick hands gripping that side of the bar, his wiry brows shading skeptical, brown eyes.

I pulled a twenty from my wallet and slid it toward the business side of the bar. "Thank you, partner, we sure appreciate it."

He swept the bill from the bar top and turned to the register behind him after a quick frown toward my partner.

I nudged Floyd. "Lighten up, man."

Floyd, taking a swig from the frosty mug, "What?"

"You're doing that thing you do."

"What thing?" he asked, looking at me incredulously.

The blonde stood, slid a half-empty glass toward the bartender, and said, "Thanks, Troy." Then she walked away, running a hand across the back of her navy-blue skirt, deflecting the wrinkles but not the stares.

Troy, the bartender, picked up her glass and swept the surface of the bar with a towel that appeared from nowhere, the motion fluid and practiced. "See ya, Tina," he said, glancing back to catch the two of us watching her walk away. Then he moved to the far end of the bar, picked up a remote control, and began surfing through the channels of a television that protruded from the wall above him. He settled on a sports channel with two broadcasters, one black and one white, the two of them out of place in suits with their thick necks and flat noses, scar tissue accentuating oversized faces.

"What'd I do?" Floyd asked, his attention coming back to me.

"Two things: one, you pissed off our bartender. I've always asked that you not do that. Bartenders and lawyers, we don't piss them off if they're working for us."

"I don't know what that big asshole's problem is anyway, unless that's his daughter or something. You suppose that was his daughter?"

"She's probably an airport employee, I'd guess, since she obviously knows the bartender and wasn't carrying anything other than a purse. When's the last time you saw anyone travel without a carry-on? Second thing, *Troy* probably thinks you're a pervert—a cocky one at that. Three—"

"You said *two* things."

"—he looks like the type who doesn't mind a good scrap."

"Yeah, well, I'm his huckleberry there. And why the hell would he think I'm a cocky pervert? You should be ashamed, Dickie, for the insinuation."

"Who knows why anyone would *ever* find you cocky or think you're a pervert. It's beyond me."

"I was just being funny," Floyd said, "offering to buy a cosmopolitan for a nineteen-year-old. You don't see the humor in that?"

"The hell's a cosmopolitan?"

"Technically, it's a martini, sort of a yuppie version though. Not like the James Bond martinis that taste like turpentine. These have all those foo-foo flavors, the ones chicks like. That's what she was drinking, I think, and she looked like she was about nineteen, so—"

"And you decided she was your friend."

"I'm a friendly guy, Dickie. You know that."

"I doubt Troy is," I said. "You'll be lucky if he doesn't bash you over the head with an empty mug, the looks he gave you."

"I'd run circles on that fat bastard, Dickie. Come on, this place sucks. You wanna go back to that restaurant, get a burger? We've got an hour before they board us."

"Sure," I said, "let's finish these beers."

"JAMES SCOTT IS CLEAR, NO DOUBT ABOUT THAT," I SAID AS A WAITRESS collected our menus and walked away with our orders in her head. "What remains to be seen is what, if anything, his brother, Randy has to do with any of this."

"You mean other than trying to kill us, right?"

I thought about it for a second. "Other than that."

"You're not buying into that one shot, one kill bullshit, are you?"

"You don't think there's any validity to it?" I asked. "I mean, he's a combat sniper."

"Thirty years ago," Floyd said. "The guy might not be able to see across the street now. Name me one other person who would've been up there shooting at us."

"Maybe you're right," I said, "I just have a hard time putting this all together, Fudd, Donna and company, the shooting . . . There's a lot that doesn't make sense."

"So what's your point?"

I stared off, thinking about my point. Trying to reason my way through all of the information, the issues, the players.

"My point is this case isn't any closer to being solved than it was the night you showed up drunk at the crime scene."

"Whatever, dude."

"We need to get somewhere with it before the next rotation. If we're not lucky enough to pick up another walkthrough—a good old-fashioned murder-suicide or a no-witness gang shooting—we're going to be buried and this case will go cold."

Floyd sank into the red, cushioned bench seat, leaned his head back with a look of exasperation, and said, "I need a vacation, Dickie."

I continued. "We've eliminated James Scott and the gangster—"

"Cedric," Floyd said, "the gangster with the smoking hot attorney. I'm thinking Hawaii, Dickie, is where I need to go."

"Yeah, Cedric. We still have Charlie Wright—"

"Who didn't do it."

"How do we know?" I asked.

"The guy's an asshole," Floyd said, "but I don't see him killing his kid just because he wears dresses. You've never snorkeled, have you?"

"I'd say there's a little more to it than that, if he's involved—"

"You don't even like the beach, for Christ's sake."

"—whether or not he did it, is what we need to resolve. Eliminate him or charge him, cross his name off the list. Who's left? And no, I don't snorkel, and no, I don't like the beach."

Floyd sat up. He looked around the restaurant, still apparently bored with the conversation. "No one, unless you want to put your Chinaman buddy on it."

"Lanh Hoang?" I said, the name coming out loud, fast. "You've got to be kidding me."

"Why not?"

"I don't know why not. And, he's Vietnamese, you idiot. Why would you even think of him for this? What're you trying to do, jack this case up more than it already is?"

"Just throwing out ideas, Dickie. The guy's a weirdo, just the type to do some weird shit like this. Sitting up there watching through his binoculars, getting his jollies when he should be downstairs with the little missus.

Who, I might add, isn't too shabby herself, really. You never did have a thing for Asian girls, did you, Dickie?"

"I'll give you he's weird, but come on, man."

"Maybe the queens got him excited, pushed him over the edge. He learned something about himself he couldn't deal with. I've seen it happen."

"What would he have done? Follow them down to Lynwood, see where they're doing their tricks and whack 'em for getting him excited?"

"Maybe he was with them first, couldn't take any chances."

"Crazy."

"Well," Floyd said, arranging his silverware now, "it will give you something to think about anyway. That's what makes you happy, having shit to think about. Where's that waitress?"

Lanh Hoang, for Christ's sake.

Floyd seemed to hear my thought, and he grinned.

"Running around the country with your uptight ass is a chore sometimes. You know it, pal?"

"I suppose," I said, listening but thinking about Lanh Hoang, wondering if my partner just took a blind swing and cleared the fences.

There had been stranger developments in a murder investigation. Much stranger. It only made sense to consider Donna and her dirtbag friends as possible suspects, and even more so to take a look at a guy like Elmer Fudd. But to consider one of our own? A deputy? That seemed a real stretch in a case like this. But, no matter how difficult it could be at times, I knew to keep an open mind, consider all possibilities until they've been positively eliminated.

"But Lanh?"

"Never know," he said.

We waited in silence as the waitress placed our meals before us. After she walked away, Floyd picked up his fork, looked up to me and said, "I think I'll put in for a couple weeks off when we get back, take some vacation. Let you wrap this case up by yourself. Because honestly, Dickie, you're really starting to bore me."

COMING OUT OF THE AIRPORT PARKING STRUCTURE IN SUNNY LOS Angeles, I fished my shades out of my briefcase as Floyd slid his down from the top of his head.

"Who're you calling now?"

"I was going to have the desk run Charlie Wright, see if he's still in custody."

"Why? You're not wanting to go see him, are you?"

"I was thinking maybe."

"I say if you're wanting to talk to someone, we go see your buddy, Long Dong."

"Lanh Hoang."

"Whatever," Floyd said.

We left the airport headed east on the Century Freeway toward the office.

"What would you say to Lanh?" I asked, *"Hey Lanh, you're kind of a strange dude, did you have anything to do with whacking those trans-sexuals?"*

"I don't know, Dickie. Just stress him out a little, see how he reacts. I actually was mostly kidding. I'd think you'd be more concerned with getting home at a decent hour, see your wife before she leaves you for a fireman."

"It's two-thirty, and we've got work to do. And she would never leave me for a hose jockey. You know that."

"It's been a long week—two weeks, actually," he reminded me, glancing over and then back at the road ahead. "Go home for Christ's sake, before you end up sleep—"

"Watch out!" I yelled, seeing the van swerve toward us in my peripheral vision.

"Jesus!"

Floyd glanced my way and yanked the wheel to the left, the vehicle jerking violently, the tires squealing against the pavement. As we straightened, the van crossed into our lane again, coming right at us.

I yelled, "Look out!"

"What the hell," Floyd yelled, swerving again. "Shoot that asshole if he comes at us again."

We were back in our lane and he in his, but there was no escape, the crowded freeway confining us to our lane with the van beside us, matching our speed. We were still traveling at about 50 mph.

"What's his problem?"

"He's trying to kill us, Dickie. Shoot that son-of-a-bitch!"

I had drawn my pistol after the first near-miss, but thus far had not pointed it toward the assailing vehicle, unsure of the intent of its driver. The van suddenly veered away from our vehicle, out of his lane and into traffic on the other side. There were sounds of screeching tires and horns, followed by the unmistakable sound of metal hitting metal. The van then moved toward us again.

Floyd yelled, "Shoot him goddammit!"

I now had my sidearm pointed at the driver's door, unable to see the driver through his tinted window. I waited, ready for one more assault, my mind racing with the thoughts that accompany questionable shootings: *What is his intent? Will the shooting be justified? Are our lives in imminent danger? . . . Where the hell are the cops when you need them?!*

I had the tunnel vision and its slow-motion effect that is common during these types of shoot or don't shoot scenarios. I continued to focus on the van, which moved slowly but directly at us again, the third time now. Coming at us inch by inch, seemingly with intent, an apparent assault, our lives in imminent danger. Floyd had it right, the son-of-a-bitch was trying to kill us.

Floyd's voice seemed distant now, his words processing slowly in my brain as I prepared to defend us, my finger beginning to squeeze the trigger, my sights locked on the driver's door of the vehicle as Floyd shouted, "Shoooooooot! . . . *S H O O T !*"

25

LIEUTENANT JORDAN PULLED onto the eastbound shoulder of the Century Freeway about a half-mile west of the Long Beach Boulevard off-ramp. He parked to the rear of several emergency vehicles: two California Highway Patrol cars, an ambulance, two fire engines, a paramedic's truck, and three black and white sheriff's patrol cars. That put him about a hundred feet or so behind the white van involved in the incident, which now sat on the back of a flatbed tow truck, not far from where Floyd's recently battered Ford Taurus came to rest.

The lieutenant walked toward us slowly with one hand in the pocket of his pleated navy-blue slacks. The other hand first caressed his tie and then pushed wire-rimmed sunglasses up onto the bridge of his nose, the lieutenant seeming to take in all the action along the way. There were deputies wearing tan and green, highway patrolmen with their tan uniforms with blue stripes, and a couple of LAPD motor cops with helmets and large mustaches, who had stopped to help with traffic control. Cops seemed to be spread throughout the scene, pointing this way and that, sharing information and discussing the incident among themselves. Firemen stood in bulky yellow pants with reflective stripes, suspenders over white or blue t-shirts under the shade of a shiny red fire truck. Two paramedics wheeled a gurney toward the opened rear doors of an ambulance parked just ahead of the firemen.

Traffic had backed up for miles. Three of the four lanes had been closed off by road flares where emergency personnel redirected the slow-moving vehicles through an alternate route. The sounds of police and fire dispatch voices crackled from handheld radios and intertwined with idling engines and the occasional blast of a horn.

Floyd and I stood near his battered green Taurus, silently evaluating the swipes of white paint along the passenger side, the dented doors and fenders, and the flat front tire. The two of us stood stoically, shades on, our sleeves turned up to our elbows, arms crossed as if we were taking in a ballgame, nothing special happening here. The lieutenant arrived at our location, shaking his head.

"Quite a mess," Lt. Jordan said, positioning himself to the side of Floyd.

The three of us now stood shoulder to shoulder, each looking toward the ambulance and watching paramedics heave the gurney into the back of the wagon. The large shape of a body shifted beneath a sheet with the motion. The gurney's wheels folded beneath itself with two thwacks—the sound of metal hitting metal—and with that the ambulance buttoned up and departed, lights and sirens parting the way.

The lieutenant leaned forward, craning his neck toward us. "You boys ready to run this by me? The captain wants a call right away. He's about to have a coronary in the office."

Floyd looked at me.

I shrugged. "It's your circus, pal."

"The man who just departed in the back of that ambulance, was the pilot of that beast over there," Floyd said, as he gestured toward a tow truck holding a white van with steam still rising from under the hood. "He sideswiped us twice, and nailed a couple of those other cars up ahead." Floyd turned to look further up the freeway. Lieutenant Jordan leaned back, looking around us to follow Floyd's gaze, up the freeway toward a black BMW, a red Chevy Impala, and a white Ford pickup truck, a line of smashed up cars parked along the shoulder.

"When he finished bouncing off half the cars on the freeway, he hit that guardrail over there," Floyd continued, now with a nod in the direction of a battered steel railing, "came back out and hit another car, then finally came to a stop."

The lieutenant shook his head, saying, "Man."

"That's when my partner tried to kill the poor bastard."

"Excuse me?" I responded. "Who was yelling for me to shoot the guy?"

Jordan snapped his head around and said, "You didn't—"

"No," I said, "but for a second or two . . . I mean, it was close."

"We had no idea what he was doing, boss," Floyd said. "For a minute there, I thought it was another Elmer Fudd attack. Seriously seemed like he was trying to kill us."

"Elmer Fudd?"

"That's what we call the guy who shot Dickie's car up," Floyd said, "out there in Downey."

"Who we think did it," I added.

"So, what's the deal with this guy in the van?" the lieutenant asked. "Was he drunk?"

"Maybe a heart attack," Floyd said, "we're not entirely sure. He was out of it when we got to the van. In fact, at first it looked like he was dead, hunched over the center console. We pulled him out, checked his vitals, and started CPR. Told one of the idiots standing around watching to call 9-1-1."

"Paramedics arrived and put the paddles to him," I added. "There were able to get him jump-started. That was just a few minutes ago, right before you showed up. How the hell'd you get here so fast, anyway?"

"I was right over there in Inglewood," Lieutenant Jordan said, nodding to the west. "You don't want to know why."

"Why?" Floyd and I said simultaneously.

"Charlie Wright filed a complaint against the two of you, alleging excessive force and false arrest. Captain wanted me to talk to him, see how adamant he is about pursuing charges."

"Did you remind him he started the fight?" I asked. "We only went there to talk to him."

"You started that fight, Dickie," Floyd said. "Don't lie to your lieutenant."

"When do I get my new partner?" I asked.

The lieutenant, accustomed to the banter, said, "Fourth car in two weeks, good chance the captain will have you both back in uniform next month. Listen, I'm going to the hospital, see if this gentleman makes it through. If so, I'll try to get a statement from him. Could one of you talk to the chippies, see to it we get a copy of their report sent to the office? This is a goddamned mess."

"No problem, boss," I said. "I'll take care of it while my partner changes the flat on his Taurus."

Floyd said, "In my Joseph Abboud? You know what I paid for this suit?"

Lieutenant Jordan smiled and turned to walk away.

I turned to Floyd and said, "Better get crackin', asshole."

IT WAS NEARLY FOUR BY THE TIME WE LIMPED INTO THE PARKING LOT OF our office in Floyd's Taurus with a donut-sized spare tire and white racing stripes against the green paint. On the bright side, my Crown Vic had been returned from the shop; the bullet holes were patched and painted, and the broken glass had been replaced, and apparently it had a new transmission. I dropped the Ford Tempo keys on my lieutenant's desk, and nearly kicked up my heels.

Maybe the day wasn't so bad after all, I thought, noticing the captain's office door sat closed and the lights were off. I wouldn't have to deal with him for at least one more day, and I had my car back. Plus, I didn't shoot anyone while they were trying to die of a heart attack.

Then I thought about the transfer, the recent complaint by Charlie Wright, another crashed county car, and I decided that Floyd and I really were having a run of bad luck.

We decided there had been plenty of excitement for one day and agreed to call it quits. We parted ways in the parking lot, and as we passed each other on the way out, Floyd flipped me off.

Merging onto the freeway, I called and left a message for my wife, telling her what a hell of a day it had been and how happy I was to be on my way home. I had started to tell her more, say the things that had been on my mind the last two days: how much I loved her, how I regretted being hard to live with at times, how I would try to keep the job in perspective and keep the home fires burning no matter what it took. Ready to say all these things but cut short by a hollow tone announcing the end of the allotted time.

Probably for the better, I thought; I'd save it to tell her in person. Get a bottle of wine on the way home, hold her and whisper these things in her ear. Make nice with the little woman.

I thought about the day I had come home to a quiet, half-empty house where an ominous envelope sat on the kitchen counter waiting to announce the divorce. The job had taken its toll on my first marriage, there was no doubt about that. But that was a long time ago, a time when the job and its inconvenient schedules and long hours made up just part of the problem. The other part of the equation—not unique to cop marriages and subsequent divorces—was that I was young, immature in many ways, and camaraderie with my partners seemed paramount. That meant nightly gatherings at cop bars or parking lots because drinking with the boys seemed more important than coming home in those days. We referred to these gatherings as debriefings, justifying them as the way we reduced the stresses of the job. A way to calm the nerves before returning to civilization.

There had been all the warning signs: complaints of the crazy hours, requests that I try to go to day shift—like normal husbands who work during the day and are home with their families in the evening—comments about too much drinking eventually escalating to accusations of alcoholism. Several requests for marital counseling, and finally her need for a few weeks away to clear her head. All of these signs but it took coming home to an empty house and a short note to hear a word she said. Then it came across loud and clear.

A couple years after the divorce, Valerie and I met through mutual friends. Soon after, we fell in love. Neither of us had children, though both were previously married. By the time we tied the knot, I had been promoted to detective.

Getting off the streets offered fewer hazards in some ways, more in others. Working patrol came with the potential for violence on every call, every traffic stop, and every contact. For that matter, every hour of each shift was a threat to the uniformed cop who had become a target to some in our society. Being promoted to detective certainly negated the target part of the equation, and no longer would I be asked to place myself between two adults who wanted to kill one another, or maybe decide that killing the cop between them would be just as satisfying. Most contacts as a detective were on the detective's terms, and therefore safer and better controlled. We decided when we would contact a suspect or witness, and generally we would know their backgrounds beforehand and be appropriately prepared. But there were other hazards to the detective's overall health and well-being, such as longer hours and more mental stress, both primarily due to an overwhelming caseload. The duty of investigating death was accompanied by the burden of unsolved cases, which weighed heavily on the broadest of shoulders. It wasn't long before I was propelled into the workaholic state that I seemed to embrace.

Now I found myself in another strained relationship and I hadn't even seen it coming. Like the previously destroyed marriage, I had been blind to the simple needs of a reasonable woman. Unable to see or hear the messages until it was too late, or so I worried, as I continued the drive home in silence, no radio or phone conversations with my partner to distract me. No thoughts about Susie or Tawny or any of the other unsolved cases that plagued me. Just me, alone with my memories and worries, marinating in regret and apprehension.

Turning onto my street, I eased past the well-manicured lawns of a middle-class neighborhood. I watched children play in the presence of normal parents who were home with their families in the evening, not visiting crime scenes or chasing killers or drinking with their partner in Chinatown, celebrating another near-miss with death. One or two waved as I passed, and it occurred to me that they likely envied my career. The big-time homicide detective who parked an unmarked cop car in his driveway, wore a gun on his hip, and had all of the exciting stories. It was all perspective, I guessed.

I turned into an empty driveway with a heavy heart, my mind racing as I imagined the possibilities of what awaited me beyond the warm, red door of our previously predictable and safe abode. None of which could compare to what I actually walked in to.

26

I STOOD AT the threshold of my front door, scanning the living room, the dining room, the visible portion of our kitchen. Everything seemed to be in place; even the coffeemaker sat in its assigned position on the counter. She wouldn't leave and not take the Cuisinart, I reasoned, if for no other reason than revenge.

"Honey?" I called out, though somewhat tentatively. I placed my briefcase, jacket, and hat on the dining room table, and walked into the kitchen expecting a note or a letter, anything for a clue. I set a bottle of wine on the counter and turned toward the hallway. "Honey?"

No reply.

I walked down the hall in the direction of our master bedroom, aware of faint noises coming from the back of the house. Stepping cautiously into the doorway, I noted a light on in the master bath. There was a strong scent of perfume, and it wasn't one with which I was familiar.

Feeling unsettled about the peculiar presence in my home, I placed my hand on the pistol at my side and moved toward the bathroom, I scanned the bedroom for luggage of an unexpected guest or anything out of the ordinary. Val's sister from Tacoma came to mind, but the room lacked evidence of overnight company.

Before turning into the master bath, I paused at the trickling sound of stirred water. I held my breath and cautiously peered around the corner.

A woman with fiery red hair stood with her shapely backside toward me, lowering herself into the oversized tub full of bubbles. She had a glass of wine in one hand and a highball glass filled with ice, a clear liquid, and a wedge of lime in the other. She settled into the bath and placed both drinks on the tub's ledge.

I couldn't recall knowing a single woman with red hair, much less one who would be lowering herself into my tub.

Setup! I thought.

Could Valerie have planned to leave me, and this woman was the decoy of a private investigator, sent to lure me into an adulterous act? That'd be a sure way to get half of my retirement without much of a battle, I thought. Stories of contentious divorce cases were common grievances among cops.

With slow gentle strokes of her hand, this redhead in my wife's tub pushed the bubbles around in front of her body, the motion revealing an occasional glimpse of glistening skin. I assumed it had to be unintentional; she couldn't have known I was standing behind her. But then she startled me by speaking in a low and nonchalant tone, her back still to me. "Care to join me?"

As I stood dumbfounded and speechless, this lady slowly turned, spiraling through the water like a mermaid until her back and bottom floated above the waterline, the bubbly water receding from skin. She kicked her heels up behind her and rested her chin on the side of the tub.

I stood aghast.

"Gin and tonic?" she asked, wrapping her fingers around the moistened glass, her red nails drumming the side. "I hear it's one of your favorites."

She was gorgeous. Stunningly beautiful. Playing the part all the way, continuing her seduction. "Well, Detective, are you going to join me or stand there holding your pistol?"

I pulled the knot out of my tie and began unbuttoning my shirt, kicking off my shoes at the same time. Then I pulled my belt from my trousers, catching my badge and gun and carefully placing those items on the bathroom countertop. I tugged at a sock while hopping on one foot and leaning against the doorway. My heart pounded with excitement as I cast all caution to the wind.

She watched as I finished disrobing and made my way to the tub, her bright eyes seeming to twinkle just a little, the corners of her mouth turned up in a coy smile.

She handed me the gin and tonic after I settled into the roomy tub and rested my back against the opposite end. The hot water—almost too hot at first—instantly soothed my tired body and I felt the tension dissipating. Our legs touched beneath the bubbles, the softness of her skin luring me further into temptation. She sat up and slid toward me, closing the space, and leaned in to kiss me lightly on the mouth. Her breath was warm, fresh, and inviting.

She kissed me again and then pulled back, but just a few inches. She stared deeply into my eyes and whispered, "Maybe you should come home early more often, Detective."

For the first time in two days, I felt good again, the domestic worries now erased from my mind. I smiled back at the sexy lady, the redheaded stranger in my tub, and said, "I'll make an honest effort at it. You can count on that."

"EVERYTHING OKAY AT HOME?" FLOYD ASKED WHEN I SLID INTO MY DESK chair late the following morning. "I tried to call you last night," he said, now turning his chair to face me, posturing himself for an interview, his partner now the one to be grilled. "You didn't answer at home, your cell was turned off, and you ignored your pager all night long. I damn near deployed myself on a mission to locate a missing Dickie."

I didn't respond, just busied myself moving some papers and files around on my desk, opened and closed a couple drawers with no real purpose.

He persisted: "Dickhead, I'm speaking to you. What the hell's going on at home? How are you and Val?"

"Good."

He crossed his arms and frowned. "That's it? *Good?*"

"Which is exactly why I ignored you last night, and why I'll be ignoring you for the next several days. You and every other asshole in this place."

"That's not very Christian-like, Dickie."

"Also," I said, rising out of my chair, "I'm leaving early today, and if anyone tries to stop me, I'll shoot my way to the door."

"I've seen you shoot, Dickie; I'm not even a little nervous."

Ignoring his comments, I continued, "Valerie and I have plans for the weekend, and nothing's going to stand in the way. Got it?"

I looked over, finally giving him my attention. He leaned back in his chair, folded his hands behind his head and grinned, no doubt enjoying all of it.

I nodded in the direction of the kitchen. "C'mon, asshole, I'll buy you a cup."

Floyd stood from his desk and followed me across the squad room, through the front lobby, down the hall past the captain's office, and into the kitchen. All along the way asking me what happened, where was I going for the weekend, what did I do to make things right with Val, did I get the wine like he suggested and slap her on the ass? I ignored his continued interrogation, greeting various detectives along the way, smiling, shaking the occasional hand, likely making a few of them wonder what happened to the *real* Dickie, the guy who'd normally give you a grunt, maybe a nod, or just an *up yours*. I had even greeted the captain, to a degree, a very slight nod through the window as we had walked past his office. Even somewhat of a smile, or maybe a grin. I wanted him to wonder what I was up to, maybe be a little concerned.

"What the hell is up with you?" Floyd asked, the two of us now stopped at the coffee pot.

I picked up the pot and poured him a cup, then helped myself. "Nothing. I just had a nice evening. It was good to be home."

"So, things are okay with you and Val?"

"Better than okay. We had a great night, something that's been way overdue. You ready?"

Floyd stood there, a cup of coffee in one hand, the other gripping his hip. He cocked his head to the side and squinted. "Ready for *what?*"

"We've got shit to do," I said, glancing at my watch. It was 10:39 a.m. "You pick, Charlie Wright or Donna Edwards, one or the other. I'm leaving at two, I don't care if we're in the middle of a gunfight. Got it? I'll toss you my spare ammo and tell you good luck, let me know how it goes. You can tell me all about it later, exaggerate the story like usual."

He shook his head, turned, and headed down the hallway with me on his heels. "Charlie Wright," he said without looking back. "That'll be the best shot I got at screwing up your weekend. Maybe this time *I'll* start the fight."

"You sure this is a good idea?" Floyd asked as we stepped out of the gray Crown Vic. We had parked on the street in front of the Inglewood apartment complex, a place enclosed by wrought-iron fencing that gave it that warm, cozy feel of prison. Floyd tapped a finger on top of the car, pulling my gaze his way. "In case you forgot, dickhead, the last time we were here, they torched my car. Then you started a fight, and now Internal Affairs is on our ass. This doesn't go well, it will seal our fate."

"They torched our car *after* the fight, and how is it I started it?"

He closed his door and turned toward the apartment complex. "You know."

No thugs out front this morning, too early in the day I supposed. I felt a little relief, not wanting to report another car fire or riot.

Before we had left the office, I mentioned to Lieutenant Jordan we were going back out to talk to Charlie. He asked why we couldn't call Charlie on the phone, ask him to come in for an interview. I told him that wouldn't work and walked away, not having the time nor inclination to explain why.

Upstairs, standing to either side of the doorway to Apartment 201, Floyd and I exchanged glances and nods, communicating to one another we were ready. I reached toward the center of the security screen door and rapped my knuckles against it.

Leilana Wright opened the door and scowled at me. "What the hell y'all want?"

"Ma'am, we need to speak with Charlie," I said.

"Don't you mean you want to whoop up on him again?" she asked. Then she looked at Floyd, still squinting beneath lowered brows. "And you, saying you was gonna shoot his ass, I didn't hand you them handcuffs. Y'all can kiss my ass now, Mista Po-lices!"

"Ma'am," I said, removing my sunglasses and pushing my hat up to reveal more of my face, "we don't want to make this a big deal, just ask Charlie a few questions is all. We never did get a chance to talk to him last time, with all the commotion. I hope you can understand, maybe accommodate us a bit. I'd hate to have to go see a judge, get a *Writ of Habius Grabbus* for Charlie."

"Hay—be what?"

"It's a court order, gives us the right to grab Charlie, take him to the station. *Habius Grabbus*. Usually, a judge issues one of those, he's inclined to include an *Order to Ramshackle*, or just *O.R.* as we call it. Then we'd have to tear your place up, ramshackle the apartment searching for evidence of a crime. Now we don't want to have to do that, not to a nice lady like yourself. All we want is to talk to Charlie, real polite like, man to man. Right here through the door is fine, ma'am; we don't want no trouble and we're not looking to take anyone to jail."

She turned her confused look back to Floyd. He held up his hand, his index finger and pinky pointed upward, the two middle fingers curled into his palm along with the thumb. The sign of devil worshipers, heavy metal fans, or maybe a catcher signaling two outs to the rest of the team. I had no idea what the hell it meant.

He said, "Scout's honor."

After another moment of studying the two civilized-appearing thugs standing at her door, she sighed and said, "I'll get him up."

I glanced at my watch: 11:42.

27

CHARLIE WRIGHT STOOD inside the closed security screen door, the whites of his eyes a contrast against dark skin. "I ain't got nuttin' to say to all y'all, them's my rights."

Floyd shrugged with a tightly closed mouth, essentially giving me the nod.

"Charlie—"

"Don't you *Charlie* me. We ain't buddies, remember? What'd you say, 'I ain't never seen you at the dinner table?' Yeah, that was it . . . you remember that, *Detective Jones?* Well, now you gonna talk to me, you gonna 'dress me as Mista Wright."

"Mr. Wright—"

"Tha's mo' like it," he said, his chin rising a bit with the new posture.

"We don't have to be buddies—"

"We ain't."

"—or even like each other—"

"We don't."

"—but we do have something in common here," I said, pausing but receiving nothing beyond his gaze.

Floyd stood to my side, his hands on his hips, scanning the apartment complex behind us more than looking at me or Charlie. As usual, he had our backs.

I said through the door, "You lost a child—your own flesh and blood—to a senseless murder. You may not like it, but the fact is we're the ones who are trying to find out who did it."

I held it there, waiting for a reaction but not getting much more than the continued glare.

Man, this guy was tough.

"Listen, Mr. Wright, it doesn't seem right to us that you're listed as a suspect in your son's murder."

He responded in a high-pitched voice. "I'm what? . . . How'm *I* a suspect? What kinda bullshit is that?"

"It just means you're someone we have to eliminate from the list during the course of our investigation. You're only on our radar due to some history, you being abusive toward Shane. Plus," I said, and tried to soften my tone, "we heard you might've had some issues with Shane's lifestyle."

"Wouldn't you?" he asked.

"I understand how you feel, Mr. Wright, but I also know you have a heart. You can't tell me it doesn't affect you he was killed."

He looked down.

I stayed with it, saying now, "You do want to know who did this to your boy, right? You're not going to let someone get away with this, are you, some asshole killing your son?"

"Y'all think I did it, apparently," he said, his voice now calm, quiet. "Might as well lock my ass up, throw away the key."

Floyd said, "We don't want to lock up the wrong guy, Charlie. Can I call you Charlie?"

"I s'pose that'd be okay."

Two old friends.

"We want to find out who did this to your son, Charlie," Floyd said. "How he lived don't mean he deserved to die. Not the way he died, Charlie. That was my son? I'd—"

Floyd held his tongue, not saying what it is he'd do. I knew, and he knew, and Charlie Wright probably had a good idea by now also, the two having been previously acquainted.

Charlie said, "True, man, true," now looking at Floyd, the two of them on a first name basis. "How's I s'posed to help y'all find out who done it? Y'all's the detectives."

"We have to eliminate you as a suspect, Charlie," Floyd said, "that's how we solve cases. We start with a list of people who might've done it, then cross off the names of the ones we can prove didn't do it. We do that until we get to the last name. You can help us get your name off the list."

"Just like that," Charlie said, seeing how it worked, getting into it now. "So, who we got on the list, 'sides me?"

Floyd said, "We can't really tell you too much about that."

"The list is secret?"

"Something like that, Charlie. See," Floyd continued, "there's some DNA—you know about the O.J. case, right?"

"Yeah, I seen it. The po-lice tried to frame the brotha. Nuttin' new there."

"The thing is," Floyd said, "DNA can be real important in a murder case—"

"Maybe, if it ain't planted by the po-lice," Charlie added, thinking it all through, philosophizing.

"—and we happen to have DNA in this case," Floyd said. "Whoever did this to your boy left some evidence behind. All you'd have to do, to eliminate yourself from our list, is give us a sample of your DNA. Let the guys at the lab compare it to our evidence."

"If I trusted you, I'd might think about doing that. For my boy, Shane, God rest his soul." Charlie looked toward the ceiling.

"Easy as pie, Charlie," Floyd told him, pulling a sterile-wrapped swab and the accompanying cardboard container from his shirt pocket. "Just run this around in your mouth for us. Then, you put it in the box, like this here,"—showing him—"seal it yourself, making sure we can't do nothing to it. You don't need to trust us, since you do all the work."

"And if I don't wanna give you none of my D and A?"

"It's up to you, Charlie," Floyd said, stepping back from the door, giving Charlie room to open it.

Charlie stood still.

Floyd, still presenting the swab, said, "Help us out and we'll be out of here, off your ass. C'mon, man, what do you say?"

"I don't know, man."

"Charlie, we know you didn't have anything to do with this. Why make it harder for all of us?"

Charlie paused another moment before cracking the door open. "I hope this ain't no trick," he said, reaching a tentative hand through the small opening. "Now go on, give it here."

The woman's voice from inside: "You betta not, boy. You know what dat lawyer say."

"Shut-up, Mama. This here's for my boy," he said loudly over his shoulder. Then quieter, now facing us, "Mind y'own damned bid'ness."

Charlie's hand snatched the DNA swab and disappeared, the door closing behind it.

"Okay," Floyd said, demonstrating it again, this time using an empty hand. "Do it like this here, Charlie . . . just kind of roll it around the inside of your cheeks . . . there ya go, like that. Now the other side . . . perfect. Okay, just drop it in that container and seal it up. That's all there is to it."

The door cracked open again and Charlie pushed the sealed box toward Floyd. "A'ight?"

"Thanks, Charlie," Floyd said. "We really appreciate your cooperation."

Walking away I heard Charlie say, "My lawyer still gonna sue yo' ass."

"What DNA evidence do we have?" I asked, glancing back and forth from the road to Floyd as we drove toward the office. "Other than semen, which we both know is useless in this case, especially if you think Charlie's our suspect. Do you know something I don't?"

"We don't have time to talk about all the shit I know that you don't, Dickie. But as far as DNA, no, we don't have anything other than the semen." Floyd leaned over to tune the radio, finding Dr. Laura and leaving it there. "None I know of anyway."

"So, we got Charlie's DNA, what, just in case?"

"Charlie don't know we don't have DNA, Dickie. I just wanted to see if he would give us a sample, see if he would cooperate. I figured if he gives us a sample, it's unlikely he had anything to do with killing Susie."

"I'm surprised he gave a sample at all, either way. Turn it up," I said, nodding toward the radio, "this'll be good. You always know when someone starts off like that, Dr. Laura's going to get in her ass."

"She cracks me up," Floyd said, "telling these broads they better get to it, treat their man better. Get in there and take care of him soon as you hang up. I think we can cross Charlie off the list now."

"I'd have to agree," I said.

"By the way," Floyd said over the girl telling Dr. Laura she didn't have any choice but to shack up with this guy, it was her baby's daddy . . . "what's new with your girlfriend, Donna Edwards? You talk to Dwight lately?"

"They still have her under surveillance. She hasn't gone anywhere or done anything exciting lately. In fact, we need to let D know if we want them to follow her over the weekend or not. What do ya think?"

"Fine with me," Floyd said. "Not like we have anything else on this case."

I waited until Dr. Laura finished telling the young girl to move back in with her parents, drop the low-life . . .

"Well, there's still Elmer Fudd, right?"

"Yeah, Elmer. Only where do we start looking for him?"

I glanced over and said, "I don't know where, but I can tell you *when.*"

"Okay, *when?*" Floyd asked, turning the radio back down, on a commercial now.

"Monday. Because when we get back to the office, I'm dropping your ass off and heading out. I'm not even coming in, taking a chance of getting hung up on something, or having your captain piss me off."

Floyd looked at his watch. "How do I get hours like that?"

"What, you have something needs to be done, can't wait until Monday?"

"I'd like to figure something out about Fudd, now that you mention him. Like where that asshole is. You have any idea how pissed off Cindy is about having the cops sitting out in our driveway? I'm ready to call it off, take my chances with Fudd coming back, blow his ass up myself. I don't need Metro to do my shooting for me."

"Judging by your last shootout, you might."

"You can kiss my ass," he said. "I didn't see you bleeding anyone out. Now you're disappearing for the weekend, taking off with the little woman. Isn't that special."

"It happens to be our days off," I said.

"Well, you just enjoy yourself, dickhead, don't worry about me and Fudd. I'm going to dump the protection and get back to a normal life. You ever mow the lawn with a couple cops staring at you from behind a windshield? Jesus, what the neighbors must think."

"If they know you," I said, "they probably think the cops are there to watch *you*, keep you in line. Probably think the captain put 'em up to it."

"I think I'll run them off when I get home."

"You can't take that chance, bud." I glanced in my rearview mirror, then checked the car along our right side. I seemed to watch my surroundings lately with a renewed vigilance, added meaning and purpose. "You've got the kids to think about."

"I didn't tell you?"

"What?"

"Cindy's parents have the kids," he said, "which is a whole other Oprah. Get this, my mother-in-law thinks the kids are *overly involved* in extracurricular activities. Well, no shit, lady, why do you think I pitched a bitch when Cindy talked about going back to work? Who the hell's going to get them to their practices, the games, the recitals, church. Shit, for that matter, to and from school? Me? Yeah, because my hours are real flexible. My partner's not a psychotic, workaholic asshole or anything, and our lieutenant doesn't put us first up in every goddamned rotation."

I glanced from the road and frowned at the back of Floyd's head as he checked his hair in the side-view mirror.

"Anyway, this is getting old," he said, turning his head to check the other side. "Metro sitting outside 24/7—though holy shit, I didn't tell you about the hot little cha-cha deputy that was out there the other night, did I? Jesus, I come home, there's this little head, dark hair in a ponytail sitting behind the wheel of this big Caprice. They're backed into the driveway, windows down, a little music playing on the radio, right? This big goon with a buffalo head and scraggly beard sitting next to her, kind of giving me the eye. I think we know him, seen him around at least. Anyway, the guy's all sprawled out with his hairy arm across the seat behind her, his big gut hanging over his jeans. He's sitting there chewing sunflower seeds, slobbering into a Styrofoam cup while the little doll is just sitting there pretty as can be, smiling at me as I walk up. This huge gorilla and the little minx. Anyway, I walk up and she says—all cute like—'Good evening, Detective.' I'm like, 'Hey, how's it going?', all cool like, and I give her the slicky-boy nod, right? And I'm thinking, Jesus, I *have got* to invite her inside for a couple beers, right? Let the hairy goon watch the house. Not like she was doing any good out there anyway."

"Cindy would've loved that," I said.

"I'd be all, 'Hi honey, look what I found in the driveway.' Holy shit, can't you just see it? *'Can I keep it?'* "

We both laughed, Floyd likely amused with himself. I laughed, picturing Cindy, the pretty little blonde cheerleader Floyd's been with since high school, sitting there waiting for her man to come home, then Floyd coming in with the cute deputy in tow. I pictured Cindy dragging the little minx out the front door by her ear, Floyd appalled, thinking, what's she pissed about?

"I'd love to see that," I said, turning onto Rickenbacker Road, coming up to the office. "Listen, you need to get ahold of me this weekend—something urgent comes up—page me. Otherwise, I'll check in with you Sunday night on our way back."

"You're not telling me where you're going?"

"No."

"You don't want me to show up with Cindy and my new little minx?"

I glanced at Floyd, who was grinning ear to ear. I said, "No offense, but yeah, no, I really don't want to see your ass till next week. I don't want to see you, I don't want to hear from you, and I don't want to have Cindy calling me up, asking if I have any idea where you are, saying she hasn't seen you since she threw the minx off the property."

"Fine," he said, "but you're the one missing out. I'll have to see what I can do to really piss you off while you're gone. Maybe shoot Elmer Fudd or arrest Donna Edwards."

"You should do it the other way around, shoot Edwards and arrest Fudd. Either way, wait until Sunday to let me know about it."

I turned into the rear parking lot and stopped as Lieutenant Jordan crossed in front of us, coming out the back door headed toward his car. He looked over at us, changed directions and walked up to my window. "You guys done for the day?"

"Wrapping it up," I said. "Looking forward to a weekend off."

"How'd it go with Charlie?" he asked, resting a hand against the top of my car, the sun reflecting off his wire-rimmed cop sunglasses.

"No problems," I said, "we had a nice little chat and got a DNA sample from him. Him and Floyd are buddies now."

"Except he's still going to sue us," Floyd said.

Jordan leaned down, his cologne coming through the open window. "Did you hear about the guy in the van?"

"No," Floyd and I said in unison.

"He's a judge. Alexander Nessbaum, Inglewood Superior."

"You're shittin' me!" Floyd said, leaning toward me and looking up at the lieutenant. "Did he make it?"

"Yeah, it looks like he did. I guess he had a heart attack, but he's supposed to recover. Not his first, apparently. You guys know him?"

"No," I said, shaking my head. I glanced to see Floyd shaking his also. "Don't think we ever heard of him. We don't get cases in Inglewood very often."

"Jesus, Dickie," Floyd said, "good thing you didn't shoot the poor Honorable bastard."

"Good thing you were there to stop him, huh Floyd?" the lieutenant said, now standing erect, straightening his tie and then combing his fingers through his thick blond hair. "You boys will probably be credited with saving his life. Saving a superior court judge's life might get you a medal."

Floyd and I exchanged glances, each of us grinning a little now.

"Anyway, you gentlemen enjoy your weekend, get some rest. I have a feeling we'll be busy next week."

"See ya, boss," I said.

"See ya, L.T.," Floyd said.

Floyd, still showing the wide grin, said, "Jesus, Dickie, I saved the judge's life!"

Sunday night concluded a magnificent weekend away from the job, away from the city, away from the stress of worrying about cases, crooks, and captains. Valerie and I were enjoying the rush of cool evening air through the opened windows of her Lexus as we traveled down a winding mountain road when the shrill beeps of my pager pierced the howling wind.

Valerie smiled as I reached for my belt. "Probably your partner," she said, reaching over and stroking my leg. "You know how he hates having to share you with me."

A smile crossed my lips as I confirmed her suspicions; it was Floyd.

I powered up my cell phone thinking how relaxed and comfortable things were after the short but much needed getaway. Thinking it was good spending time with Val, prioritizing my personal life for a change, putting things into perspective now as the mountain air massaged my face. I leaned toward the door and caught a glimpse of my smile in the side-view mirror, liking what I saw for the first time in a while.

The phone's display came to life with a full signal so I made the call.

"What's up?" I asked when Floyd answered.

"I shot Fudd, arrested Donna, and ran away with the minx, just like we had all planned out. Thought I'd better let you know."

"You're an idiot. What do you want?"

"I found your boy, Fudd, and Donna Edwards is in custody."

After a moment of silence, Floyd said: "How do you like me now, Dickie?"

28

DO YOU HAVE to go in?" Valerie asked, as I ended the call with my partner.

"Nope, I'm all yours. Work can wait."

"I'm honored," she said, glancing over from behind the wheel with a smile.

I stroked the brown ponytail jutting through the back of her L.A. Dodgers ball cap, and said, "No way I'm cutting this weekend short."

FOUR HOURS LATER I PULLED INTO THE PARKING LOT AND WALKED through the back door of the East Los Angeles Sheriff's Station, turned through a short hallway past the gun lockers, and stepped into the detective bureau. Floyd sat at one of the dozen or so empty desks, his feet on an adjacent chair and a cup of coffee in his hand. "It's about time," he said, and glanced at his watch. "Did you go by the office?"

"No, why would I?"

"You don't have to be testy."

"After you called the second time," I said, "I hauled ass home, dropped Val off, picked up the county car, and headed straight here. You have any idea how much I didn't want to see you tonight?"

"Not nice, Dickie, but I'm going to shake it off. I know you love me and didn't mean anything by it."

"How long have you been here?"

Floyd dropped his feet to the floor, stretched and yawned, maybe exaggerating a little. He looked at his watch again. "Good hour or so."

"I thought we said eleven."

"Yeah, well . . ."

"What's the deal with Donna?" I asked as I slid into an adjacent chair.

He handed me an arrest report.

As I began reading it, Floyd filled me in. "Dwight's team watched her and that dazzling urbanite in the Tahoe make a buy. Two-kilo deal with a little Jamaican asshole and a couple Bloods from the jungle backing him up."

"That where it went down, the jungle?"

"Jesus, no," Floyd said, his hands locked behind his head now, leaning back in the chair. "There's not a surveillance team in the state that could go into those projects and not get burned. Went down a couple miles from there, a little parking lot off of La Brea. Sorry about jacking up your weekend, brother, but when Dwight called and said she'd probably make bail, I figured we'd better come up with a plan."

"Where'd you get the coffee?" I asked, ignoring the apology since I didn't feel like forgiving him.

Floyd nodded in the direction of the door I had just walked through. "Up at the jailer's desk. It sucks, but it's better than nothing. Plus, you don't have to pay two bucks for it. So, what do you think, take her on for a while, see if she gives something up now, or flat out offer to make the dope case go away?"

"Did you forget she lawyered up last time around?" I rose from my chair and nodded for him to follow. "C'mon, get me a cup."

"You think she killed Susie, or the other one?" Floyd asked as he rose from his chair.

"No. You?"

"No," Floyd said. "I don't think she was involved in any of this, truthfully. I can't even imagine she knew about it. That's why I don't care if she lawyered up. Worst thing that can happen is her statement's inadmissible against *her*. She gives up Gilbert, or dipshit in the Tahoe, we're good. Won't matter how we got there."

"I don't know, man, it seems a stretch to think Gilbert and company could be involved, and she wouldn't know about it."

Floyd opened the door and stepped into the hallway, glancing over his shoulder to say, "She'll put it on them for sure, if they're involved. And that's fine, we'll use that to get them to turn on her. Gilbert's a puss, and all of them are going to have different attitudes sitting on a two-kilo rap. You watch and see."

We walked into the jailer's office, a small room constructed of cinderblock walls painted slate gray. The booking cage, a small holding cell with nothing more than a metal bench, sat unoccupied, which told me Donna had been moved to the back and placed in a cell. Or she had been released.

"You talk to the jailer?" I asked, concern in my voice.

"Yeah," Floyd said, looking around as if we could have missed him in the small room, "he said they'd hold her for us."

I nodded, looking at the metal desk with a phone and an assortment of three-ringed binders with handwritten labels: *CUSTODY LOG, SECURITY LOG, JAIL PROCEDURE MANUAL*. I flipped through a small stack of magazines: *Men's Health, Body and Fitness, Outlaw Biker's Tattoo Review* . . . Floyd reached to fill two Styrofoam cups from a metal urn on an adjacent table.

"Have you talked to anyone from Narco?" I asked.

"They'll let her walk if it solves a murder," he said. "Terry Washington —you remember him from Century, right? He worked Gangs."

I shook my head.

"You'd know him if you saw him," he said, and handed me a cup while propping half his ass on the edge of the jailer's desk. "He said either way we want to go with it was okay with him. They'll let her walk if she gives us something, slam her if she doesn't. So, are you going to tell me about your weekend, or what?"

"It was fine, until you called. I swear she thinks we're gay."

Floyd laughed. "So, she's pissed you had to go?"

I took a sip of the coffee. Thirty-weight. Maybe forty, I thought, with the second sip. Typical inmate coffee. I winced before continuing. "No, actually, things are pretty good. She said thanks for the great weekend, now get your ass in there and solve that case so your partner doesn't call here crying again. I haven't told her the captain's splitting us up. Did you tell Cindy?"

"Yeah, matter of fact."

"Oh?"

"She said, 'Great, who're they putting you with, Fitzpatrick?' She's had a hard-on for him ever since he was caught cheating on Joanne, her new best friend since the Christmas party. They talk on the phone every day, get their nails done together. Joanne's constantly bitching to her about Fitz, then I get to hear about it all night, during dinner, after dinner, in bed. Last thing she wants, is me working with him."

"Fitz was caught cheating on his ol' lady?"

"About a year ago, Dickie. Do you ever talk to anyone other than me?"

"No."

Floyd picked up the *Outlaw Biker* magazine, flipped through the pages as I stood in the center of the small room sipping bitter coffee. Listening to distant sounds of police radio traffic and intermittent laughter in the old *barrio* station on a quiet Sunday night.

"You plan on telling me about Elmer Fudd?" I asked, after a moment of silence.

"Jesus, I almost forgot about that. You're not going to like it."

"Try me."

Floyd closed the magazine and tossed it on the desk. "He's at Cedars-Sinai, recovering from open heart surgery."

"What?!"

"It gets better. He went in the day before our little shootout. Apparently, he'd gone to the V.A. for a psych eval and got shipped to the E.R. when he complained of chest pain."

"You're kidding."

"Guess what day he had surgery?" he said, rifling through desk drawers now, no doubt checking to see if he could use anything that was just laying around.

"The morning we were dodging bullets in front of his house?"

"How'd you guess?"

"Just figured. I guess it seems to be about our luck. It's his good luck for sure."

"Good alibi, huh?"

"Being under the knife? Yeah, I'd say it's as good as it gets. So, have you figured out just who the hell it was shooting at us, if it wasn't Fudd?"

Floyd stood. "Whoever it was has to have something to do with the murders. No way that was a coincidence, not if our resident nut case didn't do it. Which means our murders have something to do with Donna and her band of merry Mexicans, or whatever. Which means you need to get your ass in there and get that snarky little lesbian talking. She and I aren't speaking."

The distinct rattle of jail keys drew my attention toward a solid metal door behind me, telling me the jailer was returning from the cells. I turned back to Floyd and said, "If this case isn't solved when we split up next month, it's yours."

The gray door opened to reveal the presence of a uniformed deputy sheriff, his shirt sleeves tailored for a tight fit around bulky arms that revealed portions of colorful tattoos. These were not the type of tattoos seen on bikers, convicts, military personnel, or even cops; these were more the type found on young men and women with spiked hair and multiple body piercings, tattoos of brilliant colors, cartoon-type or maybe comic book characters, swaths of colorful ink recklessly strewn about his body. Nothing artistic about any of it.

"What's up?" he said as the heavy door closed behind him with a thud. He tucked the ring of heavy, brass jail keys into his waistband and stood with his chest out, his hands planted on his hips as he strained to keep his muscles taut.

"We're from Homicide," Floyd said, "I called earlier about Donna Edwards."

He looked up toward the ceiling. "Edwards . . . Edwards . . ."

"Surveillance team brought her in," I said, "Sergeant Dwight Campbell? Probably charged with Possession for Sales."

"Oh," he said, dropping his hands but maintaining his posture as he stepped toward his desk. "*Donna.* I thought you said *Donald.* She's in the back. You dudes need her? I can drag her out for you, if you can give me a minute." He looked at his watch, pulled a cooler from beneath the desk, and retrieved a plastic container filled with a thick brown liquid. "I'm behind on my meals."

I looked at Floyd and rolled my eyes as the young deputy chugged dinner.

"Whenever it's convenient, slick," Floyd said, puffed up a bit also. "It's not like we have anything else to do."

"Yeah, no hassle at all, man," he said, completely missing the sarcasm. He had another chug and said, "That girl, Donna, she's a cool chick. I was rapping with her in the back, asked her about the dope bust. She said it wasn't her dope. That's messed up, man, a bum rap on the babe. Anyway, then we talked about some cool clubs, and it turns out we hit some of the same places, clubs over on the west side."

Floyd said, "You don't say."

He paused to drain the remaining contents. Floyd and I exchanged glances as he placed the empty container back in the cooler and slid it under the desk. Then he stood and stuffed his thumbs into his waistband.

"Yeah, dude, she's real cool. In fact, it turns out—if she's telling me the truth—she's half owner of a strip club in Hollywood, on Santa Monica Boulevard. Club Cabo? I haven't been there yet, but I told her I had a transfer pending to West Hollywood Station, so that's super cool to know. She said that's totally cool, and said they like having cops come by, as long as they're not dicks. She said it would be totally cool if I came by, and if I'm off-duty, she'd hook me up with a couple free drinks and maybe even the V.I.P. room. Sort of a professional courtesy."

I couldn't believe it.

"You happen to ask what she wants in return?" Floyd asked, his head cocked now to the side, his jaw jutted out. Incredulous.

"Hey, I'm not stupid, bro" he said, an awkward grin convincing me otherwise. "I told her she wouldn't get anything special here, don't even bother trying. She said she knew that, and it was totally cool."

I said, "Really? She didn't even ask for a cup of coffee, a sandwich or anything?"

"She doesn't drink coffee and wasn't hungry. She did ask if I had anything to drink around here, you know, alcohol. Said she could really use a drink. I laughed and told her, come on, dude, you know I can't do that. Then she said how about just a smoke, said she'd give about anything for a cigarette."

Floyd said, "You didn't—"

"Not like I bought some, man. We have a bunch of confiscated stuff right here in the drawer," he said, and reached for a metal cabinet next to the booking cage. He opened the drawer to show us a collection of cigarette packages, lighters and matches. "They're not allowed to keep this stuff when they go inside, so we have all this crap here that just gets thrown out, or taken by the trustees, so—"

"You gave her some smokes."

"A partial pack, already opened. It would've been thrown out anyway." Then he looked from me to Floyd and back. He shrugged. "I figured, what could it hurt, man?"

We followed the young deputy through the gray door heading into the jail with the big man's footsteps and his joyful whistling leading the way. I said to his back, "Club Cabo is a transvestite bar."

"Dude, no way," he said, stopping to turn and look at me.

"Way."

I turned to Floyd, the thought just hitting me. "There was a murder at one of those drag bars about seven, eight years ago, when we were fairly new to Homicide. May have been the same place, I don't remember the name of the joint. There's a couple of them up there, the Kitty Kat, China Blue, Club Cabo . . . You remember that?"

Floyd shook his head.

"Well, it was one of them freak joints, and I remember the victim was a transvestite. Jerry Newhouse handled it. Remember him?"

"Of course I do," Floyd said, "big, fat guy with a red nose. He came out on a couple of murders when we worked patrol, and he was still here when we came to Homicide."

The three of us had stopped to face each other, finishing the conversation before walking in to see Donna.

"I still remember him briefing the case after it happened," I said. "Jerry was one of those guys who could get away with saying whatever he wanted, anytime, anywhere. The captain was standing right next to him when Jerry's briefing his case and goes, 'So it turns out this broad's got a johnson bigger than my partner's' . . . his partner at the time was Maurice Tillman, a black guy."

Floyd and I chuckled. Buff-puff stood there frowning, which made me wonder if he didn't get the reference, or if he was stuck on Club Cabo being a tranny bar.

I continued: "Then he laughs himself into one of his coughing fits, his big face turning bright red as he holds his hands out, a foot apart, and says, 'biggest tool I ever saw.' The captain—I think it was Mullens at the time—just stood there shaking his head, and Newhouse keeps going: 'You should've seen the nuts on that son-of-a-bitch!' Honestly, it was unreal. The entire bureau was dying. Nobody else could get away with that kind of shit."

"Big balls in Cowtown, Dickie. That's what I'm talking about."

My smile faded as I finished up. "Jerry was a pretty bad drunk, from what I remember."

"Go hard or go home, Dickie; that's my motto."

"Probably what killed him," I said. "Anyway, kind of a strange coincidence. Maybe something we should look into, see if there's any connection at all."

We continued down the hallway to the end, stopping behind the jailer at the last door on the right. The sound of keys rattling and then clanking against metal preceded a heavy clunk of the lock turning over. Buff-puff stepped through the doorway in his tan and green uniform, stopped, stood still for a moment, then turned with a frown on his face. His arrogance had been replaced by fear, or maybe confusion.

I stepped up, unable to see around the deputy, his large frame blocking the doorway. I knew something was wrong. "Where's our girl?"

"Dude, I think she's dead."

29

MONDAY MORNING TRAFFIC rarely flowed at all, so today's average speed of about ten miles per hour seemed normal but had me agitated nonetheless. I steered the gray beast into the carpool lane and flipped on the blue and amber *excuse me* lights to the rear, just to keep the highway patrol off my ass.

When I successfully reached the Alvarado Street exit free of CHP intervention, I phoned my partner to confirm our plans for the day: he would go to the off-site Homicide library and search for the murder file from seven or eight years ago, the case Jerry had handled, while I followed up with last night's incident involving Donna Edwards, buff-puff the jailer, and a medical emergency. The first stop would be the crime lab where I would hope to glean a little information about a certain package of cigarettes. Then, if all went well, I would meet my partner at Cedars-Sinai Hospital around noon, where we would have a go at the recovering heart patient, Randall Scott, aka Elmer Fudd.

Floyd answered on the second ring. "What?"

His tone irked me. I came to a stop light, rolled down my window and called out to a homeless man with a sign that read *Hungry and Homeless Vet – Please Help.*

He stepped toward my car with due caution, his shifty eyes scanning the interior. He likely recognized me as a cop.

"Yes sir?"

"What's your name, partner?" I asked with my hand covering the mouthpiece of my phone.

"Wayne."

Floyd saying through the earpiece: *"Dickie?"*

"Do me a favor, Wayne," I said, extending my cell phone toward him, "I'll donate five bucks if you tell this guy he's an asshole."

"What guy?" he said, looking into the back seat again.

"The guy on the phone," I said, shoving the phone toward him while displaying a five-dollar bill. "Tell him he's an asshole and you've got five bucks, buddy."

A grimy hand materialized from the soiled sleeve of a brown sport coat, Wayne reaching out to take the phone. He continued watching with scrutinizing eyes as he lifted it to his face.

"That's good," I said, "don't put it in your beard . . . there you go, now tell him."

"You're an asshole!" the homeless man shouted into the phone.

"His name's *Floyd*."

Wayne narrowed his eyes at the phone, intense now. "Hey Floyd, you're an asshole, you sumbitch!" Then he smiled, revealing a mouth of rotted and missing teeth.

I reached out for the phone.

Wayne pulled it back and started yelling at the device: "Asshole! Asshole!"

Earning every cent.

"That's good," I said, handing him the money. Wayne took the folded bill, laughing now as he returned my phone. He then retreated to his over-turned milk crate and sign, seemingly pleased with the effort and reward.

"Thanks, Wayne," I said, while wiping the phone against my trousers. I raised the phone to my ear.

"What the hell?" Floyd asked through a chuckle.

"That's my new buddy," I said, turning south onto Alvarado, "and apparently, he thinks you're an asshole."

Floyd laughed. "Who the hell was it?"

"*Wayne*, my new buddy. He lives under the freeway at Alvarado. This guy's got everything it takes to be a captain on the sheriff's department, maybe a commander. He'd be a big improvement over Stover."

"Wayne, huh?"

"Wayne. So, what are you so pissed about this morning anyway?"

"Nothing."

"Nothing?"

"Nothing, Dickie, why do you think I'm pissed?"

"You sounded like a dick when you answered your phone."

"Just tired," he said. "What'd I get, four hours sleep?"

"You sounded pissed. Oh well, my bad. Sorry about that. It *was* kind of funny though."

"I'll give you that," he said. "Hey, I'm at the library now. Let me find this file and I'll call you later."

"Sounds good. I'm almost at the lab, I'll let you know what I find out."

AFTER NEARLY A TWO-HOUR WAIT, KAREN PROVOST, PH.D., RETURNED TO her office in the Narcotics section of the crime lab where I passed the time dictating a report. I turned the recorder off and lowered it along with a blue Homicide notebook to greet the doctor who wore no stethoscope.

I rose from my seat. "Well?"

She closed the door behind her and removed a lab coat, revealing a beige-colored silk blouse tucked into a tight, black skirt. The very tasteful ensemble was at the edge of professional, maybe more in the vicinity of evening apparel, but very complimentary of her shapely figure. She hung her coat on a hook behind the door. "Finish your dictation?"

"Almost. Did you find anything?"

She handed me an envelope sealed by red transparent tape, *CRIME LAB* and *EVIDENCE* printed in black ink. "You were right, the cigarettes are laced."

"With?"

"Ketamine Hydrochloride," she said, pulling out a chair at an adjacent desk. She lowered herself into the chair and crossed one leg over the other, gently brushing her skirt before her hands settled over bare knees. "You've heard of the Date Rape drug, *G.H.B.?"*

"Sure," I said, taking my seat again. "I've heard of it, never tried it though."

My awkward smile faded as she continued without appreciating the joke.

"It's a relatively new addition to the growing list of predator drugs. Special K—that's what they're calling it on the street—is legal here in the U.S. for use as an anesthetic for humans and animals, though it's mostly used on animals. It's available in liquid, powder, or pill form. Your evidence cigarettes are laced with the powder form.

"The drug is likely to cause hallucinations and amnesia, which makes it an effective drug for date rape. Do you have any idea how many she smoked?"

The doctor, all business as she laid out the facts, a no-nonsense black woman behind designer eyewear. Educated, intelligent, maybe a bit uptight? Probably a very different woman with a cocktail in her hand.

"One," I said, picturing the jail cell in my mind, seeing Donna on the bunk and the one burned cigarette on the ground beneath her, "is what the evidence would suggest. But I can't be certain."

"No matter," she said, less than interested.

"Why's that, Doc?"

"It's not likely a person would smoke more than one laced cigarette, if even finishing the first. The effects are realized rather quickly, so it is very likely she would be lethargic after just a few inhalations, and essentially incapacitated."

"Now that you mention it, the one butt we found was on the floor directly beneath her bunk, almost under her, as if she dropped it."

"She likely passed out and it dropped. It's fortunate it dropped on the floor, rather than her bunk. I assume the floors are concrete in those cells?"

"Yes."

She cocked her head and appeared to be thinking, maybe picturing the inside of a jail cell. She nodded and pursed her lips, "mmmm."

"Where does someone get their hands on this stuff, Doc, in the powder form?"

"Drugs of this type are typically stolen from veterinary clinics, or at least that is my understanding from what I've read. Apparently, people who seek this type of drug know they are primarily used as animal tranquilizers, so it's a logical step to target the vet clinics."

I nodded but remained silent, processing the information.

She shook her head, "It's shameful that these types of drugs are used by adolescents. Or, worse, in many cases, against them."

I studied the envelope, visualizing the opened package of cigarettes I had placed inside it the night before. My mind flashed back to Donna Edwards curled on her bunk, the bluish tint to her skin, the cool feel of her hands. Then the earlier image of buff-puff standing next to the drawer of contraband: cigarettes, lighters, and matches, the grin on his face. His words gnashing my brain, *"I figured, what could it hurt?"*

My eyes came back to Dr. Provost who seemed to be waiting for a response that hadn't come. She sat patiently, giving me plenty of time, but after a moment, she said, "Will there be anything else, Detective?"

I stood from my chair and paused briefly. "How often do people die from this stuff, Doc?"

"A fatal dose is rather uncommon," she said, standing now also. Her eyes were level with mine, putting her close to six feet tall in her modest heels. "It would take a gram or more, a lot more than the amount used to lace a cigarette. That, Detective, is why the young lady came through relatively unharmed. Though I wouldn't expect a great deal of cooperation from her for a day or two. She most likely won't be coherent."

"Thanks, Doc," I said, reaching out to shake her firm but gentle hand. "I appreciate you rushing this through for us this morning."

"My pleasure, Detective. Good luck on your case."

I PHONED MY PARTNER WHILE DRIVING NORTH ON ALVARADO STREET FROM the crime lab. He answered in a snarky tone, like the one he had used earlier in the morning.

"You want to say hello to my friend again? I'll be passing Wayne's World here in just a couple minutes."

"I think you ought to bring him in, tell the captain you found a new partner."

"Probably get me in less trouble," I said. "He'd definitely be better backup, especially during shootouts. He is a vet, you know."

"So is Fudd. Speaking of, are you headed to the hospital?"

I passed under the Hollywood Freeway and noted Wayne had abandoned his post. The crate and sign were there, but Wayne was nowhere to be found. Maybe he had taken the five bucks and headed to town for a lunch break, or more likely a drink.

"I'm on my way there now," I said, "just getting ready to hop on the freeway. You get the file?"

"Yep. Picked it up and figured I'd drive by the club while waiting for you to finish up at the lab. You were right, it was Club Cabo."

I scanned the surrounding area, almost concerned now about Wayne's whereabouts. I was preoccupied, and it took a minute for Floyd's words to sink in, his saying he had the file and decided to drive by the nightclub.

Refocused on the conversation, I asked, "Wait, you went to Cabo?"

"I'm here now, sitting in the parking lot. Having a look at these crime scene photos and comparing them to the actual location, getting a feel for this place. Doesn't look like much has changed, other than maybe the graffiti on the walls."

"You want me to meet you there, have a look around? Then we can head to Cedars from there."

"You going to buy me lunch?" he asked.

"I might do that."

"Well then, get crackin', Dickie. I'll be the straight guy in the Taurus, in case you have any trouble spotting me. The only white guy not wearing a dress."

"At least not at the moment."

"Exactly," he said. "Now get your ass up here."

I ARRIVED IN THE PARKING LOT OF CLUB CABO, STEERING WITH ONE HAND while turning my sleeves up with the other, the unseasonable weather taking its toll. I unbuttoned my collar and loosened my tie.

Floyd nodded as I swung the Crown Vic in front of his car and backed in alongside him, taking in the view of the building as I shifted into Park. The bright blue paint with *Club Cabo* across the top in yellow letters with red shadowing spoke to the bold nature of the establishment. An adult book store with blackened windows sat to one side, a Hollywood souvenir shop to the other. Club Cabo had no reason to be ashamed in this neighborhood.

I stepped out, leaving the car running with the air-conditioner set at the highest level, and greeted my partner. "What's up, asshole?"

"Well, I don't think the murder Jenkins had up here has anything to do with ours," he said, looking up through his open window, Ray-Bans concealing his eyes. "I've been reading the file while you're out screwing around."

"Oh?"

"Yeah, it was solved. A lover dispute, nothing else to it."

"Okay, it was a long shot anyway. So, it looks like your buddy buff-puff stepped on his dick, giving our girl them smokes."

Floyd stepped out and closed his door, meeting me between the two unmarked sedans. Two guys in shirts and ties conducting business in the parking lot of a transvestite bar in Hollywood over sputtering exhaust and the smell of urine, hip-hop music in the background. Just another day behind the badge in Los Angeles.

"They were laced?"

I leaned against the side of my car and pushed the straw dress hat up a bit in front, giving my forehead a little relief. "Ketamine Hydrochloride—"

"G.H.B., huh?"

"How'd you know that?" I asked.

"How would you not know that, Dickie? It's the date-rape drug. When'd you switch to straws?"

"When the weatherman said it would hit eighty today." I pulled it off my head and held it out for display. "It's new. What do you think?"

"I like the felts better. You think it was an accident, the drug thing?"

That it was anything other than a major screw up had not occurred to me. “What do you mean?”

“Maybe that’s his style, buff-puff.”

My brows furrowed. “Jesus, you think?”

“Never know,” Floyd said. He pivoted to face the building. “You’ve got to see the freaks inside this place, Dickie, you want to talk about weird shit. C’mon, turn off your car, I’ll introduce you to Madam Marquis.”

30

WEREN'T YOU GOING to buy me lunch?" Floyd asked as we stood next to our vehicles outside the Emergency Room entrance of Cedars-Sinai Hospital.

With the sign *Emergency Vehicles Only* as a backdrop, I pulled my suit jacket from its hanger and closed the rear door. I looked over at Floyd and said, "I figured we'd grab something here, in the cafeteria."

"You're kidding me, right?"

"No," I said, pushing the knot of my tie up, but not too much, just enough to hide the opened collar, "the food here's good."

"You dine here often?" He was looking at his reflection in his window as he shrugged into a beige-colored Hickey Freeman suit jacket.

We turned as if on cue and stepped over the red curb in unison. Walking on the sidewalk toward two sets of sliding glass doors for emergency patients, we passed a man and lady in blue coveralls and black boots wheeling an empty gurney our way. There were courtesy greetings and smiles as we passed.

"You remember my buddy from high school, Lance?" I asked, glancing back at the paramedics. "I've told you about him."

"Yeah, I think you've mentioned him. The guy's an attorney now?"

"That's the one. Does divorce cases. His mom had brain surgery here a few years back. I ate in the cafeteria once or twice when I visited. It really isn't bad, you might be surprised. I mean, it's not King Taco, or Manny's, but it's better than Denny's."

"Maybe they could do a brain surgery on you," Floyd said, pushing his Ray-Bans up into thick brown hair as we stepped through the automatic doors, "as long as we're here."

OVER THE SOUNDS OF CLANGING DISHES, CASH REGISTERS, AND IDLE chatter, I told Floyd the details of my visit to the crime lab, including my analysis of Karen Provost, the sexy doctor with restrained appeal. Floyd said, "No shit, Dickie, where the hell have you been? You mean you'd never met Doc Provost? She is smoking hot. Plus, she loves me."

"Don't they all?"

"Not all of them, Dickie. But most; I'll give you that."

I said, "Maybe you were right about that jailer. Maybe it wasn't an accident. Makes me wonder."

"I knew buff-puff was an asshole, soon as I saw him drink that brown shit. Nothing would surprise me about him."

Then I told Floyd about the conversation I had had with Lt. Jordan on the way here, surmising that Internal Affairs would probably rake the kid over the coals, even if he had no knowledge of those cigarettes being laced.

Floyd said, "I.A.? Those guys are assholes too."

Then I told him I was taking Thursday and Friday off this week, but I'd be back for our on-call rotation which starts Saturday night at ten. He paused with a tuna-melt suspended beneath a gaping mouth and gave me the look.

I said, "I know, I'm an asshole too, right?"

"Right," he said, "and I'll tell you something else—"

I waited as he chewed just enough to allow him to continue.

"If they're still splitting us up next month—which is what, two weeks away?—I'm protesting being in the rotation with your dumb ass." He wiped his mouth with the back of his hand. "That's bullshit. We've got plenty of active cases to divide up; we don't need any more. And if you're taking time off—"

I leaned back and grinned, breaking his train of thought.

Floyd took a swig from his Diet Coke, watching me over a semi-translucent red cup. Then he set it down and said, "What? What are you up to now, Dickie?"

I enjoyed the moment, taking advantage of his appetite for immediate satisfaction, knowing he realized I knew something he didn't. I sipped my soda and took my time, glanced around the cafeteria noticing the colorful scrubs: green, blue, and floral-patterns too. A pair with bicycles without riders, and another with fish: seahorses, puffers, and clowns, a great white pursuing an otter—predator versus prey. *Life in Los Diablos.*

"Dickhead?"

"I must've forgot to tell you."

"Yeah, you must have, asshole. Now get to it."

"Captain's not splitting us up now."

"What?"

"Well, I talked to Jordan on the way here—"

"Yeah?"

"—turns out the Honorable Judge Nessbaum, the guy on the freeway you wanted me to shoot, called the sheriff to thank him for two of his finest deputies saving his life."

"We are a good bunch of men."

"I guess he even apologized for wrecking our car."

"Well that will make your captain feel better."

"Apparently," I continued, "the judge and your sheriff know each other, have some type of association. Probably golf together. So the sheriff turned around and called Stover and said he was putting us in for medals of valor. He said he looked forward to personally recognizing our heroism. You believe that shit?"

Lifting his sandwich again, he said, "Jesus."

"Jordan said no way was that asshole going to split us up now, take a chance of me mentioning it to the sheriff as he's draping medals around my neck. Can you see it? 'Thanks, Sheriff. By the way, did you know that prick Stover's trying to split me and my partner up?'"

Floyd said around another bite, "You can't split up Dickie Floyd.

We're a dynamic duo, like Batman and Robin, the Lone Ranger and that Indian."

"Cagney and Lacey."

"He knows you'd do it, too," Floyd said, "front him off like that in front of the sheriff."

"Hell yes, I would." I watched as Floyd shoved the last bite of tuna-melt into his mouth. "You ready?"

He pushed his chair back and stood quickly, dropping a napkin onto his empty plate. "Born ready, dickhead. Let's get at it."

A HEAVYSET MAN IN GREEN SCRUBS STOOD AT THE FIFTH-FLOOR NURSE'S station pointing to his right, nodding that way, saying, "You can take him with you when you leave, far as I'm concerned."

Floyd said, "You don't like our buddy, Elmer Fudd?"

"Whatever you call him," said the nurse, "no."

I chuckled and said, "That's odd, we just love that guy."

"First day he's on the floor," the nurse says, "the guy asks if I'm the doctor who cut his chest open with a chainsaw. I said, 'No, but I'll be your nurse for the next twelve hours and the rest of the week on day shift. Is there anything you need?' The jerk asks if I'm gay."

"He's not real sensitive to others' feelings," Floyd said, "not what you'd call a *people person*."

"We won't be long," I said, smiling politely.

Floyd and I turned and headed to Room 502.

As we stepped inside, I noticed the pasty-white complexion of our boy, Fudd, and smiled at the sight of the clear fluid dripping from a bag above his head, most likely filled with morphine. His droopy eyelids fluttered before settling half-open, his dull, hazel eyes peering our way. He lifted an arm covered with tubes and tape, offering a lazy wave with two fingers. Then he said through a dry and crusty mouth, "Howdy, boys. C'mon in."

Floyd and I looked at each other and I beat him to the nod, a traditional passing of the torch in these situations. He frowned at me, then stepped closer to the bed.

"Mr. Scott," he said in a serious but affable tone, "I'm Detective—"

"You're the guys was across the road there, looking for that little colored girl. You ever find her?"

"Yes sir," Floyd answered, "we did. Listen, we have some questions for you about your place over there—"

"My brother's house," Elmer said, a clear tube bouncing over his upper lip. "I been looking in on it for a couple months now since he's been in Arizona, on account of them people across the way there, dealing drugs and running whores. You know, someone broke into the house when my brother first left, him and his ol' lady, and I bet it was them people over there—"

"We had a little trouble out there, Mr. Scott, a few days back. Someone shot at us from your brother's place, and to be real honest, we thought it was you until we found out you've been here."

"You thought it was me? Why the hell would you think that? I'm a law-abiding citizen—a veteran too, damn it. You want my opinion," he said and paused to cough and hack for a moment, "I'd say that nig—sorry, that *black girl*—and her friends had something to do with it. Did you know they got one of my rifles last time they broke in? Remington 700 in three-oh-eight, had a four by twelve variable scope. Son-of-a-bitch was a shooter too, sub-MOA for sure, it'd group five in a half-inch at a hundred yards if you knew anything at all about shooting. I've got night vision on another rifle, but they didn't get that one. What'd they shoot at you boys with?"

"Not too sure," Floyd said, "some type of high-powered rifle. But you're saying they broke in, again?"

"Well hell yeah they did . . . who the hell else would've done it? The whole neighborhood's gone to shit lately."

"Your neighbors might agree," Floyd said, "after the big shootout."

"Big shootout?"

"Yeah, it's what I just told you, someone shot at us from your brother's house."

Randy Scott, the man we had called Elmer Fudd, the one we believed had tried to gun us down in front of his brother's house, smiled and rubbed the salt and pepper stubble on his chin. "See there," he said, "had to be that girl or one of them Mexicans she runs with. Anyone using a rifle, and you two lived to tell about it, ain't never shot one before. There's your proof it wasn't me."

"We were told you were a sniper," Floyd said.

"Damn right, boy."

The veteran sniper then looked out the window and gazed into the distance, likely beyond the view of Hollywood below. In almost a whisper, he said, "Yes sir."

I stepped forward to the foot of the bed. "Mr. Scott, when they searched your brother's house, they came up with some photographs. They were taken by someone at your brother's house, all of them toward the neighbor's place across the road. Most of them were pictures of Ms. Edwards and her friends, but there were others too, some that we found very interesting."

"You talking about them ones of you boys?"

"Yeah," I said, "that's been bothering us quite a bit, to be honest. Why would you take pictures of us, out there doing our job?"

"I remember thinking you fellas looked kinda good out there. You with the hats," he said, and then he nodded toward Floyd, "and him with that Hollywood cop look, those shades and his pretty hair. You know, like that young fella on Law and Order?"

Floyd grinned.

Fudd smiled back at him, likely enjoying the company. He said, "Hell, you boys gave me something to do, once them others disappeared."

"There were some pictures of a couple black girls too," I said.

"That's what I've been trying to tell you. They been running whores out of that place, have been for months, long as I been staying there anyway. You're talking about them black hookers, right?"

"How do you know they're hookers?"

"Because I've been paying attention, boy, and that's what I've been trying to tell you. That's why I've been taking pictures. I told the Downey cops about the whole deal, but they didn't care. All they're interested in is harassing law-abiding Americans like myself. So, to hell with them. I started my own little investigation, did a little reconnaissance, you might say. I started keeping track of who's who in the zoo, if you get my drift. Hell, I even followed them around a little bit too, once I started figuring out what they were up to."

"You followed them?" Floyd asked.

"That's what I just said, junior. Hell yeah, you bet I did. I can show you where they do their tricks. It's a sleazy little motel down there in the ghetto on Long Beach Boulevard. I used to drive a wrecker down there, know the area well. Nothing but a bunch of animals 'round there. Reminds me—"

"You've been there, the motel on Long Beach Boulevard?"

"One night," he said, "them two whores in those pictures came out of that nigger girl's house—*sorry 'bout that*—along with that dirty little Mexican dude with all them tattoos. They all got to fussin' in the front yard, cussing one another and carrying on. You know how them people are. The Mexican mostly just watched, but the one that lives there was mad as hell at them two whores. I started snapping pictures with a zoom lens, black and whites, like we used to do on recon missions.

"Then when them two in their little whore outfits left, that Mexican and the *black girl* got to fussin'. She was yelling at him for a couple minutes, waving her arms around, then the two of them got in her car and drove off. That's the night I followed them down there to that motel."

"Did you happen to get any pictures at the motel?" I asked.

"Oh yeah," he said, raising the bed with a remote control, taking a minute to hack and then spit into a pan on the table hanging over his bed. "Well, first, they stopped over there in East L.A.—beaner town—and the Mexican went into a house. He came out with another greaser, an older one. Then, the three of them went to Hollywood, some fag club, and the colored girl went inside. The two Mexicans left, so I followed them, figuring they were the ones that looked like trouble. They went to some shit-hole motel down in the ghetto, went into a room up on the second floor, and stayed in there about twenty minutes. Came back out, but didn't go anywhere."

"What do you mean?"

He looked around the side of his bed and mumbled, "I need that queer nurse in here."

"What do you mean, they didn't go anywhere, Mr. Scott?" I asked, bringing him back to the conversation.

He stared for a minute, a blank stare as if he had lost his train of thought. Then he said, "The beaners. Well, yeah, they drove around, but they didn't leave the area. They went around the block, through the alley, up and down the street a few times, like they was looking for someone. I followed them around a bit but decided I'd better leave before I got robbed. Damn savages were everywhere. Place is more dangerous than 'Nam."

"Let me make sure I've got this straight," I said. "The black girl, Donna, and the Mexican with the tattoos, they went to a house in East L.A.?"

"That's what I just told you. Are you paying attention?"

"Then they picked up another male Hispanic, an older guy, and went to a club in Hollywood."

"Hispanic or Mexican, one of the two. He was one of them *cholo* types, a tattooed wetback looks like he just got out of the joint. And yeah, the three of them all went to some fag joint right over here," he said, pointing out the window.

"Then the two men left, the girl stayed there, and you followed those two men to a motel on Long Beach Boulevard where they went into a room on the second floor?"

"Ain't that what I just got done telling you, boy?"

"You have those pictures?" Floyd asked.

"I gave 'em to the Downey cops, told 'em this's what's going on around here, them there whores and drug dealers ruining the neighborhood. They didn't care, the dumb bastards. They're too damn busy harassing veterans, writing chicken-shit tickets and whatnot. You guys want those pictures, you're gonna have to get 'em from them. Check with that weasel, Sergeant Ely, sawed-off little shit college boy who could stand to have a little respect for his elders. That's who's got most of 'em. Negatives too. I wasn't going to give him the negatives, but he insisted, took them away from me along with the pictures, the bastard. And that's why nobody helps the cops anymore, and for that matter, it's why nobody likes any of ya, neither. You guys are a bunch of assholes. 'Cept maybe you two. You two ol' boys are okay by me."

I looked over to see Floyd grinning. I thanked Mr. Scott for his time and wished him a speedy recovery. Floyd thanked him for his service to our country.

He held up a hand to stop our exit, and we waited while he coughed and spit mucus into the tray. He said, "You know, you boys need any help watching them folks, getting some pictures and whatnot, I'll be out of here in a couple days. I did three tours in Vietnam, sixty-seven through sixty-nine, worked around some of them spooks in the agency, operating up near the border of Cambodia. I still got a few tricks up my sleeve, and I ain't afraid to drop the hammer when it's time, neither."

"We'll keep that in mind," Floyd said, and we headed for the door.

He called out to our backs: "You see that queer nurse out there, send him in here, would ya?"

31

SERGEANT ELY OF the Downey Police Department handed me an envelope as he stepped into the lobby of the station, choosing to meet with us amongst the public rather than inviting us into his office for a cup of coffee.

The envelope revealed photos of Donna Edwards and Gilbert Regalado in front of Donna's house, Donna with an angry expression, her lips pursed. Next, they were in front of a rundown house. It could have been East L.A., as Fudd had described. The other male Hispanic joined them there, the one who looked like he was fresh out of the joint according to Fudd. I would agree with that assessment, from the photographs. The next photos showed the three of them at the Club Cabo in Hollywood, then Donna out of the car, walking toward the club, and the two gangsters leaving without her. The last photos showed the two men, Gilbert Regalado and the unidentified vato at the Regal Inn on Long Beach Boulevard. There were pictures of the two men starting up the stairs to the second floor, but only a view from behind, and then others showing the same two waiting outside the scene of the crime, Room 217. One photo showed Gilbert looking this way through dark sunglasses, a positive identification of him. The older man with him stood sideways, offering only a side profile. He was a thick-chested man, heavily tattooed—even more so than Gilbert—with a black mustache that covered his mouth and half his chin. The last photo showed a woman in the open doorway as Gilbert was stepping into the scene, the mustached Mexican looking back. But the picture caught him with his left hand reaching toward his head, blocking much of his face.

Returning the photographs to their envelope, I looked at the man to my right, the detective wearing short sleeves and a wide, red- and gray-striped necktie, a black belt contrasting his brown pants and loafers. His pale blue eyes darted from me to the photos while he fidgeted with a wiry red mustache over what I figured to be a permanent smirk.

I held the envelope up and said, "We're going to need these, Sergeant."

"Let me check with my lieutenant," he said. Then he turned and disappeared into the hallway behind him.

"What a punk," Floyd said.

"Let me check with my lieutenant," I scoffed.

Floyd turned to a display on the counter and began thumbing through pamphlets: *Drug Abuse Resistance Education, Family Violence Prevention, Gang Intervention* . . . pamphlets in English and Spanish, colorful photos of men, women and children, all colors, shapes, and sizes on the front. Picking them up one at a time, perusing them while speaking to Ely in his absence. *"You do that, Sergeant . . . go check with your mommy, see if it's okay if these homicide detectives take your pictures."* He turned to me. "What's he going to do if we just walk out? I'll seize this shit as evidence right now."

"Easy, buddy," I said. "We'll get the photos and be out of here in a few. We don't need any international incidents."

"It's just, some people . . ."

"Yeah, I hear ya. But hey," I said, glancing at my watch, "on the bright side, we should be able to make it to the lab before Gentry's gone for the day."

"What're we doing at the lab? Wasn't this going to be our last stop, then beers?"

"I'd like to get these photos enhanced," I said, "the sooner the better. Especially the one where our friends are standing up there at the opened door. Aren't you dying to see who it is standing inside?" I pulled the photos back out of the envelope and began thumbing through them a second time. "My guess," I said, showing a black and white photo to Floyd who was now leaning into me, "that's going to be the hooker from the motel right there. What's his name, Stephanie?"

"Stephen Dubois," Floyd said.

I paused as a dispatcher in uniform, a light blue blouse with shoulder patches over a dark blue skirt, passed through the lobby and disappeared into a room constructed of mirrored glass to our left. The sounds of police radio traffic faded as the door closed behind her but the scent of her perfume lingered in the lobby. I looked back at Floyd. "How is it you always remember the weird shit?"

Floyd shrugged as he stuffed two or three of each pamphlet in his jacket pocket.

I continued, "If we can prove that asshole boyfriend of Donna's—"

"Gilbert."

"—and this *vato* with the 'stache were the last visitors of a dead hooker."

"That'd be good for Sandy's case for sure. Probably ours too," he said. "But traffic's going to suck if we go to the lab this time of day."

"You remember Elmer saying these two assholes cruised around for a while after they left the motel. What the hell were they doing, cruising around Lynwood? Or should I say, who were they looking for?"

"Susie."

"It's what I'm thinking," I told him.

"So, what's our motive? If we think Donna wanted them whacked, sent the Mexicans to do the manual labor—no pun intended—we're going to need a motive, something that can stand up against the defense saying Susie's her best friend, the other was an associate. They will also point out that if she is actually pimping them out, they're a source of income to her."

"So is cocaine," I said, looking past Floyd at the mirrored glass. Picturing the dispatcher on the other side. She was probably watching us. Maybe talking about us with another dispatcher, wondering who are the two guys in suits, this one with a fedora?

Floyd nodded to signal the return of Sergeant Ely, the little man coming up behind me.

The detective handed me a form and said, "My lieutenant said no problem, but you'll need to fill out this form, Evidence Disposition."

Floyd stepped away from the counter and positioned himself near the glass doors, *DOWNEY POLICE DEPARTMENT* in white lettering behind him, backwards from inside. He stood with his arms folded across his suit jacket in silent protest. I scribbled our names and contact information across the top of the white paper with green and pink duplicates beneath. The sergeant licked his thumb and separated the pink copy from the bottom, handing it to me with his smirk in place.

I forced a smile. "Thank you."

"Anytime, Detective. We're here to please."

Floyd pulled a can of Copenhagen from his pocket when he stopped at the passenger's door of my Crown Vic parked out front. He scooped two-fingers and a thumb full of tobacco into his lower lip, pocketed the can, and began brushing his hands together in front of him. Then he spit into the gutter and wiped his mouth with the back of a hand.

"Do we hate Sergeant Ely, the South Pole elf?"

"That shit's gonna kill you," I said.

Floyd appeared thoughtful for a moment, his tongue fiddling with the tobacco behind his lip.

"I've been hooked up with you for the better part of eighteen years," he said, pausing as he retrieved a pair of Ray-Bans from his inside jacket pocket, "and *that* ain't killed me."

I turned to walk around the car.

Floyd staying with it: "You've dragged my ass into half-a-dozen shootouts, a couple dozen donnybrooks, two full-blown riots, and one church social. And you say *this* is gonna kill me."

"It could happen," I said over my shoulder.

"I'm popping pills for blood pressure," he continued, pushing the shades over his eyes, "trying to drop twenty pounds without giving up booze. You feed me fast food twice a day, and I can't remember the last time I popped a vitamin or choked down a vegetable."

I paused at my door, looking at him over the top of the car with a big grin.

He chuckled and continued: "My liver probably looks like an old wino's, the ones you see at the coroner's office, gray and black and full of holes, look like recycled sponges from the Compton Carwash.

"My brother-in-law," he said and paused as we ducked into the car, "says he's going to stick a shank up my ass when he gets out of the joint, and he's one of the few who's said it, might actually have the balls to try."

"Not sure I'd blame him," I said. "If my brother-in-law beat my ass and sent me to prison, I'd consider shanking him when I got out too."

"Exactly," he said. "Then we've got the dozen or so assholes sitting on death row, courtesy of *Dickie Floyd*, and that's a lot of homeboys and family members that've got our number too. So, I have to pack a gun everywhere I go nowadays, taking the kids to school, sports, church—"

"Wait a minute, partner; when's the last time you went to church, there wasn't a dead guy somewhere?" I pulled into traffic, adjusting the air-conditioner.

Floyd paused, thinking for a minute. He said, "That's not the point. What I'm trying to say here, Dickie, is if this Copenhagen's what finally kills me, that'd be an ironic son-of-a-bitch. Where did you say we're headed?"

"The crime lab."

"Well get crackin', dickhead," he said, and glanced at his watch, "I'm thirsty."

AFTER TEN MINUTES OF DRIVING IN SILENCE, FLOYD ASKED, "SEX OR murders?"

Our short list of preferred topics.

"Your choice."

"I'm gonna kill my wife if she doesn't figure out a way to get to bed before midnight, pay a little attention to the man of the house."

"So, we're doing both?"

"Huh?"

I checked the mirrors, giving him time. Still with that lost stare on his face. I said, "Sex *and* murders."

"Oh," he said, "yeah."

"What's she doing, keeps her up so late?"

"Ebay."

"Buying or selling?"

Floyd had sprawled out in the front seat, his left arm stretched behind my seat and his right arm resting on the door, one leg crossed over the other. "Oh, she's spending. Spending like we grow it on trees. Remember that fight we had about garage sales, couple weeks back? She cleaned the garage one weekend while you and I were working. The next weekend, she sold everything we haven't used for more than six months. All the camping gear, clothes, toys—everything."

"Yeah?"

"Ever since," he said, "she's been busy buying it all back. Swear to God. Half the shit she's buying, she sold for a buck at that stupid garage sale. What're you looking for?"

I glanced over to see Floyd watching me. "Over there," I said, nodding toward the left side of the underpass almost behind us now, "is where Wayne lives."

"The bum you had on the phone this morning?"

"Vietnam vet."

"He told you that?" Floyd asked.

"It's what his sign said, *Hungry and Homeless Vet.*"

"I think you're going soft on me, Dickie."

I parked along the red curb in front of the crime lab and stepped out of the car, calling back to Floyd, "Bring the photos, asshole."

"Don't you start bossing me, Dickie," he said, getting out of the car with the photos in his hand. "I'm the one person you don't boss."

"You just keep reminding me that, partner."

32

STEPHEN DUBOIS WAS a relatively attractive man with delicate features, light brown skin, and sparkling eyes. He was what cops and men in the joint call *soft,* very feminine in many ways.

As a woman, he was a knockout. *Stephanie.* There in the photo with his short skirt and pumps, bare legs, long black hair falling over the side of his face.

Jesus, to think it, let alone *say* it.

"Seriously," Floyd said, holding the photo in front of Phil Gentry, "he really was pretty hot, for a dude."

Phil shook his head, appalled.

We stood viewing the enhanced photos of the young man in pumps, there in the doorway of Room 217, The Regal Inn in Lynwood. Wearing the same outfit he wore when we found him strangled under the bed, not twelve hours after these pictures were taken by our boy, Elmer Fudd.

Floyd said, "You know, if a guy had too many beers—"

"My God," Phil said.

Maybe we really *weren't* normal, the thought occurred to me, now and other times too. Maybe too often.

We thanked Phil for staying over for us, getting the photos enhanced while we waited. He told us no problem, asked if he could see us out, as if in a hurry for us to leave. He appeared a bit flushed in the face.

Floyd and I stepped off the front steps of the red brick building tucked into the century-old neighborhood of Los Angeles, not far from Hollywood or downtown, just around the corner from the famous Tommy's Burgers, and a short drive to Dodger Stadium. We walked to the Crown Vic under a sky showing its last light of the day, with Floyd saying behind me, "I'm starving. Plus I still need a beer, and you are pissing me off, again. You think Phil thinks we're nuts?"

"It's very likely; he's no dummy. You know, I worry sometimes that people take us serious."

Floyd looked over and said, "We are serious, Dickie. This police shit is nothing to joke around about."

I rolled my eyes as I pulled from the curb, flipping a U across Beverly Boulevard.

Floyd said, "It's just as easy to head straight, this time of evening. Take surface streets rather than mess with the Hollywood. Less traffic, plus there's places to eat along the way: the Thai place, that barbecue joint, Philippe's downtown . . . what else?"

I turned right on Alvarado and he said, "Jesus. You're still looking for Wayne, aren't you?"

"No," I said, wondering what it was that bothered me about him not being under the bridge. "Hadn't even thought about it, to be honest."

The effects of the G.H.B. would be dissipated by now, we figured, two days past the overdose. Unfortunately, Floyd and I agreed, we couldn't interview Donna Edwards even if she were sober as a judge, now that we had to seriously consider her a suspect in the murders of Shane Wright and Stephen Dubois. Not after she had invoked her right to counsel the last time we tried to interview her.

Having heard the traffic report every ten minutes for the last half hour, I turned the radio off. I needed to focus only on my thoughts and use the time alone in the car to sort things out, come up with a plan.

The photos, Floyd and I had agreed over Thai food and beer last night, weren't enough to get the case filed. They were good pictures; there was no doubt about that. We had the one showing Donna Edwards and Gilbert Regalado arguing with the victims in front of Donna's house the evening of the murders. Then there was Donna and Gilbert picking up the older gangster at the house that was probably in East L.A., before dropping Donna off at the club. Then, within a few hours after the big argument in front of Donna's house, the two gangsters were at the scene of the crime, placed there by photographic evidence. The two of them with Stephen Dubois opening the door in his skirt, the last time—as far as we knew—anyone had seen him alive. Then the duo left the motel a short time later, and there was no sign of Stephen from that time on.

This, of course, had a major problem: it all came from Elmer Fudd. Floyd had said over beers last night, sure, it would be the most humorous trial of all times, Elmer Fudd, the prosecution's star witness. He had almost spit beer, laughing, saying, "Jesus Christ, Dickie, can't you see it?"

I stared at the skyline of downtown Los Angeles as I crept south on the Hollywood Freeway, still a good fifteen minutes from the office in this traffic, maybe a half-hour. Thinking what a pretty city it could be on a clear morning as the sun blossomed behind the skyscrapers, quiet and peaceful from this view, beyond the sight, sound, and smell of its cancerous underbelly.

I thought about Gilbert and his buddy leaving the motel, driving around Lynwood, according to Fudd. They leave the motel and Stephen Dubois is never seen alive again. Then they're looking around for something, or more likely, someone, and Susie Q ends up dead on the street, right across from the motel. How's that for a start? Mostly circumstantial, I argued to myself, but not bad.

What would be the motive? Not that motive is necessary to convict someone of murder, but Jesus, it'd sure help in this case. Without it, the defense would have a field day poking holes in our case, given the relationship between Donna and Susie.

I stayed in my zone, recalling the details, trying to put it all in perspective with the newfound information, photographs that changed everything we thought we knew about the case. I pictured the crime scene: Susie on the sidewalk, strangled, her lifeless body leaving us few clues about her death. Tissue from beneath her fingernails, no doubt our best evidence if they were able to extract DNA. The other source of DNA, not likely relevant, given both her profession and the fact she was fully clothed; there was no evidence of this being a sexual assault murder. No, this was not the work of a predator or a disgruntled customer; these murders had an entirely different motive than the average dead hooker case.

And suddenly it all seemed a little clearer.

We had the statement of Gilbert Regalado: Gilbert saying Donna pimped the two victims through a club in Hollywood. He had worked for her as a driver, getting the hookers transported to and from various hotels and motels, supposedly an exclusive clientele. He also mentioned there had been a move toward extortion, some of these clients willing to pay to keep their dirty little secrets concealed. Who were these clients?

But what would the motive be? That continued to gnaw at me. Why would Donna want to kill the ones who were making her money? Why would she kill her childhood friend? What were we missing? What had they argued about out front that night, if we believe what Fudd had told us over what Donna had said.

Then I wondered, what if the girls, Susie and Stephanie, for whatever reason, had chosen to get out of the game. Decided they didn't want to be pimped any more, or maybe they didn't like the extortion part of it. Or the drug dealing part. Clearly, they had a disagreement about something, according to the testimony of Fudd.

Was that a mistake, to believe what Fudd had said? His story made sense, and the photos seemed to back up his statement. But it also stood in stark contrast to what Donna had told us about that night, about Fudd being out front, words exchanged between him and our victims. Who was telling the truth? Who was the more credible witness?

Jesus, that was a tough call.

There was something we were missing still, but I couldn't put my finger on it. The last piece or two of a puzzle that would likely reveal the whole picture to us and unravel the mystery.

"We need to do a search warrant," I said to Floyd when he

answered his cell phone. "We've got enough probable cause to hit Donna's place, right?"

He sounded slow this morning, maybe tired, or a little hung over. "I'd imagine we could stretch what we have, come up with enough to convince the right judge."

"You at the office yet?"

Floyd said, "Yeah, Dickie, I'm at the office. Where the hell are you, the driving range?"

"I'll be there in about fifteen, twenty minutes," I said, speaking rapidly, a list of things to do now clear in my mind. "If you could start an affidavit, I'll write the search warrant when I get in. Whoever finishes first can line up a judge, then find us a few volunteers to assist with the searches."

Floyd said he'd be on it as soon as he got another cup. Saying it'd been a madhouse in the office this morning, but I wouldn't know, coming in as late as I do.

By the time I reached the office, my mind raced with another idea. I hurried to my desk from the back door of the office, passing rows of desks along the way. The squad room bustled with men and women in business attire talking to one another or staring at computer screens, some of them speaking into their phones. I shed a tweed coat with elbow patches, rolled up my sleeves, and loosened my gray patterned tie. Tossing a straw Dobbs with a two-inch brim onto my desk, I said to Floyd, "The club."

Floyd, hunched over his laptop, working the keyboard with two fingers, looked up. "What?"

"We need to hit the strip club too."

He turned to face me. "We love strip clubs, Dickie."

"The one thing we're pretty sure Madam Marquis *didn't* lie about," I said, "is that Donna has a partnership in that club. There has to be something there, if she's running whores like Gilbert says. Ledgers, client lists, a black book, something."

"Cabo," Floyd said, giving it a subtle nod.

"Two locations for the warrant," I said, "we hit them both at once. I'll take Donna's house, you can have the club. I know you'd prefer to be in a strip club, even if it is transformers doing the stripping."

"You know me, Dickie, always willing to take one for the team."

Floyd picked up a white mug with NYPD in blue letters, a gold shield on the side. It brought back memories of one of our most adventurous excursions, kicking doors in Brooklyn with the Cold Case Squad, some of the best cops I'd ever had the privilege to know. I nodded toward the mug, "You ready for a refill?"

LATER THAT AFTERNOON, FLOYD CALLED ME OVER THE POLICE RADIO AND said when I had a chance, find my damn cell phone and get ahold of him. They were almost wrapped up at the club and he had a few things to tell me. I asked Sandy Landers if she could keep an eye on things inside while I made a call, Sandy and her partner assisting with the search warrant at Donna Edwards's home.

"Sure," she said. Then she said to the new guy, "Rick, you want to finish up searching that room? I need to keep an eye on things around here."

I hadn't meant for her to quit what she was doing.

"Anything good?" I asked when Floyd answered his cell.

"I think so," he said.

"Well, do tell."

"I've got a detailed list of men," he said, "clients of the call-girl operation, I'm sure. Different notes about preferences, which girl the client prefers, the outfits—one here says *French Maid*—hotels, cell phone numbers . . . Some of the people on this list are very interesting, to say the least."

"Like who?"

"Probably shouldn't say over the phone," he said, "but there's a lawyer's name here, one you and I both know—"

"You're shittin' me."

"—a cop we know . . . well, maybe; it's a common name, so I'll give him the benefit of the doubt for now. There's a doctor—"

"A doctor?"

"—maybe a couple other VIPs. I'll show you at the office."

"We know for sure the list is Donna's?"

"It was locked in her desk," he said. "The madam didn't even have a key to get in there. Lucky for us, Dwight here's got a few tricks up his sleeves. You know how these surveillance guys are."

"You guys buddies again?"

"I'll meet you back at the office, Dickie, you're starting to bore me."

"Hang on a sec," I said.

"What?"

"Don't you want to hear what we got?"

In the early evening, Floyd and I sat at our desks surrounded by paper bags and cardboard boxes containing evidence and items of intelligence collected from the two locations searched earlier in the day. Floyd pulled the black book from a box and wheeled his chair next to mine, pushing the evidence at my feet out of his path. He began flipping through the pages, reading the names as I labeled evidence tags with our case number, the date, time, and victim's name.

Floyd said, "Right here, Dickie, Dr. Brandon Gladstone, three-ten area code. The pervert lives in Beverly Hills or Brentwood, most likely."

"Let's piggyback the warrant and get subscriber info on his number. Might as well get subscriber info on all the numbers in that book, while we're at it. You never know, and we definitely have the probable cause now."

"Here's the cop," he said, pointing out the entry. "Larry Walker."

"Jesus, Floyd, you get cop from *that?* How do you know it isn't the baseball player?"

"You think he pays for girls?"

"There was a guy in my high school named Larry Walker. Big goon with a full beard by tenth grade. It's not an uncommon name. That's the point I'm making."

"Yeah," Floyd said, "but you know the guy I'm talking about, right? That asshole who worked a radio car for about twenty minutes before he transferred to Headquarters. Now he's a sergeant up at the Information Bureau, where all the suck-asses go."

"House fairies," I said. "Yeah, I do know who you're talking about, and he is definitely a punk. But that doesn't mean he chases drag queens."

"The guy's a freak," Floyd said, "you ask me. So, what did you get out of her house that was so terrific?"

I pulled a small envelope from my shirt pocket, handed it to him, and watched his hazel eyes as he opened it and reached inside with two fingers.

He pulled a small key from the envelope and held it in front of him, looking at it and then glancing back to me. "That's it, a key?"

"Not just a key, dumbass. A safe-deposit box key. Bank of America."

Floyd tossed the key in the air and then caught it, his eyes tracking it back into his hand. He said, "Guess we add B of A to the piggyback, huh?"

33

FLOYD STUDIED THE first photo from a small stack in his hand, turned it sideways for a moment, then slid it to the rear. He looked at the next photo, glanced up with a malicious grin, and then flipped to the next.

The sick bastard.

"What?"

Floyd chuckled. "You've got to see these."

"Le' me see."

"We may be onto something, Dickie. Why do you suppose . . ." he said, drawing it out as he stepped next to me, "Donna would have these photos? The old man here doing the nasty with your girl, Susie."

I glanced at the photo. "Jesus."

"No shit," he said. "Looks like Gilbert told the truth about her extorting the clientele, or at least planning to."

"Wonder how they got the pictures."

We were both leaning on the hood of my gray Crown Vic behind the Bank of America in Downey. Floyd holding the dirty pictures recovered from a safe deposit box registered to a D. Edwards. Floyd hoarding them, showing me one at a time. "Oh . . . my . . . God!" He'd turn some sideways, tilting his head, "Ho-*ly* shit! Dickie, look what she's doing here."

"C'mon, let's go. You can study them on the way to the office. We need to get this pervert ID'd."

We turned out of the parking lot, the morning sun to our back now, the digital clock on my dash reading 10:33. Floyd, with his Ray-Bans on top of his head, flipped through the photographs, one after another, commenting on each one. Impressed with some, fascinated by others. He said, "Who do you think this guy is?" holding a photo of the same old man in a different pose.

I glanced over. This time the man sat on the edge of a bed in boxer shorts, black socks, and dress shoes. Sitting there with his pale, sunken chest revealing white hair and faded blue ink over his left nipple, a tattoo from the fifties.

"We get back to the office," I said, "we'll pull the DMV photos on all those names from the black book, see if we can figure it out."

Dr. Brandon Gladstone appeared respectable in his collared shirt and V-necked sweater, smiling, every hair in place for his DMV photo taken three years prior. I compared it to the photos from the safe-deposit box, the one of the old man in his boxers and dress shoes, studying the two side by side. It may have been taken three years ago, but these two guys were one and the same. I convinced myself of it. Almost.

"Hey Frank," I called out to a passing detective, "have a look at these."

He leaned over my shoulder and peered at the photos on my desk. "Who's that, your dad?"

Why had I asked Frank Lewandowski, I wondered.

"You're such an asshole. Seriously, Frank, you think it's the same guy, that one there," I said, pointing to the DMV photo, "and this freak in the shorts?"

I felt the moisture of his breath on my neck as he snorted through a chuckle. "How the hell should I know? I ain't got my glasses on, and I can't see shit without 'em. Can't remember shit either, to be honest about it. Hell, I probably won't be able to find my glasses now either, won't remember where the hell I put 'em. You want, I can try and find my glasses and come back, have a look."

"It's okay, Frank. I was about to head out anyway."

"Where the hell's your partner?" he asked, looking around the squad room. "I never see that asshole anymore unless we're somewhere there's girls and booze." He glanced at his watch. "Which reminds me, I've got places to be."

I returned to my study of the two men, convinced they were the same even with no help from Lewandowski. It was nearly nine and few detectives remained in the squad room this late in the evening. Those who did sat behind desks and computers, likely unaware of the time, maybe catching up on reports or running with new leads on a case. Some just preferred to not go home.

My desk phone rang, distracting me from the photos for a moment. I stared at it, wondering who would be calling me at this hour. Maybe my partner, or my wife, neither of whom would be happy to discover I was still at the office. I ignored the phone and stood through aching knees and a sore back, and thought a cup of coffee was what I needed.

Returning to my desk with a fresh cup, I decided to call it a night, make it a *coffee to go* order. I slid my chair under the desk, grabbed my briefcase and walked out the back door, into the parking lot under a dark and cloudy sky.

Twenty minutes later I found myself fighting traffic on the Hollywood Freeway, wondering if it was Valerie who had tried to call. Probably not, I decided; she would have tried my cell or at least paged me. My partner would have called the office, called the cell, paged me six or twenty times, and if he hadn't reached me by then, he would have come up with a new plan over a six-pack of beer. It had probably been a victim's loved one, I reasoned, wanting to ask what the hell I do with all my time since I haven't bothered to solve their darling's murder.

That settled, I switched off the cell and tuned the AM radio to catch the late innings of a Dodgers home game. To say Vin Scully *called* the game would be to say Leonardo *painted* a picture. No, Vinny's words went beyond mere play-calling; he transformed radio waves into vivid imagery of uniformed men wearing caps and gloves and chewing seeds or tobacco on a glimmering diamond of manicured grass and its contrasting red clay, playing America's game under the brilliant lights of a place he fondly called *Chavez Ravine.*

WHAT I HATED MOST ABOUT THE CORONER'S OFFICE, I THOUGHT, WHILE tearing off a disposable paper gown, matching blue slippers, plastic goggles, and latex gloves, were the inadvertent contacts, the disgusting parts and particles of death and decomposition that seemed to jump out like the bogeyman and assail you from all directions. During examinations, technicians would carelessly wash the bodies, spraying water from a short hose, trying to direct the fluids and tissue toward the stainless-steel sink at the end of a table. But somehow they seemed to, more often than not, splatter foreign matter in the direction of those of us who stood nearby. If that wasn't bad enough, there were the hallways filled with bodies, fresh corpses all over the place that you would inevitably bump into or the dead guy would reach out and grab you if you weren't careful. Or so it seemed.

What I have never figured out though, as I recalled now on my way out, passing through Receiving, is why the hell they bothered to decorate for Halloween. I thought about the paper skeletons and strings of ghosts that, in the fall, hung across the wall behind the receptionist, a remarkably well-adjusted woman who answered phones and checked in visitors, both temporary and permanent ones. It was as if they thought that maybe, with a few cutouts and cobwebs, they could make the place more ghoulish.

I dropped the officer-involved shooting notebook in my brief case as I slid into my car, glad to put another autopsy behind me. The image of an Asian gunman now memorialized on the stainless-steel slab, no longer a part of—or problem to—society. The would-be bank robber shot to death by Hawthorne officers, another case of cop-assisted suicide, the way this asshole selfishly chose to end his life. The officers would be burdened with his decision for the rest of theirs.

FLOYD LOOKED UP FROM HIS DESK AS I WALKED PAST HIM AND DROPPED my soft-sided briefcase on the floor between us.

He said, "You look like shit."

"Back atchya, asshole."

"You have a rough night?"

I plopped in my chair and loosened my tie. "You might say that."

Floyd grinned, maybe happy to see me suffer. "You didn't go out last night, did you? Did you go out without me, dickhead?"

I turned, powered up my laptop, and made a point of ignoring him.

"You did, didn't you? Well you two-timing little bitch. What'd you do?"

"All right," I said, leaning toward him, "but you aren't going to believe it."

"Try me."

"This is strictly between us, and I'm dead serious."

"Yeah, yeah, get on with it."

"I went to that club last night, Club Cabo."

Floyd's eyes brightened. "Yeah?"

"Well, I had had this hunch—"

"Uh-huh."

"—having thought about what you said about the cop, that Larry Walker guy, being in Donna's little black book."

Floyd watched me like a dog waiting while his master ate a ham sandwich. If I kept teasing him with the information, taking small bites and chewing slowly, he would soon whine or growl or try to snatch it out of my hands. I had him, hook, line, and sinker. "Yeah?"

"If it did turn out to be the cop, that prick from Headquarters, we'd probably better find out right away, you know, and figure out how we're going to deal with that. Right?"

"Out the bastard, is how we'd deal with him."

"Right. Well, anyway, I get to thinking, maybe a guy like that would be hanging out at the tranny club, you know? Just enjoying the show, maybe picking out a new girl or two since there seems to be a sudden shortage of drag queens."

"Thanks to Donna Edwards."

"So, I decided to stop by on my way home, maybe have a couple beers and mingle, and who do I see?"

"Walker?" Floyd asked, his brows raised.

"No. Your captain, Stover."

"Get outta here."

"Yeah, really, he was up on stage. I almost didn't recognize him, the black dress with sequins, a slit up one side showing some leg."

"You asshole."

"You know," I said, standing from my desk, "that asshole actually shaves his legs."

I headed for the kitchen with Floyd on my heels, passing several detectives in the hallway along the way.

"You are such a dick. No wonder your mother named you Dickie."

"That was you who named me that."

"Oh yeah. But seriously, man, where'd you go last night?"

I gestured pouring him a cup, after filling mine.

He grabbed a fresh Styrofoam cup and held it out for me. "Come on dude, you're killing me."

I chuckled. "Nothing exciting, really. I stopped at the V-room on the way home, thought maybe I'd run into Waters. Had a couple beers—H2O wasn't there—and then I went home and had a couple more. Couldn't sleep, so I pulled out my notebook and the case file, started reviewing the case, just going over shit. Next thing you know, I had switched to gin."

"Do we hate it when we switch to gin?"

"Sometimes. Today being one of those times."

"So, in your pickled state of mind," Floyd said, now leading the way back to the squad room, "did you come up with any brilliant conclusions?"

"Yep."

He stopped to hear it.

I sipped my coffee, making him wait for a minute before letting it go. He'd say I was nuts, say my theory sucked and tell me the problem was I spent too much time thinking about this shit. I'd argue my point for a while and sooner or later, he'd probably say all right, let's see how your theory works out, Columbo. Or he'd tell me I needed to avoid gin, or maybe he'd suggest I should drink more of it.

I said, "The doctor did it."

Floyd stood with a hand planted firmly on his hip, a coffee mug in the other, frowning. He watched me for a minute, apparently in thought, maybe questioning my sanity, maybe wondering if I was trying to put him on again, the second time this morning. Finally he said, "So we just forget the pictures, the ones putting Donna's boyfriend and his homeboy at the crime scene?"

"I haven't worked that part out yet."

"For Christ's sake, Dickie. You just come up with this shit while looking through a bottle of Bombay, and expect me to throw out the only real leads we've got? What the hell makes you think the doctor did it? What's his motive? How's he go to Lynwood and find these hookers, one in the motel and the other out on the street, whack 'em, and get out of the neighborhood without being jacked for his Mercedes, or jammed by the cops because he's in the wrong neighborhood? Have you lost your mind?"

I wavered a little. Maybe he was right, I thought, staring at his squinted hazel eyes. Looking at my partner but seeing the crime scene in my head, picturing the pervert doctor there on Long Beach Boulevard strangling the well-dressed hooker. Watching him straddle Susie, maybe giving it a grin as he stepped away, the madman having completed his mission.

My eyes were still on Floyd and his white cotton shirt loosened at the collar, a gray- and blue-checked tie with its fat knot hanging low. But in my head, I saw the escape, the doctor moving away from the body, looking over his shoulder and then hurrying toward the lot where his Mercedes sat waiting, stepping in the planter along the way.

I thought about the gangsters on the balcony, outside the motel room, Fudd saying he followed them there after the argument in the front yard. And I thought, it could be a coincidence, and maybe when they left there she was alive and well. It was a stretch, but . . .

So I said to my befuddled partner: "Stranger things have happened."

34

THE GOOD DOCTOR, who apparently suffers from advanced stages of Sexual Deviance Disorder, an unrecognized medical condition I discovered during a silent analysis of my partner, had several strikes against him. That's how I saw it, thinking about it on the way into the office this morning.

No doubt the duo of Donna Edwards and Gilbert Regalado had snared the doc, getting explicit photos of his private moments with Susie. A Beverly Hills doctor would dread this type of bad publicity, and seven figures a year could afford to pay for silence. That's probably the way they saw it, the good doctor gladly stuffing twenty large into an envelope to protect his dirty secret. Maybe fifty, who knows?

However, we were surprised to learn that his forte was plastic surgery; neither of us had seen that coming. I had told Floyd it bolstered my theory, figuring he probably performed the gender reassignment surgery of Shane Wright, and the breast augmentation for Stephen Dubois, and maybe he had worked out a deal, something along the lines of ongoing companionship in lieu of payment. But when the pressure started, and the extortion began, maybe he saw them as disposable.

Or maybe the doctor paid the extortion demand and then the two hookers decided they would get in on the big cash-out, make a demand of their own. That could have been enough to send him over, make him realize he had a substantial problem that needed a permanent solution.

It was a huge stretch, and I knew it. But it intrigued me nonetheless. Though I had to admit I wasn't even close to convinced of it myself, and the other theory was a far better one. But the shoe impression kept me there, the remark by Gentry saying it appeared to be a men's casual dress shoe. *Dress shoe.* Not gangster shoe, or prison shoe. Dress shoe.

The rain had brought traffic to a crawl this morning, but I preferred it over another unbearably hot day in early spring. It'd be a long day, I surmised, thinking of everything we needed to accomplish, which meant I probably wouldn't have to contend with traffic during the drive home.

I thought again about the doctor theory and began to gloat beneath the gray Dobbs, a snappy straw dress hat with a two-inch brim turned down in the front and back, suddenly realizing that if my theory proved true—against all odds—it would be Floyd eating crow.

The physical evidence needed to bolster my theory would be a match of the shoe impression. "If the shoe fits, you must *not* acquit," I said over the traffic report on my radio. Talking to myself, alone but surrounded by idiots. I smiled, saying it again, this time with some rhythm to it. *"If the shoe fits, you must NOT acquit."* I laughed at myself, and thought, maybe I'd suggest the little ditty to the district attorney, something he could use during closing arguments. Johnnie Cochran probably wouldn't mind too much, I thought, the play on his famous courtroom declaration, God rest his soul.

Then I thought about the doctor's defense. What could he say? If the shoe impression matched, he'd never be able to explain being in that part of town, much less in that part of town afoot, and just a couple feet from the scene of the crime. The man with his big house in Bel Aire, his business in Beverly Hills. What could he say to justify being in South Los Angeles? He went to the store, wound up in the ghetto near that dead hooker? I don't think so.

Not even an L.A. jury would buy that. Not unless the doctor was a celebrity, a sports figure or rap star maybe.

I STOOD INSIDE THE BACK DOOR OF THE OFFICE AND COLLAPSED MY umbrella, a frown creeping onto my face as I noticed a crowd near my desk. There were a couple of guys in green raid jackets, *SHERIFF* printed across the back, most likely gang cops, and two others, a man and a woman wearing blue raid jackets, *PROBATION* on the front.

Floyd sat center stage, telling his story as I walked up behind him: ". . . high-caliber rifle rounds tearing through the metal of our car, glass flying everywhere. Dickie comes flying out of the car, lands on me, I'm trying to see who the hell is shooting at us but now I have his big ass on top of me —oh, speak of the devil."

"Excuse me," I said, giving the guy leaning against my desk a hint. I nodded as he moved, doing my best to be polite given my level of irritation. Floyd telling his war story rubbed me the wrong way for some reason. Sitting back in his chair, arms folded, telling it like it was no big deal, another day at the office. The cool guy with his flowered tie. Never mentioning the terror, the moments wondering if we'd live through it, the sweat pouring off our foreheads, the fear we each saw in the other's eyes.

It occurred to me I was being a bit grumpy, that Floyd was only doing what he does, entertaining. Everyone seemed to like him and he easily drew a crowd. I had never been a fan of crowds, especially on my home ground. Like coming home and having someone parked in my driveway, it irritated me to come in and see people sitting at my desk, on my desk, or even standing around my desk.

Maybe I was also a little bitchy that my partner still scoffed at my theory about Dr. Gladstone.

He'd see soon enough about the doc . . .

Floyd said, "Looks like my partner's grumpy today, probably that time of the month again."

There were a few snickers as the newly founded fan club slowly dispersed.

"You going to buy me a cup, asshole?" Floyd asked, entertainment hour now behind him.

He followed as I silently rose and drifted toward the kitchen.

"I'll take that as a yes," he said to my back.

When we reached the kitchen, I finally spoke. "Who were those idiots?"

"Florencia Gang Task Force," Floyd said. "They're assisting Team Six with search warrants. What's your problem?"

"Nothing."

He let it go.

"I talked to Phil Gentry about the shoe impression. He said it's definitely good enough for a comparison, but he wants every shoe the doctor owns to make sure he can get a definitive, if you're still dead set on wasting our time with that theory."

I ignored the comment, instead thinking about an affidavit, wondering if we had enough probable cause for a search warrant of the doctor's residence.

"You think we have enough for a warrant?" he asked, maybe reading my mind.

"I don't know, maybe. Yeah, probably."

"We could always knock on his door, ask him real nice could we have a look around. Then swipe all of his shoes, tell him we'll get back with him later."

"You think this guy doesn't have a team of lawyers on his speed dial?"

"Good point, Dickie. I guess you'd better get crackin' on a warrant. After all, the doc is all yours, from start to finish. Personally, I think it's a waste of time."

The thought went through my head that he was right, that I was way off track on this theory. But I ignored my gut on this one, the stubborn side showing its colors.

Floyd poured us each a cup and we headed back to *the floor, the squad room*, a sea of desks with computers and fluorescent lighting where A-type personalities killed themselves trying to find out who killed someone else.

DR. GLADSTONE FINISHED PERUSING THE SEARCH WARRANT, A COPY OF the original Floyd told him was his to keep. He lowered it to reveal a smirk on his face. "You're wasting your time here, Detectives."

Oh, is that right?

It was just what I expected from the arrogant bastard, this man in his silk robe and house shoes smoking a cigarette at seven o'clock in the morning, the second straight day of rain in the southland. The rain being as rare and about as welcomed as our search warrant at the Bel Aire estate.

Floyd said, "Why's that, sir?"

"I was traveling abroad when those pitiful youths were slain," he said, in his English accent.

Now I knew we hated him.

But Floyd continued: "Where were you, Doctor?"

I did a mental eye-roll, wanting to tell Floyd, *Let him take the witness stand, say it there.* It annoyed me that Floyd entertained the man's alibi, even if he didn't believe it. This doctor who no doubt would think he was smarter and more important than the two cops coming in from the rain. The way I saw it, he expected our visit, another sign he was our man. Why else would he have an alibi prepared? This doctor smoking his Virginia Slims, or some other girly cigarette, in his robe and slippers.

I left the two of them standing in the marbled entryway with chairs and a bench seat covered in red velvet, a room bigger than my first apartment, and I proceeded up the spiral staircase to my right, the search warrant giving me unrestricted access to the home. I'd bring back a box full of shoes, interrupt Floyd saying, *Really, sir, how impressive* . . . Tell both of them, *We'll see about that alibi, doc,* and walk out with the evidence. Send the perverted Englishman to the pokey, tell him his new name's going to be *Peaches* in the California Department of Corrections. Maybe tell him in an English accent.

Be able to say to Floyd, *See?* . . .

Shortly after I began my search, the sounds of friendly chatter downstairs faded and soon thereafter I felt a presence in the master bedroom.

"You can go ahead and take his shoes, if you're set on it, Dickie, but I think he's right, we're wasting our time."

I was on my knees in the carpeted walk-in closet. A collection of dress shoes in a box soon to be labeled *Evidence* sat next to me. I glanced at Floyd over my shoulder, then returned to my search without a response.

"I know you're not going to like this, but the man has more than just a good alibi."

"He convinced you, huh?"

"The problem is," Floyd said, squatting down next to me now, "Doc wears an eight and a half. Look at them, those little shoes there, they damn near look like women's shoes. Phil estimated tens or elevens, nothing near an eight or nine."

"He did?"

"Yeah, Dickie, he did."

"I don't remember that," I said, doubting him.

"And the doc's got proof he was in Atlanta the night of our murder."

I lifted my hat and wiped sweat from my forehead with the back of my hand. "You ask him how it is he knows what day they were killed? It's not like this case made the papers."

"Donna told him the day after," Floyd said. "She told him Susie and Stephanie had been killed, told him it happened the night before. He remembers she called after he got home from the airport Saturday afternoon. He's looking for travel records as we speak, trying to find his itinerary, airline tickets, hotel receipts . . ."

I sensed there was more. "Yeah, and?"

"The call was an extortion demand."

I stopped and turned to face him.

He continued: "Donna told Doc about the two girls being killed, then told him to check under his mat, said he'd find something of interest. Actually, what he told me was, *'of significant matter'*"—Floyd giving it his best English accent—"but I don't think that's actually what Donna would have said.

"She stayed on the phone while he checked under the mat and found an envelope. He opened it up, and there's these photos, similar to what we took from her safe-deposit box, from what he described. She told him there's another set, says it'll cost him a hundred thou to get those and the negatives."

We both stood and faced one another in the walk-in closet, though I still had nothing to say.

Floyd continued, "Doc tells Donna he'll have her incarcerated—yeah, that's what he said, *incarcerated*—and her response was basically that it would be his word against hers, as far as the phone call. Then she asked if he was really so stupid that he would go to the cops."

"What'd he say?"

"He told her they'd get her prints off the letter, compare her writing and she'd be done. That's when she said Susie wrote the note, what did he think, *she* was stupid?"

"He told you all this?"

"Yeah," Floyd said, "and there's more. Donna told him if he went to the cops, her gangster friends would pay him a visit, maybe at his office. I mean, basically our sweet little Donna Edwards had Susie and her friend whacked and threatened the doctor with the same."

I shook my head in disbelief, struggling with the story, not wanting to let go of my theory. I said, "Well, at least according to *this* suspect."

"Come on, man, you can't get around those pictures. Gilbert and the other thug at the hotel the night of these murders. Then cruising around like they were looking for someone. You have to admit, buddy, the doctor theory is thin, especially in light of his story on this, and his alibi."

I couldn't believe it, Floyd believing every word the man said to him. This asshole doing Hugh Hefner in his pajamas on a rainy morning in Los Angeles, probably wishing we'd have a good fog roll in, the *bloody arsehole.*

"So is he willing to testify to all of that?"

"He will if we need him to. He actually said he has nothing to hide. He's single, openly bisexual, and he said he loved Susie."

I didn't know what to say. It was a lot of solid information, but it was also a big pill for me to swallow.

Floyd continued: "This also makes sense about them arguing in the front yard. Maybe Susie wasn't too keen on the extortion, or at least the extortion of Doc Gladstone, since he's who made her a woman. Whatever Susie said to Donna in that front yard, is what got her killed, Dickie. I'm convinced of it. Maybe she told her they were through, done with working for her, done doing her dirty work, done watching her destroy lives. Doc said he loved Susie, and I would bet Susie knew it."

"Okay, okay" I said, somewhat defeated, "you're probably right. So what's our next move, Sherlock?"

"We need to get Donna's cell records, show that she called him the day after the murder to corroborate the doctor's story. Then we need to identify the tattooed thug that was with Gilbert, and then find both of their dumb asses, and beat a confession out of them."

"Yeah, and then what?"

Floyd thought about it for a minute, and said, "You can buy the steaks and beer. How's that sound?"

35

I SAT AT my desk biting at the end of a ballpoint pen while staring at the back of Floyd's head. He sat at a computer beyond a cluster of desks along the squad room wall, computers that provided access to law enforcement applications such as FBI and DOJ criminal histories and personal records. The pimple on his neck annoyed me as I sulked over the death of my theory, the brilliant though perhaps ill-conceived hunch that it was the doctor who killed Susie and her friend. The obnoxious, rich, Englishman with his robe and girly cigarettes.

Both of them were actually pissing me off, I thought, the doctor with his English accent and Floyd with his fifty-dollar haircut, the two of them teaming up to tear me down today. The whole day gone to shit, the search warrant and all the extra work that went into it having caused the loss of nearly a full day. Or so it seemed. If I had to be fair, I would admit that the doctor's information was certainly helpful for our case against Donna and the boys . . . *if* I had to be fair. Ah *bloody hell.*

The clock read eight and we had missed dinner again, the second night in a row. After leaving the doctor's house, we had spent the day driving through the soggy streets of Los Angeles, the traffic barely moving as panic had struck Angelenos. It became the top story of the southland, this dangerous—if not deadly—phenomenon where water came from above and wetness blanketed the streets, the cars, and the few pedestrians who were so foolish as to venture outdoors during such treacherous conditions. People had been forced to close their sunroofs, put their tops up, and close their windows. Weather warnings were announced throughout the day by reporters clad in yellow or blue plastic raincoats, who risked their very lives to report the natural disaster in dramatic fashion.

The bulk of the day included stops at the crime lab, where we submitted evidence for analysis, the courthouse, where we filed our search warrant, Manny's in East Los Angeles, where we consumed Hollenbeck burritos, and the hat store at Fifth and Main, where my mood didn't allow me to enjoy shopping for hats. But it had been a nice try on Floyd's part to get me out of my slump.

The office seemed unusually busy for this time of evening. Most of the detectives were likely waiting out traffic, or maybe the weather. Raindrops drummed against the squad room's windows, and I pictured the streams of water cascading from the roof forming rivers across the sidewalks and turning the parking lot into a pond. It was a perfect evening to catch up on paperwork, if I was stuck here anyway.

I thought of Val and wished I were home eating popcorn and watching a show, or sitting in the hot tub as rain battered the gazebo, not a thought of the city on my mind. But the reality of it was, I wasn't home, and I wouldn't be for a long time, even if I left work at this minute. So, I decided to get my head back into the game, quit sulking and do what I do best.

With this renewed commitment, I said to Floyd, "You find anything yet, partner?"

He leaned closer to the radiating screen and mumbled something about East Los Angeles.

"What? I can't hear you when you mumble."

"It looks like his mom lives in East L.A., I said." He had turned in his chair to face me as the adjacent printer came to life. He spat tobacco in the trash can next to his chair, and said, "I'm betting that's where we'll find little Gilbert, home with his mama. Shit, this might be the same place they picked up the old gangster, the place Fudd described. It's in the right general area. I think we need to go knock on a door, Dickie."

I held on to a look of indifference, not willing to acknowledge that it seemed to be the right path. "You in a hurry, we need to check it tonight?"

"I think it's a good idea. Don't you? He's the only one we can talk to. Donna, looking at a trafficking beef, sure as hell isn't going to talk to us. What else do we have? Gilbert and maybe this other asshole, once we figure out who he is. That's it."

I shrugged nonchalantly.

Floyd grinned—the smart-assed Floyd grin—and said, "You want to go visit with the doctor again?"

"Look, I get it, Doc didn't do it, most likely. But if Gilbert and the mustache did it, do you think they're actually going to talk? We don't have enough to arrest them yet—in my opinion—so I'm not sure what your strategy is."

"My strategy, Dickie, is to take you out in the rain, splash through some puddles and see what happens. Weren't you ever twelve?"

"No."

"I believe it."

"We get Gilbert to talk again, prove to him we've got him by the balls, maybe even show him the photos of him and *vato* at the crime scene with Stephanie, and what's he going to say? He'll lie and deny like he did in Texas, or maybe he'll put it all on Donna—again. He isn't going to give up a homeboy, especially a hardcore looking asshole like the mustache-wearing *vato* who just got out of prison. That's my concern. I'm just not sure we gain anything."

"Are you going to sit there and complain all night, or suit up for a famous Floyd Outdoor Adventure? I swear sometimes you drive me crazy with this shit. Come on, dickhead, helmets and shoulder pads, we've got police shit to do."

I glanced toward the windows. "In the rain?"

"It ain't gonna kill us, Dickie, I promise."

THE REGALADO RESIDENCE WAS ABOUT A FIFTEEN MINUTE DRIVE FROM THE office in the rain. And not far from Third Street and Ford Boulevard where King Taco dispenses carne asada twenty-four hours a day to the citizens—

and non-citizens—of East Los Angeles. As we drove through the soggy streets, I used the time to convince Floyd he'd have to feed me before we looked for Gilbert, buy me a plate of tacos and a Coke if he wanted me to cover the back while he knocked on the front and tried his luck with Mrs. Regalado. Otherwise, I told him, I'd keep the window cracked just enough to hear him scream, but not so much that the rain could get into the car as I waited in the comfort of a dry Crown Vic. He called me an asshole and said go ahead, stop at King Taco, he could use a bite himself.

After dinner, I loosened my belt one notch, putting it back to a well-worn hole. I had dropped a few pounds over the last couple of weeks, which caused my pistol to tug at my belt, so I had cinched it up a bit, and it felt good. The weight loss had probably been the result of working fifteen hour days, substituting food with high-test caffeine and alcohol; it certainly had nothing to do with any form of diet or exercise.

"The thing is," Floyd said as I pulled out beneath a glowing neon sign, my belly full and warm, "we find Gilbert, it's going to be a long night. You know we'll spend a few hours interviewing him, a couple more booking him and doing the paperwork, and that doesn't even take into account what happens if the old gangster is there when we knock on the door."

"So, you've changed your mind? It can wait until tomorrow?"

"No, Dickie, I haven't changed my mind. But what I'm telling you is I think we should pick up some beer, just to be safe, and put it in the trunk for later."

There was a moment of silence as I tinkered with the controls, getting the wipers going and the defroster working. "Just to be safe?"

"Hey, I fed you, didn't I?"

"Chances are," I said, "this little asshole's not going to be home. I'll get to take your ass back to the office and then I'm going home to have a beer in my Jacuzzi."

"In the rain?"

"Why not?"

After stopping for beer, we drove to the address Floyd had found for Gilbert's mother. I slowed as I turned onto Evergreen, a narrow street with scant lighting, cars parked along both sides of the street and in driveways and on lawns.

"What're the numbers again?"

"Thirteen-twenty," Floyd said, "should be on the right, just up ahead a little more."

We crept along on the quiet street trying to find numbers that seldom existed on these old houses and were difficult to see on the few that had them, especially on a rainy night.

"Thirteen twelve on the curb right there," I said.

"Probably going to be two houses down, Dickie."

"There, that one right there, looks like the house in the photo."

"Two assholes on the porch. You see 'em, Dickie?"

"They're moving—"

"That's Gilbert!" Floyd exclaimed.

In the same instant, the passenger's door flew open and Floyd was gone into the darkness, into the rain.

"Shit!"

By the time I jerked the car to the curb and slammed it into park, the porch stood empty and Floyd was nowhere in sight.

Rain pelted my face as I surveyed the neighborhood. This wasn't the first time he'd done this, and I could hear him already, like all the other times, promising not to do it again. I considered driving around the block, hoping to head them off, one of the more common tactics all ghetto cops used. But something told me not this time . . . I thought to call it in, ask for backup, and tell them my partner was in foot pursuit of a murder suspect, but questioned whether it had even been Gilbert we saw run, or maybe just two random turds who recognized the cops looking their way. Something told me the two from the porch ran into the house, and if I knew my partner, he wouldn't hesitate to run in right behind them.

The Crown Vic waited behind me, her motor running and wiper blades swiping at the dancing raindrops as I set out for the front of the house in question. The porch held a floral-patterned couch, dry under the shelter, and showing no sign of its prior occupants. Beer containers were scattered about the wooden railing and concrete steps ascending from the front lawn.

As I approached at a jog, I heard voices from within, shouting in both English and Spanish, some cursing, and the sounds of doors slamming closed. I hit the middle of the three steps with one foot and landed on wood slats with the other, my H&K 9mm pointed at the closed door. The momentum carried me across the six feet of covered porch with one step and my next step included a foot landing flush against the door, just above the lock. The door shattered, hardware and splinters of wood exploding inward, and I came to a stop just inside the threshold.

I expected to see my partner on the other side, maybe the two gangsters from the porch on the living room floor spread eagled, but the room sat empty.

At that exact moment, I realized, standing in the center of this dark and musty room, that if Floyd had come through the front door, it would have already been knocked off its hinges.

Shit!

A robust woman appeared out of nowhere, now standing in a doorway to my right. I instinctively spun toward her, the front sight of my pistol homing in on her forehead until I saw the child plastered to her side. I lowered my gun. She snarled and yelled something in Spanish. Before I could speak, she had disappeared into the dark hallway behind her.

I scanned the remainder of the living room, seeing an empty armchair, a lamp with no shade on the adjacent table, the bulb shining faint light against a dark wall of wood paneling. *Cops* played on a small television in the corner, the theme song blaring as credits rolled, cop action showing in the background.

"Floyd?"

There was no response.

"Floyd?!"

Still nothing. No more shouting or screaming, no sounds of movement beyond this room. Nothing but *Cops* playing on the television, dim blue light flickering from the screen, and a sick feeling in my gut as I stood alone in this strange house, my partner missing in action.

I moved into the kitchen, my front sight popping up to cover the direction I traveled, while glancing back toward the dark hallway, a black hole where the mystery woman once stood, a potential area of threat now behind me. A pot of beans simmered on the stove and dirty dishes sat piled on the countertops and filled the sink. I continued toward a laundry area beyond the kitchen, becoming aware of an open back door.

I caught a quick movement out of the corner of my eye, and it startled me. I spun to my right. As I did, a blinding flash lit the room and an explosion rattled the windows. I felt a sudden burning in my shoulder, and another flash followed immediately, and another explosion. A bullet slammed into my stomach, and I felt myself falling. It was like being slugged with a baseball bat, not at all what I thought being shot would feel like. But I knew it had happened, and in that instant, I pictured the bulletproof vest beneath the box of beer in my trunk. I thought of Valerie, but only for an instant, and then I focused on the man who stood before me.

He screamed at me, spittle flying from the mass of dark hair that covered his mouth. His dark, harsh eyes stared at me with hatred through the smoke that now hung in the room. His voice was muted by the noise of the blast that still reverberated through my head. It all seemed surreal, nightmarish, and as in a nightmare my body was slow to react although my brain demanded that I shoot this bastard with his hateful eyes.

Flames erupted from my pistol as I squeezed the trigger with all my might again and again. I collapsed against a table and slid to the floor, my stomach and chest on fire. A fan twirled above my head, slowly stirring the hanging smoke, and my ears rang in the suddenly silent room.

Then I could hear voices, mostly speaking Spanish, and another speaking loudly and angrily. At first the words were indecipherable, but then I heard my partner, and knew I wouldn't be left to die here alone in this old and musty room on a dark and rainy night in East Los Angeles.

The room filled with sounds of a fight, yelling and cursing accompanied by the dull thuds of violent blows striking human flesh. My brain insisted that I get up, fight through the fatigue and the pain and help my partner who was likely fighting for his life—or maybe for mine—but my body refused to comply. I tried to look for Floyd but was unable to see him, my vision limited to the fan that still twirled above me. But in my mind, I saw my partner fighting ferociously, a thing I had seen many times before. He would win, there was no doubt about that, and then he would be pissed at me for lying there bleeding, helpless and without a plan. We always needed to have a plan.

A thick haze engulfed my mind as if I were drunk, and as the minutes passed I became less able to understand what was happening around me.

The fan moved more slowly now, winding down to its inevitable stop, and the pain subsided and the sounds faded. There were no more angry voices, no more sounds of a fight, as the smoke settled and darkness descended on me.

I drifted into a slumber, at peace now with what was next to come.

Bad boys, bad boys . . .

36

IT HAD BEEN six days since Jorge Regalado, Gilbert's uncle, had shot me with his .38 Special, once in the abdomen and once in the shoulder. Floyd stood at the side of my bed in jeans and a beige V-necked sweater, telling me how it went down: "Man, I damn near lost my mind when I heard those shots, Dickie . . .

"While you were screwing around out front, looking for a place to park, I chased Gilbert and some other asshole around the side of that house. Gilbert went into the back yard while his buddy took a left into the alley. I stayed with Gilbert and caught the little fat turd when he tried to go over a fence. I was in the back of that house trying to handcuff Gilbert—he's a lot stronger than you'd think—when I heard the gunshots. I went, *Jesus, what was that?* I mean, I knew what it was, but it took me a second to process it. You know, like, what the hell's Dickie shooting at while I'm back here rolling around with Gilbert? So, I pretty much decided, screw this, I don't have time for any more of these reindeer games, and I bashed him over the head with my flashlight.

"He went out cold, but I didn't want to leave him there, let him come to and maybe lose him again. Plus, I was like, I'm not in that big of a hurry to see who you'd shot, right? Jesus, Dickie,"—he said, and took a deep breath, his eyes glassy but just for an instant—"it never occurred to me it could've been you that was shot. I mean, we don't *get* shot."

He paused, maybe reliving it for a moment, and then he seemed to snap back, maybe before it felt too heavy.

"So, I dragged Gilbert's dumb ass over and handcuffed him to the fence, ran to the back door, and barreled through it only to run straight into this big-assed, Indian-looking asshole with bloodshot eyes, a big ol' soggy cocksucker who took up the whole goddamned doorway. Now, I've already got Vanessa ready to go," he said, tapping his hip though he stood in my hospital room unarmed, "and my first impression of this Tonto-looking bastard is he don't come across as real accommodating, the friendly type, if you know what I mean. So I don't bother introducing myself and making nice, I just cracked him across his forehead with the barrel—*bam!*—right across here"—Floyd said as ran his index finger over the center of his forehead—"and he folded like a cheap lawn chair."

I drank up every word, thirsty for the knowledge. Most of it had been previously unclear as I had tried to recall the scene, the action, wanting to know what happened and what went wrong on that dark and rainy night in East Los Angeles. Now, as I listened to my partner, I could see it in my mind, Floyd pistol-whipping the big Mexican there in the doorway, my partner vicious as any man could be when necessary. I could see the laundry room off the back door, the last thing I had remembered seeing before it all happened, before the flash of light, the explosions, the pain . . . I remembered hearing Floyd's voice that night as I faded beneath a slow-twirling fan, Floyd cursing as he charged into the home of Gilbert Regalado. Now I put it together with what Floyd described like an action-packed detective novel, maybe an Elmore Leonard or Mickey Spillane.

"After Tonto hit the ground, I saw you on the floor, just outside the kitchen . . . Jesus, Dickie," he said, and paused, sniffed and abruptly changed course.

"There was this kid," he continued, "some fifteen-year-old punk-rocker with long hair and a leather jacket standing over you, so I kicked him in the nuts and punched him in the face, knocked him on his ass. What the hell, you know? At that point, I had no idea who shot my partner. I saw blood everywhere and you were out, and I didn't know how bad it was. No way I was taking any chances with any of those assholes. Turns out the kid didn't have anything to do with any of this, just a nephew who was too stupid to get away from a downed cop. Same with Tonto, actually, as it turns out. Just two guys in the wrong place at the wrong time. But that's what happens when you associate with assholes, right?

"Then I see your boy, Jorge—that would be *the late* Mr. Regalado—sprawled out on the floor, not far from you. Dead, apparently from leaking to death, by the looks of the blood around him. Turns out he's Gilbert's uncle, been out of the joint less than a month. There was a Rossi .38 Special in his right hand, no doubt the gun you were shot by."

I shook my head, nothing to say and too much to process.

"It gets better," he said. "They're comparing his prints to a partial print that was lifted from my car after it was stolen. There's some similarities, I guess, with the pattern. Nothing concrete yet, but it might be a match. Can you imagine that? How's that asshole find my house, and why would they steal my car and take it back over to Fudd's? My thought is they wanted to frame him for all of this, and that's why they shot at us from his house. What do you think?"

I just shrugged.

He continued: "That's something we might not ever know, and honestly, it's the most disturbing part of all of this—other than you being shot of course."

After a moment of silence, I mustered the strength to ask, "What's the story on him?"

"Jorge? The asshole you shot?"

I nodded.

"He's got robberies, assaults, an attempted murder beef, some burglaries, couple pages of dope charges, and wouldn't you know it, a couple GTA's. No loss to society, if that's what you wondered.

"Funny thing, soon as I saw him, laying there on the floor, it all came together. I recognized him from the photos, the mustached dude with Gilbert at the motel, and I thought, holy shit, man, he's the one who killed our girls. He did it, the dirty son-of-a-bitch, and now he's shot my partner.

"I tried to tell you about him the other day, but you were too far out of it still. Kept falling asleep, irritating the shit out of me."

"You were here?"

"Yeah, Dickie, I've been here every day. Can't hardly get any work done with you laying around like this. You talked to me a little, in between sleeping. You don't remember?"

I looked around the room as if it was the first time I'd seen it, though it seemed I'd been here a long time, and everything felt familiar. Valerie wasn't there, and I wondered why.

My partner continued, still a little bit of excitement in his voice. "So, with this guy dead, I'm thinking Gilbert might talk, but I don't know. He'll probably put it all on his late uncle, the weasel he is. But with the shoe impression, the photographs, and the doctor's statement, I'm pretty sure we've got him now, and Donna too."

Floyd waited as I processed what he said. It took me a minute, my brain still a bit fuzzy, but then I realized he was saying that the man who shot me was the same guy in the photos, the guy at the motel with Gilbert. The one who killed Susie and her friend.

I wanted to know more, but the questions bounced around in my head and seemed unable to find their way out. I began fading, and for a moment, I saw the fan twirling above my head again as the darkness returned.

Floyd was saying, "How're you feeling, partner?"

THE NEXT MORNING, I WOKE TO FIND VALERIE STROKING MY HEAD, THE flowery scent of her perfume opening my eyes and putting a smile to my face.

"You're awake," she said.

Yes, awake and alert with a clear head. No more fuzziness, at least for the time being. I said, "Hey babe, it sure is good to see you."

"I've been here for a week now, right here in this chair waiting for you to come to. The first time you woke up in three days, I had gone home to get a shower and a change of clothes. Floyd told me you were awake while I was gone. It figured. He had insisted I get home and take a break, assured me you'd be sleeping the whole time but he'd keep an eye on you."

"Val . . ."

"Did he wake you up? I know he was dying to talk to you, tell you everything that happened."

"Yesterday?"

"Yesterday, the day before . . . I think maybe another day before that. He's been here every day, same as me. We've kind of taken shifts. But it seems like whenever I've left, you've been awake for a while. I was starting to worry he was waking you when I wasn't around, which the doctors said not to do."

"He seemed worried."

"We've all been worried, Richard."

"It was good to see him, to hear about what happened. I had no idea—"

"He must have worn you out. By the time I got back, you were out of it again. This is the first time I've seen those blue eyes in days."

"It's good to see you."

She smiled.

"Why don't you get me out of here, babe? Take me home and I'll be good as new in no time, I promise. Hell, we can get some dinner on the way home. I'm dying for a steak and beer."

"Your doctor says you'll be here another week, maybe more. Your injuries—" she raised a hand to her mouth and closed her eyes, trying unsuccessfully to stifle the tears.

"I'm going to be okay, honey, you know I am. It's going to take more than this to put me down." I reached around, picking at the white gown over bandages and tubes, straining my neck to look down at my torso. "Look here, honey, they've got me all patched up, good as new."

She nodded and forced a bit of a smile as she dabbed the corners of her eyes with a tissue. "You lost a kidney, Richard. You also lost a lot of blood and they've left that bullet in your shoulder, said it's too risky to take it out."

"And it won't hurt anything to leave it, right? They do that all the time, it's not a big deal. You go down to South L.A., Compton, everyone has bullets in them."

She huffed.

I heard Floyd's voice beyond my room. "Floyd's here?"

She nodded toward the door. "Out in the hallway."

"Who's he talking to?"

"Probably a nurse. Richard, you need to take this seriously."

I grimaced as a pain shot through my stomach, but tried to hide it from my wife.

"Jesus, Dickie," Floyd said, sauntering in with an ear to ear grin, "how long you planning on milking this thing? We got shit to do, partner."

He stopped at the edge of the bed next to Valerie, glanced at her and smiled, then looked at me and frowned. "Your lieutenant was by earlier—you were sleeping, same as all day yesterday—said he was putting me in the rotation with Lewandowski this weekend. So don't think you're getting any sympathy from me, partner. I'd rather be shot, lay here in bed and harass the nurses, than catch a case with that idiot." He looked toward the bag hanging at the side of my bed. "You still on morphine?"

I shrugged.

"Good shit, eh? You remember talking to me yesterday?" He didn't wait for my response. "You looked out of it then, too. You remember me telling you what happened?"

I nodded.

"Well, it gets better. Phil Gentry says he can say with near certainty the shoes Jorge Regalado wore to the coroner's office"—he stopped and laughed at his clever remark—"left the shoe print at the scene."

I pictured the crime scene, the impression in dirt, but didn't have the energy to respond.

"We definitely have enough to charge them now, murder and conspiracy to commit murder. We solved a tough one, Dickie."

"Honey," Valerie said, "you feel like you need to rest yet?"

"Jesus," Floyd said, "all he's done since he got here is sleep."

Valerie glared at him.

Floyd didn't notice. "You know who needs some rest around here? Well, it damn sure ain't Dickie *Two Shots in the Ten Ring Jones*. Did I tell you how you nailed that prick? *Bam . . . bam,"* he said, poking himself twice in the center of his chest. "Not bad shooting, dickhead, and I might say, it's about time."

"My God," Valerie mumbled.

"Sorry, Val," he said.

I looked at Valerie and nodded toward the table next to my bed, the one Floyd pushed out of his way when he came in. "Honey, would you mind getting me some ice chips? I'm dying of thirst."

"You probably need a beer, Dickie."

Val glared.

I said, "Man, that sounds good."

"I'll let you two have some time to yourselves," Floyd said, "I need to get home for a few hours anyway. See you tomorrow?"

"You bet."

He stood for a minute, looking around the room. I wondered what he was thinking, or what he planned to steal on his way out: gauze pads, tape, bedpan, bag of morphine?

He stepped toward the door and paused to check the bathroom, a quick glance in there—apparently nothing of interest—and then back toward me. "Listen, you need anything, Dickie . . ."

I nodded and gave a slight wave using my good arm. "I'm fine here, buddy."

"Buddy? What's this *buddy* shit? What happened to partner or asshole, whatever . . . *Buddy?"*

I attempted to smile, but doubt it showed, the fatigue taking over again. My eyes burned as I strained to stay awake, the *happy button* doing its job, keeping the allotted dose of narcotics flowing into my veins.

Floyd, still making his way to the door, stopped one more time to say, "Hurry back, Dickie. You're honestly driving me crazy with this laying around, all-day nappy-time bullshit."

Just being Floyd.

And I loved him for it. He wasn't about to sit there and cry, mope around like there was no tomorrow. No, Floyd knew damn well—same as me—what *no tomorrow* really looked like; we saw it every day. We lived by the Homicide Bureau's motto: *Every day above ground is a good day*. As long as I stayed above ground, he wasn't going to cry. In fact, it was more likely he'd smuggle in pizza and beer by the end of the week, pull up a chair, kick his feet up on the bed, and ask what's good on TV. Or he'd be planning to break me out, find something fun to do.

How could I *not* love him? The man at the door in his cargo shorts and a gray hooded sweatshirt today, Ray-Bans protecting his eyes from the fluorescent lighting. My partner and friend, Pretty Boy Floyd, with the attention span of a puppy, and the charisma to go along with it. If I could only get him house-broke.

"You are coming back, aren't you, Dickie? . . .

"Dickie?"

I hope you'v enjoyed this novel, the first book in the Dickie Floyd Detective series.

If you would take a moment to write a review wherever you purchased this book, it would be greatly appreciated.

Thank you!

Next up: Preview of

Door to a Dark Room

Book 2 in the Dickie Floyd Detective series

Door to a Dark Room

A Dickie Floyd Detective Novel

by Danny R. Smith

THEY WERE EASY prey. Complacent, like a herd of sheep, unaware of their vulnerability. Oblivious to the presence of a predator.

Concealed in darkness, he watched them. He relished the power he had over them, knowing it was his choice whether they lived or died, not theirs. Not the decision of God or Satan or some bitch named Karma. It was *his*.

He almost pitied them for their weakness.

Almost.

The mothers, busy on their cell phones, unaware that their children trailed behind, babbling, whining, some staring at phones of their own. He could easily pull one into his car and be gone, *whisk*. How long would it take an oblivious mother to notice? The self-centered bitches were ignorant of his grace.

He waited.

Leonard watched them all, women, girls, and boys. He had no desire for mature women, though the idea of young girls stirred him greatly. In prison, he had managed his own sexual gratification, with only the occasional aid of another man. Young men only, though. Those who were new in the system and as frightened and malleable as he had been when he was locked up at age sixteen.

The real thrill had always been the stalking. Creeping through the darkened homes of others, watching strangers as they slept. Death was their houseguest, though most of them never knew it; they were the fortunate ones. Those who did know, only knew for an instant during their final moments.

Leonard didn't always kill; most times he had not. The first murder had been the result of panic—he had been only thirteen. The others were by choice.

An electric thrill shot through Leonard as he thought of the fear in the eyes of his chosen ones. How they begged, squirmed, tried to escape. Their efforts were futile. His preference was strangulation; it was so intimate. Bare hands allowed him to feel their final pulses, smell their last breaths, stare into their unbelieving eyes. Some of the killings had been more violent, a swift and easy death with a single blow to the skull. Once he had used a hammer; another time it had been a pipe. Each experience had been an education. Though the more violent attacks were efficient, and there had been little suffering, they had been less gratifying.

Leonard was more compassionate than the news stories had painted him. Always, he kissed them goodbye. Most would not have been capable of understanding the intimacy of their death, nor of appreciating it. But he knew, and he wanted to share his affection with these chosen ones. It was his gift to the newly dead.

Leonard had dreamed of killing during his years of confinement, treasuring and reliving his memories of those he had watched, those he had killed. He remembered them all. They were his. They would always be his.

He thought of the first, an elderly woman alone in her bed. He had meant only to observe her, but she had awakened and begun to scream, leaving him no choice. There had been no desire for sex, although he had explored her lifeless body. He had seen naked women and girls before by peeping into their windows, and this experience had solidified his taste for the young ones. When Leonard was eventually arrested, three years later, they didn't even ask him about it. Nor did they ask about any of the others, not even the five-year-old boy who had lived—and died—right next door.

Leonard thought the boy's mother might have been considered a suspect, but he never heard what became of her.

His only arrest had come after he killed his mother. By that time, he had become efficient at killing. His mother had deserved her death, and she had not been entitled to his grace; he did not kiss her goodbye. He turned himself in; what else could he do? It had been just the two of them all of his life, and now she was dead. This he pondered for hours as he sat on the porch, a cordless telephone in his hand and his mother's body cooling inside the house. He knew the call would end the killing. Or would it?

His lawyer said his mother had sexually abused him, had tormented him physically and psychologically. "What monster would do this to her own son?" the attorney had asked of the jury, rhetorically. They had bought it. They believed the adolescent when he took the stand and allowed the tears to roll down his cheeks. While on the stand, he had kept his head low and softly answered the questions. *Poor boy.* He had been sentenced as an adult, but his life had been spared. He received twenty-five years and was sent off to Raiford, Florida's infamous penitentiary.

Leonard considered his time there mostly tolerable, once he understood what was required to survive in prison. He had learned quickly.

The last ten years had been wonderful. He had been assigned a new cellmate, Whitey Blanchard. Whitey, a member of the Irish mafia, had been the youngest man ever convicted of a mafia-related murder in Florida. He was a legend in the crime world, having taken out two top hitmen of a rival family. The two mafioso were known to be vicious and precise, always wary, yet a mere boy had walked in and popped them both as they sat among friends in a crowded diner. Then he casually walked out. Leonard and Whitey were nearly the same age, and, over the years, they had become like brothers. Each enjoyed sharing with the other details of their crimes, reliving and relishing the memories, the accomplishments.

Their last year together had gone by too quickly. Leonard was released knowing Whitey would never see freedom again, having been sentenced to two consecutive life sentences for the double murder. Though freedom awaited him, Leonard shed tears when he told Whitey goodbye.

Whitey had taken care of things for Leonard though. From prison, he had arranged for Leonard to be introduced to upper management of *the family*, and that had led to a sit-down with the boss. The interview was brief. The boss knew of Leonard's accomplishments. He knew of the killing that had landed Leonard in Raiford, and he knew of the unsolved cases as well. Leonard had divulged certain details of each to Whitey, who in turn had fed them to management. Once they were verified through an FBI agent who was on their payroll, Leonard was in. The dirty cop confirmed there were cases just as Leonard described that remained unsolved. The Irish mafia boss admired his work.

No longer confined, he was now a contract killer, a pro. Neat and efficient.

But never had he been as bold as Whitey. He often thought of the story he had heard many times about the hit in the diner. To prove himself, someday Leonard would do something similar. He'd have to learn to shoot a gun though. How difficult could it be? He had always admired Whitey for his courage in walking up to two killers and doing them in front of an audience. That was a different kind of killing than Leonard knew, and because of it, he saw his friend Whitey as the bigger man. Maybe one day Whitey would read about him in the paper and be proud of his friend.

A woman stopped directly in front of Leonard, startling him out of his reverie. She never looked his way. In a moment, she moved on. Leonard let out a breath he had not realized he had been holding. She would have been the one, he thought, as he watched her walk away, if only he were allowed. But he would no longer choose his victims, that was part of the agreement. Although Leonard had silently questioned his concession to kill exclusively for them. Impulses might dictate otherwise.

He refocused on the target and continued to watch, hoping tonight would bring opportunity. He had been supplied with everything he needed to know, which did not include the *why.* That was the agreement: a name, a location, and a death warrant issued by *the family*. It was all he would need, and all he would receive. This one was to have no sexual component, and efforts to conceal the victim's identity would be made. Simple enough. Killing is killing. You needn't hear trumpets to bask in its glory.

FLOYD SAID, "LOOK it there, he's back."

Mongo looked up from his work.

I STEPPED THROUGH the back door into the squad room, a sea of desks beneath fluorescent lighting where men and women sat or stood or walked about in business attire. They were speaking into their cell phones or landlines or staring at computer screens or visiting with other detectives. It was a typical Wednesday morning at the Los Angeles County Sheriff's Homicide Bureau. No different from the way it had been the last time I darkened that doorway, though there were several new faces. The turnover rate rivaled that of a combat post in the middle east.

But for me, this was no ordinary Wednesday in the office. Not just another week, another bureau meeting. It was the return from a year's absence. The return from a traumatic injury, two gunshot wounds that resulted in the loss of a kidney and a lengthy rehab. Physical and mental.

At times I had silently questioned if I were ready to return. Ready for the cheerful greetings and welcome backs and handshakes and high fives. Ready for the questions: How was I doing? How's the wife? What's it like being shot? Cops were direct like that, at least with one another.

How would I answer?

Great.

Wife's gone. Strike two.

Being shot sucks.

I had concealed my concerns about coming back from those in my inner circle. Which had been reduced to my partner Floyd, my doctor, and my shrink. I assured each of them I was fit for duty.

It felt different, all of it. As if I were a stranger in this place I once called home. A place in which I'd spent much of my life over the past decade. Much more of it here, with Floyd, than at home.

Everyone seemed to look up at once from their work or conversations, some still holding phones but not speaking, maybe on hold or listening to the party on the other end. For a moment, the room stood completely silent; everything had come to a stop. It was awkward. Almost embarrassing.

My heart beat rapidly and sweat beaded under my hat. Then, suddenly, as if on cue from a director, the characters resumed their activities. They were back to speaking into phones, typing on computers, and talking to one another. The greetings began. Colleagues were welcoming me back. Some from afar, but others approached and gave me hugs or pats on the back. There were genuine smiles and friendly greetings, and I began to feel comfortable again in this place I called home.

My attention was drawn across the room and I locked eyes with those of a friend. My old partner. An ex-wife, I would often call him. Detective Matt "Pretty Boy Floyd" Tyler sat across the room, behind his desk, watching. Studying. Waiting patiently, a burgeoning grin on his face.

FLOYD'S PARTNER, MONGO, as Floyd called him, Detective Manny Diaz according to the placard on his desk, looked up over reading glasses that hung on the end of his nose. He was editing a report that Floyd told him needed to be finished by the end of the day. They had a meeting with the district attorney the next morning and it was the new guy's job to have the case prepared for filing. Mongo had never met his partner's former partner, though he had heard much about him. Maybe too much. Floyd never stopped talking about him, about their cases, about how well they worked together and how everything seemed balanced and cohesive. Floyd often spoke of the night that had become legendary around the bureau, a dark and rainy night in East Los Angeles that resulted in Dickie being shot. Floyd would recount the night, sometimes with a distant stare, and tell Mongo about finding his partner in a pool of blood. He told how Dickie had shot and killed the man who shot him, a convict who had murdered several prostitutes, a big case they had solved. Floyd would recount how he charged through the back door after hearing the shots, searching frantically for his partner. How he had gone bat-shit crazy and damn near killed the two assholes he encountered on the way in. One of whom was twice Mongo's size, Floyd would say, "in both directions."

Mongo had often felt like the new wife who couldn't match up to the former, and he already hated the other woman. He leaned back in his chair, all two-hundred-and-fifty pounds of his five-foot-seven frame and watched as the man in the fedora walked slowly through the bureau, greeting at least every other detective along the way. He heard the various greetings, "Welcome back," "Great to see you," blah, blah, blah. He watched as some stood and approached him, embracing him with a hug or a handshake. Others, mostly the newer guys, sat and watched. It seemed overdone, maybe a bit of a spectacle.

Mongo had dreaded the arrival of this day.

He glanced over to see his partner, Floyd, leaned back in his chair, chewing on a pen and smiling with his hazel eyes, watching as his former partner made his way through the sea of detectives.

Mongo looked back at Detective Richard Jones and saw that through all the greetings and short conversations and distractions along his way, he continually looked in their direction. Back and forth, but regularly, as if he were homed in on Floyd. The two watched each other in the way only best friends or mortal enemies would, as if nothing around them had any significance compared to that which awaited them each.

Soon the man in the hat, Dickie Jones, stood near their desks. He was tall, probably six feet or better, and of average build for a man in his mid-forties. He had a thick mustache that was mostly gray, but hints of red were still there. The room had fallen silent as the two old partners held their gazes. Finally, Dickie smiled at his old partner. It was a closed mouth smile, or maybe it was more of a grin.

He let out a breath and looked at Mongo. "You're in my seat."

I love staying connected with my readers through social media and email. If you would like to connect, find me on Facebook, Instagram, and Twitter. You can also sign up for my newsletter and receive bonus material, such as the action-packed short story, Harder Times.

As a newsletter subscriber, you will receive special offers, updates, book releases, and blog posts. I promise to never sell or spam your email.

Danny R. Smith
Dickie Floyd Novels

Dickie Floyd Detective Novels

- A Good Bunch of Men
- Door to a Dark Room
- Echo Killers

Dickie Floyd Detective Short Stories

- Harder Times: A Cop Goes to Prison (Free to Newsletter Subscribers, visit dickiefloydnovels.com)

Danny R. Smith spent 21 years with the Los Angeles County Sheriff's Department, the last seven as a homicide detective. He now lives in Idaho where he works as a private investigator and consultant. He is blessed with a beautiful wife and two wonderful daughters. He is passionate about his dogs and horses, whom he counts among his friends.

Danny is the author of the *Dickie Floyd Detective Novel* series, and he has written articles for various trade publications. He publishes a weekly blog called The Murder Memo, which can be found at dickiefloydnovels.com.

He is a member of the Idaho Writers Guild and the Public Safety Writers Association.

facebook.com/Dickie.Floyd.Novels
twitter.com/dickiefloyd187
instagram.com/dickiefloyd

27757102R00186

Made in the USA
San Bernardino, CA
03 March 2019